THE
STAR
DWELLERS

Book Two of The

Dwellers Saga

David Estes

This book is dedicated to all the members and moderators of my Goodreads fan group.
Your kindness and support is beyond generous, and I'll always value the way you make me laugh, cry, smile and sometimes just shake my head.

Prologue
Tristan
Two years ago

My mom didn't show up for dinner tonight.

Come to think of it, I haven't seen her all day. Although my schedule was jam-packed—sword training all morning, an interview for a silly telebox show in the early afternoon, a painful two hours of "life lessons" from my father in the late afternoon (where the President "his highness" imparted his unending wisdom upon my brother and me), and barely a half hour to myself to clean up and get ready for dinner—I would still usually cross paths with my mom at some point. But not today. And now she isn't at dinner, which is very unusual, her designated spot at the foot of the table empty save for the untouched place setting.

"Where's Mom?" I ask from the center of our mile-long table.

From the head, my father looks up from his juicy prime beef. "She's gone," he says so matter-of-factly I think it's a joke.

"Gone?" I snort. "What's that supposed to mean?"

There's no compassion in my father's dark stare. "Are you dumb, boy? Gone means gone. Vanished, disappeared. She left you." He wears a smirk, like the joke's on me.

"She wouldn't do that," I say firmly. I know she wouldn't. She loves me. My brother, Killen, too, who sits across from me watching our exchange with unreadable eyes.

"She would and she did," the President says. "Her handmaiden found her cupboard empty this morning. She packed up as if she's never coming back. If you're ever going to be a man, Tristan, you have to face the truth. She's abandoned you."

But that's not a truth I can face. Not now—not ever. She didn't leave. She was driven away.

"You did this," I growl. For a second my father's face is vulnerable, his eyebrows raised, as if I've struck a nerve. A moment later, he's himself again, unflappable.

"Watch your tone, son," he says back, his voice simmering with hot coals.

I know not to push him too far, but tonight I can't stop myself. "I hate you," I say through clenched teeth. Pushing back my chair, I add, "I'm going to find her."

Before I can get to my feet, he's up and moving, barreling around the table, his face a swirling mixture of wrath and fire and his idea of discipline. I've seen him bad, but never this bad, and it takes me by surprise, so much so that I'm frozen for a split-second, just enough time for him to reach me.

There's no hesitation in him as he towers over me; despite my recent growth spurt, he's still taller by a head. And his frame is that of a man, chiseled from his daily personal training sessions, while I, though athletic, still sport the body of a boy. The strike comes so fast I have no time to react.

CRACK!

My head snaps back as the vicious uppercut lands just beneath my chin. Still half on the plush red velvet cushion of my cast-iron chair, I feel my feet tangle with the chair legs as I go down in a heap, unwittingly pulling the heavy seat on top of me. Pain is shooting through my jaw but I don't even have time to massage my chin before my father's vise-like hands are clutching the top of my tunic, pulling me to my feet, and then further, lifting me in the air, my legs dangling helplessly beneath me.

I'm looking down at my father, and I feel the warm trickle of blood from my mouth. I must've bitten my tongue when he hit me. Out of the corner of my eye I see Killen watching, his face that of a ghost, white and powdery. I look back at my father when he shakes me, once, twice, thrice, a reminder of the power he holds over me.

"You will NOT speak to me like that!" he spits out. "If anyone's to blame for your mother's disappearance"—another shake—"it's you."

He drops me, and although I land on my feet, my legs are weak and rubbery, unable to sustain my weight as my knees crumble beneath me. His shadow looms over me and I shudder. Why won't he just let me be, leave me to my own grief? Because that's not who he is. I suspect that his cold, uncaring shell of a heart stopped beating years ago.

"You will not leave this house again until I say so," he commands, and despite the rebellion in my heart, I know I'll obey him. But someday, when I'm stronger, I won't.

I never saw my mother again.

One

Adele

The thunder of marching boots sends shivers through the rock and through my bones.

When I was young my parents used to tell me stories about monsters that roam the underground world we live in. Serpents with glowing eyes the size of dinner plates, longer than ten houses, slithering and slipping through the underground rivers and lakes. Faceless boogeymen, walking the caves, searching, searching…for a child to snack on. I now know my parents were just trying to scare me into not going out alone at night, to trick me into not wandering the outskirts of the subchapter.

These days there are worse things than monsters in the Tri-Realms.

Tawni and I hold our breath as the convoy of sun dweller troops pass us. When we heard them, we managed to extinguish our lights, pull back into our tunnel, and duck behind a finger of rock jutting out from the wall. We're lucky—they're not in our tunnel. Instead, they're passing perpendicular to us, through a tunnel that intersects ours, shooting off to the left and right, the first crossroads we've seen since leaving the Moon Realm. Thankfully, they don't seem to understand the concept of stealth, or they might have seen us before we even knew they were there.

It's weird: even though he's nothing like them, the sun dweller soldiers remind me of Tristan. I guess because they're from the same place. The Sun Realm. A place I've only seen on the telebox. A place I will probably never go.

Compared to the ragtag legion of star dwellers we saw back in the Moon Realm, the sun dwellers are polished and professional, with pristine red uniforms adorned with medals and ribbons and the symbol of the Sun Realm on the shoulder—a fiery sun with scorching heat marks extending from the edges. Their weapons are shiny and new, their swords gleaming in their scabbards, their guns black and unmarked. They have bright flashlights and headlamps, which make it easy for us to see them. If one of them aims a light in our direction, they will spot us.

My muscles are tense, as line after line of soldiers march past. Without counting, I know there are more of them than the star dwellers in subchapter 26. If they were to fight, it would be a massacre. But they don't turn at our tunnel, don't head for subchapter 26. They pass straight through the crossroads, moving somewhere else—I don't know where.

Some of them speak. "Damn endless tunnel," one of them says.

"Damn the star dwellers for their rebellion," another replies.

"I've got to take a piss," the first one says, breaking off from the pack. He heads right for us, the light on his helmet bobbing and bouncing off the rock walls.

"Well, turn your damn light off," a guy says. "We don't want to see you doing it."

"Shut your pie-hole!" the small-bladdered soldier says, but reaches up and switches off his light, thrusting him into shadow.

I feel Tawni grab my hand as the guy's boots scrape closer. We can hear his breathing, heavy and loud from his long march. I am coiled as tight as a spring, ready to shove my foot into his groin, or my finger into his eye, if he stumbles on our bent legs.

He stops, and I know he is close, practically right on top of us. Cloth scuffles as he gets his thing out. We hear the soft *shhhhh* of moisture as he pees right next to us. It splatters on the rocks, spraying tiny droplets of liquid waste on my leg. Tawni is even closer so she gets the worst of it.

He is so exposed I could hurt him badly in an instant. As much as I want to, it would be suicide. The rest of the soldiers would be on us before I could say *Pee somewhere else, sucker!*

I resist the temptation, trying not to throw up as the tangy scent of urine fills my nostrils.

He finishes, scuffles his clothing some more, scrapes his boots away. I breathe out slowly, and I hear Tawni do the same. The guy flicks his light on and reunites with the other

11

men just as the last line passes through the intersection. Darkness is restored as the torches disappear into the outgoing tunnel. The thunder fades away.

We don't speak for a half hour, barely move, barely breathe. It could be the first of a dozen convoys for all we know. I feel that if we stumble into the crossroads, a bunch of lights will come on, a net will be thrown over us, and we'll be dragged away.

My legs are aching from lack of movement. I feel like screaming. I am trying to outlast Tawni, but what she lacks in toughness, she makes up for in patience. I can't take it anymore.

"You smell nasty," I whisper.

"Speak for yourself," she hisses.

"That was really gross."

"It was worse for me."

"True." Silence for another minute. Then I say, "Do you think it's safe?"

"No."

"Neither do I, but I don't think I can sit in a puddle of urine any longer."

"Okay."

"I mean, I'm sure there's some spa in the Sun Realm that claims urine has healing powers, or is good for the skin, or something, and offers urine baths and urine scrubs, but I just don't buy it."

Tawni snorts. "You're nuts," she says. "Thank God for the modesty of the sun dwellers."

"Yeah, we were lucky. If they were like the guys in the Moon Realm I know, the whole platoon would've peed against the wall, lights blazing full force."

I pull myself to my feet and help Tawni to hers. We don't turn our lights on, opting to feel our way along the wall to the intersection. When the rough rock gives way to empty air, we know we've reached the crossroads. Tawni holds my hand and pulls me across the mouth of the intersecting tunnel. A bead of sweat leaves a salty trail on my forehead as my anxiety reaches a fever pitch.

No lights come on. No net falls on us. No one drags us away. Not yet.

We make it to the other side safely, and then walk another five minutes to put a safe distance between us and the intersection, before turning our lights back on.

Tawni's white tunic is yellowed with filth. I don't look at mine.

"I don't know if I can go any farther wearing this," Tawni says, motioning to her soiled garb.

"I'd prefer a hot shower before changing clothes. Check the map and see if there's a five-star hotel nearby."

Tawni smirks, but pulls out the map anyway, one of the ones that Tristan's friend, Roc, gave us before we left them. I shine the light for her while she locates the 26th subchapter in the Moon Realm. She finds it and nods when she identifies the inter-Realm tunnel we are in. Using her finger, she traces our path along the tunnel. The line ends at the edge of the map.

"We need to switch to a Star Realm map," she says. Fumbling through her pack, she selects a new map and unfolds it. She turns the map clockwise until she sees an edge with a tunnel going off the page that reads *To Moon Realm, subchapter 26*. When she pushes the new map against the old one, they match perfectly. "I guess we're done with this one for now," she says, folding the Moon Realm map and returning it to the pack.

I've officially left the Moon Realm for the first time. It feels weird, like I'm in a foreign land, not on earth anymore. As a little girl, I always dreamed of traveling the Tri-Realms as part of my job as a famous novelist, seeking inspiration for my books. Now I just wish I was at home, with my family.

Turning her attention back to the new map, Tawni continues tracing her finger along the straight blue line, until she reaches a red intersecting line. She taps the key in the bottom right-hand corner of the map. "Blue is for inter-Realm, red is for intra-Realm."

"Those sun dwellers were traveling within the Moon Realm," I say.

"Doing what?"

"Helping to squash the rebellion," I guess.

Tawni nods, goes back to the map. "So if we're here…"— she places her finger on the blue line just past the red one— "…then we are at least two days' march from the first subchapter in the Star Realm—subchapter 30."

"And the nearest hotel?" I joke.

"Probably an hour away," she replies, "but it pretty much looks exactly the same as where we're standing right now."

I groan. I guess the builders of this tunnel didn't really consider comfort to be a top priority.

"Wait a minute," Tawni murmurs, peering at the map and once more consulting the key.

"What?"

"Eureka! There's a blue dot not that far away!"

"Thank god!" I exclaim. "That's amazing, wonderful! Uh…what's a blue dot mean?"

Tawni laughs. "Watering hole."

Yes! Now I really am excited. Our canteens are dry. We are filthy. A watering hole is just what we need. "Perfect," I say.

Tawni and I are both smiling when we start walking again, our legs no longer sore, our steps bouncy and light. Funny how a little good news can have a physical impact.

We float along for an hour, expecting any second to hear the gentle slap of moving water against a rocky shore. When the second hour passes, I am getting antsy. Perhaps the map is wrong and there is no watering hole. Or maybe the underground lake has dried up, no longer fed by one of the many life-giving tributaries that flow in between and through the Tri-Realms.

"Where is it?" I say when a few more minutes pass without any change in the dull gray scenery.

"I'm not sure," Tawni says.

"You said it was close."

"It's hard to judge distance on this map. Everything looks so close when there are really miles between."

"We've walked for at least eight miles," I point out.

Tawni shrugs and keeps walking. Having no other choice, I do the same. That's when I hear it.

At first a soft tinkle, the noise becomes louder, a swishing— and then a gurgle. Water, has to be. Tawni looks at me and we both smile. The map was right!

For only the second time since we entered this godforsaken tunnel, the monotony is broken as the passage opens up to our left. The right wall remains straight and solid, but to the left there is an empty darkness. I feel cool air waft against my face, ruffling my hair. At our feet is water, lapping against the edge of the tunnel floor.

We go a little crazy. Or maybe just I do. Letting out a *Whoop!* I sling down my pack and thrust my cupped hands into the cool liquid. First I throw a handful into my face. My breath catches as the icy water splashes over my skin. But I don't shiver—it feels wonderful. It's like the water is healing me, rejuvenating more than just my skin: refreshing my soul. The wet drips off my chin and dribbles down my neck and beneath the neckline of my tunic. It feels so good I can't help myself.

With no room in my mind left for embarrassment, or modesty, I pull my tunic over my head and toss it aside, leaving just my undergarments. Oh, and my shoes, too, which I pull off, along with my socks. I leave my flashlight angled on a rock so I can see.

I splash into the knee-deep water, relishing the soft caress of the cooling elixir. The lake bed is covered with long, smooth rocks that massage my sore feet. As I scoop water onto my arms, stomach, and legs, I remember a story my grandmother used to tell me about the Fountain of Youth, a pool of water with life-extending power. The cool touch of this pool feels equally potent, and I half-expect to see myself growing shorter, shrinking to reveal a younger me, the size of my half-pint sister perhaps.

I don't shrink, but I am cleansed. When I turn around, Tawni is grinning. She tosses me a sliver of soap, which I manage to juggle and then catch. As I use it to wash my body, she methodically uncaps each canteen and fills them. She is the responsible one.

Seeing her with the canteens reminds me of the hungry thirst in my throat. I finish with the soap and hand it to Tawni to use. She is already undressed and daintily steps into the pool, looking as graceful as a dancer, particularly when compared to my own clumsy entrance.

I turn around and splash some more water on my face.

"Where'd you get that scar on your back?" Tawni asks.

Looking over my shoulder, trying to gaze at my back, I say, "What scar?"

She moves closer, places a hand on my back, and I shiver, suddenly feeling cold. Her fingers linger somewhere near the center of my back, where I can't possibly see, just below my undergarments. "Curious," she says absently.

"What is it?"

"It's a crescent-shaped scar, small, but slightly raised off your skin. It looks like a recent scar…"

"Maybe I got it in the tunnels somewhere—or from Rivet," I say, but I know that's not right—there would have been blood, and someone would have noticed the wound seeping through my tunic.

"No, it's not *that* fresh. Just looks like it's from something that happened in the last few years. If I didn't know better, I'd say it looks just like…"

I turn to face my friend, taking in her quizzical expression in an instant. "Like what?" I ask when she doesn't finish her statement.

"Nothing, I don't know what I was thinking," she says unconvincingly.

"You were going to say 'Tristan's scar', weren't you?" I laugh. "You're nuts, you know that?"

She laughs, high and musical. "And you're not?"

I grin at her and cup my hands, once more using them as a scoop to lift a portion of water to my face. As I open my mouth to receive the glorious liquid, I see Tawni's face change from mirthful to one of confusion. It looks like she's playing with something in her mouth, moving her tongue around, side to side. Her eyebrows are lowered. I plunge the water into my mouth, delighting in the slick feel as it slips over my tongue, down my gullet.

"Ahh," I murmur softly, just before Tawni grabs my arm. Her eyes are wide—she is scared. "What?" I say.

"Spit it out!" Tawni shrieks. Now I am the confused one. "Spit it out!" she says again, reaching around and thumping me on the back.

"I can't," I say over her shoulder. "I've already swallowed it."

Tawni releases me and says, "No, no, no, no…this is not good."

That's when I taste it. Something's not right about the water. Like Tawni, I make a face, swish some spit around in my mouth. Overall, the water was refreshing, delicious even, but the aftertaste is not good. The water is…. "Contaminated?" I say.

Tawni nods slowly. "I think so."

Not good.

As kids, all moon dwellers are taught to look for the signs of contaminated water. Strange coloring, frothy film on the top, a unique odor, strange taste: All are possible clues that the water is not good to drink. At home we used a testing agent every four hours to check our water. If the water turns blue when combined with the agent, it is okay. If it turns green or brown, your water is bad. Even if we had the stuff we needed to test the water, it is too late. We've drunk it.

I peer into the water. It looks okay. No film, no discoloring, no malodor. The nasty aftertaste might just be a result of trace metals in the water, picked up somewhere along its winding path through the depths. I doubt we're that lucky.

"What do you think it is?" I ask. There are a lot of dangers associated with drinking bad water. In mild cases, you might just get a bad case of diarrhea or perhaps light vomiting, but there are many worse diseases and viruses that can be picked up, too. Like…

"Bat Flu," Tawni says.

"What? No. I doubt it. Can't be. Why do you think that?" Bat Flu is the worst of the worst. Infected bats release their infected droppings into a water source, which then becomes infected. The symptoms of Bat Flu are numerous and awful: severe stomach cramps; cold sweats and hot flashes in conjunction with high fever; mind-numbing headaches; relentless muscle aches; hallucinations; and in many cases, death. There was a mild outbreak at my school in Year Three. Four kids, a dog, and one of their parents got the Flu. The only one that survived was the dog.

Tawni steps out of the water, leaving a trail of drips behind her. She picks up the flashlight and shines it across the pool. I follow the yellow light until it stops on the far wall, which is pockmarked with dozens of small caves. Bat caves. "That's why," she says.

I feel a surge of bile in my throat as I see piles of dark bat poo littered at the tunnel mouths. Each time the bats emerge from the caves, they will knock the piles into the water with the flap of their wings. Evidently, they're sleeping now—the caves are silent.

I choke down the bitter, acidic taste in my mouth and say, "But this is a key watering hole for an inter-Realm thoroughfare. It's even on the map." My words don't change

19

anything. The water is likely contaminated. I don't want to be in denial. I just need to deal with what has happened as best I can. My mother always told me to "face the truth with grim determination and a smile on your face." I'm not sure about the smile. "Okay, let's assume it's contaminated. We need to vomit it out, Tawni. Now!"

Without watching to see what Tawni does, I stick two fingers down my throat, gagging immediately, the stomach fire rising so fast I can barely get my hand out of my mouth before I spew all over myself. I retch, gag, cough twice, spit as much of the vile liquid from my mouth as possible. At my feet, my own vomit is floating around my ankles. At my side, Tawni is throwing up, too.

Clenching my abs, I say, "We're both going to get very sick. But we'll get through it together."

"What do we do?" Tawni asks, her voice rising precariously high. Her lips are tight. I'm afraid she might lose it. Since I met her, Tawni has always been strong, even when her best friend was viciously murdered. But now she looks seriously freaked out. She must've seen firsthand what the Bat Flu can do to someone.

"Who do you know that had the Flu?" I ask, stepping out of the bile-choked water, Tawni flitting out next to me. We are still filthy, but there's not much we can do about it now.

Tawni's eyes flick to mine and then back to the water, to the bat droppings. "My cousin," she says.

"What happened?"

"She passed."

"That's not going to happen to us."

"It was awful."

"Tawni."

20

Her eyes dart back to mine and stick this time.

"We're going to be fine," I say. "Stay with me."

Tawni's steel-blue eyes get steelier, and then, after reaching a hardness level I'd never seen in them before, soften, returning to their soft blue. "Right. We'll be okay," she says, almost to herself.

I take the soap from Tawni and chuck it, along with the two canteens, across the pool. They clatter off the far wall and plunk beneath the surface.

"We should dry off with our dirty tunics and then chuck them away, too," I say.

Although it's kind of gross soaking up the water with our filthy old clothes, we both do it because we have to. It's the nature of things in our world. Out of necessity you have to do a lot of things you don't want to do. I wonder if it was the same in the old world, before Armageddon, before Year Zero.

When we are dry and our old clothes have been thrown into the foul water, we each don one of the fresh tunics from our packs. It feels good—the simple act of putting on clean clothes. It's like a rebirth, a second chance, a new beginning. At least usually. This time neither of us wants to turn the page on our story. But like so many things in life, we have no choice.

"How far to the Star Realm?" I ask.

"We're in the Star Realm now, technically."

"But how far to the first subchapter? Subchapter 30, right?"

Tawni consults the map. "Yeah, first we'll hit subchapter 30. I'd say at least a twelve-hour hike if we move fast."

"We've got to make it in eight," I say. "Just in case we have the Flu. First symptoms will come fast, perhaps in three hours or so. Worse symptoms after six hours. The very worst at around eight hours. So we have to move fast."

"What about water?" Tawni asks. Water will be a problem. We had to get rid of our contaminated canteens. We are already dehydrated.

"Any more blue dots on that map of yours?"

Tawni scans the page. "None in this section of the tunnel. There are blue dots all over the place in subchapter 30, but nothing between here and there."

"We're just going to have to suck it up. Can you make it?" I don't know if I can, but I will do everything in my power. I don't want to die without at least trying to find my mom.

"I don't know," Tawni answers honestly. I nod absently. "If I don't make it, leave me and find your mom."

"I won't leave you," I say.

Tawni opens her mouth, presumably to argue, but then snaps it shut and nods. She remembers who she's dealing with. I'm not known for changing my mind.

"Let's go," I say, shouldering my pack.

Two

Tristan

"I'm just a guy," I say.

"And barely even one at that," Roc adds, smirking. Sometimes I wonder why he's my best friend.

Mr. Rose shakes his head. "No, you're more than that, Tristan, and you know it. You're an idea."

"Yes, and you're betrothed to my sister," Elsey chimes in eagerly.

I laugh, half because the notion of ideas and betrothals is ridiculous, and half because Adele's ten-year-old sister is really growing on me. "I've just barely met your sister," I say to Elsey.

"I saw the way you looked at each other. You're practically engaged."

I want to get off the subject because I feel embarrassed talking about Adele and me—whatever we are—in front of her father. Without looking him in the eye, I say, "What do you mean *an idea?*"

"Like sliced bread?" Roc asks unhelpfully. "Because I'd say sliced bread is a way better idea than Tristy here."

Adele's father chuckles and shakes his head again. "You two are worse than brothers."

"You haven't met my brother, Mr. Rose," I say grimly, automatically reaching up and touching the area under my eye. The last time I saw my fifteen-year-old brother, Killen, he and his cronies beat me senseless. My eye is still black and swollen.

"It's Ben."

"Right...Ben," I say, still feeling weird about calling Adele's father by his first name.

"You're more than just a guy because of who you are." I raise a hand to object but Ben waves me off. "Hear me out. Just because you're from up there"—he motions to the high rock ceiling above us—"doesn't mean you are one of them. And that's my whole point. Despite the fact that you're the son of the President of the Tri-Realms, the chosen one, the next great leader of this world, you aren't a tyrant. You don't support your father's politics, am I right?"

I nod slowly, trying to understand where he's going with all this. "But that just makes me an enemy to the government. I'm a thorn in their side—a criminal who must be brought to justice. I'm sure my brother has already told my father what I've done. They'll be hunting me with everything they've got."

24

"We could dress you up like a woman and then they'd never find you," Roc suggests. He's being particularly unhelpful this morning.

Ben ignores Roc and says, "You're thinking about this all wrong. You're an *idea*, Tristan. The idea that someone from the Sun Realm could be on the side of the people in the Lower Realms; the idea that someone from within the highest government ranks is helping the Moon and Star Realms; the idea that injustice will not go unpunished. If we can get the moon dwellers to believe in that idea, maybe, just maybe, we can unite the people."

I gotta hand it to this guy, he knows what to say to get the blood pumping. He is a born leader, and I'm just a guy. He should be the one leading a rebellion, not me. I'll help, sure, but I don't want to be the one. Ben is a big man, strong and capable. When I first met him—when Adele and I broke him out of prison—he looked haggard, his black hair and beard long and disheveled, his body strong but battered. After only just two days he is a new man. First he used my sword to trim his hair, cropping it medium length and getting it off his ears, and then to remove his beard, leaving a neat goatee as his only facial hair. Next, he got cleaned up in the subchapter 26 reservoir. When he was done, I barely recognized him, and probably wouldn't have known him at all, if not for his piercing emerald-green eyes, the same eyes born by Adele.

"I don't think I'm the right—"

"Yes—you are."

I can tell he's not going to back down, and the last thing I want is to argue with Adele's father. "What do you want me to do?"

Ben smiles, as if he knew all along I'd listen to him. "For a start you need to meet with the Vice Presidents of the Moon Realm."

"There are dozens of them."

"We'll start with one—one I know will listen. She'll get the rest of them to one place for a meeting, and then you can work your magic."

"I have no magic."

"I guess we'll see, won't we?"

I sigh. Before I left Adele, I told her I was willing to do whatever it takes to help her people, the moon dwellers. The time has come for me to keep that promise. "Okay," I say.

"You'll be wonderful, I just know it!" Elsey says excitedly, clutching my arm. I flash her a smile, which doubles the size of her own smile. There are so many of Adele's features in her face, and yet her temperament is so different. Elsey is bright, cheery, formal—a miniature woman. Adele is sarcastic, tough-minded, slightly solemn at times. I close my eyes and whisper a silent prayer for her safety.

Roc is staring at me, the edges of his lips curled slightly in his classic *I-know-what-you're-thinking-and-I-think-you're-a-dork* smirk. His naturally brown skin makes him blend in with the brown rock of the cave wall behind him. I ignore him. "So where are we headed?" I ask.

"The place where it all started," Ben says, his eyes serious. "Subchapter 1 of the Moon Realm."

I've been there, of course, but I don't really remember it. I've been everywhere as part of my duties as son of the President.

"That's the subchapter with that big fire parade, isn't it?" Roc asks. Roc is better at geography and culture than I am.

26

"Correct," Ben says. "And the home to Theresa Morgan."

I lean my head back and close my eyes, trying to remember why that name sounds so familiar. *Ahh, yes. Middle-aged woman, sharp as a tack, short red hair.* "I remember her. Vice President Morgan. One of the few VPs who wasn't a complete puppet. She negotiated hard—finally got my father to lower the taxes by a few percent. We even threw in some free boxes of medicine. I liked her."

"She's a close friend of mine," Ben says.

I want to ask how he knows her, but I don't think he'll tell me. Behind his sparkling green eyes I sense there are fathomless mysteries.

"I'm growing tired of this place, Father. It's cold and dank in this cave. When shall we depart for subchapter 1?" Elsey's head is cocked to the side and her nose is all scrunched up. I can't help but smile.

Roc mimics her facial expression and tone of voice. "Yes, Father. It's cold…and *dank*. We must leave before all bounce has been removed from our step."

Elsey giggles and jumps up, trying to grab Roc, but he leaps out of the way, besting her with his agility and speed. He gets behind her, picks her up, and tickles her around the sides of her stomach. She giggles louder, desperately trying to pry Roc's hands from her. Ben is chuckling heartily, his dark stubble throbbing up and down with each chortle.

I laugh, too, but stop when Adele's face flashes into my mind. She's not laughing, not even smiling. Her face is serious, grim, straight-lipped, and heavy-eyed. Even in this form, her face makes my breath catch in my throat. I wonder whether I am seeing a memory, or whether my mind has invented the image of its own volition—or whether I am somehow seeing her across the miles, through rock and stone. If so, I feel bad. We are laughing and she is not.

"What's wrong?" Ben asks, looking at me suddenly. His smile is gone too. I can still hear Elsey's unfettered laughter, but it feels distant.

I shake my head. "It's nothing."

"I felt it, too," he says.

I nod. I'm not sure why I've been chosen to have such a powerful connection with Adele, but I'm glad for it. She's changed my life. "I'm worried about her," I admit.

"Me, too," Ben says. "But she's strong, like her mother. She'll be okay."

I find it odd that he compares Adele to her mom, particularly when referring to her strength. He seems so strong, and from what she's told me, it was he who trained her to fight. There must be something I'm missing.

I realize it's quiet again in the cave we've been hiding out in. Roc and Elsey are once more sitting on the rock floor close to each other, panting from the exertion of their tickle fight, listening to my conversation with Ben.

"Adele is okay, right, Father?" she asks.

Since Adele left to start her journey to the Star Realm with Tawni, a full forty-eight hours have passed. We've spent it hiding out in a cave on the edge of subchapter 26, but Adele has likely spent the time marching through a tunnel potentially filled with sun, moon, and star dweller troops, any of whom could have easily mistaken her for the enemy.

"She's fine," he says, and I take as much comfort from the confidence in his words as Elsey does. "And we can leave this cave right now—I think we've taken more than enough time to recover."

"Let's leave this *dreadful* cave right now," Roc says, once more imitating Elsey, which brings another scream and peal of laughter from her. She has really taken to him and I am glad. Although Roc gets on my nerves sometimes, he has such a good heart and has always made me laugh. I feel moisture in my eyes and I blink it away quickly, but not before he notices.

"Aww, is Tristy getting emotional on us? Wah wah!" he says.

Now it's my turn to attack and although Roc's fast, he's not fast enough. I spring to my feet and close the gap in seconds, knocking him flat on his back as he tries to twist away. Using my knees for leverage, I pin his hands over his head. "Who's your master?" I say.

"Umm, Elsey," he says, which makes Elsey giggle again.

Pushing one of my knees into his midsection, I say, "Wrong! Who's your master?"

"Uhhh!" he groans. "Okay, okay, your dad, President Nailin, is my master!" he yells.

"Wrong again!" I shout, releasing his arms and dragging my knuckles across his scalp.

Roc yelps and tries to grab me but I'm already back on the other side of the cave. Elsey is giggling uncontrollably and even Ben is chuckling. I can tell Roc is mad, but one look at Elsey's mirthful grin and his face softens and he joins in the laughter. I feel happy for another moment, but once again, I feel bad about it. Adele can't be a part of it.

After gathering our few measly possessions—Roc's pack and our swords—I start to stretch out my body, preparing for the long trek we have ahead of us.

"What's that for?" Ben says, motioning at me as I touch my toes.

"I don't want to cramp up after only ten miles," I say, feeling sheepish all of a sudden. I really am bad at geography, and I wonder if perhaps subchapter 1 is closer to 26 than I think.

"I would agree with you if we were going to walk."

"We can't take the trains; they'll be looking for us."

"Not on *our* train," Ben says cryptically. Evidently he's not going to tell me any more than that, so I just let it go. Darkness is surrounding the cave mouth, casting eerie shadows across the opening. In this case, darkness is our friend, our co-conspirator. It's time to go. We snuff out the dual torches we've been using to light our cubby hole and move out, Ben first, then Elsey, then Roc. I bring up the rear. It's the most dangerous position and I want it.

Outside, the underworld is a mystical place. The thin day/night panels on the roof of the expansive subchapter 26 cavern are slowly dimming, veiling the city in the murky haze of unnatural twilight. Looking in from the outskirts, the city is quiet. From our vantage point, subchapter 26 appears to be just another silent moon dweller city. The reservoir that circles the city blocks us. We had to ford it to reach the cave—we'll have to cross it to get back. The black water threatens us, but I'm not scared.

There's not much that scares me these days.

Ben noiselessly slips into the water, leaving barely a ripple as evidence of his entrance into the man-made stream. He turns and extends his arms, wordlessly beckoning to Elsey.

"I jumped from much higher than this before," she whispers. He is being an overprotective father. And she is being a young girl coming into her own. Elsey easily drops the three feet to the water, which churns silently and steadily clockwise, ceaselessly patrolling the city it provides sustenance to.

Roc is next and is less confident. He has never liked the water. After casting a furtive backward glance at me, he lines up to perform an awkward jump. I shouldn't do it, but I can't help myself.

I kick him in the butt.

His arms windmill two, three times, and then he drops in a tangle of arms and legs. Because the distance is minimal, his splash is weak, albeit greater than his predecessors'. I follow him into the water, timing my jump so that the slight wave I cause hits him in the face just as he comes up for air.

Spluttering and wiping at his eyes as if they've been sprayed with Mace, he blubbers, "That was mature."

"From the king of maturity himself," I say, laughing.

Ben bobs up next to us. "Guys, I know it's hard for you, but let's try to take the next ten minutes seriously. This may be the most dangerous part of our journey."

My face feels warm as I wish I hadn't let Adele's father down already. I have to do better. But it *was* fun.

Roc wipes the final drop of moisture out of his eyes and smirks at me. "Can't you ever be serious?" he says.

"It's not in my nature," I say.

Ben and Elsey are already across the moat and scrambling up the rocks on the other side.

"C'mon," I say, using the palm of my hand to splash Roc in the face. He lunges at me, but I am already gone, swimming underwater to the other side. I clamber out and wait for him. His slow and steady doggie paddle turns a thirty-second trip into two minutes.

When he gets to the edge, I reach out to help him up, tensing my muscles in case he tries something. He doesn't. Instead, once on the rock slab outside the city, he says, "Nice one." I don't believe that he means it. His dark eyes are already plotting his revenge.

Rather than sneaking into the city to the train station like I expect, Ben and Elsey are working their way around the city, sticking tight to the edge of the bending reservoir. They are holding hands and she's skipping along gaily, as if we are just out for an evening stroll. Again, the difference between Adele and her sister is stark. Roc and I begin a light jog to catch up.

As we walk, I admire the beauty of this subchapter, nicknamed Waterfall Cave for obvious reasons: Waterfalls of various heights and shapes spill down the sides of the enormous cavern, providing everlasting life to the reservoir and sustaining the city.

Strangely, there are no windows on the outside of any of the buildings along the city perimeter. Instead, bare rock stands like a fortress, sometimes rising ten stories high on heavy stone blocks. Maybe the occupants don't want to see the beauty of the waterfalls, as they prefer to numb themselves with negativity. I don't blame them—*can't* blame them. I might do the same if I were them. I look away from the falls, feeling bad that I ever enjoyed their beauty.

As we approach the end of each city block, Ben slows and peeks around the corner and down the cross street. No one is out. I wonder what happened to everyone. Many would have died at the hands of star dweller bombs, but there would have been survivors, too, like us. I hope the star dwellers are treating them kindly, but I fear they are not. War brings out the worst in people.

We make it five blocks before Ben stops and turns around, his green eyes appearing gray under the dusky lights. "One more block and we head back into the water. Follow me exactly and don't ask any questions." I have a few questions, but I hold them in. Despite having only just met this man, I trust him. His quiet, calm demeanor is a welcome change from my father's ruthless and anger-filled outbursts.

The final block flashes by and we approach another cross street. Ben takes his standard peek around the corner and then motions us to follow. We are halfway across the gap in the buildings when a throaty sneeze shatters the silence. Ben and I turn at the same time to see Roc standing frozen in place, eyes wide and white, his hand over his nose and mouth.

"C'mon," I hiss. "Don't just stand there."

Too late.

We hear a shout from the city. I whirl around to see a half-dozen troops wearing sky-blue uniforms with bright yellow star insignias patched on the shoulders running toward us. Star dwellers. They have guns and we are sitting ducks.

Roc cries out and starts running. I wait for him to pass me before I chase after him, preferring to defend the rear. Maybe I'm not a born leader like Ben, but I *can* fight.

We get around the building without being shot at, probably because the troops know they can pick us off one by one on the open slab between the city and reservoir. Pushing Roc and Elsey behind him, Ben barks, "Tristan—I'll take the first three, you get the last three." I jerk my head down in a quick nod. He knows what I can do, and I know what he is capable of. But we still need a miracle.

Although we haven't run far, I can already feel the heat of the adrenaline pumping through my veins. My muscles are tense and slightly shaky, but not in a bad way. I am ready. I was born for this. I've trained for this all my life. This is our world. I slide my sword out of its sheath.

It's not always good to be fast. The fastest star dweller trooper rounds the bend first, wrongly assuming that we are still running out in front of him. Before the guy has any idea what's happening, Ben's knee is thrust in his midsection and he's sprawled out on the rock, wheezing. The next one should be more prepared, but she's not, and evidently Ben has no qualms about hitting a girl, particularly when she's carrying a gun and trying to kill us. He takes her head off with an uppercut that will leave her senseless for hours. I am starting to think he might take out all six on his own.

But he runs into trouble on the third trooper, who realizes something isn't right. Rather than barreling around the corner like his friends, this guy leads with the black nozzle of his gun, which is blindly pointed right into Ben's chest. With a grunt, Ben grabs the nozzle and thrusts it downwards at his feet. The guy pulls the trigger.

Boom!

As close as I am to the gun, its roar echoes in my ears, momentarily deafening me. However, I don't need to see Ben's face to know he's hit. His mouth is agape and his eyes are closed as he continues to grapple with the guy with the gun. Even in the dim lighting I can make out the glossy sheen of blood spilling from his leg.

I have to help him.

I don't have time.

The final three troops—my responsibility—charge around the corner after hearing the gunshot. Two girls, one guy. Despite the favorable gender ratio, I don't relax. I've seen what

Adele can do. Perhaps there are other moon and star dweller women who are similarly capable. Perhaps they are all that capable. Probably not—Adele is amazing—but still, I don't underestimate these women.

They are all in a cluster—one in front, two on either side and behind—which is good for me. It makes them a single target rather than three. The one in front wants to shoot me. She takes aim at my head while running at me. I anticipate the explosion and dive for the stone slab.

POP!

The gunshot sounds dull and thin to my deafened ears, but I know I avoided the shot because I don't feel anything. Not even a pinch. Just a twinge of pain as my forearms and then hips and then back skid across the stone. I come out of the intentional roll at full speed, ducking under my attacker's gun, which she tries to jab me with. I am too close to use my sword, so I crash straight into her, rocking her back and into her two friends.

We go down in a heap on the ground, me on top, then the shooter, then her two friends. If we were a sandwich, the shooter would be the meat in the middle, or the cheese perhaps. I'm the top layer of bread and her friends are the bottom crust. Apart from a few bruises and scrapes, everyone in the sandwich is unhurt, so I push to my feet and kick the metaphorical cheese in the head. Her eyes roll back and her tongue lolls out as she tumbles off the pile.

The other two were so surprised by my attack that they've dropped their guns. I pick up one of the weapons and aim it in their general direction. They raise their hands above their heads while still lying prostrate on the rock. Their eyes widen as they see me—*really* see me for the first time. They know who I am;

at the end of the day, whether I like it or not, I'm still a celebrity.

We don't have time for prisoners, so I move in close and give each a moderate-strength tap on the head with the butt of the gun.

My job finished, I spin around and survey the scene before me. It's not good. Ben is on the ground, clutching his wounded leg and bleeding from the side of his head—his ear I think. A gun lies discarded a few feet away, but out of his reach. The last remaining soldier has his sword out and is waving it wildly at Roc, who stands in front of Elsey with his own sword, protecting her from the onslaught. Roc's a maniac, growling between bared teeth and blocking each attack with a fervor I've been trying to get out of him for weeks. He's a man possessed.

As I consider my options, I watch as Roc blocks another sword stroke and then flicks his wrist, rapidly slipping his own blade around his opponent's weapon, slashing him on the hand. The guy cries out and drops his sword as blood spills from his mangled thumb. Dashing forward, Roc lands a hard kick to the guy's gut, knocking him onto his back. I've got to hand it to him—Roc looks amazing, a mere shadow of his former timid self.

But he's not done yet. He strides forward, his face awash with fury, his sword raised high above his head.

With no time to think, I rush ahead, closing the distance in three long strides. Roc thrusts his blade to the ground and I dive.

Clang!

My hearing returns just in time to appreciate the full extent of the impact of metal on metal, as I slap Roc's blade away from the downed soldier.

From the ground, I look up at my best friend. Roc stares back at me with horror and anguish, his teeth no longer bared, his eyebrows no longer fierce. All strength sapped from him, he's just a scared teenager again. "I'm…I'm sorry," he says weakly.

"Roc, it's okay. You were just doing what you needed to."

"But I…I didn't need to kill him." His brown-skinned face is ashen, appearing paler than I have ever seen it.

"You didn't."

"Only because you…" He trails off.

"It doesn't matter how," I say. "It's over."

From beside me on the ground, the soldier sucks the air sharply through his teeth, grimacing in pain and clutching at his severed thumb. "What are you going to do with me?" he asks.

In one swift motion, I snap my elbow across his skull, delivering another knockout blow. He slumps over and becomes still.

I stand up and take Roc's sword, which is dangling precariously from his loosened fingers. I don't want him to lose a toe when he accidentally drops the blade point-first onto his foot. Closer to him, I can see him trembling slightly, his body's reaction to the burst of adrenaline he received during the fight.

I place a hand on his shoulder. "You did well, my friend. You were amazing actually."

"But I almost…"

"He was trying to do the same to you," I say.

"Roc," a tiny voice says from behind him.

Elsey is wide-eyed and serious, her brow furrowed, her lips bunched and tight. As soon as Roc turns, she rushes to him, throws her thin arms around him, pulls him to her. "I owe you my life," she says solemnly.

At her words, Roc's face finally relaxes and his body goes slack. He hugs her back. He's going to be okay.

"I need to help Ben," I say.

"Father?" Elsey says, her head popping up.

"I'm okay," Ben says, lifting a hand to his mangled ear, which is still bleeding heavily. "We don't have time to linger."

"You need medical attention," I say, kneeling down to inspect his leg. The bullet entered his skin just above the knee. I search for an exit wound but there isn't one. "The bullet's still inside you."

"No—I'm fine. There will be time for that later. More troops will be here any second." His face tells me he's not fine, but he is right. We have no choice but to keep going.

"Okay, let me help you."

"I'm fine," he says again. I think he's saying it to convince himself—like a self-motivation sort of thing. It seems to work as he manages to push himself to his feet, favoring his uninjured leg. "Follow me. Hurry."

Elsey clutches her dad's side as he limps toward the reservoir. She doesn't ask if he's all right, just takes his word for it.

With no other choice, Roc and I follow in their wake, watching carefully to make sure he doesn't stumble. Ben stops at the water's edge and gazes into it. I wonder what he's doing. Has the loss of blood affected his mind?

He dives into the water headfirst.

Three
Adele

The first two hours are fine. We maintain a light jog, trying to use our relative health to our advantage. Tawni stumbles once when she trips over a stone, but I catch her arm and we keep going. No one dies. I consider it a victory.

Although our fitness levels are improving since we left the Pen, we are still in no shape for an eight-hour run, so we eventually slow our pace to a hurried march. Tawni's long strides force me to take two steps for every one of hers. Her white ponytail swishes from side to side, like the ticking spindle on a clock. Ticking away the minutes on our lives.

Halfway into the third hour, Tawni says, "Uh-oh." It's the first thing either of us has said, as we are concentrating on our breathing. It's not the first thing I hoped to hear out of her mouth.

"What is it?"

"I have a headache."

"It might just be a headache," I say.

"It's not."

"The symptoms are too early."

"You can't predict these things, Adele. Three hours is just the average. Plus we didn't leave right after we drank the water."

I know she's right. Since I've known Tawni, she's never complained of headaches. It would be too much of a coincidence that she gets one now. I don't believe in coincidences.

"We have to go faster," I say.

We start to jog again, even though we both know it's not sustainable. A half-hour later my legs are on fire and I can't seem to swallow enough air to satisfy my hungry lungs. A silent drumbeat begins to thump in my temple. A headache. I don't say anything. Just keep jogging.

"I need to stop for a minute," Tawni pants.

I pull up short and look at my friend. She's not doing well—that much I can see. She's breathing even heavier than I am and her face is knotted with pain. "Any new symptoms?" I ask.

Tawni shakes her head. "Just the headache, but it's getting worse."

"I've got one, too," I admit. "But it's not bad yet."

"We need water."

I close my eyes, wish with all my might that water will appear out of thin air. When I open my eyes we still don't have any water. "Damn, didn't work," I say.

Tawni manages a wry grin, but I can tell even that's a struggle.

"Let's walk fast again. Every step forward gets us closer. We might still make it." I'm trying to be optimistic, which is hard for me. Secretly I'm praying we stumble upon someone—I'd take anyone at this point, perhaps even some bloodthirsty star dweller soldiers.

We start up again and the thuds in my head sync with my footsteps. *Thud, thud. Thud, thud. Thud!* With each step I feel like my headache reaches its maximum point of pain, but then the next step hurts even more, pounds a little harder. It feels like my skull is trying to break free from my skin. Tawni's headache started earlier, so she must be hurting even more, but I don't look at her because I have to concentrate on my own steps.

After three hours we have to stop to rest. I sling my pack in the corner between the wall and the floor, sit down next to it, lean my back against the rough stone. Tawni slumps next to me, huddling close.

Not for the first time since we parted ways, and surely not for the last time, my thoughts turn to my mother's note.

You'll know him when you see him.

A cryptic message, one that both Tawni and I have decided is about Tristan. It has to be. I mean, how many other *hims* will cause me physical pain the moment I set eyes on them? Probably, definitely, exactly none. Except Tristan. What her note means or why she asked my father to give it to me, I don't know. He didn't seem to have a clue either.

Since my final hug with Tristan, since I last saw him, the tingles on my scalp and the buzzing along my spine have lessened with each step, until finally, an hour or so ago, they vanished completely, as if our physical connection will always depend on our closeness. Our nearness.

Or it could all just be related to the Bat Flu.

Although we've been walking for two days solid, Tawni and I, trudging down an endless inter-Realm tunnel, making our way slowly to the Star Realm, the last two hours have been by far the worst. Although I know we are, I don't feel like we're getting anywhere. Every step forward feels like two backward. It's like wading through water, as if the air has substance, its viscosity slowing our every move.

It's not just the act of walking that frustrates me. It's the monotony of the tunnel. The tunnel is wide enough for half a dozen people to walk side by side, and tall enough for me to give Tawni a piggyback ride, although given she's about six inches taller than me, the physics might not work so well. The tunnel floor is smooth, packed hard by thousands of tramping feet, but the walls and ceiling are rough and jagged, as if it was excavated haphazardly by a century-old tunneling machine. Modern-day tunnelers create perfectly arched passages, with smooth edges and glassy sides, at a rate of five miles per hour. This tunnel looks more like three guys with shovels and pickaxes carved their way through at about five feet per hour.

Huge pipes run along the ceiling: air pipes, carrying fresh, filtered oxygen to the star dwellers. It's scary to think about the fact that we'd all be dead if not for these kinds of pipes, our air used up, leaving nothing for our thirsty lungs. I've always taken it for granted that my subchapter had fresh air pumped in through the roof, while the old air is sucked out and back to the barren surface of the earth. I remember learning in school how the air on earth contains noxious fumes—as a result of what happened in Year Zero—which required the scientists to come up with an advanced air filtration system to ensure there was enough clean air for everyone. Well, the pipes I've been staring at as we trudge along are part of the system.

For two days, the tunnel has sloped gently downwards, which should make the hike easy, but since we've contracted the Flu, it's as if gravity has reversed itself, pitting even the laws of nature against us, making the downhills feel like uphills. It's getting warmer as we go deeper into the earth, which was another thing I learned in school, but could never really believe until experiencing it firsthand. Or it's the fever setting in, I'm not entirely sure.

My thoughts turn to my mom. Is she okay? Although I rescued my sister, Elsey, and my dad, I don't dare to hope that my mom is still alive. How could she be? There are no happy endings in my world. Not even happy beginnings. And the middle parts, they are the saddest of all.

"Are you okay?" Tawni manages to ask, snapping me out of my grim mood. I'm not sure how long we've been resting.

I nod, lick my dry, chapped lips, try to swallow.

"Why haven't we seen anyone since the sun dwellers?" I ask.

"I don't think the star dweller troops are going home anytime soon," she says. "Not until they get what they want, anyway."

Just before we entered the tunnel we are in, two days earlier, we saw thousands of star dweller troops pass by. They looked rough and weary, but determined. Determined to get the moon dwellers to join their rebellion…or die trying.

"So many people will die," I say.

"Not if your dad and Tristan can get the moon dweller leaders to listen. I mean, they *will* get them to listen. I know they will." Tawni is just being herself. Optimistic by nature. Despite all she's been through, still optimistic. I marvel at her character.

"I'll agree with you the second the sun dwellers invite us all up for a big Tri-Realms unity party," I say.

Tawni smirks, but tries to hide it.

"I meant never."

"I know," Tawni says, laughing at first and then coughing.

It's the most we've talked in a long time and I'm glad we can still joke. I doubt we'll be able to in a few hours. Tawni looks at me curiously.

"What?" I say.

"I've been thinking—"

"Always dangerous," I comment.

"And…" Tawni says, ignoring me, "I think Tristan and Roc were hiding something from us."

"Like you think one of them might be a woman?"

Tawni cracks up and doesn't even cough this time. It's like the laughter is healing us. I might believe that if not for the throbbing in my forehead. "Not what I was thinking, but good guess. I'm thinking something more important, like about the meaning of life."

"You don't think Tristan being a woman is important?" I say, attempting a smile of my own which ends in more of a grimace.

Tawni laughs hard, which results in another coughing fit. So much for the laughter-healing theory.

"I guess that would be pretty important to you."

"You guess?"

"Okay, yes, that would be important. But I'm talking important on a world scale, not just a personal level."

I'm giving Tawni a hard time, but I know exactly what she means. I felt it, too. A couple of times I thought Tristan was about to tell me something big, but then he would make an offhanded comment, a joke usually. It's as if he was waiting for the perfect time to tell me something, but that time never came. Or maybe he was debating whether he could trust me with some secret. I guess if I were him, I wouldn't trust me either, not after having only just met me. It's not like I completely trust him yet either. I mean, I want to, especially because the fate of the world seems to be resting precariously on his shoulders. Oh yeah, and because we held hands for like two hours one night. Which was a big deal for me, who doesn't know a slide into first base from a base-clearing homerun.

"I think so, too," I say.

"You do?"

"Yeah. Remind me to ask him about it on our next date."

Tawni laughs again, her face lighting up, the laugh reaching her pale blue eyes. I'm happy I can make her laugh even in our current condition. She deserves some measure of happiness. I know I complain a lot about the hand life has dealt me, but Tawni has it bad, too. At least I know my parents are good people, even if I may never see them again. At least I want to see them again. Tawni, on the other hand, has told numerous times that seeing her parents in a million years would be too soon.

And then…Cole.

He was the only family she really had left. I mean, maybe he wasn't tied to her by blood, and certainly no one would mistake him for her brother, what with his dark skin against her white.

But he was her family—there is no doubt about that. But now he's gone. Laid low, like the dust on our shoes. Torn from this world with the same ferocity that his entire family was taken from him by the Enforcers.

I realize I'm gritting my teeth and Tawni has stopped laughing. Nothing like my dark thoughts to bring down the mood.

"What are you thinking about?" she asks.

"Nothing," I lie.

"Cole."

"Maybe."

"Yes." We haven't talked about Cole since we tearfully entered the tunnels. I've heard Tawni's muffled sobs both nights, but when I whispered to her they stopped, and she didn't respond. Maybe she was embarrassed or something. She shouldn't be. Her tears are only showing what we're both feeling.

"Yes," I admit.

"I'm not sure I can cope." Her face is blank, unreadable. Her laugh lines have disappeared, her cheeks and forehead smooth once more. One of her hands is unconsciously tugging on her single lock of blue hair, tinged with white near her scalp, where her regrowth is pushing it away.

"You will. We both will," I say, trying to imbue confidence in my shaky voice. It's a lie. Maybe we will find a way to cope, but I don't know for certain.

Tawni looks at me, shivers because of the oncoming fever, but I can't tell if she believes the lie. Her words don't give me any clue either. "It's weird," she says.

"What is?"

"Death."

I just look at her, wondering where she's going with this, wondering if we're both headed for a breakdown.

"It's like, one moment a person you know and love is there, right next to you, and the next they're gone, taken. Their body is still there, but you know that *they're* not."

I don't know how to respond. Her words seem so calm, so rational, so precise. Free of emotion. *Almost.*

"He's gone forever," she says, her voice quivering slightly.

"Deep breaths," I say, stopping to heave in and out a few times, taking my own advice. It's what my mom used to say when I got upset about something that went wrong at school. She was always a master of controlling her emotions. I never saw her lose her temper, or even cry, not once.

Tawni follows suit, crosses her arms, closes her eyes, breathes in deeply, holds it for a second, and then releases it. When she opens her eyes, the tightness in her lips is gone.

"Thanks," she says.

I try to find the right words to say. One thing springs to mind. "My grandmother was my best friend," I say slowly, trying to get my words right, make them perfect. Tawni is watching me closely, her head leaned back against the wall. "She used to tell me stories, read me books, treat me like an adult and a child at the same time. She was…she was…" My voice catches in my dry throat.

"She sounds like an amazing woman," Tawni says, coming to my rescue.

I force down a swallow, nod my head once. "Yes, she was. Amazing. She died when I was six."

"I'm sorry," Tawni says.

"It's okay. At the time I was a wreck. I wouldn't leave my room, wouldn't eat, wouldn't speak. I didn't even want my dad to teach me how to fight anymore."

"Your dad was teaching you how to fight when you were six?" Tawni asks, her eyebrows raised, her lips curling slightly.

"He started when I was three," I admit.

"That explains a lot."

I laugh, and Tawni does, too. Now she is helping me.

"My dad told me to celebrate my grandmother's life, not mourn her death. We spent a whole day just sitting on the floor across from each other, telling stories about her. How she made us laugh, how much we loved her smile, all the happy memories we had of her. When we were finished I was still sad, but it felt different somehow. Like she was still with me—not gone forever."

"I don't know if I can handle that," Tawni says.

"Well, if you ever want to try, just let me know."

Tawni stares into space for a minute. I just sit there, too, hoping she'll open up to me.

Finally, she says, "Okay, I'll try, but I might have to stop."

"Okay. Do you want me to go first?"

"Please."

I didn't know Cole for long, but the time I had with him is precious to me. I close my eyes and try to remember something special about him, but the first thing that pops into my head is a horrifying vision: Rivet wrapping his arms around Cole's neck, wrenching his skull to the side, snapping his neck; my screams; the blood on my hands as I stab Rivet in the chest; the pain of losing Cole replacing my lust for revenge; Tawni's shaking, sobbing breakdown later that night. *No!*

I squeeze my eyes shut tighter, hoping I can regain control of my thoughts. This was my idea, after all, and if I can't control my memories of Cole, how can I expect Tawni to?

Suddenly I remember something good. "Remember when Cole took that punch for me, during the prison riot?"

"I didn't see it, but I remember how his eye looked afterwards."

"Like he'd run headfirst into a wall," I say.

"And he had a hard skull. Imagine what your face would've looked like if the guy had punched you."

"I would've been unrecognizable," I say. "Remember how stubborn I was after? How I said I could take care of myself?"

"I've seen you take care of yourself. You're more than capable."

"Yeah, but in that situation I was in way over my head. That dude was a giant. He might've killed me. It was then that I knew Cole was special." My voice catches, but I plow ahead, trying to mask it. "It's so weird. I knew him for such a short time, but I would've done anything for him. He was just so…"

"Pure?" Tawni suggests, making eye contact.

I brush my dark hair off my face with my hand. "Yeah, exactly. Like all the bad stuff that happened to him didn't muddy his soul at all. Like he was above it all, better than this world. In the muck, but not part of it." My soul feels like it's slowly healing. This therapy session is for Tawni, but I'm benefitting, too.

Tawni smiles. "I'm glad you felt that, too. Although I knew Cole for five years, I can still remember when I first met him."

"How'd you meet?"

"He saved me, too," Tawni says, closing her eyes. I can almost see Cole's strong face behind her eyelids. "Even though we were rich, my parents sent me to a local school. They said it was so I could live a normal life, but looking back, I think it was just another way to get close to other moon dwellers. You know, so they could report back to the Sun Realm on what the mood was in the Moon Realm." Tawni's eyes are open again and she's frowning. I need to steer her thoughts away from her parents, who only make her angry.

"You met Cole at school?" I ask.

Her eyes soften and she glances at me. "Yes. The kids gave me a hard time at school. First off, I've always been freakishly tall. They called me things like Tawni the Giant, Ogre-Girl, and Freakazoid."

"But you're so pretty," I say. I'm honestly shocked. I thought she would have been one of the cool kids at school, little miss popular, with good looks, lots of money, guys lining up for her attention. I never considered the possibility that she was bullied.

Tawni blushes. "Thanks," she says. "Cole always said that, too. Even though the kids made fun of me, it didn't bother me too much. They were just words. It was my parents that caused the real problems."

"What do you mean?" I ask, my mind filling with thoughts of her dad beating her, her mom verbally abusing her—perhaps they locked her in her room for days at a time.

As if reading my mind, she says, "My parents didn't do anything to me directly. But because of who they were and the money we had, the kids at school took their bullying to a new level. They still yelled names at me, but they also started spray-painting my locker. *Rich bitch* was one of their favorites. But that didn't satisfy them because I ignored it, pretended not to see it. So they took it up another notch. They knocked my

50

books out of my hands, pulled my hair in class, tripped me in the halls. I remember lying to my parents about the scrapes on my knees and elbows, telling them I fell down playing basketball at recess."

I pull my mouth into a tight line. I remember when I found out about the lavish lifestyle that Tawni had. A big house. Servants. Gobs of money. My first reaction was anger. I never considered that Tawni paid the price for it at school. I feel ashamed.

She continues. "It was getting pretty bad, and I was considering telling someone. The principal, maybe. A teacher. Anyone but my parents. One day I was outside the school, eating my lunch by myself, trying to make myself invisible."

Her story reminds me of how I was in juvie, in the Pen. I was the same way. Always alone. I wonder if it's why she approached me in the Pen in the first place. Because she knew how I was feeling.

"There was this guy, Graham, who, along with his girlfriend, Tora, had been messing with me lately. They came up behind me and pushed me over. My food spilled everywhere. When I tried to pick it up, they stepped on it. A few of their friends saw what they were doing and came over to join in the fun. There were eight of them, four guys and four girls. I had never seen them this bad. I could see in their eyes that they wanted to hurt me. Not just humiliate—but physically injure me, maybe kill me. I'd never been so scared in my life."

Tawni is not like me. She's not tough. She's fragile. All I want to do is protect her. I pray I'm strong enough.

"Some of them picked up stones and were ready to throw them at me. That's when I met Cole. My knight in shining armor. He burst through the circle like a bull. Two of the guys went flying. The other two guys tried to hit him, but Cole was made of steel. He blocked their punches and knocked them out. He wouldn't hit the girls although I could tell he wanted to. Instead he growled at them to run away and they did. He got suspended for two weeks, and I started spending all my time with him. No one messed with either of us again. He was my best friend."

Her eyes are moist, but not with sadness. Her pride at having known Cole is just spilling over. I hug her.

We've lingered for far too long, but it seems to have energized both of us as we stand up. Although we're sick, there's a slight bounce to our steps. I feel like we might still make it through this.

But those feelings can't possibly last.

Four
Tristan

Elsey is about to follow her father into the water, but I grab her arm. "Elsey—no!" I shout.

She looks at me blankly. "But Father told us to follow him," she says. I have a feeling she would jump into the lava flow if he did first.

"I don't think he's thinking clearly," I say. "I'll go pull him out."

My head jerks up as I hear a splash. Ben is bobbing in the center of the reservoir, staring at us. "What are you waiting for? There's a tunnel here." Without further explanation, he ducks under and kicks downwards, sending tiny ripples chasing each other to the shore.

Elsey manages to squirm away from me and dives in, making almost no splash. Roc looks at me and shrugs. "After what we just did, I wouldn't mind a quick dip." I can always tell when Roc is lying—like now. His lips are pursed, his eyebrows raised slightly. He wants to look brave, but I can tell he's scared. Like I said, water's not his thing.

"You first," I say. I want to make sure no one follows us. I still have no clue where Ben is taking us, but I have to trust him.

This time I don't kick Roc in the butt. He's scared enough as it is, so I let him dabble a toe in the water and then wade in slowly. Once he's waist deep, he pauses and I can tell he's trying to gather his nerve. Plugging his nose, he plunges into the inky stream.

Before following, I turn and scan the area up to the buildings. There's no sign of movement. The shadowy silhouettes of the downed troops blot the edge of the city. I catch a whiff of burning when I breathe in. Whether it is a lingering reminder of the bombing from three days ago or a new fire, I don't know.

I turn back to the water and slip in, pushing off of the rocky embankment to propel myself forward. Expecting complete darkness, I don't bother to open my eyes, sweeping my hands to each side to dive deeper, while churning my feet like a propeller.

Ten seconds pass and still I go deeper. I push forward with my hands, reaching out, trying to touch something, an arm or a leg, anything to tell me I've caught up to Roc, but I feel nothing. Nothing. And then…

Crunch!

Sharp pain lances through my fingers as my knuckles glance off hard rock. I pull them back sharply, tucking them to my chest for a moment. I've reached the reservoir floor without finding anyone. Finally, I open my eyes and feel the cold water swarm around my eyeballs.

As expected, blackness surrounds.

I swivel my head to the right, seeing nothing but oil. Twisting back to the left, I see it. A light. A beacon. A surprise. Off in the distance, something bright is bobbing through the pool, moving away from me.

I'm not sure how long I've been underwater, but my breath is becoming short. My instincts are urging me to kick to the surface and breathe, but I know I can't. I try to push all thoughts of air out of my head as I kick hard, chasing the light.

As I swim, more lights appear on either side of the first one, except these are stationary, like the sentry lights that guard the tunnels of the many inter-Realm trains. I am gaining on the light.

When I reach the stationary lights, I find they are embedded in the wall, illuminating the entrance to a tunnel. An underwater tunnel! Ben isn't crazy, after all. He knew exactly what he was doing.

The moving light is in the tunnel and I can barely make out shadowy figures flitting about it. I'm not sure how long has passed since I entered the water, but my lungs are aching for air. From its entrance, the tunnel appears endless, a never ending chute to nowhere, or somewhere—it's definitely one or the other.

I grit my teeth and kick harder, shoveling the water to either side with my hands. Thankfully, the tunnel is wide enough to use my whole body to move me forward, and I feel a surge of water around my ribs as I move faster through the abyss. Chasing. Chasing. Chasing a damn light that seems to move ceaselessly away from me.

My movements grow frantic as my body, my blood, my brain demand air. I push harder and harder, straining against my own limitations. The light moves upwards and disappears, and I fear it's gone out, plunging us all into darkness and death.

I push on.

My vision gets blurry and I feel lightheaded.

I push on.

One kick. Two kicks. Three kicks. I have nothing left.

But I find something more. I push on.

I feel strong hands grab my tunic and pull me up. I gasp, splutter, take deep breaths that are half-air, half-water. Choking, I cough, trying to expel the intruding liquid.

"Slowly, Tristan. Breathe slowly," Ben says, rolling me over onto my back.

I obey, deepening my breaths—in between each gulp I'm still coughing—and trying to relax my heaving chest. Gradually, I open my eyes to see Roc, Elsey, and Ben hovering over me. They all appear to be perfectly fine—while I'm a mess.

"Who hates the water now?" Roc says, smirking.

I'm too tired for a comeback. Plus Roc does appear to have handled the long swim better than me. I take three heavy breaths and start to feel better.

"Where are we?" I ask.

"See for yourself," Ben says with a wave of his arm. I roll over and look past him, at where he's gesturing. Everything's blurry at first, so I blink a few times to clear my eyes. Something comes into focus. It's a...a...

"Train?" I say, not really believing my own description.

"Traaaiiinnn," Roc repeats slowly, sounding out the word for me like I'm stupid. "T-R-A-I-N. Spell it with me, Tristan."

I ignore him and push up to my feet. Indeed, it's a train, gleaming silvery and metallic, even under the dim glow of the lights inset into the brownish-gray rock walls. We are in a small bunker, accessible only via the train that stands before us, or the watery tunnel from where we arrived.

"Does it run?" I ask stupidly.

"Of course," Ben says. "All of the secret trains have been maintained by the Resistance for many years."

"The Resistance…" I murmur, remembering my history lessons. From what I can remember, the Resistance was formed and destroyed in the same year, in 475 Post-Meteor, before I was born. My father and his armies crushed the Resistance like a bug before it could ever really do any real damage to the government. "But the Resistance was destroyed," I say.

"You've been reading sun dweller history books, I see," Ben says. "The real story is much darker and more complicated than your father wants anyone to believe."

My mind whirls. But if there are still secret trains maintained by the Resistance, then that means the organization still exists. That there are still people out there fighting. "Tell me," I say, my throat aching from swallowing too much water.

"Maybe later—we've got a train to catch."

I have so many questions, but Ben hasn't led us astray yet, so I follow him to the train doors, which open automatically as he approaches. Elsey is clinging to his side.

"Will the train whisk us away to a better place?" she asks innocently.

"I can't see how it could take us to a worse place," Roc grumbles.

"We'll see, Elsey, we don't know whether subchapter 1 has been hit yet," Ben says, not sugarcoating the situation, even for his youngest daughter. I can see how Adele got so tough. Her father probably always gave it to her straight—the real story, not some children's fairy tale. A harsh truth perhaps, but the truth nonetheless.

We step onto the train, which is spotless, in better condition than even the sun dweller trains. The seats are gray and hard, lined up efficiently along the edges like a military convoy, with plenty of room in the middle for satchels of weapons and ammunition. At least that is how I guess the space was being used by the Resistance. Correction: *is* being used by the Resistance. I'm still trying to get my head around what Ben said.

While Roc and I take a seat with Elsey between us, Ben presses a black button on the wall and speaks into an intercom. "It's Ben, requesting immediate train transport from subchapter 26." His leg is covered in blood, and I start ripping shreds off my tunic so he can bind his wound.

There's a bit of static, and then a female voice comes through loud and clear. "Ben? Is it really you? We thought…we thought you were dead."

"It'll take more than a traitor prison camp to kill me."

"And Anna?"

"Anna is below. My daughter is going after her."

"Do you think she's—"

"Yes," Ben says firmly, glancing at us. "She's alive, I know it."

"Adele has been all over the news," the voice says.

58

"Look, Jinny, I'd love to catch up, but…"

"Right, sorry. I'll get you moving right away. We'll have plenty of time to talk later…but Ben?"

"Yeah."

"I'm sure glad you're alive—and we'll be pulling for Anna, too."

"Thanks. Over."

Before Ben can sit down, the train starts moving, beginning slowly and picking up speed as the lights flash off and we're thrust into absolute darkness.

I feel a scrape against my arm as Ben sits next to me, grunting slightly. "Mr. Rose—I mean Ben—are you okay?" I ask, handing him the strips of my tunic.

"Thanks," he says, taking the fabric. "I think so. I'm not sure, but I think the bullet missed the bone and lodged in the muscle. At least that's what I'm hoping."

"What happened to your ear?" I ask in the dark.

"That horrible soldier with the sword sliced it off," Elsey interrupts from my other side. I turn, half-expecting to see that face that reminds me so much of Adele, but see only a black void.

I turn back and say, "He cut your ear off?"

Ben chuckles, which seems odd given we're talking about his missing ear, which is likely being examined by the star dweller soldiers as we speak. "Nah. Just the tip, I reckon."

"Oh, *just* the tip. No big deal then," Roc says. "Sorry, guys, I'm not used to all this violence. I think I might just catch a transfer back to the Sun Realm at the next stop."

I laugh and it hurts my throat, but still feels good somehow. "Oh, I think you fit right in, buddy. I'm not sure what won you the battle—your clunky sword work, or the deranged look on your face while you swung that pointy hunk of metal like a madman."

"You taught me everything I know."

"I don't remember the day I taught you Fearsome Expressions 101."

"Yeah, you were absent that day, so I had to do self-study," Roc retorts. Elsey giggles. I can sense Roc grinning in the dark. Somehow we are always able to joke. Somehow it makes things easier.

"Ben, can I ask you something?" I say.

"I'll tell you all about things later," he says.

"No, not that," I say. "Something else. About Adele."

"Sure."

"Why'd you teach Adele to fight?"

"Because she wanted to," he replies simply. It's not the answer I expected at all. I thought he might say *So she could defend herself*, or *Because it's all I know*, or even *Because it's a dangerous world out there, son*. I don't know, something like that.

"How'd you know that she wanted to learn?"

"Because one morning I took Adele out back, behind our house, and showed her a few things. You know, how to kick, how to punch, that sort of thing. I was mostly just messing around, having fun with her. Roughhousing. The next morning when I went out back to train, Adele was already there, practicing her kicking. She always loved to kick. Every day after that she showed up, without being told. When Elsey was born, she never seemed interested, so I didn't push her. We did other things together, but with Adele it was all about the training."

"I liked cooking with Mom," Elsey interrupts.

"And your doll."

"Molly!" Elsey exclaims. "Oh, dearest Molly, my only doll. She and I used to go on the most incredible adventures together. To defeat evil witches and dark wizards and meet fantastically handsome knights."

I can't help but to laugh. Roc's cracking up, too, and Ben's deep chortle rises above us all. A proud father.

"How'd you learn to talk like that, El?" Roc asks.

"Like what?" Elsey says innocently.

Ben chuckles. "She loved reading old throwback books with my wife, about princes and princesses and kings and queens. Something about the formal way they spoke just stuck with her."

"Well, I think it's pretty silly," Roc says, tickling Elsey on her stomach, which earns another squeal of laughter from her.

We sit in silence for a few minutes, each lost in our own thoughts. I think back to what Ben said. *Because she wanted to.* He's the opposite of my own father, who always *encouraged* us to do certain activities with the back of his hand or his belt. It was never a choice. Learn to fight or face his wrath. Ben is a good man. The best kind of man. A role model. I've barely just met him, but already I want to be like him. I'll follow him to the molten core of the earth if he asks me to.

I'm in the game.

* * *

A few hours later the lights come back on and the train slows, pulling to a stop next to a dimly lit stone platform. A half-dozen people are gathered to meet us. They remind me of Ben: strong and capable, heads held high, tight lips that are quick to smile and then spring back to serious again. They are each wearing various shades of brown tunics that have seen better days, littered with patches and ragged edges.

To my left, Elsey is asleep on Roc's shoulder, and he on her head. To my right, Ben is wide-eyed and alert, as if he hasn't slept at all. I couldn't sleep either, but chose to pass the time in silence.

As the train doors ease open I feel my stomach lurch with hunger. The greeters push their way inside. "Ben!" the woman in front shouts as she sees us. Ben is on his feet in an instant as the woman charges him, hugging him fiercely. She looks to be in her early forties, with the beginning of wrinkles under her amber eyes and creasing her broad forehead. She wears a long, brown ponytail with just a touch of gray around the edges. Her jaw is firm, her lips full. I stand up next to them and wait in uncomfortable silence as they embrace. I feel somewhat embarrassed at the emotion they display, especially given Ben is a married man.

My confusion is erased when Ben releases the woman and says, "Tristan—meet my sister, Jinny."

I break into a smile and extend a hand. *Smack*□ Instead of shaking my hand, she slaps me across the face, stunning me. "That's for being the son of the President," she says. Then she hugs me tightly, pulling her head into my chest. I don't hug back—my arms flail helplessly past her back—because I'm too shocked.

When she releases me, she says, "And that's for joining the Resistance."

"I, um, I, well…" I blubber.

"What he's trying to say is that he's pleased to meet you," Roc says, extending his hand. When Jinny takes it, he says,

"Can you show me how to do that slap you just laid on Tristy here? It could definitely come in handy."

Jinny laughs while I continue to try to figure out what the hell is going on.

"My sister can be rather opinionated," Ben says.

"Father?" Elsey says, rubbing her eyes groggily.

Ben's head whips around, as if he's forgotten about his youngest daughter. With a single large step, he moves to her side, puts a tender arm around her shoulder, and says, "Elsey—there's someone I'd like you to meet."

Jinny steps forward, reaching her hand out slowly, as if she's afraid she might frighten her. "Hi, Elsey, I'm your Aunt Jinny."

For a second I think Elsey might be angry as her eyes narrow, but then she rushes forward past Jinny's outstretched arm and throws her petite hands around her back. When she pushes back to look up at her aunt's face, she says, "But why didn't you ever visit?"—her head swivels to face her dad—"And why didn't you ever tell me you had a sister, Father?"

Ben's eyebrows arch and he smiles lightly. "I'm so sorry, El. I had to keep Jinny's existence a secret for everyone's safety. There are bad people that wanted to take her."

"Like they took you and Mother?"

"Exactly like that."

As she pulls away from Jinny, Elsey's hands move to her hips and a scowl appears on her face. The expression reminds me so much of Adele. "Are there any other relatives I should know about?"

Ben laughs. "I'm afraid not," he says. "Your mom is an only child and it is just Jinny and me."

"Then I suppose I can forgive you…this time," Elsey says, once more smiling.

"Ahem." Someone clears their throat at the train door. I turn to see a towering, dark-skinned guy with a day's worth of stubble. He's wearing a dark brown tunic cut off at the shoulders. Powerful, muscular arms hang loosely at each side, like rock-crushing sledgehammers. "We should really move inside," he says.

"Ram," Ben says, "it's good to see you again."

"I'm glad you're alive."

"Thank you."

"Ramseys—meet Tristan Nailin."

"I know who he is," Ram says, his eyes dark and glaring. "Follow me." Without another word he leaves the train, clearly expecting us to follow. He doesn't like me—that much is obvious.

"Sorry about him," Ben says.

"No problem," I say. "I'm used to all kinds of reactions to me. I think I prefer Ram's to most."

Ben's head cocks to the side, as if he's surprised by my statement. "I have a feeling you're just like an onion," he says, taking Elsey's hand and pulling her off the train before I can ask what he means.

Five

Adele

The fourth hour passes and we don't stop. Neither of us speaks. The only sounds are from our heavy breathing and the scuff of our shoes on the rock tunnel. The fifth hour passes and my headache escalates into a fever. I feel cold and shivery and empty, but my head is boiling. Sweat drips in my eyes, and when I blink it stings.

I sneak a look at Tawni. Her face is so gaunt and pale that she looks like a ghost. A thin sheen of sweat coats her skin.

Somehow we manage to maintain a steady pace to the sixth hour. My muscles are on fire, but not because of our long, strenuous hike. The virus is attacking my body, and from the feel of things, my body's not putting up much of a fight.

Next to me, Tawni stumbles. She manages to stay on her feet, but then a minute later, she stumbles again.

"You okay?" I ask.

She opens her mouth to speak, but no words come out. She points to her legs. *Her muscles are failing her.* Mine will do the same soon. We have to hurry.

"Here." I reach out and grasp her hand. We're going to have to support each other the rest of the way.

We keep walking. Tawni stumbles every few minutes, but I keep her up. Her right leg is doing this weird dragging thing with each step. Left foot up, step, right foot drag, repeat. It makes for slow going.

I stumble for the first time, but Tawni holds me up this time, which I acknowledge with a nod. Speaking will waste precious energy. It is weird, losing control of your body. It almost feels like I've been sucked into the past, when I was a toddler, unable to fully control my arms and legs. It's like I know they're there, and capable of doing cool things, but I just can't quite get them to do what I want. My left arm is no longer swinging while I walk, like it should; rather it hangs lifeless at my side. Dead. Like it's not part of my body anymore, just a strange growth. My other arm is only held up because I'm holding Tawni's hand.

I know my headache is bad, but I can't really feel it anymore. My muscles are aching more.

Seven hours pass, but I know we aren't moving fast enough to make it to subchapter 30 in only eight hours. Even if Tawni's guess as to the distance was correct, we might be four hours away still. We won't last that long. Not without water. Not without medicine.

"Ahhhhh!" Tawni screams next to me and I practically jump out of my skin. Instinctively I release her hand and pull away, moving flush with the tunnel wall. She is clawing at her face, tearing light scratches down her cheeks with her fingernails. A thin layer of blood rises to the surface. "Get them the hell off!" she screams.

I know she's hallucinating, but I don't know what she's seeing. It doesn't really matter—just that she's scared and needs my help. Without hesitation, I grab her hands and pull them away from her damaged face. She's lucky. Somehow she missed poking herself in the eye.

She struggles against me, tries to lift her hands back to her face, tries to claw at herself. Having no other choice, I release one of her hands and slap her hard across the face before she can raise it to her cheek. She stops struggling and collapses into my arms. Gently, gently, gently I lower her to the unforgiving rock bed. Her eyes are wide open, watery and red. She makes a weird gurgling, squealing sound from the back of her throat. "Shhh," I say. "You're okay, Tawni. They're not real." Whatever *they* are.

Tawni's chest is heaving but as I talk her breathing seems to slow, so I keep doing it, speaking softly, like I'm talking to a child. "Hush, hush, hush, my friend, danger's far away…Hush, hush, hush, my friend, the monsters go away." It's part of a poem my mom used to sing to me when I had nightmares, although my mom used to say *my princess* instead of *my friend*.

Not knowing what else to say, I cradle Tawni's head in the crook of my arm and hum to her, finishing the rest of the poem without words. Partway through, her eyes close and her body relaxes, going limp in my arms. The worst of the hallucination is over. When I finish I think she might be asleep, but when I move, her eyes open, blue and misty, but snaked with red veins, brought to the surface by the virus.

"Thanks," she says.

"It's okay."

"They were eating my flesh."

"What?"

"Maggots, insects, *things*. They freaked me out. I could see them on me, feel them chewing on my skin. It was so real."

I nod. "We're both going to have to try to ignore them, try to remember it's all part of the Flu.

Tawni sighs. "I'll try."

"We have to keep moving."

"I know."

Standing up again is torture. In the few minutes we've been on the ground, it seems every muscle in my body has frozen. My right arm is better off, so I use it to straighten my left arm, flex it, massage it. I feel a spurt of warmth as some blood rushes back into my arms. Next I work on my legs. Tawni is doing the same thing. Then we use the wall and each other to pull ourselves up. It probably takes us ten minutes to get to our feet.

Ten precious minutes.

I am dreading my first hallucination.

We continue walking, Tawni dragging a foot while I manage to lift both feet off the ground far enough to take real steps. At some point we switch from holding hands to huddling against each other, arms around each other's shoulders. She is my crutch and I am hers.

My fever is out of control. When the sweat isn't pouring down my face, I am shivering uncontrollably, shaking from head to toe. We are a mess. First Tawni shakes for a few minutes and then stops just in time for me to start convulsing. Soon our shaking begins starting and stopping at the same time. It's weird, almost like how they say girls who spend a lot of time with each other somehow synchronize their periods—we've synchronized our shaking.

I hear a sound. A thunder, of sorts. It sounds like a train is heading our way, moving down the tunnel. But there is no train station, no tracks. It's no train, of that I am certain.

I see what is making the noise, but it's too late. The water is moving too fast, charging toward us, a deluge of power, bubbling and raging and bursting. I scream, loud and long, and try to pull Tawni in the other direction, back the way we came.

She resists my pull and I don't know why. Perhaps she has given up; perhaps it is all too much for her; perhaps she just doesn't have the strength. Whatever the case, my hand pulls free from hers and I run alone, but not fast enough. The torrent sweeps me off my feet with the power of a mining machine, lifting me up and slamming me on the rocky floor. I roll and bounce, battered by the white bubbly rapids.

My only hope is that the force of the water will sweep me all the way back to the contaminated lake, where it will exit the tunnel, washing me up on dry land before I drown.

Tawni is already lost.

But the flood doesn't push me along. Instead, it encompasses me, leaving me churning on the tunnel floor, desperately straining to hold my breath for another second, another ten, another minute. It's like all my childhood nightmares about drowning—brought on by my near-drowning when I fell down a well as a young girl—are muddled into one horrible reality. My lungs are on fire, setting my chest ablaze with pain. Agony. Somehow I'm crying underwater, blubbering and sputtering, my lips parted and my eyes closed. The water should enter my mouth, suffocate me as I take one last breath.

It doesn't.

Tawni is by my side, holding me. The water swirls over and around her. It's as if she's in an air bubble, protected from the current. Not even her hair is wet. Her eyes are soft. Still red, but soft. Her lips move.

"Not real, honey," she says softly. "Hush—not real."

I realize I'm yelling something amidst my blubbering. I'm not sure what I'm saying, but I stop. The water looks strange. Almost too blue to be real. Too perfect.

Before it begins to ebb away, I know it's a hallucination. The waters subside and I'm left in Tawni's arms, much like she was in mine not that long ago. I'm soaking wet and shivering.

"So cold," I murmur between blue lips.

"No," Tawni says, shaking her head. "Not cold. Not real."

"But I'm all wet," I say, hugging myself, trying to get warm.

"Not wet. Completely dry."

Even as her words sink in, warmth returns to my body and I watch as my clothes stop sticking to me, the slickness on my skin vanishes, and the soggy, dripping locks of my black hair are replaced by soft, loose locks around my face.

I take a deep breath, trying to fight off the surreal memories of the life-taking water. "I'm okay," I say, wiping the unwanted tears from my face. I'm embarrassed, even though I know the hallucination was so real. I knew it was coming, but couldn't combat it. I need to do better with the next one. "We need to go."

"Maybe we should just stay here and ride it out," Tawni says. Her face is shining with sweat, her white hair tight and knotted, twisted together from the sweat on her neck and cheeks. Her words are a temptation. I can feel my face flushed with the fever and my muscles are battered and bruised. I couldn't handle the hallucination, but I *can* handle a little pain.

"No," I say, pushing myself up, biting back a groan as my muscles and bones scream at me. "That would be suicide."

Tawni knows I'm right so she lets me help her up without complaining. "I'm scared, Adele."

"We will make it," I say. *Won't we?*

With the Flu, things just keep getting worse. Thirty minutes later, Tawni is a ghost, pale and gaunt. She looks like she's sweated off ten pounds that she can't afford to lose. Her bony hands are clutching me at the elbow, depending on me to stay on her feet. I'm not much better off, but am coping with the achy muscles better than she is. I've been grinding my teeth in determination for so long I can feel the enamel flaking off on my tongue, gritty and dry.

Thankfully, neither of us has hallucinated for a while, and, despite the pain we're in, we are making steady progress, although I don't know if we're minutes, hours, or days from our destination. Nor do I know what to expect when we arrive. For all I know, the star dwellers might kill us on the spot. They are not the friendliest of people at the moment.

My mind is becoming a problem. One minute it is sharp and clear, and then the next it's hazy and groggy, like I'm sleepwalking through a deep fog. The foggy times are fast becoming the majority. I want to slap myself, but I can't get my hand up to my face; nor can I move it with the speed required to hurt enough to snap me out of my numbed state.

Tawni's fingernails dig into my arm and I know something is wrong. I slowly turn my head toward her to see what's going on, but it's too late. My face swivels right into her punch, and I feel a dull impact when her clenched knuckles collide with my cheekbone. It doesn't hurt exactly, but does force me off balance, and my legs are in no position to correct my momentum.

I tumble hard to the earth and try to roll away from my friend, who is now my attacker. My body disobeys me once more and I remain pinned to the ground. All I can do is hope that whatever hallucination is clutching Tawni will release her.

It doesn't.

Tawni leaps on top of me, grapples with my outstretched arms, tries to get the tips of her fingers into my eyes. She is screaming at me, shouting horrible things, obscenities, things I've never heard come from her mouth. Disgusting, vile things.

I try to remember that she's hallucinating, but she's trying to hurt me, and I have to defend myself. When she tries to hit me again, I grab one of her hands and get it under control. "You're hallucinating, Tawni, get off me!" I cry, but she doesn't listen, just keeps fighting with me.

A knife flashes, shiny and deadly. I can barely make it out in the dim light provided by our flashlights, which we have cast aside haphazardly during our fight. Where did she get a knife from? Why would she even have a knife? Tawni is the least violent person I know—more prone to run or hide than fight back. And yet she has a knife—and is trying to cut me open.

I grab the wrist of the hand with the knife and try to force it away from me. But Tawni has somehow become stronger from the Flu, gaining superhuman strength. The knife moves closer to my chest. She's going to kill me. I have no choice.

I close my other hand around her neck. The Flu has weakened me beyond recognition, but I use every last ounce of energy to squeeze my fingers shut, hoping to get her to drop the knife. The feeling is sickening. Horrifying. Knowing that you are literally squeezing the life out of someone. But I don't stop, because Tawni doesn't stop. It's weird. Although she's being choked to death—that much I can tell by the wretched gurgling sounds she's making—she won't drop the knife. It's like killing me is more important than her own life.

So this is how it ends for us? With friends killing each other?

Her lips are moving, trying to tell me something, but I can't understand her. Is it a trick or should I relax my grip? I'm afraid if I do she'll cut me to ribbons. "Ha…" she chokes out.

Her face is turning blue. I loosen my grip slightly. "What?" I grunt. The knife is so close to my skin, inching closer, but I have to know what Tawni is trying to say.

"You're…you're hal…luc…in…ating," she breathes.

Huh? I'm hallucinating? She's the one with the knife, the one trying to kill me. The cold steel pricks my skin, just below my neck. It doesn't hurt, doesn't bleed. I try to consider for just one moment that I might be the one having a waking nightmare. As soon as I do, the knife disappears. My world spins upside down and I am on top of Tawni, rather than the other way around.

I'm trying to kill her.

I'm hallucinating.

My body shakes and I wrench my hand from Tawni's neck. Twisting to the side, I throw myself against the hard rock, panting heavily.

Next to me I can hear Tawni gasping for breath, half-gagging.

I did it to her.

I spit once more and desperately wish for water. I'd even take a hallucination of water—they are so real, after all.

I turn back to Tawni, who looks like she might throw up, her head between her knees, her matted hair clumped around her face, which has no color in it. She's not gagging anymore, but her breathing is ragged and forced.

I did it to her.

The fact that the Flu caused me to do it provides no solace. I still tried to kill my own friend, my only friend, and I hate myself for it. I hate myself even more when I pull Tawni's hair away from her face so I can look at her, and she visibly twitches, pulls away sharply. She's afraid of me. She should be. I'm dangerous. Lethal. I've killed before and I can do it again, even if I don't want to.

Her neck is marked with red stripes where my fingers gripped her skin and I frown as I look at them. They will surely bruise, reminding me of my sins for the next few weeks. If we make it that long.

"Tawni, I'm—"

"It's okay," she croaks, suddenly looking from the ground to my eyes. Her eyes are watery—not from crying, but from the pain I put her through. I start to object, but she cuts me off again, once more in a voice two octaves lower than her natural timbre. "You were hallucinating, Adele. I would've done the same thing. It's not your fault. Let me guess, I transformed into a goblin, some evil monster with big eyes and tentacles?"

In spite of the way I'm feeling, I laugh. "No, you were just yourself, but you were like a wild woman, ten times stronger than normal. You were trying to stab me in the heart with a knife. But I should've known—"

"No, it's fine. Really. Promise me you won't apologize again, won't even speak of this again."

I shake my head. I don't want to promise, don't deserve to be able to make such a promise.

"Promise me."

"Okay."

"We've got to go," Tawni says. She is playing my part.

We go. We are moving even slower than before, hobbling along like a couple of oldies. At some point we strap the flashlights to our wrists because we can't grip them anymore. I don't know how we even manage it, as all dexterity is gone from my fingers. Seconds pass like minutes, minutes like hours, hours like entire days.

Somehow we keep going.

My head is down; I am watching my feet scrape the ground, barely rising high enough to move forward. Instead of holding each other up, we are slowly dragging each other down into the dust. Tawni falls first, not even trying to break her fall with her hands. I try to help her up, but she has nothing left. "Go," she says. "Find help."

I don't want to leave, don't want to abandon my friend, but we will both die if I don't. "I will come back for you. That I promise," I say.

I leave my pack with Tawni and will my body forward, using the wall to support my left side. Struggling along, I pray for a miracle. The walls start closing in, the ceiling falling on top of me; the floor even rises slightly under my feet—all moving together to crush me. It's a hallucination—has to be. *Not real, not real, not real,* I tell myself, but it doesn't help. The stone walls keep coming.

I am crouching now, trying to get out of the tunnel before it destroys me. I see a light in the distance, dim but visible, a mere hiccup in the endless darkness before me. Stretching, reaching, extending my arm, I fight toward it, beyond desperation. My vision blurs.

I am going to die.

My legs crumble.

Without seeing my mom again.

My vision blurs.

Without asking her about her note.

Without seeing him again.

The dim light is gone, once more replaced with utter blackness.

Tristan.

Six

Tristan

I wake up thinking about secrets. My secrets; Ben's secrets; whether Adele has any secrets. Heck, I am even starting to get paranoid about whether there are things I don't know about Roc, who I think I know everything about. I guess I'm just used to knowing things, because of my father. How could I be so stupid, so naïve? After everything my father has done, after everything I know about him, how could I have trusted him so blindly? How could I have actually believed that he told me the truth about our world? Could it be that he doesn't know the truth? I doubt it. I think he was just too arrogant to admit the truth to his own son.

And so now I wonder what other secrets he has kept from me.

When we left the train, we followed Ram and the others through a stone archway and into a tunnel lit by staggered torches on either side. I wanted information, to ask the zillions of questions I'd been thinking about on the train, but they took me directly to a stone box room with a dozen beds, leaving Roc and Elsey and me to get some rest. I didn't want to sleep, didn't think I *could* sleep, but as soon as they turned the lights out and closed the door, my head sank into the pillow and I drifted away. I guess I was more tired than I thought.

I hear movement to my left. Roc, shifting in his sleep, or perhaps—

"Roc, you awake?"

A grunt. "Barely."

"Oh."

"Are you awake?" Roc asks.

"I'm talking to you, aren't I?"

"I've heard you talk in your sleep before," Roc says. I can feel the grin in his voice.

"Shut up, I don't believe you."

"Believe what you want. It's true. Especially recently. You keep saying some name in between snores. What name was it again? Oh yeah—Adele."

"You're full of it," I scoff.

"Something about how you want to kiss her and hug her and marry her."

"Dork."

"Butt monkey."

I can't stop myself from laughing. "*Butt monkey?* Really, Roc?"

"I never said I was mature."

"Good point."

"What are we doing here, Tristan?" Roc asks, his tone turning serious in an instant.

"I wish I knew."

"That Ram guy didn't seem to like you too much."

"You think? I was thinking he might be my new best friend," I say.

"Very funny."

"I thought so."

"Do you miss her?" Roc asks cryptically.

"Who?"

"Adele?"

"I don't know," I say slowly.

"So yes then."

"Yes," I say.

"We'll see her again, don't worry." Easy to say; hard to do. I want to believe she'll be fine, but any one of a million different terrible and tragic things could befall her in the Star Realm. I try not to think about it.

"I can't sleep anymore," I say.

"It's okay. You go. I'll stay with Elsey. I'm not really into all that political stuff anyway."

I don't need any more encouragement than that. Throwing off the thin sheet I'm under, I roll off the bed and stumble blindly to the door. Locating the iron handle, I pull hard. Nothing. I try pushing and am met with the same result. The door won't budge.

We're locked in. Like prisoners. We are sun dwellers in the Moon Realm, after all. Not welcome.

"It's locked," I say.

"Great," Roc says, "and I'm starving." Just like that, my hunger from the train comes raging back.

"Me, too."

"What's going on?" a small voice asks.

"Everything's fine, El," Roc says.

We hear her yawn. "I'm famished," she says.

"Join the club," Roc grumbles.

I pound on the stone door. *Thud, thud, thud!* The sound is dull and likely doesn't carry more than a few feet into the hall. I turn to feel my way back to my bed when I hear a metallic click and a grinding sound as the door moves away from me, letting a growing triangle of light into the room. I flinch back when I see who's standing in the doorway.

Ram.

His gigantic, dark frame takes up the entire gap between the door and the frame. His lips are turned up in the center, nearly touching his nose, as if he's just caught a whiff of dirty socks. "Your presence has been requested," he says robotically.

"We're hungry," I say.

"Food will be provided," he says.

"And my friends?"

"They'll go somewhere else for food."

"Roc, Elsey—c'mon," I say.

I step into the tunnel hall, slipping past Ram as if he isn't there. Giving me a look, he starts down the hall without looking back to see if we're following. *He's better than a bunch of random girls asking you to marry them*, I think to myself. Which is true—but being hated still kinda sucks.

Roc steps through the doorway, his black hair full of sleepy disarray. "Nice do," I say.

"Your blond curls could use a good brushing too, my friend."

Elsey's right behind him, her eyes tired but alert, her long, straight black hair falling perfectly down her back, like she's just combed it. "Good morning, gentlemen," she says brightly.

"Your chariot awaits," I say with a smile, extending a hand. She takes it and links her other hand with Roc's, walking between us. Ram is well out in front of us, waiting for us to catch up with his back to us, but we take our time, as if we're just out for a leisurely stroll. Making him wait gives me childish satisfaction.

When we are a few steps away, Ram moves forward, leading us away from our sleeping quarters. He's wearing heavy black boots with dark brown camouflage pants tucked into them. He's got a few inches and more than a few pounds on me, but I still think I could take him. Not that he's the enemy, although it's starting to feel that way.

The tunnel is plain, roughly cut through the rock, just high enough so Ram doesn't have to stoop and just wide enough so the three of us can walk in a row. The ground is hard-packed dirt and smells earthy. Water trickles from cracks in the roof, staining the walls black.

A few minutes later, we exit the tunnel into a tall cylindrical space, full of long, gray, stone tables and people. *The Resistance.* Eating breakfast. Men and women, laughing and talking, eating and drinking. If I didn't know better, I would say the scene looked rather normal.

The aroma of fried rice and potatoes sends my stomach into a frenzy.

Squeezing my stomach muscles to quell my demanding gut, I gaze upwards and see that the room rises six or seven stories high, ending in a craggy roof full of stalactites. Magnificent. The circular walls contain dozens of cave mouths at every level up to the ceiling, like an open air theater with layer upon layer of balconies. It reminds me of something I once saw as a kid. My father took me and Killen to the bee plantations, where they make honey. The bees swarmed around their hives, hard at work. I guess that's where the expression *busy as a bee*, comes from. My mom liked to use that one. Anyway, the head beekeeper cracked open one of the hives for us and the inside looked like a miniature replica of what I'm seeing now. *A honeycomb*, he called it.

My attention is pulled away from the honeycomb walls as a familiar face stands up from one of the tables and approaches us. "Mornin', sleep well?" Jinny says.

"Oh, yes, Aunty, the bed was surprisingly soft, and I had the most wonderful dream about Mother. Father was there, too, and Adele, and you. We were all together again."

I watch Jinny's eyes as Elsey talks about her dream. Her amber eyes cloud over, and although her face wears a smile, I can tell the tale troubles her, like she knows it's just a dream, one that will likely never come to pass. The hard lines of her face tell me that this is a woman who has been through violent times, and come through them hardened and pessimistic. Maybe she still believes that her cause can be achieved, but it is a clinging hope, just a thread of faith left holding her together. I am just guessing, but my thoughts feel right.

"Come, El," she says, taking Elsey's hand. "You can tell me all about it at breakfast." She leads her away to the table.

"Follow me," Ram says.

I start to follow, with Roc next to me, but Ram bars his path with an arm. "Not you," he says.

"Roc's coming," I say firmly.

"No—he wasn't invited."

"I won't go without him," I say. Roc and I might argue a lot, but he's still my friend and advisor. I want him there with me.

Ram shrugs and says, "Fine. But it's on your head."

As Ram leads us through the honeycomb room, Roc whispers, "Thanks." It's not necessary.

We pass Elsey, who is sitting next to her aunt, laughing at something she said. She looks happy. This, I remind myself, is what we're fighting for.

Under another stone archway, through a short tunnel that curves gently to the right, up a set of jagged stairs: We approach a heavy, metal door. It's the first thing I've seen that isn't stone. Whatever room it is guarding is more important than the others. To the right of the door is an open space and I can see that we're up a level, overlooking the common area where the people are eating. They can see us, and we can see them. We're in the honeycomb.

With a sharp tap on the metal, Ram announces our arrival, and the door swings open with a creak. Four faces are framed by the doorway, all staring at us as we enter the long, rectangular room. Ignoring the faces, I scan the area. On one wall is a large map, dotted with orange, yellow, and blue pins. On another wall hangs a giant mural, woven from black thread, etched with symbols in white: a hammer; a chisel; a sword; a harp. In the center of the tapestry is a large symbol I have never seen before, made up of three smaller symbols that I know well. The sun dweller symbol: a red and orange sun with curling heat lines churning from the edges; the moon dweller insignia: a bright yellow crescent moon crossed by a black sword; the star dweller emblem: a blue star outlined in dark black. The marks of each of the Tri-Realms. Each is encircled by gold thread, overlapping and meeting in the middle. Beneath them, the words *Forever United*.

A cough. My gaze has lingered too long and everyone's waiting for me. It was Roc who coughed to get my attention. He's already sitting on one side of the table. I take a seat next to him.

"Welcome, Tristan—Roc." It's Ben who speaks from the head of the table. His green eyes are sparkling from the candlelight and I can only think of Adele, her pale skin and vibrant lips, her fearless eyes, her slim figure and great legs—

"Tristan?" It's Ben again and I think I've missed something.

"Uh, yeah?" I say, sounding exactly how I feel: stupid.

"Would you please introduce yourself and Roc to the group?"

"Yes, sir—I mean Mr. Rose—I mean Ben," I say, glancing at Roc, who's grinning at me like I've got sauce all over my face.

I clear my throat. Clear it again. Finally, take a moment to look at the other faces in the room. First, a woman, probably in her twenties, sitting across from me, smiling at me with soft pale blue eyes. She's pretty, in a sisterly sort of way. A friend, I hope. Next to her is a guy who looks about her age, with a buzz cut that is the same length as his well-trimmed beard. He looks athletic, like me. I make a silent bet with myself that he's a good swordfighter. His expression is unreadable. Friend or foe? The jury's out. At the other head is another woman, with deep blue eyes that remind me of my own. Her hair is short and red and spiky. I'd know her anywhere.

84

"Vice President Morgan," I say with a nod.

"Tristan Nailin—fancy meeting you here," she says with a slight wink. I've always liked her. She's one of the few moon dweller VPs who have tried to stand up to my father's obscene politics. Now that I know the Resistance is still in operation, it doesn't surprise me that she would be one of them, or at least in communication with them. She nods for me to speak.

"I am Tristan Nailin, reluctant son of President Nailin, ruler of the Tri-Realms." My voice is surprisingly firm and I gain confidence from it. "This is my friend, Roc, and we've come to help the Resistance in any way that we can."

Standing in the corner, Ram snorts. "You expect us to believe that?"

All heads turn toward him. "I don't expect you to believe anything," I say, my voice rising. "But I hope that you will let me prove it to you."

"And allow you to sabotage all of our careful planning?"— Ram snorts again—"We would be better served to simply turn ourselves in."

"He wouldn't do that!" Roc shouts. I look at him. His nose is slightly turned up and his fists are clenched together on the table. A hint of the protectiveness I saw from him in subchapter 26 has once more manifested itself. He is my brother to the end.

"It's okay, Roc," I say, putting a hand on his shoulder. "Let it play out." He shrugs and his fingers relax.

I look around the table, meeting each person's eyes for a moment before moving on. I end with Ben. "Is that what you all think? Because, if so, I'm clearly wasting my time."

Ben is silent and I wonder if I've misjudged him. He had seemed so supportive of me being a part of this—had seemed to want it—and now, silent. His face is a puzzle that can't be solved, emotionless.

The young brunette across from me says, "I'm Maia."

I don't know what to say, so I allow the good manners taught by my mother to kick in. "It's nice to meet you."

"And you. I for one think we should hear Tristan out. I mean, what do we have to lose?"

Ram is out of the corner and circling the table, heat in his narrowed eyes and clenched fists. "Only the last chance we might have to overthrow this *boy's* father!" he spits out with a roar. "I cannot support this."

"And you are not a member of this council," a firm voice says. The voice commands attention, clear and authoritative. It's a voice I've heard before, but not like this. Ben's voice. I turn back to him, and his previously expressionless face wears a slight grin. He is calm, but beneath the grin lies a fierce determination betrayed only by the steel in his gaze. When he looks at me, I get the message: I was right about him; he will support me in this cause to the bitter end.

When I turn back to Ram, his lips are tight and his face is red, but not from embarrassment. It's anger, coursing through him like an electromagnetic pulse, seeking an outlet. He takes two deep breaths from his nose, collecting himself. When he speaks, his voice is remarkably level. "Then why do you drag me along to these sessions?"

"Because we value your opinion—always have."

"Not so much as of late, it appears." Surprisingly, he sounds sad, and for the first time I feel bad for him. I try to put myself in his shoes. Would I trust someone from the Sun Realm, particularly someone like me, who's been embedded from birth in the very government the Resistance seeks to overthrow? I cannot say for sure. Only that I would have to trust my gut, which is perhaps exactly what both Ram and Ben are doing. Their guts are just saying different things.

"I trust him," Ben says. "He helped me break out of prison."

Silence.

Even Ram seems surprised by the revelation, although he tries to hide it by turning his back and moving to the corner once more. Thirty seconds pass, and then Vice President Morgan says, "Is this true?"

I nod once. "I didn't do it because he's a member of the Resistance," I admit. "I happened to be following his daughter, and she was trying to rescue him, so I...I just helped."

"You did more than just help, Tristan," Ben says.

"Look, I left the Sun Realm because I hate my father's politics—I hate *him*." It comes out as a growl. My hands are aching and I realize they are gripping the table, my knuckles bare and white. My eyes flit to Morgan, and I see she's staring at my hands. Slowly, I release them, letting the throb of hot blood to return to my fingers. I tuck my hands together under the table. Take a breath. "I won't betray you," I say, mustering as much fervency as I can. They have to believe me.

"I believe you," Vice President Morgan says. "It's a risk we have to take, anyway."

"I do, too," Maia says, flashing a quick smile.

The young guy next to her says, "I'll go along with it, but if you try anything, I'll personally see to it that you're taken down." *Fair enough*, I think—but I don't speak, just nod.

"You're all making a big mistake," Ram says, breaking his silence.

"Only time will tell," Ben says. "For all our sakes, I hope you're wrong." He's looking at me when he says it, almost like a challenge. I meet his gaze and, although it's slightly uncomfortable, I hold it, for fear that looking away will be a sign of weakness, of deceit. Ben breaks the stare first, his eyes wandering to Morgan's. "Do you want to start the proceedings?" he asks.

Morgan's expression is filled with warmth. "Ben, I've been keeping things moving in the right direction while you've been gone, but I'm not the Resistance leader—you are. After everything, it's still you."

Ben nods, his jaw tight. "Jonas—please administer the oath," he says.

Jonas; the guy has a name. "To both of them?" he asks.

Ben says to Roc, "It is your choice—one we cannot force upon you."

"I'll do it," Roc says, his voice determined. This is a side to Roc I have rarely seen. He is coming into his own. I am proud of him.

"Stand, please," Jonas says. We obey, pushing our chairs back. "Place your right hands out, palm skywards." A strange choice of words, *sky*wards. It almost makes me wonder…

"Repeat after me. I, say your name, vow to support the Resistance, to do whatever it takes to unite the Tri-Realms—the Sun, Moon, and Star Realms—as one." Roc and I repeat the oath in unison, and Roc even manages to say his name, rather than repeating 'say your name,' like I know he wants to. He really has changed.

When we finish and sit back down, Ben says, "Excellent. Now to business. Vice President Morgan, how soon do you think you can gather the subchapter leaders?"

"Give me three days to get them all to subchapter 1."

"Done. Tristan, may I have a word with you in private?"

I feel an ache in my belly. Ram had told us food would be served, but that was apparently a lie. "Can it wait until after breakfast?" I ask. Roc nods vigorously.

Ben laughs. "Of course. We don't want you passing out before you do anything for us. Ram," he says, and I groan. Our supportive escort, back on duty, babysitting.

The look on Ram's face shows he's about as happy about it as we are. "C'mon," he growls.

Seven
Adele

My eyes blink open. It is dark, of course, so I can't see, not well anyway. I must've dropped my flashlight when I fell. It's not on, so either the batteries died or it broke. I'm surprised to even be waking up. I thought the Flu or the dehydration would take me away.

My next thought is Tawni. Is she still alive? Did the Flu spare her life, too?

I put a hand on my head. There's a bulging lump on my forehead but it's not warm. I don't feel shivery or sweaty. The fever has broken.

I want to test my legs, so I place a hand on the ground to push off. The ground has some give to it, like it's not made of stone. It's weird. Maybe I'm still hallucinating, my fever still raging on while I dream. Or I might still be asleep, in a viral coma, dreaming of soft ground and blackness.

As I touch the floor again, I confirm: The ground is definitely soft. I try to stand up anyway, but I can't seem to get my legs under me, either because of the plush ground or my failing muscles. I might still be dying; just not dead yet.

One more time I push upwards with my hands and I feel my muscles grip, firm and strong. They don't hurt. Perhaps I'm in shock. I am up but unsteady on my feet, wobbling and swaying and holding my arms out to try to get my balance, like a baby trying to take its first step. Losing the battle, I topple over, but I don't hit the soft ground quickly like I expect. Instead the ground is farther away, as if I'm falling into a hole. And when I collide with it, the floor is no longer soft, but hard like…well, like rock. I scrape my arm and bang my knee and cry out.

"Who's there?" someone asks. The voice sounds so familiar. So very familiar. My mind churns, but like the rock-cutting machines, I come up with only shattered rocks as thoughts. Nothing makes sense. I'm alone in the tunnels and yet…

"Tawni?" I say, knowing the voice was hers but also knowing it couldn't have been. Surely I'm still hallucinating.

"Adele?" the hallucination says.

"Yes, it's me," I say, right away feeling stupid for talking to an apparition.

"Thank God. Where are we?"

If it is Tawni, she's hallucinating too, confused by the fever that continues to plague us both. "Are you real?" I say.

"I think so," Tawni says, her voice rising in the dark.

"Keep it down!" a third voice grunts. "I'm trying to sleep."

Tawni squeals and I cover my head like someone is about to hit me.

When I pull my arm from my eyes the darkness is being fought off by an incoming light—a lantern. It bounces and sways as it approaches. I'm scared of the hallucination but I won't show it. My mouth is a snarl.

"Who's there?" Tawni says and I trace her voice to her face, which is now lit up by our mysterious visitor's lantern. She is scared and it shows on her furrowed brow and wide, white eyes.

I look back to the light and have to shield my eyes with my hand as the bright beams flash in my face. A hand reaches over the lantern and covers it with a thin fabric, dimming the light. "You're awake," a young male voice says. The voice places the lantern on the ground and steps forward. Backlit by the light, our visitor is a dark profile, just a shadow in the shape of a human.

"Who are you?" I ask, my eyes never leaving the shadow. I'm still on the ground and I finally realize something: We're not in the tunnel anymore. Tawni is elevated on a low bed, similar to one I was lying on, which is why I had so far to fall when I toppled over. Although I can't see much of it, in my peripheral vision I can make out rows of beds extending in either direction. The room is large. "Where are we?" I add to my initial query.

Instead of responding, the shadow steps forward and extends a dark hand. If he wants to hurt me, he will regardless of whether I take his hand now. I hesitate, but then take his hand, tightening my muscles in preparation for a fight. His hand is warm but not sweaty, strong but not angry.

He pulls me to my feet with ease and I struggle to maintain my balance, but he adds a second hand to the small of my back to steady me. I don't like this—relying on someone else. It makes me uncomfortable.

Gently he guides me to Tawni's bed, and she lifts her knees to make room for me. "Sit here," he says. I obey, only because I'm not sure I can stay on my feet any longer.

With a deft spin, he turns and sits on the bed I was on originally. His face is thrust into the light. As I guessed from his voice, he's young, no more than twenty. His hair is chestnut and curly, and his eyes light brown. He's smiling, but it's constrained, like he's afraid of being too merry given our present condition.

"I'm Trevor," he says. "Welcome to the Star Realm." His eyes are dancing in the light.

"What? But how?" I ask.

Trevor laughs. "We heard you."

"Heard us what?" I say, stupefied by how anyone could have possibly found us. Then I remember: the dim light I saw up ahead, fighting to reach it, failing, passing out; darkness surrounding. "I was at the border," I say, before Trevor can reply. "But I didn't make any noise."

Trevor smirks. "From what I hear, you were screaming like a banshee. The border guards found you delirious on the tunnel floor, yelling and screaming about floods and bats and sun dwellers."

I don't remember any of what he is saying so I'm not sure whether I can trust him. But I'm here, I guess, so it makes sense.

He continues: "They managed to calm you down, but you kept mumbling about your friend in the tunnel. At first they thought it was just the fever, but you kept persisting so we sent a few men and they found her." He motions to Tawni.

I look at Tawni. She looks much better. Her normal pale-pink color has returned, and her eyes are no longer a tortured red. "You saved me," she says to me.

"No."

"Yes. I couldn't make it any farther, but *you* did."

I shrug. "I just got lucky."

"Luck had nothing to do with it," Trevor says and I look back at him. His grin is gone and the brown in his eyes has darkened. He runs a hand through his long hair. "Let me guess: You drank from the reservoir in the inter-Realm tunnel?"

I nod, feeling somewhat sheepish. I expect him to mock us for our stupidity. He doesn't.

"Impressive. You made it nearly forty miles before the Flu took you."

Even I raise my eyebrows. *Forty miles.* But I keep my mouth tight. "All the more reason why we were lucky."

"If you say so," he says.

"I do. What is this place, anyway?"

"The infirmary. Kind of like a hospital. We get a lot of sick people down here. The conditions aren't great."

Looking down the row of beds to either side, I can make out a few arms, legs, and heads poking from beneath the sheets. "I need to get out of here," I say.

"Not gonna happen."

"What—are we prisoners?"

"Not exactly."

"Then why can't we leave?" I don't like being told what to do, even by the people who have helped us.

"You're not well enough yet."

I take a deep breath and plan my next words carefully. Tawni, always the mediator, steps in for me. "Thank you, Trevor. Thank you for everything you've done for us. But we're here on an urgent matter. There's someone we have to find."

"Who?"

Tawni looks to me for guidance. I sigh. "My mom."

"She's a moon dweller?"

"Yeah, so what?"

"There aren't many moon dwellers down here."

"I think she's in the Max," I say.

Trevor's eyes light up with understanding. "A prisoner, huh? Well, you can't see her."

I frown, clench my fists, try to stay calm. Fighting won't get me anywhere—at least not yet. "Why not?" I ask.

"You have to see the General first."

"Why?"

"The General asked me to bring you as soon as you woke up. It's been three days and the General is not very patient."

"Three days!" I say. I can't hide the surprise in my voice.

"You were nearly dead," Trevor says. "Dead like the Star Realm." It's a weird expression, but somehow it feels appropriate.

"And after the General?" I ask. I figure we'll go see this dude and then be on our way, free to visit the Max and find my mom.

"The General will decide that." I'm barely able to contain my anger, but I do, following Tawni's lead.

"When do we leave?"

"It's the dead of night," Trevor says. I can't ignore his second reference to death. Despite his cheery face, there is something dark about him. I can't quite put my finger on it. It could just be my imagination. Or it could just be the way people are down here—in the Star Realm. "Look, just try and get a few more hours of sleep and I'll come to collect you in the morning."

A thought occurs to me. "Why were *you* here in the middle of the night?"

"Rounds," he says simply. I don't believe him. He doesn't look like a doctor, or a nurse, or a guard, or anyone that should be watching over us while we sleep. He was here for a reason. Either an order or his own agenda. As if sensing I am not satisfied, he hurries on: "Get some sleep, Adele. There are clean tunics under your beds to change into in the morning."

"How did you—" I start to ask, but he is already up and floating away, a ghost in the dark, his lantern casting eerie shadows in his wake. Darkness returns, but my eyes have adjusted and I can still see.

"He seemed nice," Tawni says, putting her typical positive spin on things.

"More like a creep."

Tawni looks at me and laughs. "I can tell you're feeling better."

I can't help myself. Seeing my lost friend safe and healthy is enough to coax a smile to my lips. "I guess so," I say. "Are you okay?"

Tawni nods. "I feel fine. They must have given us medicine."

I return her nod absently. Something doesn't feel right about this whole setup. Trevor's tone; the all-powerful General; our miraculous recovery; Trevor knowing my name: I can't seem to make sense of it all.

Tawni reaches out a hand. "What are you thinking about?"

I take her hand and she gives mine a light squeeze. "Nothing," I say, not wanting to worry her with my muddled thoughts. "Let's get back to sleep."

Although I hope Tawni will be able to sleep, I know I won't. I have too many questions, too many puzzle pieces to make sense of. It feels like my entire life is a mystery all of a sudden. Trevor must know my name because we were all over the news after we broke out of the Pen. So he must know Tawni's name too. But that doesn't explain why his tone was so dark, why he kept using the word *dead*. I mean, I guess he only said it a couple of times, but still, it was creepy. My thoughts cause me to shiver under my thin sheet.

What keeps me going is my dad's confidence in me. Before we parted ways, he told me I was courageous and strong and that he was proud of me. He also told me trust my heart. Now my heart is telling me that I have to find my mom and get out of here as quickly as I can. But not tonight. Tonight Tawni needs to sleep, even if I cannot.

With hours to kill, my thoughts turn to my dad, my sister, and then Tristan, in that order. I am afraid to start giving Tristan priority in my thoughts to the detriment of my own family. Somehow I know if I do it will put them in danger. Ridiculous, I know, but I can't help it.

I fear for my dad. He will do everything in his power to protect Elsey, but he's also not very good at picking his battles. If he sees an injustice he's compelled to do something about it. It's a rare quality to have these days. In my world, it's a dangerous way to be. It's what got him and my mom in trouble in the first place. And Elsey and me too, indirectly. I hope he'll focus on taking care of Elsey and staying out of trouble.

I'm worried about Tristan, too. He was injured when I left, and although he seemed capable of taking care of himself— very capable actually—as the President's son he is a target for the star dwellers. Which is why I need to get my mom and get home, so I can look after the ones I care about. Besides Tawni, they're all I have left, and I can't trust anyone else to do the job.

For the first time I notice the sounds of the infirmary. It is spooky, lying in the dark with the hushed whirs of breathing all around you, like the sounds of tiny waterfalls plunging into the depths. I try not to think about the multitude of diseases and ailments that likely afflict those around us.

My mind wanders as I try to unlock the mysteries of the universe, the things that have troubled me for days. Like what was Tristan trying to tell me? And who convinced the star dwellers to attack the Moon Realm? Was it this General that Trevor kept referring to? I roll these questions around in my head for hours, until behind my closed eyelids I sense the room lightening.

I open my eyes and jerk back against my mattress, which isn't thick enough to prevent my head from thumping off the stone beneath. Trevor is standing over my bed, grinning. "What the hell?" I bark angrily. "Were you watching me sleep?"

"Good morning to you, too, Adele."

I stare at him, eyes narrowed, as I try to decide whether to drive my foot into his ribcage. That'll wipe the grin off his face. The room is indeed lit by dim panels on the ceiling. Although not bright by any means, relative to the abject darkness of the night the room appears luminous.

"I wasn't watching you sleep, because you weren't sleeping. You were flopping around like a fish out of water. Not like your friend, Tawni. She slept like the *dead*." There it is again—the word "dead." What a creep.

I don't want to admit he's right. "Maybe I was just dreaming heavily," I say.

"Maybe not," he says.

"In any case, you should get another hobby. Something you're better suited to, like knitting or something."

Trevor shrugs and ignores me. "It's time to go meet the General."

"Fine." I gingerly swing my legs over the bed and get to my feet, hiding my discomfort beneath an indifferent expression. Although the aches from the Flu are gone, I'm stiff from all the bed rest. Ignoring Trevor, who watches me the whole way, I coax Tawni from her deep sleep with a gentle hand on her shoulder.

Her eyes roll open lazily. "Mmm."

"Time to go." I stand up and point a finger at Trevor. "You—out."

Trevor's eyebrows rise in surprise, but he recovers with a quick grin. "I'll be back in five. Be ready."

He turns robotically and weaves his way past the other beds. While I watch him to the door, I take in the room. Dozens of beds litter the room, strewn haphazardly at strange angles, no attempt made to line them up. There are bodies everywhere. Even in the light, they look dead. We are the only ones moving, so they might be, although like before, I can hear the soft sounds of sleep.

"Why were you so mean to him?" Tawni asks from behind me.

I turn to face my friend. "That was nothing—you should have heard me earlier, before you woke up."

"He's just trying to help." She's on her feet, hands on hips, her face tight and frowning. She's taking this pretty seriously.

I sigh. "I don't know, something about him just bothers me. He was watching me sleep."

"He probably just walked up when you woke up." Ahh, Tawni who sees the best in people. I can't fault her for it. She saw the best in me even when I could not.

"You're probably right. I'll try to be more civil." I don't promise because I know I can't keep it.

I scoop a folded tunic off the floor under Tawni's bed and hand it to her. Her lips curl into a smile, as if she can't stay mad at me. Not after everything we've been through together. I retrieve my own change of clothes and hurriedly remove my sweat-stained tunic, catching a whiff of its Flu-stained scent. I make a face, toss it on the floor, and replace it with the new one. Tawni does the same and we're ready to go.

Across the room, the door thuds open, sending echoes bouncing off the walls, unlike before when Trevor managed to sneak in and to the foot of my bed. The previously dead bodies stir, producing a cacophony of wake-up sounds. Groans, stretches, and yawns create a symphony of exhaustion.

Trevor stands between the door jambs. "Let's go," he says.

Cutting a path through the beds, I try to avoid looking at the faces of those we pass, but I can't help it. It's like the more you try not to look at something, the more your subconscious forces you to. I spot a woman with red pustules all over her face. Her eyes are an unnatural white, all color wiped from them by whatever disease assails her. She stares unseeing. Another man twitches again and again, wrought with seizures. I find it odd that we haven't seen any nurses yet. Perhaps this is the place where they leave people to die. But not us. They helped us. Why? I do not know.

Without acknowledging either of us, Trevor leads us from the room, which leads directly to the outside, to the cavern that is subchapter 30 of the Star Realm. You can hardly call it a cavern. Compared to our massive caverns in the Moon Realm, this subchapter is set in a cave that's more like a shoebox, the roof rising a mere fifty feet above our heads. The Sun Realm must have deemed the cost of further excavation not worth the benefits.

We pass through a cracking, crumbling courtyard surrounded by cracking, crumbling stone buildings. A statue of President Nailin stands pristine in the center. It is the only thing I see that is well maintained.

From the courtyard we enter an alley barely wide enough for three people to walk astride. Well, not an alley, apparently. Various similar-sized streets shoot off on either side. Evidently these are the standard roads in this subchapter. The buildings on either side rise up only three or four stories before connecting with the rocky cavern ceiling, almost like the buildings grew from the stone, like roots. There are no good views in this town.

At first Tawni and I walk side by side in Trevor's wake, but are soon forced into single file as we pass beggars camped out with their backs to the buildings. They raise their jars and try to grab the bottoms of our tunics while muttering incoherently. I feel sick as I step over and around their legs, scraping past their outstretched fingers. They are gaunt, pale, dying. Things are bad in the Moon Realm, but nothing like this. I never realized.

I never realized.

Now I see that the gap between the moon and star dwellers is as big as the gaping crevice between the sun and moon dwellers. If the gap between the Sun and Moon Realms is a mile, then the gap between the Moon and Star Realms is more like two miles. Life seems to be hard enough as a star dweller without having to conduct a full-scale rebellion against the Moon Realm. I mean, if they barely have resources to keep their people alive, how can they afford to fight a war? Where are they getting the money for bombs and weapons and supplies? Based on the poverty around me, it seems impossible. Even the medicine required to cure us of our Bat Flu would've cost a fortune. A fortune that these people don't have. Trevor must know the answers to these questions and more. Instead, I ask something else.

"Why is the General here and not fighting in the Moon Realm?" I blurt out.

Trevor stops and turns around slowly, his lips curling slightly as he looks me in the eyes. "Feeling chatty all of a sudden?" he says.

"Look—cut the crap. We appreciate your help and all, but we need answers. Something bigger than all of us is happening here."

"You think?" Trevor says.

He turns around and keeps walking and we're forced to follow. I don't think he's going to answer my question until he says, "Not that it's any of your business, but the General has just returned from a successful campaign in two moon dweller subchapters."

"Which ones?" I ask, pushing my luck.

"Fourteen and twenty-six."

My breath catches and I glance back at Tawni. Her wide, blue eyes tell me that she realizes, too. The General happened to be in the same subchapters that we were during the bombings. A coincidence? I don't believe in them.

I nearly trip on another beggar who's squirmed his way into the center of the thin laneway. "A Nailin for the poor," he croaks. Feeling bad as I do it, I tiptoe around him. We still have money left from Tawni's little prison trust fund set up by her parents, but we can't afford to use any of it frivolously.

"Did you say fourteen and twenty-six?" I ask.

"Yeah, so what?" Trevor says without looking at me. "Ah, we're here," he adds as the alley empties out into another circular courtyard. There doesn't seem to be any rhyme or reason to the layout of the subchapter. Another perfectly manicured statue of President Nailin rises majestically in the center. He has his leg raised and set on a stone block, like he's looking out upon his kingdom. I don't understand why these people would have so many monuments to the dictator that rules them.

Before I have a chance to calculate the odds of being in the same two subchapters as the general we're about to meet, especially because they're separated by hundreds of miles, Trevor ducks into a stone entryway, motioning with one hand to follow him.

I glance up at the building before I enter. It's a monstrosity—not beautiful by any reckoning, but sturdy, fortress-like, with heavy stone columns supporting a cement overhang. The walls are huge, undecorated stone blocks, straightforward in their utility.

Like everywhere in this town, it's dimly lit inside. We pass through a thin passageway and then follow Trevor up a flight of stairs. An empty foyer welcomes us with more of the same stark stone solidity. From the foyer, Trevor moves without hesitation to the far side of the room. A heavy stone door bars our way.

"You're expected," Trevor says with a wink, like we should be impressed.

I roll my eyes at Tawni while Trevor drags open the door. We enter and I crane my neck to see past the chestnut waves on Trevor's scalp.

The General is sitting behind a desk.

My heart flutters and a shiver rolls down my spine as pure elation fills my soul.

The General is her. The General is my mom.

Eight
Tristan

"Uhhh!" I groan as my back slams into the rock wall.

"Let go of him!" Roc yells, rushing at Ram. With a lazy swipe of his big left hand, Ram backhands Roc in the face, knocking him back a dozen feet while holding me in the air with his right. He's even stronger than I expected.

His face is red again, seething with fury. His words are laced with venom and spit as he says, "You may have fooled the rest of them, but not me. I'll be watching your every move, while you eat, while you sleep, while you piss—"

"That's gross," I say, choosing the wrong time for sarcasm.

Ram punches me in the stomach and I feel all the air go out of my lungs. "Shut it!" he roars as I suck at the air, wheezing through my throat. "One false move and you'll wish you had never been born." He throws me to the ground and stomps away.

I feel like throwing up. Why couldn't he have hit me *before* we ate? Now the potatoes that I scarfed down not ten minutes ago threaten to reemerge from the wrong end. I crawl to my hands and knees and pant, trying to calm my nervous stomach as perspiration pours from my brow. Roc groans and through my sweat-clouded vision I see him roll over.

"You okay, man?" I manage to grunt.

"I feel dizzy," he says. "I hope it doesn't leave a mark. Then I won't be able to get anywhere with the Resistance ladies."

I laugh and then cough, which makes my stomach roll again. "No jokes," I choke out.

"That wasn't a joke," Roc says, which naturally makes me laugh and choke again.

Using the wall, I pull myself to my feet, somehow managing to keep the potatoes down. Roc is up too, although he's stumbling crookedly toward me. He probably has a concussion.

I look at him and see the beginnings of a black eye darkening his cheek to the right of his nose. And that's on top of the injuries he previously sustained at the hands of my brother's goons.

"There's no mark," I lie.

"Really? Because I don't feel anything so much here"—he points to the left side of his face—"but it hurts like hell right here," he says. "You sure there's no mark?"

"Nope."

"Okay, good," he says, laughing. "Next time we become mortal enemies with someone, can we make sure it's not someone six-five, two hundred and fifty pounds?"

"Good call. Are you gonna be okay?"

"I'll survive—you?"

"I'm good, I think. Let's find Ben."

We head in the direction Ram left, seeking a neon sign or flashing lights, or something else that points to "the Isolation Room," where Ben said he would meet us, where Ram was supposed to escort us. We come to a crossroads and I look left, and then right. Both tunnels appear identical, gray stone at the bottom and black at the top, as if it's been scorched by fire. "Which way?" I think aloud.

"Right," Roc says. "If we always go right, we can't go wrong."

I smirk. "That makes no sense."

"Okay. Then go right because it smells worse to the left, which means Ram probably went that way."

I shrug. It's as good a reason as any. We turn right and make it two-thirds of the way down the hall before passing an open door. Flickering orange flares spill into the dimly lit tunnel. "Come on in, guys," Ben says from within, although we can't see him through the gloom.

Roc looks at me, grinning. "It was a lucky guess," I say.

"Slice it however you want, but the truth is, my logic worked."

We enter the room, which immediately brightens as Ben uses the single torch lighting the room to light another torch, and then a third. He's lying on a stone bench, his leg propped on a flat boulder. His thigh is heavily bandaged.

When we approach, his eyes widen. "What happened to you?" he asks, staring at Roc.

"You see, the thing is—" Roc starts to say.

"He walked into a wall," I interrupt, glaring at him.

"But…"

"He can be so clumsy sometimes."

Roc looks at me, blinks. Pouts out his lips in frustration and then concedes. "Right—a wall. How *clumsy* of me." I get why he wants to rat on Ramseys, Lord knows I want to, but I also want to prove myself to Ram—that I'm not a rat. I don't know why I care what he thinks, but I do. Despite his fierce temper, he *is* technically one of the good guys.

Ben looks at us strangely, his gaze bouncing back and forth between us. He knows we're lying but doesn't push it. "Have a seat," he says with a wave.

We lower ourselves onto a bench perpendicular to Ben.

I wait for him to speak, but he's silent, staring at one of the crackling torches. I stare at it, too, my mind wandering. What is this all about? What secrets does this man hold? Secrets buried so deep he would keep them from his own daughters? Secrets that my father would keep from me?

"Who the hell are you?" I blurt out.

Ben's head twitches as he's pulled from his thoughts. "Just a guy," he says.

I laugh. "You sound like me."

He nods. "I think we're more alike than you might think," he says.

"Look, my father told me all about the Resistance. How it rose up in 475 PM, before I was born; how you tried to control the freight train system, thus controlling the flow of resources; how he sent his armies pouring out of the Sun Realm; how he killed every last one of the traitors. And yet here you are—and I don't know what to believe."

"Not your father," Ben says.

"Maybe he just thought you were all destroyed." I'm not trying to defend my father. I'm just trying to understand why he didn't tell me. Because I'm surprised. My father may be a terrible person, but he never tried to hide his evil ways from me, although sometimes I wished he would.

"No. He knows. He lied to you."

"Why would he do that?"

"I don't know—pride maybe. Or because in his arrogant mind he truly believes that the Resistance is still weak, of no concern to his dominion."

"And how do you fit in?"

Ben sighs. "I never wanted to be the leader, which I'm sure you understand, Tristan." I do. I am also reluctant to be at the forefront of the Resistance. Not because I don't believe in the cause—because I do—rather, because I'd prefer to just be another soldier, nothing special. Just a guy. I'm sick of being singled out because of who my father is.

"So you're the leader of the whole Resistance?" Roc asks for me.

Ben chuckles. "Yeah. All two thousand of us."

"But that's not even half the size of one of the sun dweller platoons," I comment.

"We have a lot of heart, though," Ben says wryly. "But that's where you come in. We are nothing while there is dissension between the Moon and Star Realms. We need someone to unite them. Someone who knows the truth about the inner workings of the Sun Realm. Someone like you."

I shake my head. "Why should they listen to me? Ram was right about one thing. No one has any reason to trust me."

"I'm not saying it'll be easy, Tristan. Just that it's necessary. You and my daughter—you both have important missions."

"Adele," I murmur. Just speaking her name sends flutters of excitement through my chest.

"Yes. She has to find my wife. Anna will know what to do from her end. If we do our job from this end, we just might be able to pull this off."

I stare at him blankly. I comprehend his words, but they don't make sense to me. *Adele. Her mission. Important.* If she's fighting against the odds then I can too. I have to.

"Do you know the population of each of the Realms?" Ben asks.

"I have a good guess, but Roc would—"

"One point five million star dwellers, one point five million moon dwellers, two million sun dwellers," Roc rattles off. "Give or take a hundred thousand." With higher life expectancies and enough wealth to support more children, the Sun Realm has the highest population of the three Realms.

"Right," Ben says. "Do the math."

Easy—three against two. So we'd have the advantage in sheer numbers, but—

"They have heaps more resources," I point out. "Weapons, equipment, armor. Plus the people up there—I point to the rocky ceiling—are in much better shape: well fed, well-trained, prepared."

"So we shouldn't try?" Ben says, throwing up his hands. "This sounds like a different Tristan than just a few days ago."

"We have to try," Roc says.

I look at him. His eyes are a deep, steady brown, no hint of his usual comedy in them. Ever since leaving the Sun Realm, he's been the one pushing me toward my destiny—whatever it is. "I know," I say.

"I want to show you something," Ben says. Raising his back slightly, he slides a book from beneath him. Its cover is leathery, marred by scrapes and black marks and time, but in relatively good condition. He hands it to me and I see that a strap curls around from the back and clasps in the front.

"What is it?" I ask.

"Open it."

I gently unfasten the leather strap, afraid I will break the brittle material, and turn to the first page. The pages are yellowed with age, but not torn. On the inside of the cover is written "A girl's first diary, by Anna Lucinda Smith."

Roc leans in to see. "Anna—you said that's your wife's name, right?"

We look up and Ben's eyes smile, but not his lips. "Just a coincidence," he says. "But it's one of the many reasons I like it."

"So whose diary is this?" I say, implying I want to know more than the name written on the inside.

"Turn the page," Ben says.

Obediently, I carefully separate the page and slide it over. It's the first page of the diary and it's dated—

"Year Zero!" Roc exclaims. "You mean—"

"Yes. It's the diary of one of the survivors of Year Zero. A little girl, only twelve years old. Her mother gave her the diary so she could remember all the experiences she had, pass them down to her children. Later in the diary she tells all about her and her family. But I want you to start reading from page one."

111

I'm interested now. I've never heard of there being any eyewitness accounts left over from Year Zero. Conveniently, many of the diaries and journalistic accounts were destroyed over the years, in anything from fires to cave-ins. All very convenient for a secretive government.

I start reading in my head, but Ben stops me right away. "Out loud," he says. His eyes are closed and he's waiting for me to begin. I read:

"They are calling it Year Zero. The start of a new life. But not for everyone. The Lottery was yesterday and I got picked. A one in a hundred chance, they said. The President of the United States himself congratulated me on being selected. Not in person, though, because all the government people are already underground. That's where I will be soon. Safe and sound and away from the earth's surface, where the meteor will crash.

"I got a video from him, and through the fuzzy picture Mr. President said I am one of the lucky ones, but I don't feel very lucky. My mom didn't get picked. Or my dad. Or my grandmother, Aunt Gina, Uncle Tony, or Uncle Jerry. They even left behind my older sister, Tina. Only one of my friends got picked. I guess she was lucky, like me.

"My mom was crying yesterday. I asked her if she was sad, but she said they were tears of joy, because I got picked. My dad didn't cry, but he got really quiet. I'm only twelve but first thing tomorrow I'll have no family.

"In a day I'll be in the Caves, far under the earth, where it's safe. The government people say I'll be given a new family, even though I don't want one. They say life will be better; that it'll be a fresh start for humans, for Americans. I try not to think about things, but when I do, my palms get sweaty and I get really cold, like I'm sick. I don't cry, because I don't want to upset my mom again.

"They're coming to take me away tomorrow."

I finish the first entry and look up. "My father told me the Lottery was bad, but I didn't realize they split families up," I say.

Ben nods, his eyes still closed, and says, "Keep reading."

I flip to the next entry and read:

"Tomorrow has come faster than I thought possible. The streets are full of shouting people. Some of them have sticks, some shake their fists, all wear angry faces. The armored truck is here and the crowd presses around them until the soldiers start shooting their guns in the air. When the bullets start flying the people quiet down and back away. The serious men who get out of the truck are wearing heavy armor and carrying big, black guns. I don't want them to take me away, but I put on a brave face and hold all the tears inside of me.

"My mom's hug is so tight I can't breathe, but I don't complain, I just hug back harder. 'Everything will be okay, sweetheart,' she says, but I know she's lying.

"Finally my dad is crying, which scares me the most. He's a man, big and strong and proud. I've never seen him cry, not even when Grandpop and Grandma died in the same year. I blink away the tears and stick my chin out. 'I'll be okay, Dad,' I say. Now I'm the one lying. He nods and pulls me close and then pushes me toward the men.

"I don't struggle, because I've already seen the men use the Tasers strapped to their belts on other people on my street. They always get you in the end.

"My eyes are wide as the men lead me through the crowd, but I stare straight ahead and pretend I'm all alone. Before the big soldiers help me into the truck, I look back at my house and notice things I've never noticed before. The bright yellow paint that always felt so cheerful after a long day at school looks brown and flakey. The white shutters on the windows are gray with smog. The bright red door is the mouth of a beast, and my stark-faced parents are its teeth, cold and uncaring. Why don't they do something? Why don't they save me?

"When I linger outside the truck, a strong hand shoves me forward and into the tinted interior—and Year Zero begins."

There's a blank page, which I pass quickly in an effort to get to the next entry. I'm gripped by the young girl's words, speaking from beyond the grave. The history books don't tell it like this. They're all patriotism and new beginnings and marvels of engineering.

I read the next page:

"Just like me, the elevator shakes and trembles as it descends deep into the earth. We are packed into the metal box like the yucky sardines my dad likes to eat are packaged into their smelly cans. My stomach feels funny as we drop, like when my dad took me and my friends to ride the rollercoasters at the amusement park. The elevator is bright, lit by yellow fluorescent light that hurts my eyes. I close my eyelids, because there's nothing to see anyway. I imagine I'm still with my family, playing in the backyard with my sister while my dad mows the lawn and my mom does yoga. My imagination tells lies.

"When we exit the elevator it is dark. We are in a cave full of gray rock walls and pointy stones popping from the floor and ceiling that I know from school are called stalactites and stalagmites. The cave is the biggest cave I've ever seen, even bigger than the ones in Laurel Caverns, where my family went spelunking on one of our family vacations. This cave is so big that I can't even see the other side of it, which seems to disappear into the gloom at the far end of my vision. The roof is so high that I have to squint to see it, and I can only make it out then because of the dim overhead lights strung up on the ceiling.

"They give us hardhats with lights on them. Mine is too big, but they say it's better to be too big than too small. They tell us we have to hurry, that the scientists are predicting the meteor will hit earth very soon.

I can't hold back my tears any longer, but I wipe them away quickly with the back of my hand.

"We all line up with our helmets on and sit on the hard stone floor, which pinches my skin beneath my jeans. They tell me to put my head between my knees so I do. Silence. A child whimpers. Not me. Someone shushes him and he's quiet again. Silence. A bead of sweat trickles from my helmet down my forehead and into my eyes. I blink it away, ignoring the stinging.

"The impact is so powerful I think the earth will be torn in two. I'm flung to the side and I land in a tangle of arms and legs. There are bodies all around me. People screaming. Kids crying. I cry. The lights flicker and go out. The earth is shaking, shaking, shaking to pieces. The sky is falling and my head hurts when I feel the stones crack against my helmet. Sharp pebbles sting my skin, but I keep my head down like they showed me.

"I am scared."

I take a deep breath and look up. "I can't imagine what it was like," I say.

"One more entry," Ben replies.

The next page is dated two weeks later. I read:

"It's the first time I haven't cried in a week. My family is dead, they told me. Nothing could have survived it. I don't understand it all, but they say that it wasn't the meteor that killed everyone. Mostly it was the oceans, which rose up and covered everything when the meteor hit. They say we are lucky to be alive. There they go with the lucky thing again. It bothers me, but I just listen.

"One kid asks when we can go back outside again. I can tell he's scared of the dark. I'm glad I'm not, because it's dark most of the time. They told him never. That it would be hundreds, or maybe thousands, of years before anyone could go back up. They told us this is our home now—in the caves.

"I feel so alone."

I feel something tickling my cheek and when I touch my face with my hand it comes away wet. A single tear, filled with the girl's desperate tale, moistens my cheek. I don't know why I'm moved by something that happened five hundred years ago, but I am.

"Why did you show me this?" I ask, looking up.

Ben doesn't answer right away and I think he may have fallen asleep, weary from the gunshot wound and our harried flight from subchapter 26. I'm about to ask again, but his eyes flash open suddenly. "I just wanted to change your perspective," he says.

My perspective? My perspective is that my father's a creep and he needs to be stopped; that I want to help; that I want to forge a new life for myself; that I want to get to know Adele better. What's wrong with that? I puzzle over Ben's words, trying to understand what he means. What does our fight have to do with a diary from five centuries ago?

Something clicks in my brain, and I realize how dense I am sometimes. Everything I want is for me, selfish. I want to stop my dad because he drove away my mom, and because he didn't love me or her, not really. I want to help because I think it's what Adele wants, or maybe because Roc thinks it's my destiny, I don't know. I want to forge a new life and figure out why being near Adele brings me pain while leaving me breathless because I think it will make *me* happy. I want, I want, I want. I am stunned when I realize how self-centered I've been. It all comes together in an instant.

"You want me to see that this is bigger than just me, just you, just any of us."

There's an invisible smile on Ben's face and I know I'm right, even without him saying it. "If we're not doing this for the right reasons, we won't make the right decisions," he says simply.

I know he's right.

Nine

Adele

"Mom!" I cry out, bumping Trevor from behind as I dash past him. She's on her feet, moving around the desk, and we meet partway. And then my arms are around her and hers around me.

I'm dreaming. I'm dreaming. I'm waking up for sure. Any second. Any moment. I'll be back in the inter-Realm tunnel, feverish and delirious with Bat Flu. I'm not sure my heart can take the loss of my mom again, and I hold on tighter, willing her not to disappear.

I realize I'm crying, sobbing into her shoulder, my nose running like a faucet. Maybe it would be better if it was a dream. I don't want my mom to see me like this.

"Adele…" the melodious and familiar voice murmurs. "You found me. You're okay and you found me."

Before I pull back so I can look at her, I wipe my nose and face on the shoulder of my tunic. It's gross but I don't care. She's looking at me. My mom. Anna. *The General?* Reality flashes back and I have so many questions.

"Mom—what are you doing here?" I ask.

Her hazel eyes are full of compassion, just like I remember, soft and somber. She lifts a hand and gently wipes a lingering tear from my cheek with the backs of her fingers. "There's so much I have to tell you," she says.

Her head jerks to the side as she remembers we're being watched. I follow her gaze and notice Trevor staring at us, his eyes narrowed, his lips contorted into a slight frown. An unwanted shudder passes through me. Tawni is behind him, smiling bigger than I have ever seen before. Or at least since before Cole died.

"Mom, I want to introduce you to my friend," I say, motioning with a hand. She steps forward. "This is Tawni—Tawni, meet my mom, Anna."

My mom releases me from her embrace and shifts forward, ignoring Tawni's outstretched hand, hugging her. Tawni takes it in stride, hugging back.

When they pull away, Mom says, "Any friend of Adele's is a friend of mine. Thank you for coming all this way with her." The way she says it makes it sound like she knows exactly what we've been through—every challenge, every heartbreak, every success. But of course, that's impossible.

"It's nice to meet you, too, Mrs. Rose," Tawni says respectfully.

"Call me Anna."

"Of course."

"Thank you, Trevor," she says, her eyes flitting to the door. One side of my lip turns up when he gets the unspoken message: *You're no longer needed here.* His eyes dance from my mother to me and then back again, before he takes a slight bow and exits the room, closing the door on his way out.

"What is with him?" I say, not trying to hide my annoyance at our guide.

"Trevor's okay," Mom says. "He's not the one to worry about."

I search her once-young face for a mystery, but find only lines of age and hardship, despite having been away from her for only eight months. "Then who is?" I ask.

"There are many liars in our world," she says cryptically.

"And Trevor's one of them."

Tawni laughs, high and musical. "She's been talking like this since we met him."

"You've done well in winning Adele's friendship," Mom says. "It's not easy to come by."

A comment like that should make me angry, but my heart is too full of excitement at having found my mom, and it just rolls off my back like the trickle from an underground waterfall.

"C'mon," she says, tugging my hand to the side, where a stone bench sits, padded with something dark. We sit in a row, me, Mom, and Tawni.

I bite my lip as my brain pushes me to ask one of the zillion questions swirling around my head. As my mom smiles at me, her delicate features—a small, upturned nose, doll-like lips, and rosy cheeks—bring on memories of my childhood. I shake my head, willing them away. There's no time for memories.

"We have to get out of here," I say. "Dad said—"

"Tell me everything, Adele."

I sigh, trying to organize my thoughts. My mom's hand rests lightly on my leg and it gives me comfort. "Everything?" I ask.

"Take your time," she says. "Everything is important."

"But I don't understand. Why are you here? Why are they calling you the General?"

"All in good time, honey. But first, I need to hear what you know." I'm confused—so freaking confused that if my mom suddenly turned into a dog and started licking my face it would make just as much sense—but I just go with it. I know my mom too well. She's a patient woman, not one to be rushed.

I start with the Pen, about meeting Tawni and Cole—my voice cracks slightly when I say his name—how we escaped the electric fence, the bombs, rescuing Elsey, Rivet's attempts to capture or kill us. Unlike when I told my father, I don't leave anything out, including Tristan. I tell her about my headaches and body aches when I was near him, how he followed us, saved us, pursued us on the train to subchapter 26. Tawni interjects from time to time, adding important details, but for the most part she is silent, just listening. Just before I get to the part about Cole's death, she gets up and leaves. Mom raises an eyebrow and then turns back to me.

When I get to the fight on the train platform, I pour my heart out to her, telling her of the pain I felt at losing Cole, the rage inside me as I killed Rivet, my deep sadness and rebound as I got to know Tristan, learned that when I'm near to him I hurt him too. I even told her about holding his hand before we slept, how the pain subsided, how it started to feel good after a while. It's like I've been bottling up all my most powerful emotions and finally they spill over, with my mom as the recipient.

Tawni reenters the room and I relay the story of rescuing Dad, our frantic race through the city, and how we parted ways at the reservoir. I condense our monotonous jaunt through the inter-Realm tunnel to just a few sentences, focusing mainly on when we crossed paths with the sun dweller army, and end the tale when we pass out after contracting the Bat Flu.

When I finish, my mom leans back and puts both hands behind her back, closes her eyes and breathes deeply. "You're sure you saw sun dweller soldiers in the Moon Realm?" she asks.

"Yeah, in the inter-Realm tunnel. What do you think they're planning to do?"

"I'm not sure, but nothing good. And you're sure your father told you to come rescue me?"

I try to remember. "I don't think he said 'rescue,' but he did say to find you," I say, glancing at Tawni. She nods once in agreement.

"Then he really doesn't know what's happening."

It's not a question, but I feel obliged to answer. "He didn't know anything. He said they didn't get much news inside Camp Blood and Stone, just rumors. Mom, please, what is this all about?"

"And he didn't tell you anything else about me, or him, or the past?"

"No, Mom, I don't know what you're talking about. He just gave me your note."

Her eyebrows shoot up. "Ah, yes. My note. I'd almost forgotten about that."

"Mom, what does it mean? Is it about Tristan?"

"All in good time, honey. Let me start from the beginning." Her eyes open and she looks tired, like all the years and troubles and stress are catching up with her. "Your father and I are in the Resistance."

The words ring through my head, but it takes me a moment to register their meaning. A strange feeling washes over me, like I know what my mom just said won't be the biggest surprise. My initial reaction is to deny it, to even scoff at it, but somehow I know it's true. Probably because my mother has never lied to me. At least not that I know of. Evidently she's kept some secrets, but it's not the same thing as a bold-faced lie. "Okayyy," I say. "You mean, like part of the Uprising in 475 PM?"

"Correct."

"I thought the Resistance was defeated, Mrs. Ro—I mean, Anna," Tawni says.

"Sort of. The sun dweller army was too powerful. Many of us were killed, but not all. Nailin knew it, but he instructed the press to imply that all Resistance members had been killed in battle, or captured and executed." This is a different woman than the one who raised me. I've never heard her speak of death so brazenly. Nor have I heard her utter the Tri-Realm leader's name with such disrespect. Growing up, it was always *President* Nailin.

"How many survived?" I ask.

"Not many, a hundred, maybe. But most were the Resistance leaders."

I stare at her, pondering her words. I don't ask the question. Can't. Want so badly to ask it, but my tongue is tied.

As usual, Tawni comes through for me. "Were you one of the leaders?" she asks.

Despite Tawni having asked the question, my mom's eyes never leave mine. They look different than before. Less compassionate. Harder. Not somber—fierce. More like my eyes. I feel like I'm looking in a mirror, the way I normally do when I look into my father's eyes. "Yes," she says. "Ben, too." She lets it sink in for a minute and I say nothing.

"We were the two topmost members of the Resistance Council."

I say nothing, heat rising in my chest.

"They hid us in plain sight after the Uprising was quashed…"

I say nothing, the fire in my throat.

"Allowed us to start a family…"

I say nothing, my lips twitching.

"To live a normal life—"

"No!" I shout. "No, no, no!" My mom's head moves back, seemingly surprised by the ferocity of my outburst. Even Tawni looks shocked, and she's been dealing with me for a while now.

I lower my head to the floor, take a deep breath. What is going on? Have I accidentally fallen down a hole and into another dimension, one where my soft-spoken mother has become a born fighter? All these years, has she been hiding her true self? The truth slides behind my heart, flits into it, bumps and shakes. I know the truth, but *No! It can't be true!*

It is—and I know it.

With the truth, everything in my life abruptly makes sense. Why my dad wanted me to go to find my mom, and why he expected I'd be safe once I found her. Going back further, why my father always said I was more like my mom than him,

124

particularly once I learned to fight. It all makes sense and none of it makes sense; it's definitely one or the other, and I know which.

"Adele," my mom says, snapping me back to a dream world which is really reality. I slowly lift my head, meet her eyes, and she pulls me into her chest.

"Are you okay?" Tawni asks, gently stroking my hair. I think about the question, all my crazy thoughts over the last few minutes, and what it means to my life going forward. Despite how insane it all sounds, something about it just feels right. It's like a missing link, or the last puzzle piece, and now the picture is complete.

"I'm fine," I say, sitting up straight.

Mom's eyes are twinkling and I suspect she knows much of what I've been thinking. "You fought," I say, not as a question, but as a statement.

She nods.

"And the Enforcers took you and Dad away because they figured out who you were?"

"Yes. When the Resistance was defeated, we laid low for a few years. We maintained the organization, but didn't seek to grow it. Eventually, though, we had to start recruiting. Slowly at first, and then more and more as our plans advanced. We were careful and patient, vetting all potential new members before approaching them, using mostly referrals and internal connections. But no system is perfect, and at least one of the President's spies slipped through. Somehow the traitor found out about us—you know the rest."

"You were brutally abducted, I was locked and forgotten in the Pen, and Elsey was dumped in a shithole orphanage."

Her lips part slightly and I can tell she's shocked by my language, but she doesn't reprimand me. "Exactly," she says.

I feel like screaming and crying and laughing all at the same time. A smattering of emotions, all fighting for control. Instead I ask another question: "What happened after the Enforcers took you?"

"I was brought here—to the Star Realm. Locked up in the Max; the key thrown away. Dead to the world, at least in Nailin's mind. I gave your father the note just before they pulled us away."

"Why'd they take Dad to a different prison?" I ask.

"They knew who we were, how dangerous we were together. So they weren't taking any chances. Perhaps they thought two of us in one place would increase the chances of a rescue attempt."

"But why not just execute you?" I ask, swallowing hard.

My mom cocks her head to the side. "Good question, one I've pondered myself. The best I can come up with is that under the law all traitor executions must be well-documented and publicized. Maybe Nailin didn't want anyone to know, because he had been so adamant that the Resistance was snuffed out years earlier." Anticipating my next question, she rushes on. "They could have arranged a secret execution—with Nailin's power he can do almost anything—but it's almost like he wanted to add us to his collection, like trophies."

I realize I don't care why he didn't execute them—just that he didn't. "I'm just glad you're alive. Then what happened?"

"When the star dwellers rebelled a few weeks ago, they opened up the prison gates and I was free. I reconnected with some members of the Resistance, joined the star dweller rebellion, and they made me a general because of my past experience."

I've never heard my mother talk like this. So methodical, so soldier-like, as if she's conveying tactical attack plans to her subordinates. I cringe when a thought pops into my head.

"All those people," I say, unable to hide the contempt in my voice. "So many moon dwellers died from the bombings." My mother, the compassionate one. The selfless one. The murderer?

"No, Adele, it wasn't like that at all. Please let me explain."

My breaths are coming rapidly, and I inhale a deep gulp of air to try to get control, to give her a chance to explain. I owe her at least that much.

"Okay," I manage to say.

"There are seven generals. Seven, Adele. I am only one voice. Two are Resistance members, including me, and I trust my friend implicitly."

"But what if your friend is the mole?" I ask.

"She's not," she says without further explanation. "The other five generals are star dweller leaders, and they maintain control of all major military decisions. I can try to sway them, but I can't force them to do anything. I tried—tried desperately to get them to reconsider bombing the Moon Realm, but they wouldn't listen. God, Adele, do you really think I would willingly attack our people, kill innocent men, women, and children, put your and Elsey's lives in danger?"

A moment ago I *had* thought that was possible. The woman sitting next to me seems like a stranger, capable of anything. But the tone in her voice sounds like my mom, the woman I grew up with. She's still herself, just a little different.

"I guess not," I say.

Her eyes flick to Tawni, but then right back to me. "The best I was able to do was influence where and when we attacked. I tried to ensure the bombs hit areas that would be sparsely populated, at times when people would be closer to the protective shells of their cellars and storerooms. I made sure that when the bombing started, I was close to home."

My head jerks up. Trevor's words flash in my mind. *14 and 26.* He wasn't lying. "You mean...?"

"Yes. I was in subchapter 14 on the first night of bombing," she says. Tawni looks at me, her face awash with surprise, reflecting my own shock back at me. "As commanding officer, I steered the bombing away from the residential areas, knowing full well that very few people remained in the city after dark. One of the pre-determined targets was the Pen, as the rest of the generals wanted to create as much chaos in the subchapter as possible—and they thought a pack of escaped adolescent criminals would do just the trick."

"But that's when we were escaping," I say.

My mom laughs, and once again I get a glimpse of my old mom, the one who tried to make light of even the direst of situations. "Yeah, I didn't expect that. I'd positioned the bombers such that they would only destroy the electric fence and the outer walls. I was overseeing each and every minute detail, as I didn't want some rogue bomb technician dropping incendiaries in the center of the Pen where you might get hurt. I was hoping I might see you, might even be able to rescue you." At that, she squeezes my hand, instantly sending warmth through my palm. My mom is touching my hand. It still hasn't truly hit me.

"Anyway," she continues, "we were about to begin phase one of the attacks, when one of my guys spotted movement in the Pen yard."

"That was us," I say.

My mom nods. "I didn't know it was you at the time, but I wasn't taking any chances, so I ordered one of my soldiers to zoom in using the infrared binoculars." A vaporous thought swirls through my mind and I try to grab hold of it, but it dissipates before I can snatch it. "I'd recognize my beautiful baby any day, anywhere," she says.

Mom! I want to object, what with her embarrassing me in front of my friend, but I don't because her words feel so good after all this time. I smile sheepishly. "Sooo," I say, prodding her to move it along.

"So we watched as the guards chased you, cornered you, and then I ordered my team to bomb the other side of the fence, helping you escape."

I raise my eyebrows. "So it wasn't just luck?"

"More like fate, really." I've never heard Mom talk about fate before, but it sounds right coming off of her pink lips.

I can't hold back a sudden frown as a thought pops into my head. "Why didn't you rescue us then?"

"I was too far away. The rockets were shot from hundreds of feet away, on the tops of buildings. When the smoke cleared you were already gone, and we had no choice but to retreat from the subchapter."

I manage a smile. "My mind has officially been blown," I say.

"Ditto," Tawni says, laughing.

My mom smiles, the twinkle back in her eyes. "Well...I'm not quite done yet." I gawk at her like she's an alien.

129

"Remember the bomb that took out the Nailin boy and his men in subchapter 26?"

"Tristan?" I ask, sitting up straight.

"The other one."

"Oh, Killen," I say, feeling silly.

"Yeah, that one. Well, once I knew you had escaped, I tracked your progress across the Moon Realm. I knew exactly where you were headed and I managed to gain responsibility for the bombing of subchapter 26. The waiting was the worst, wondering if and when you would show up, whether you'd escape that sicko Rivet long enough for me to help you. But you did, Adele, you did, and I chipped in where I could, by using a well-aimed rocket to help you escape again. But again, I couldn't get close enough to get you out of there. I just had to trust that once you were with your father that he would know what to do."

I am surprised, but not as much as the last time, especially because Trevor gave us the heads-up. "I knew it wasn't a coincidence!" I exclaim. "I wasn't sure, but when we found the freshly singed, gaping hole in the wall of Camp Blood and Stone, I knew something was weird about it all. One time, maybe. Twice, unlikely. Three times, impossible. Dad thought so, too, thought I'd find answers down here." My mom had been protecting me all along. My guardian angel.

Mom smiles. "That's my girl," she says. "You always had good instincts. You're so much like your father."

"He always says I'm so much like you."

She laughs. "You've got both of us in you." And for that, I'm glad. "It was hard to resist charging in with the cavalry to rescue your father, but it wasn't part of the plan and would have been too suspicious. I had to trust you'd do what I could not."

"We need to go meet up with Dad," I say.

Her laugh quickly turns serious again. "Thank you for coming here," she says, "for finding me, but I need you and your friend"—she motions to Tawni, pausing as if trying to remember her name—"Tawni, to stay here in the Star Realm with some of my guards. The Moon Realm is too dangerous right now, and you need to stay safe."

What? No! Heat floods my face. I don't want to sound like a child, but we've come too far, been through too much, to just be left at home, safe in our beds. We are a part of this, for better or worse. I can't speak for Tawni, but I will for myself. "I'm coming with you," I say firmly.

"And me," Tawni echoes, her eyes shining with determination. Glancing at her, I consider trying to talk her out of it, but who am I to tell her what to do after everything she's done for me?

I wait for the rebuttal, but it never comes. Instead my mom laughs. "How did I guess you would say that? Well, I thought I'd give it a try anyway, can't fault me for that, can you?"

I cock my head to the side, smirking. Who is this woman?

"You can both be listed on the star dweller army rolls as my personal aides," she says. I'm still smirking.

"Nice try, Mom. I want to fight."

"Aide sounds pretty good to me," Tawni says, her face flushed.

My mom nods at Tawni absently, accepting her as her personal aide. Looking back at me, she says, "One problem. If you want to fight against the Sun Realm, you'll have to join the star dweller army for now."

"Never!" I blurt out, anger rising within me. "Not after what they did to the moon dwellers. They took it too far. Much too far."

"Hear me out. A lot has happened since you showed up on our doorstep. As of yesterday, the generals have agreed to a cease-fire, pending talks with the moon dweller leaders. They may be able to reach an agreement and join forces, and then it will be us against the Sun Realm."

"And if they don't reach an agreement?" I say.

"We have to trust that Ben…that your dad, and Tristan, can convince the moon dwellers to join us."

Tristan. Dad. Elsey. My desire to see them again springs up so quickly it takes my breath away. I swallow it back down. "Okay, I'll do it," I say. "But I won't fight the moon dwellers."

"I know. If it comes to that, we'll figure something out together."

"Wait. You still haven't told me about the note," I say.

She looks off to the side, away from me. "Honestly, I'm not sure. I just had a feeling someone important was coming your way."

I don't understand but she's doesn't seem in the mood to tell me anything more. I manage a crooked smile. "Okay, you can keep your little secret for now. Is there any way we can contact Dad now? He doesn't even know that I've found you."

My mom's expression turns grim. "I've been thinking about that too. I can't come up with anything. All the comms from this place are being monitored by the star dweller army. The generals get reports on any suspicious contact with the other realms. Everyone's worried about spies. We'll just have to wait for Ben to get in touch with us."

"I can wait a little longer," I say.

Mom's head jerks up suddenly, as if she's just remembered something, or had an idea. "If you're going to join the rebels, you'll need this," she says, reaching behind her and pulling out something L-shaped and black.

My mom gives me a gun. I stare at it like I don't know what it is. I ready myself, knowing I am about to wake up from a dream. Soon I'll wake up in my cell back in the Pen. No, farther back than that. At home, with my mom cooking stew, my father cleaning the dirt off his hands and face from another hard day in the mines. A time and place when my father taught me to fight just for fun and my mom didn't have a gun.

Ten

Tristan

We're all back in our little room. Roc and Elsey and me. Resting and recovering. Both from subchapter 26 and from Ram's less-than-warm welcome.

Ben loaned me Anna's diary and I'm flipping through it randomly, feeling the emotions of Year Zero through her. It was a hard time for everyone, but especially for the kids who were adopted by the survivors. Her new family didn't care about her the way her biological family had. She was a chore, a responsibility, someone they had to feed and clothe. That's all.

There was chaos that first year. Everyone was reliant on the government to provide their meals, their housing, their clothing. People worked hard, but they were only allowed to do the things that the government told them they could do. Maybe that level of structure was necessary back then, but things haven't changed that much. Things need to change and if I can help people to realize that, then who am I to fight it?

"Oh my word, Roc! Is that Tawni?" Elsey exclaims, pulling my concentration away from the diary.

Roc's blushing, his brown skin darkening under Elsey's scrutiny. "What? Uh, no. It's just a drawing."

"What kind of drawing?" I say, leaning at the edge of my bed, craning my neck to see what they're looking at. Roc tilts the paper away from me, so all I can see are his hands against the white back of the page.

"It's nothing." The way he says it, I know it's not nothing.

"It's beautiful, Roc," Elsey disagrees, nodding encouragingly. *Huh?* Roc drew something beautiful. I've never seen him draw anything at all. I've got to see this.

Hopping off my bed, I grab for the drawing, but Roc pulls away, bumping Elsey, who's sitting next to him on his bed. "Go, Elsey, go!" he says, handing off the paper to her like a baton, urging her forward.

She leaps from the bed. *Traitor.* I charge after her, corner her on the other side of her own bed. I fake like I'm going to go around one side and she squeals, moving to the other side. I go the other way and she spins and heads back the way she came. By the time I reach the other side, she's moved to where I was originally and is giggling uncontrollably.

I grin at her. "Okay, okay, let's make a deal," I say.

"No deals!" Roc cries from the bed, where he's watching from his hands and knees.

"No deals!" Elsey echoes. Roc's got her wrapped around his little finger. I never knew he was so good with kids. Then again, I never knew he could draw either. Although until I get my hands on that drawing I won't be able to confirm his drawing ability.

I leap across the bed.

As I soar through the air I see El's eyes widen—she's frozen, too surprised to run. I grab her around the waist with one arm and lift her in the air, using the other arm to tickle her. Her laugh is melodious and carefree and beautiful. As I planned, the tickling not only makes her laugh, but forces her hands open as she clutches her stomach, where I'm tickling her. The drawing flutters to the floor and I plop her onto the bed and grab it. "Aha!" I cry, making her laugh even more. "Teaches you to join *his* side," I say.

Roc's leaning back on his bed, his expression unreadable. It's almost like he wants me to see his drawing, but is embarrassed about it at the same time. Using the palm of my hand, I smooth the paper, which has become marginally wrinkled, curling up around the edges. When I look at it, my eyes widen like sauce plates, and I glance at Roc, who scrunches up his nose slightly.

It's the face of an angel, sketched with charcoal. Long, white hair. Full, pretty lips and a small graceful chin line. High cheekbones. She's smiling the most natural smile, like it comes easily to her. The drawing is magnificent, an artist's painting, not just a quick sketch by an amateur. The likeness is so well done that I can tell without a doubt that it's Tawni.

The only strange thing: the face has no eyes. Not holes or dots or ovals or anything. Her eyebrows are there, thin and white, but it's just blank paper beneath them.

I look at Roc, then back at the drawing, then to Roc once more. "You drew this?" I say, already knowing the answer to my question.

Roc nods lightly, his lips curling up at one end. "I've always liked drawing," he says, by way of explanation.

"You never told me."

"You never asked."

"It's magnificent," I say, using the same word I thought in my head when I first saw it.

"Thanks…" Roc says slowly, as if waiting for the *but*.

"But…" I say, pausing.

Roc laughs. "Here it comes."

"But it's Tawni…and she has no eyes."

Roc just shrugs. Seems I'm going to have to push a bit more if I want to get anything out of him.

"Why'd you draw Tawni?"

The blush is back, so I don't need him to actually answer me.

"You've got a *crush* on her?" I say, my eyes lighting up.

"No—nothing like that!" Roc protests. "I just thought she'd make a good subject."

"Yeah, right." Payback time. Ever since I opened up to Roc about my desire to get to know Adele, he's given me a hard time about how I have a crush on her. My turn. "What's next, a drawing with you and her holding hands, sitting on the edge of a cave, making out?"

137

"Roc and Tawni, in the cave next to meee! K-I-S-S-I-N-G!" Elsey sings helpfully, cracking me up and making Roc tuck his head into his hands.

"I knew I shouldn't have drawn her," Roc mumbles. "I'll never live it down."

"No, no, it's cool, Roc. Really cool, actually. Both that you are an amazing artist, and that you have a thing for Tawni." I say it earnestly, because I really mean it. I certainly enjoy giving him a hard time occasionally, but more than anything I want him to find happiness in our unhappy world. "Question, though: Why doesn't she have any eyes?"

"Because she doesn't see me," Roc says evenly.

Right away I feel bad that I made fun of him. Darn him for doing that. The beauty of his sketch prevents me from even enjoying the satisfaction of paying him back for all his jokes.

"I'll bet she noticed you," Elsey says. "It was just a hard time for everyone."

"You are so wise sometimes, pipsqueak," Roc says, smiling at El. "Get over here."

Elsey charges over and gives Roc a big hug. My eyes are watery but I hide it well. I can't trust Roc to cut me any slack just because I did the same for him. "Group hug!" I yell, barreling over and jumping on them, smashing them like the pancakes Roc used to serve me for breakfast in the morning.

Elsey shrieks and Roc groans and I laugh. When I release them I say, "You got any other talents I don't know about, man?"

"I think that's about it," Roc says, grinning.

"Can you show us how you do it?" I ask. I can still hardly believe how talented he is. I never actually saw his servant's room back in the Sun Realm—we usually hung out in my vast apartment—but now I picture it with walls covered in Roc's artwork. Pictures of the Sun Realm, the Moon Realm, the Star Realm. All the places we visited—the people we saw. A history of our lives, perhaps.

Roc shrugs and turns the paper over, leans on a sturdy rectangle of slate he got from somewhere. I sit on the bed next to him and Elsey leans in from the other side.

Roc deftly handles the charcoal pencil with ease, like he's been doing it his whole life, probably because he has. At first his drawing is just lines and random bits of shading, brought together in a way that seems abstract, almost pointless. After ten minutes I'm thinking he's a fraud.

But then with just a couple of effortless strokes the drawing starts to take shape. A person—a woman—sitting under a tree, holding a book. Tucked under her arms are two children, boys. One has brown skin and dark hair, the other white skin and light hair. The tree is majestic, with a huge trunk and sturdy, rising branches full of leaves. The woman is smiling as she reads to the boys, and I can almost hear her voice. A voice from my childhood—from our childhood. A memory is unleashed in my mind and I'm transported to a better time, a better place. A happy place:

Bright light from the artificial sun shines through my stained-glass window, sending brilliant red and blues and greens dancing across the white-painted stone walls. I should be up already, but I'm still groggy from yesterday's late-night festivities. It was my eighth birthday, and my mom let me stay up till midnight. Last night I was happy, but today I'm sad. Because today is Roc's eighth birthday. The day he becomes a man. My father calls it the age of accountability, which for me is awesome, because I get to stay up later, start real sword training, and brag to my brother about how I'm a man now.

But for a kid born into a servant family, like Roc, turning eight means no more fun, no more playing, time to work. Today he's my best friend, my playmate, like a brother to me; and tomorrow he'll be my servant, charged with cleaning my armor after training, serving me my meals, answering my every beck and call. Father sat me down and explained everything. Roc has to call me *sir*, and he can't laugh around me. We can't joke around, or play tricks on my brother, Killen, or do anything fun together. No more friendship, no more brotherhood. So I'm sad.

I slip out of bed and pad down the white, stone hallway. The lights are on in the presidential house, making the place feel bright and cheery. In the Sun Realm, things always seem bright and cheery. Roc said he hears his dad talking about the other Realms sometimes. That they aren't bright...or cheery. That he and Roc are lucky to be living up here, even if only as servants. That the Moon and Star Realms are dreary and not a place you'd want to visit—not even for a day. All that just makes Roc and me want to visit the other Realms even more. But I'm not even sure I believe him. Roc can be a bit of a fibber sometimes, but I don't mind.

The long dining table is empty when I arrive. Everyone else had to stick to the schedule, and they have long since finished their breakfast. But not me, not today. Because of my birthday, and because of Roc's. My mom's orders.

I even take a risk and sit down at one end of the table, instead in the middle like I'm supposed to. I sit impatiently, sliding the bottoms of my socked feet against the floor as I swing my legs. A minute later I feel a tap on my right shoulder and I swing my head around to catch the culprit. No one's there. Someone snorts to my left, a clear attempt to disguise a laugh. *Roc.*

I turn sharply to the left, wrenching my elbow to the side and behind me. *"Oomf!"* Roc hollers, as my bony elbow cracks him in the shoulder. Now it's my turn to laugh. Roc may be a better prankster, but I'll beat him in a fight any day.

Roc is rubbing his bruised shoulder, but his brown-skinned face isn't angry—he knows he had it coming. He's even sort of grinning, but wincing too, like he wants to laugh but is in too much pain to do it properly. What a dork.

He sits down next to me, still massaging his shoulder. "You should have seen your face," he says. "You were like, 'what the heck!'"

"Like you can talk," I say, pointing at his pained expression.

We are interrupted when one of the servant girls brings us our breakfasts. She's one of my father's personal servants, blond-haired and blue-eyed, with legs that are longer than my whole body, and big bumps on her chest. Roc calls them her pillows and they're way bigger than my mom's. She looks like what I think an elf would look like, except a whole lot taller, if there even are elves anymore. I'm not sure what she helps my father with, but it must be important.

We devour our breakfasts without speaking, occasionally flicking bits of food at each other with our forks and laughing. Good old Roc. My best friend. At least for one more day.

We hurry off to find my mom. It isn't hard because she's always in the palace gardens, and we find her at her favorite spot, sitting with her back against the biggest tree in all the Tri-Realms, with a thick trunk and gnarled branches that are perfect for climbing. She tells me she loves the gardens because they're peaceful, away from all the politics and hubbub of the government buildings. I like that word, *hubbub*—it sounds funny when you say it.

When my mom speaks of the gardens it's all about the beauty of nature and the *serenity*—which I think means peaceful—of wasting away the day dreaming on the lawn. When my father speaks of the gardens all he cares about is how smart his engineers are who figured out how to make artificial sun powerful enough to grow plants underground. My parents are so different.

My mom looks sad when I first see her, her eyes wrinkled and tired, and her mouth thin and drooped. But as soon as she spots us, her eyes come alive and sparkle—prettier than the flowers that dot the gardens, prettier than Father's servant girls, prettier than anything—erasing the weary lines underneath them. Her mouth sprouts wings and curls into a smile that warms my heart and soul. "Tristan, Roc—I'm so glad you're here. I was afraid I'd have to tell myself stories all day. And that can get pretty boring. Plus they'd probably lock me up for insanity." My mom's smile somehow manages to get bigger as she talks.

I crack up and Roc giggles next to me. The thought of Mom sitting there talking to herself seems funny for some reason. "You can tell us the stories," I say, right away taking control of things.

My mom ignores me and looks at Roc. "It's your birthday, kiddo, so it's up to you."

That's just the way my mom is. She treats both Roc and me like sons, which is probably why I think of him as a brother. I wonder what will happen tomorrow, when he's not my brother anymore.

Roc's brown eyes light up in a way they only do when my mom's around, and he says, "I'd love a story. For my birthday."

Mom gestures with her arms and we sit next to her, one on each side. She pulls us in close to her shoulders, kisses us each on the forehead, and says, "Once upon a time, when humans lived aboveground..."

We dream the rest of the day away in the gardens, me, Roc, and my mom. It is a perfect day and I know it's probably the last one I'll ever have.

The daydream fades away and I blink twice, trying to come back to the real world. I glance sheepishly at Roc, who's still drawing, and Elsey, who's still entranced in the elegance of Roc's pencil-strokes. They didn't even notice I was gone for a few minutes.

The woman looks different now, like my mom, but not. Well, half of her is the spitting image of my mom—I'd know her anywhere—and the other half is like a different person. It *is* a different person, I realize.

"Who...?" I murmur absently.

"*My* mom," Roc replies, finishing off the second half of her nose. She's brown-skinned, like Roc, but darker, with firm, toned muscles and full lips. She's every bit as beautiful as my mom, and they look right together, even when combined to make one person.

My heart does a backflip. Because she died giving birth to him, Roc's never met his mother. My dad didn't believe in taking photos of servants, so Roc didn't have the luxury of a photo to guide his hand, but somehow I know that the picture of his mom in his head is the right one, perfect in every way.

143

Like when Ben showed me Anna's diary, I feel so selfish again. Since my mom's disappearance, I've felt like my whole world is falling apart, and yet Roc has lived without a mom for his entire life. And as a servant, while I didn't want for anything.

Now in this simple drawing, I feel the breadth of his emotions pouring from the page. His love for my mom, his living mother. And his love for his real mom, the one he never met but wants to know.

His pencil is down and we're all just staring at his drawing, as if it might come to life and start talking to us. "It's perfect," Elsey says.

"Yes," I agree. "Simply perfect." Roc's smile is worth every word.

Eleven

Adele

Everything seems so close. The good, the bad, the neutral, the evil, the happy, the sad. It's as if the world is a thin line, everything in a row. There is no wrong, no right: only actions. These are my thoughts as I leave my mom in her office. Nothing is the same as it was before—probably never will be. After all, there's a gun tucked in a holster in the small of my back beneath my tunic. The holster is another gift from my mom. She offered Tawni a gun, too, but Tawni politely declined. I suppose I could've done that, too, but that's not me.

Trevor is leading us again, following my mom's orders to escort us to the star dweller training grounds. She said if I want to be part of the rebellion, I have to be trained like a soldier. I like that she said that—it means she respects me. Tawni will just be watching, and won't be a fighter. My mom said that on the record, Tawni will be considered one of her private aides, but really she'll just be with me like she has been since the start of all this.

We exit the fortress-like building, this time out the back, away from the claustrophobic city streets. The area behind is cold, not temperature-wise, but stark, uncaring, a barren wasteland of empty stone slabs and craggy gray boulders. Everything is in black and white, or a mix of the two. It makes the Moon Realm look like a paradise.

The expansive area is surrounded by a towering brown rock wall. Whether its primary goal is to keep rubberneckers out or the soldiers in, I do not know. "What is this place for, the gladiators?" I say, making a bad joke. I remember learning in school during history class about the Roman gladiators, forced to fight each other and professional warriors to earn their right of survival.

"Something like that," Trevor mumbles, not looking back. I can't tell if he's serious.

Across the grounds is a platoon of soldiers, engaged in some sort of training—it appears to be hand-to-hand combat. They're wearing blue training tunics, which don't look that much different from their standard-issue fatigues, complete with a faded patch of the star dweller symbol on the shoulders, although they seem slightly more worn-out. They're separated into pairs, each pair battling within the confines of circles designated by red tape on the ground. There aren't any patterns

146

to the pairings: males fight females, big battles small, tall locks horns with short. I can't expect special treatment here, and I don't.

Only two people aren't participating, a man and a woman who are set off from the fighters, watching and shouting things like, "Keep your head up, Lewis!" or "Don't let him back you into a corner, Matthews!"

As we approach, I see a smallish woman get flipped over the back of the ogre she's fighting. Her body hits the stone with a sickening *thud*, and I can't help but to cringe. Tawni visibly stiffens beside me and I glance at her. She's not even looking at the woman's prostrate body lying on the ground; rather, she's watching as another guy takes blow after to blow to the head, twisting and turning, until his legs wobble and he collapses, blood oozing from his nose and mouth.

"So brutal," she whispers.

My heart is in my throat. I'm well-trained, too, but these guys are serious, professional warriors. I take a deep breath and try to remember my father's lessons. *Never show your fear, Adele.* Gritting my teeth, I firm up my expression and try to turn the horror on my face into a believable scowl.

Trevor turns suddenly, a wicked grin on his face. "Good luck, soldier," he says, motioning me forward.

Ignoring him, I stride past and up to the woman supervising the training. She's tall and muscular, wearing a tight black tank top, camo pants, and sturdy, black boots. She's looking past me, almost as if she's looking through me, but I ignore that too. "Adele Rose, reporting for training under the orders of General Rose," I say, keeping my voice as firm as possible. I extend my hand and she finally looks at me, and then down at my hand.

"Get that limp fish out of my damn way," she says, one edge of her upper lip raised in a sneer. Her eyes are dark and steely and look like they could kill. Her face isn't ugly—even with the sneer—but it's not pretty either. It's just a face.

Dumbstruck, I drop my hand back to my side, unsure what to do or say next. Luckily, the guy next to her says, "Sergeant Buxton, where are your manners?" He lifts an open hand and I take it, following his arm up to his face, which wears a casual smile and kind, blue-green eyes. "I'm Sergeant Sean Brody, but you can just call me Brody," he says, shaking my hand firmly, but not crushing my fingers.

"I'm—"

"General Rose's daughter—I know. We've heard all about your strange appearance in the tunnels. In any case, the General told us yesterday that you'd be joining us."

My heart stops. "She did?"

"Yes—is that a problem?"

My mom is just full of surprises. She really did expect me to join the star dweller rebellion. Proud heat rises in my chest. "No—not at all," I say.

Brody releases my hand and runs his fingers through his dark bangs, pushing them away from his eyes. "Are you ready to start?" he asks.

"I, uh, I guess," I say, my confidence waning as I hear the grunts and groans of combat from behind me.

"Are you or aren't you!" Sergeant Buxton shouts, directly into my ear.

I cringe and turn away from her. "I'm ready," I say through clenched teeth.

Tawni has moved off to the side with Trevor, and I can see the two of them chatting, flashing smiles, and occasionally laughing. *Traitor*, I think.

"Han! You're up!" Buxton yells. Evidently she has difficulty controlling the volume of her voice, because she's always about a hundred decibels louder than necessary.

A dark, Asian-looking girl's head pops up from where she's got another girl pinned to the ground. She releases the girl and trots over, not even looking winded from her fight. "Yes, Sergeant," she says.

"Rose, get in the circle," Buxton growls.

My heart hammers as I walk across the hard stone, wondering what it will feel like to get slammed against it. The girl whom Han was fighting rolls out of the circle, face bloodied, apparently unable to stand up.

"At ease, soldiers!" Buxton shouts from behind us. "Feel free to watch the show!"

Great, I think. The last thing I want is an audience for my first fight.

The other soldiers pull themselves up from various levels of peer-inflicted injuries and make their way over to our circle. Out of the corner of my eye I see Tawni and Trevor move closer. Tawni's no longer laughing, her mouth a tight line. She's worried about me. *Serves her right*, I think.

Instinct and training kicks in. I settle my heart and lungs by taking deep breaths through my nose, exhaling from my mouth. All of my father's mottos ring through my head: *hit first and hit hard; a quick fight is a good fight; there's no such thing as a fair fight; play to your strengths.*

But all my thoughts vanish when the taunting begins. "You smell like a moon dweller, chickie," a guy with a black eye says. "You a moon dweller?"

My mouth is tight as I nod.

"We've been looking for some moon dwellers with balls to join us, but you don't look like you've even fought a cold before." I grit my teeth and try to ignore him, focusing on my opponent, who has just stepped into the ring, her fists clenched at her side. She looks ready; I hope I am.

"We need moon dwellers who can fight," a butch woman with no neck cries.

I stare at her sharply and say, "I can fight."

The original heckler chimes in again. "Bah! You're just a scared little girl, not a fighter." He got the scared part right. But not scared of fighting. Scared of losing those closest to me; scared of failing my parents, my people; scared of not fighting well enough for everything that is important to me.

"I'll prove it," I say.

"Fight!" Buxton shouts, even louder than she has yet. Her voice echoes through my ears, and I don't think I'll ever hear well again.

Han is like a flash of light, faster and more agile than anyone I've ever fought before. But I've got a few inches on her, am built slightly bigger, and I have the advantage of not underestimating her. My father taught me to use any advantage I can in a fight.

She moves in fast, feinting left and right, left and right, trying to lull me into a rhythm. She whips a lightning-quick kick at my head and I duck sharply, narrowly avoiding it, but realizing too late that it was a combo move. Her other leg is already in motion, sweeping the ground and cutting toward my feet. I try to jump, but all my force is pushing down and I can't get my feet off the ground. A sharp pain jolts through my ankles and I go down hard on my right shoulder, wincing as I feel it start to throb.

My training kicks in and I know the fight is moments away from being over if I don't get out of the vulnerable position I'm in.

I roll hard to the side, away from Han, and hear her boot clomp down hard on the rock, just where I was a second earlier. My mind is machine, thinking like my opponent, anticipating her next move.

She'll expect me to try to get to my feet.

So I don't.

Instead, I roll back the other way.

My surprise works, as I feel my turning shoulder bash into her legs, which are moving in the opposite direction of my roll. She was rushing to stop me from getting to my feet, trying to maintain her advantage. The joke's on her as she tumbles over me, sprawling head first. More pain lances through my shoulder and I realize it's the same one that hit the ground. Bad luck, but I can't worry about that. Not now.

Gritting my teeth, I will my body to ignore the pain and move faster than I've ever moved before. I finish the roll and use the momentum to push up with my legs and one arm, regaining my feet. In the back of my mind I know there are people watching and that they're making a lot of noise, but my head is a void, focused on only one thing: winning the fight.

Using my heel, I stop myself and charge back the other way, where Han went down. She's scrambling to her feet, but I can tell from her wide eyes and slightly parted lips that I've surprised her. I see fear. Another advantage I can use.

I scream something that sounds like "Arrararararara!"—part roar, part battle cry, perhaps?—and lower my shoulder, watching her eyes widen further before I crash into her chest, flattening her with the power of a miner's sledgehammer. Not graceful—but effective.

Another one of my father's nuggets of wisdom pops into my head at that moment—*don't stop until it's over*—and I make him proud by continuing to drive forward after the initial impact, crushing Han into the stone and landing with my full weight on top of her. She half grunts, half screams, and I can feel the air go out of her lungs with a whoosh of breath on my face.

I know it's over—there's no way her smaller frame could get up from the power of the smack that I just laid on her—so I roll off her and stand up, looking around.

Initially, I worry I really have lost my hearing from Buxton's incessant yelling, because there's no sound. But then I realize that it's just because everyone's quiet, staring at me like I've just grown a third arm and started juggling hunks of limestone. I scan the crowd, searching for a familiar face. I see Buxton, who's scowling, but with an eyebrow raised; Brody, who's wearing a big grin, as if he planned the whole thing himself; Tawni, standing out with a smile of her own, like a sparkling diamond amongst ashy hunks of coal; and finally, Trevor, who looks half amused and half like he wants to kill me.

Ten seconds pass in silence, and then: a clap rings out through the seemingly impenetrable silence, sounding like the hollow ring of a dinner bell in the caves. I jerk my head to the side and see that it's the short, black-eyed guy. The heckler. He claps again and then shouts, "WoooOOO!" getting louder as he yells. The next thirty seconds are a bit awkward as some of the other soldiers join in, some applauding, some shouting encouragement, and others just staring at me. I focus on Tawni, who is laughing, until the noise dies down.

I hear a strange sound behind me, like an old person trying to breathe through a ventilator, and turn to see Han on her hands and knees, wheezing through her mouth. She was my enemy, but now she's my comrade, and so I stride to her and help her to her feet, lifting her by her elbows. Leaning on me, she manages to walk to the edge of the circle, whispering, "Thank you," in my ear, like I've just done her a huge service, rather than crushing her sternum.

Brody approaches us. "Nice fight, soldiers," he says. "Zarra, take Han to medical to get her, uh, her ribs and her…chest, and, well, whatever else hurts looked at." A girl no more than twenty-one, with short-cut black hair and thick black eyebrows, steps forward and takes Han from me.

I turn back to face Brody, and Buxton, who has once more moved to his side. "Well done," he says, grinning again.

"It's just one fight and I didn't mean to hurt her so bad," I say. I'm not proud of having sent a girl to the medic, especially because it's just training, and she's supposed to be on my side.

"Damn right," Buxton says. "It *was* just one fight and Han is a small fry compared to a lot of the soldiers, so don't get a big head."

I don't know what her problem is, but I'm getting tired of it. "Don't worry, I won't," I say, glaring at her.

Brody pats me on my injured shoulder and I clench my teeth so I don't show how much it hurts. "At ease, soldier," he says, and I realize my hands are fisted and my arms are tight, like I'm straining against a heavy weight. He probably thinks I'm about to hit the other sergeant. Maybe I am—I dunno.

Sometimes when the adrenaline gets pumping and I'm in fight-mode, it's like I lose a bit of control, which scares me a little.

I force my hands to open, flexing the soreness out of them a few times. Then I relax my shoulders, allowing them to droop just a little. "What's next?" I ask, trying to keep my voice pleasant.

"Have you ever even fired a gun?" Buxton asks, with a note of sarcasm in her voice.

"I only learned how to fight with staffs and bows and slingshots," I say. "But mostly we focused on hand-to-hand combat."

"Yeah, we noticed," Brody says, winking. I wonder why he's being so nice to me. Maybe he's just a nice guy. I wish Buxton were more like him.

"You trained with your mother?" Buxton asks, sounding relatively interested in me for the first time since I met her.

"No—my father."

Her head jerks back in surprise. "That's interesting," is all she says, and I want to ask her why, but I don't, knowing she won't give me a straight answer. "All right, soldiers, time for target practice!" she announces, once more deafening anyone within earshot.

I follow the stampede of uniformed men and women as they move further down the gray ore slab. A few of them slap me on the back and nod encouragingly, but no one tries to talk to me, and most just ignore me.

I hang back, letting Tawni and Trevor catch up. "Took you long enough to finish her off," Tawni says.

I laugh, feeling all the pent-up tension slip away upon hearing my friend's sarcasm. "Yeah, I paid for it, too," I reply, rubbing my shoulder.

"You got lucky, kid," Trevor says, smirking.

"Whatever you say," I reply, desperately wanting to smack the smirk off his face. "But don't call me kid."

"Whatever you say," he mimics, "*kid.*" Now I really want to punch him, but I'm sure it will land me some sort of undesirable army punishment, so I manage to just flash a fake smile.

Tawni doesn't let it go, though. "You don't know what you're talking about, Trevor," she says. I give her a real smile, and finally I think maybe she sees why I hate this guy so much.

"Oh yeah? Then educate me."

"Just let it go, Tawns," I say.

"No, really, I want to know," Trevor insists. "Why do I not know what I'm talking about?"

"No, Tawni," I say, warning her off with my eyes.

"Because she doesn't look so tough," Trevor continues, raking a hand through his chestnut curls. "Hell, I wouldn't trust her to cover my as—"

"Adele killed Rivet, Trevor," Tawni blurts out, her eyes brimming with tears.

I look away and swallow hard, trying to choke down the bad memories that well up every time I think of Rivet. Because when I think of Rivet I can't help but think of Cole. *Cole.* No. No. No! *God, no! Why did it have to be him?* I ask in my mind. No one ever answers me.

Blinking furiously, I fight off the tears and try to think of something else, anything else. It's harder than fighting Han, but I manage to win the battle.

I glance back at Trevor, whose face is ashen, as if dusted with chalk powder. Luckily, we arrive at target practice and he and Tawni are forced to move to the side, out of the line of

155

fire. There are six guns, three handguns and three rifles. Each black, each foreign to me. My weapons are fists and rocks and sticks and feet. Hot metal bullets are used by Enforcers and prison guards. Bad people. Not me.

But I know I have to do this if I want to be a part of the rebellion.

"Line up, even numbers in each line!" Buxton barks.

The platoon moves somewhat haphazardly into relatively equal, straight lines. The soldiers don't seem to be the most disciplined—not like the sun dweller troops we saw anyway—but they get the job done. I choose a line on one end that seems to have fewer people than the others.

Brody raises a hand in the air, his thumb and forefinger extended in the shape of a gun. Not surprisingly, it's Buxton who shouts, "Fire!"

Pop, pop, pop! The first rounds are fired by the front soldiers in the lines on my half, the ones with the handguns. They are smaller and lighter and presumably quicker to prepare and aim.

Crack, crack, crack! The rifle fire thunders through the low-ceilinged cavern, echoing off the walls and roof.

"Hold your fire," Brody says sternly. "Dom—check 'em."

One of the soldiers in my line breaks away and jogs to the other end of the slab, where a row of canvas targets are set up. He checks each target, and then pulls the canvas upwards, removing the old target and revealing a fresh target underneath. They must have a big old roll of targets strung behind.

The guy named Dom lopes back, calling, "One, three, five, six—out! Two, four—in!" as he approaches.

"Brady, Wong, Henderson, and Raine—bad luck," Brody says. Four soldiers—three girls, one guy—step out of line and sit on big stone benches erected to the side, near where Tawni and Trevor are standing. The two who apparently had the best aim move to the back of their respective lines, to wait their turn again.

The cycle continues on, as more and more soldiers are defeated and forced off to the side, and the lines get shorter and shorter. As I slowly move up the line, my legs stiffen and I can feel my shoulder bruising under the sleeve of my tunic.

The guy in front of me is up and I watch him carefully, trying to memorize his every movement. He places his feet shoulder-width apart, steadies them, holds the gun at approximately shoulder-height using both hands, his elbows locked but not tightly. He stares down the barrel and—

Pop! I see a flash in the dim cavern and then a finger of smoke curls from the gun. The bullet is invisible, but I see the canvas visibly flutter near the edge about the same time as I heard the gunshot.

They check the results and the guy is out, trotting off to the side to join his comrades.

It's my turn. I've never held a gun until that morning, when my mom handed one to me, and I've certainly never fired one, but I hope it's like shooting a bow and arrow, or a slingshot. You know, point, aim, shoot. Simple.

I step up and grasp the gun and feel all eyes on me as I stare at it, trying to position it right. The handle—is that what it's called?—is cool to the touch, but also a little moist from the previous shooter's sweaty hands. There's something weird about the gun, but I can't figure out what and I don't have time to think about it. I mimic my predecessor's positioning, although maybe I shouldn't because apparently he didn't do very well. I take aim, trying to get the end of the gun even with the target, while I wait for the command.

One second—I'm too high. Two seconds—I'm aimed dead center. Three seconds—"Fire!" Buxton yells.

I squeeze the trigger with my finger, surprised at how easily it pushes in. Dangerous, if you ask me. The gun explodes back into my palm, and, despite my locked arms, my elbows bend and it bucks upwards, forcing me to take a step back and out of my shooter's stance. The target doesn't flutter, but I hear a *zing!* as the bullet ricochets off the wall behind, sending splinters of rock in every direction.

"Oops," I mutter.

"Pathetic," Buxton scoffs. "No need to check that one. Rose—out!"

Staring at the ground the whole way, I walk over to the rest of the eliminated soldiers, taking a seat without looking at anyone. I feel a tap on the shoulder from behind. I'm not in the mood to be ridiculed, so I don't turn around.

Tap, tap. The fool isn't giving up, so I raise my shoulder sharply like I'm trying to get a pesky fly off of it.

Tap, tap. I whirl around. "What?" I hiss.

A young guy is looking at me, mouth open. He looks around my age, with thin black stubble, full lips, and swirling gray eyes. His brown eyebrows are arched in surprise. He's not bad looking, but I'm not interested in that right now. "What do you want?" I ask again.

"I was just going to say that I missed on my first attempt, too."

My shoulders droop and I feel bad right away. The poor guy was trying to make me feel better, was probably one of the ones clapping when I defeated Han, and yet I was so rude to him. I can't let even a tough situation like this turn me into one of the bad guys. "Oh. Thanks." I manage a crooked smile although I know it's not very believable. I turn back around, trying to calm down.

Soon target practice is over and the winner is announced. It's the dude named Dom, a sturdy guy with athletic arms and legs who's about two heads taller than me.

This is meant to be training, but with only getting to take one shot, I don't feel like I've learned anything. I stand up, take a breath, and promise myself I'll do better on the next challenge.

Twelve
Tristan

When Ram came to get us, he said there was a "situation." Whatever that means. He wouldn't give us any details, but insisted that we follow him immediately. I thought about giving him a hard time, refusing to go, but decided it wasn't worth the fight.

So now we're traipsing back through the tunnels, along the familiar route to the honeycomb room. Elsey is humming softly while Roc whistles along. Some tune I don't know, but that they both seem to. They are a funny pair.

I'm watching Ram's every movement, daring him to try and hurt me again. This time I'm ready if he tries anything. To be honest, I'm somewhat disappointed when he doesn't.

We pass through the common area, which is less filled than before, but not empty. It seems as if people are always eating in this place. My heart still feels slightly warm from my time spent with Roc and Elsey. It was nice, for a change—just being able to hang out, learn something about Roc I never knew before. My guard is down, but the walk gives me time to raise it back up. Whatever this "situation" is, it's probably not good. Nothing in our world every really is.

We reach the same sturdy metal door as before, and Jinny is waiting for us.

"Auntie!" Elsey exclaims, running to her and hugging her around the waist.

"Ready for dinner?" Jinny says.

"Yes," Roc and I reply simultaneously. Seems we can always eat these days.

Jinny laughs. "They'll have food for you guys in there," she says, motioning to the door.

"That's what Mr. Meathead said last time," Roc says under his breath.

I chuckle. "See ya later, El. Bye, Jinny."

"I'll miss you both dearly," Elsey says, pushing the back of her hand to her forehead like she might faint.

"And you, Lady Elsey," Roc replies in his best theater voice, generating a peal of giggles from his new best friend. Jinny smiles and shakes her head as she shepherds Elsey back the way we came.

Ram grunts and pulls open the door, holding it for us. "Ladies first," I say, motioning for Roc to enter first.

"Age before beauty," he returns, bowing graciously.

"I'm a day older than you."

"And ten times uglier." I fake a punch to his midsection and he flinches.

The cast around the table is the same as it was earlier. The Resistance leaders. Ben, at the head. Vice President Morgan at the other head, her back to us. Maia sits next to Jonas on one side, and flashes me a smile as I enter. Jonas's expression is less friendly, his mouth a tight line. His eyes follow me to my seat.

"Thanks for coming on such short notice," Ben says.

"How could we refuse when you sent such a persuasive escort," I say, watching Roc smile as he sits down. Even if no one else gets my sarcasm, at least he does. Ram grunts again from the spot he's taken in the corner. I guess he gets it, too.

"We have a bit of a—"

"Situation? Yeah, we heard, but what does that mean exactly?" Unlike the last time I was in this room, I feel more confident. I have a better idea what to expect from the other people in the room. Vice President Morgan I know from before; Maia's got my back; Jonas is one to watch out for, but could be an ally; Ben's my biggest advocate. And Ram, well he's just a bunghole. I smirk at my own thoughts.

"The President has taken over all the airwaves," Morgan says. I like the way she calls him *the President*, and not *your father*.

"He does that all the time," I say. "Whenever he wants to spout his propaganda."

"True," Ben says, "but this time it's a message about you."

"Wha...what?" I say, unable to prevent the slight stutter.

"It's probably best if you see for yourself," Morgan says, motioning to a screen that's descended from a crack in the roof behind Ben. For living in a cave in the middle of nowhere, these people are full of surprises.

"Nice telebox," Roc says. It's the first thing he's said while in this room, and his face turns a dark shade of crimson when everyone looks at him.

"It wasn't easy secretly running lines in here," Ben comments. "But then again, it wasn't easy building a train network unknown to the government either." It's weird thinking about how Ben had another life, back before we were even born, a life involving secret trains and communication networks and the Uprising.

The dark screen turns white, and then gray bubbles buzz across it. "Acquiring signal," a voice drones.

The screen changes, bringing up a visual that I know is from the Sun Realm, because the lighting is way too bright to be anywhere else. And because I've been there many times. It's where my father conducts all his press conferences: on the steps of the government buildings. The camera pans to show the beautiful backdrop of the palace gardens. In the top corner of the screen is a message in red: *Recorded earlier today.*

President Nailin is at the podium. Before he speaks, there's light applause from his admirers. "Thank you, my friends," he says. Another round of applause. "There has been much speculation over the past couple of weeks about the state of our great Tri-Realms. Rumors of attacks by the star dwellers in the Moon Realm plague the headlines. People are worried about my son, Tristan, who went missing about the same time as the star dweller attacks began. I thank you for all of the letters and cards wishing for his safe return." A pause. He licks his lips, scans the crowd.

"I've called this press conference today and will be broadcasting it for the next twenty-four hours, as I have a very important message for all citizens of the Tri-Realms. First, I can tell you that after some strong messaging from me personally, the star dwellers have ceased their attacks on the Moon Realm, and it is my understanding that the two great Realms are getting close to a peace accord. It's a sad day indeed when any of the Realms are in disagreement with each other, and I'm so thankful I was able to step in and facilitate a peaceful resolution."

I grit my teeth and glance at Ben, who wears a wry smile. The lies are so blatant I can barely stop myself from removing one of my boots and chucking it at the screen. This is bad, even for my father.

"Furthermore, I am so pleased to announce that Tristan has returned, safe and sound."

"What the hell?" I blurt out. Ben points to the screen, urging me to listen to the rest.

"My son, bless his heart, left the Sun Realm seeking to find his mother, who, as you all know, disappeared a few years ago, breaking all of our hearts." The camera pans to show the crowd, who are nodding and murmuring words of pity to the poor President, the victim of a terrible tragedy.

"Lies," I growl through my teeth.

"Although he's not yet ready to stand in front of all of you, or resume his duties as my son, he asked me to apologize to all of you on his behalf, for putting the Sun Realm through such a trying ordeal. My youngest son, Killen, will, effective immediately, stand in for Tristan, fulfilling all the duties of the eldest son. Please show him your appreciation as I do."

As Killen walks across the white rock platform to stand behind the podium, my father claps loudly, leading a roar of applause from the crowd. My jaw is aching from clenching it so hard.

Killen's face is lit up in a smile that reminds me so much of my father. Arrogant. Smug. Looking down on his worshippers. I hate him in that moment. "My friends," he says, using the same greeting as my father, "I am so pleased to be able to serve you." Scripted. My father's words—not his—but he pulls it off. He's a natural at BS.

"My first order of business is to lead the rebuilding of the Moon Realm after the careless star dweller bombings. To the people of the Moon Realm, I say, do not fear, help is on the way."

The reply is deafening. Shouts of "Thank you, Killen" and "We love you!" fill the air.

My brother uses his bobbing arms to quiet the crowd. "And then I will personally meet with the star and moon dweller leaders to help them work out their differences, to once again restore peace to the Tri-Realms." More applause. More screams.

My fingernails are scraping the table and if Ben didn't turn off the telebox right then, I fear my fingers would be cut and bleeding soon.

I stand up, cracking my knuckles. I'm seething, my emotions out of control, like a tidal wave of rage, but I don't care. All I want is revenge. "I'll go public—prove him wrong. Turn the people against him."

Ben sighs. "He's controlling everything right now, Tristan. We can't get a message out to everyone. And even if we could, he'd just counter with another message refuting it. Who do you

165

think the people will believe? The President, or his rogue son who's desperately seeking his runaway mom?"

I stand there, my chest puffing in and out, my arms tight at my sides, my hands fisted. "Urr," I growl and then sit back down. I feel better. I just needed to get the anger out. "I'm okay now," I say. "Let's talk about it." Roc's looking at me strangely, like I'm a weird new animal species who's just demonstrated a bizarre mating ritual. I ignore him.

"There's something else," Morgan says. I groan inwardly. *What else could there be?* "Shortly after the initial broadcast from the President, he sent a typed message to all the moon dweller vice presidents. He said if any of them are harboring his son, to pass the message along to him."

"So he admitted to his lies. We've got him," Maia says, her eyes alight with excitement.

"Not exactly," Ben says. "The message also warned them that if anyone tries to make the information public, that he would deny it, and destroy them. I don't think any of the VPs, with the exception of VP Morgan here"—he motions across the table—"would be willing to go head-to-head with Nailin. They know what he's capable of."

"And if Morgan tries to do something, he'll make an example of her," I say. I know my father's tactics all too well.

"This is good news," Roc says suddenly, and all eyes shift to him. He raises a cheek and chews on the side of his mouth for a second, and then says, "If he sent the message to *all* the VPs, then he doesn't have a clue where we're hiding. So that's good, right?"

He has a point. It's not often my father is so in the dark about the goings-on in his own kingdom. It's an advantage, albeit a small one.

"That's a good point, Roc," Ben says, nodding. Roc grins. I knew there was a reason I wanted him with me at these meetings.

"So what message did my loving father give me?" I ask.

Ben has a paper in front of him and he consults it, using his finger to guide his eyes across the page. "He said, 'Tell Tristan he must contact me within twenty-four hours or I'll start killing moon dwellers.'"

I cringe. "How am I supposed to do that?"

"He provides information on how to reach him directly from the Moon Realm."

"Of course I'll do it," I say. "It's not like he can do anything to me over a videoconference."

"There's one other thing," Ben says.

"Yeah?"

"He wants Roc with you when you call him."

"Roc? Why?"

"You tell me."

Roc and I look at each other. His face wears the same expression I expect I'm wearing. Confusion. I don't have the slightest idea what my father could want with Roc. I mean, in my eyes Roc is an amazing person, my best friend, but in my father's eyes, he's just a servant. Scum. No—lower than scum. Fungus on scum. Of no concern to him. And yet…there must be a reason he wants him there. And not an honorable reason. A way to get to me.

"I have no idea," I say, while Roc shakes his head. "When can we do it?" I ask. I'm curious now, which probably means I'm falling right into my father's trap, but I don't care—I have to know what he's playing at.

"Right now," Ben says, standing up and pushing back his chair. "He said you must do it alone."

"Fine. Will you be listening?"

"He said he would know if it was being transmitted to multiple receivers or being recorded. I don't want to take the chance. You can give us the details afterward."

I nod. "You ready?" I ask Roc.

"Do I have a choice?"

"Not really."

"Then I'm ready."

Thirteen

Adele

My life feels complete for the first time in a long time. I mean, we're not one big happy family or anything, but at least my mom, dad, and sister are all alive and okay and I've been able to see them all recently. That's about as good as it gets these days. So you'd think that would mean maybe I'd be at peace, or something like it, but instead, I'm throwing everything I have into training.

And that feels the most normal of all.

I grunt as our wooden staffs connect in the middle. The raw power of my opponent allows him to shove me backwards, crushing the wood into my lip. I taste coppery blood in my mouth as it splits open. He charges, swinging the rod back and forth like a sword. *Use all parts of your body.* I hear my father's voice in my head and I obey, ducking my enemy's attempted blow, crushing his kneecap with my heel, and slamming my elbow into his jaw. I take his head off. Not literally, but his head snaps back and he tumbles to the rock, yowling in pain.

Jamming the butt of my staff into his throat, I say, "Do you submit?"

He's discarded his own staff and is rubbing his jaw and clutching his knee. "Uhhh," he moans.

"I'll take that as a yes," I murmur, moving away from him and out of the ring. It's my fourth staff victory in a row. The dude was twice my size, but in some fights, size doesn't matter.

Someone's clapping. Brody. He's been clapping after each of my victories. Beyond him I see Tawni and she gives me a thumbs-up. Next to her Trevor is glaring at me. There's something not right about that guy.

Ignoring him, I stride over to the next station, archery, and pick up the bow. It's brand new and practically sparkling. The arrow is like a violin bow as I move it along the catgut string. Although the target is at least two hundred feet away, I pull it toward me with my eyes, until it's just in front of me, the bull's eye like a throbbing red beacon. I make small movements, just like I've been taught, until I'm certain my aim is true.

Twang!

The bow sings and my arrow cuts sharply through the murky air, embedding itself in the dead center of the target.

"Another perfect shot—four for four," Brody says, resuming his clap. "You're doing well, Rose."

"I completely missed the gun target," I say, frowning.

"It was one shot," Brody says, flashing a smile. "You'll get better. I can teach you."

"Really?" I say, lowering my voice so no one will hear our conversation. I don't want to be accused of getting special treatment because of my mom, but I do want to learn how to shoot. I don't know where it comes from—my drive. For some reason, ever since I was little, I've had to be the best at anything I try. Nothing less is acceptable. Anything less is failure.

I don't want to shoot a gun, but if I have to, I will be the best at it.

"Sure. A lot of the soldiers get additional help on the side at the things they're not natural at." I make a face, and Brody says hurriedly, "Not that you're not a natural—I mean, given your proficiency at archery you might be just as good with a gun once you get the hang of it."

I crack a smile, finally releasing some of the tension I've felt all day. "I was just giving you a hard time," I say, and Brody grins, pushing his dark hair away from his eyes. For the first time I notice just how good looking he is. Perhaps it's because I've let my guard down, if only for a moment. The blue and green in his eyes seem to swirl around, sometimes mixing, sometimes separated. With his smile, a dimple forms in one of his cheeks and his strong cheekbones rise high on his face. His longish, wavy hair suits his face perfectly. Between his looks and his personality, he's the type of guy I'd like to have as an older brother.

I realize I've gone into a daze thinking about Brody as a brother and he's looking at me funny.

"What?" he asks.

"Nothing. What's next?"

"That's it," he says cheerfully. "No mandatory training until tomorrow. Meet me here tomorrow morning at oh-six-hundred hours for *personal* gun training." The way he emphasizes the word *personal* sounds odd. And then I realize: he's flirting with me.

Without a word, I spin and walk away, hoping it didn't come off as too rude, but hoping I'm sending some pretty strong signals Brody's way. I'm not interested.

As I meet up with Tawni, I try to push all thoughts of Brody out of my head.

"You were amazing!" she says as I walk up.

"Yeah, but only at the things I've done before," I point out.

"You'll improve with those nasty guns," Tawni says in a way that makes me smile.

"Don't count on it," Trevor says. "You can't be perfect at everything."

"What is your problem?" I say, letting my anger get the best of me. I know he's not worth the effort, but I just can't seem to push down the heat when I'm around him.

"I'm not sure what you mean," he says snidely.

"You two bicker like you're brother and sister," Tawni says, shaking her head disapprovingly.

"We do *not!*" we say simultaneously. The laugh comes before I can stifle it, and I realize Trevor's cracking up, too. It's a weird moment, but I see a burst of humanity in him, like he's not such a bad guy.

In an instant, his sneer wipes out the laugh with the speed of a cave-in. "For your information," he says, "I don't trust you."

"But my mom's a general," I say, hating to use my mom like that, but feeling the need to point out where my loyalties lie.

"That means nothing," he says. "There are rumors that you and Tristan Nailin were seen together in the Moon Realm. I don't trust him, so I don't trust you." I don't want to talk about me and Tristan, and I know it's not worth arguing, so I don't.

"It's not like I trust you either." There's just something strange about Trevor, and I can't put my finger on it. It's like he doesn't belong in this place. If anyone might be a traitor, it's him. "Why are you always hanging around us, anyway?" I ask, my voice sounding as rough as the cavern roof above us.

"The General's orders," he replies simply.

"Which general?"

"General Rose." What? Really? Why would my mom give us a babysitter, especially one like Trevor?

I huff, but don't respond. I'll speak to my mom about getting a new escort the next time I see her.

As we head toward the office building, a soldier comes around the corner, wheeling a cart. It's full of weapons, black and silver and new and shiny. Guns mostly, but bows and slingshots, too. My mind races back to the first time I touched the gun during target practice. I don't know much about guns, but it looked like a nice weapon. The star dweller army seems extremely well-equipped. First the bombs used during the attacks on the Moon Realm, and now a seemingly unlimited supply of high-quality infantry weaponry. Seems strange for a people who are living in poverty—I mean, I've seen poverty on the streets; they're at the bottom of the food chain.

"Where are all the weapons coming from?" I ask. Trevor is probably the last person I should be asking, but I can't help myself. The answer to that question suddenly seems like the most important thing in the world.

Trevor cocks his head to the side and gazes past Tawni, who's walking between us. He chews on his lip for a moment, as if he's mulling over the question, or perhaps how to concoct a believable lie. "That's none of your damn business," he says.

"It's a simple question," I say. "It takes money to buy weapons, or resources to make them—neither of which the star dwellers have. And yet, you've got more shiny, new weapons than the freaking Moon Realm." I'm practically growling now, sick of putting up with Trevor's crap.

"The Star Realm's got plenty of resources," he says.

"Yeah, all of which you hand over to the Sun Realm. You really think they wouldn't miss a few tons of ore? They keep track of everything. They're not stupid."

"I never said they were!" Trevor yells, and I stop. His quick temper, the snarl on his face, his unwillingness to tell me anything: all of it makes me hate him.

"I want to see my mother," I say.

"She's busy."

"Just tell her."

"Fine," Trevor says, stalking off and leaving Tawni and me alone for the first time since we woke up next to each other.

"You still think he's okay?" I say once he's gone.

"I don't know," Tawni says. "Maybe you're right."

"I *am* right."

"You think he's involved in something?"

"Yep."

"Your mom will know what to do."

"Yeah," I say. My stomach grumbles. "You hungry?"

"I could eat," Tawni says, and we laugh together. It's what Cole always used to say. Her laugh turns sullen and I see moisture in her eyes. "I really miss him," she says.

"I know. Me too."

She grabs my arm at the elbow, her touch feeling warm and safe against my skin, and we enter the building together. First we stop at my mom's office, but the door's closed and locked and there's no answer when we knock.

"I guess she's out," I say.

"I wonder where the food is."

"It would have been nice of Trevor to let us know before he stormed off."

"We've got some food left in our packs," Tawni says thoughtfully.

I'm not particularly interested in the stiff, cardboard-like wafers we've got in our packs, but I don't have a better option.

"Okay, let's go."

We retrace our way through the narrow streets, stepping over the beggars—who seem to have multiplied—and stray dogs sleeping on the cobblestone. We see a guy defecating against the wall and my stomach turns. Horrible. This place is horrible. And I thought the Moon Realm was a hard place. I don't know how my mom stands it.

We arrive at the medical building without interacting with anyone, and slip through the maze of sick beds. Instinctively I hold my breath, not wanting to breathe in the raft of potential disease and bacteria that flavor the air like an invisible cloud. I know it's silly, especially because I've been sleeping in this room for days, but when I do breathe, I cover my face with my hand like a mask.

Just before we reach our beds, Tawni shrieks as a woman grabs the side of her tunic, her hands clenched and gnarled and pale. Her gray skin is covered in sores and blisters, but beneath the flesh-eating disease I can tell she's young. Older than us, but probably only in her mid-twenties. A soldier, possibly. I'm still not sure if the wing is military only.

Tawni tries to pull away, but the dying woman's hands are stronger than they look, latched onto the cloth like pincers. "Help…me," she croaks through chapped lips. Her eyes are so bloodshot I can't determine the color.

"What do I do?" Tawni asks, her mouth contorted with horror.

Tawni is too pure, whereas I am not. I've killed already. I'm a bad person already. I kick the lady's arm, not too hard, but hard enough that I know she'll let go. Her hand snaps back and she cries out, tucking her hand back beneath the thin white sheet that covers her.

I slink past, hating myself. There's nothing I can do for the woman. I'm no doctor. And I certainly don't want to catch what she's got.

Tawni sits on the bed, breathing heavily. "Thanks," she says, looking up at me.

"I'm good at kicking," I say, trying to make a joke.

She gives me a courtesy smile, but I can tell she's not up for humor right now. The thing with the woman really affected her. "What can we do for these people?" she asks, her light blue eyes questioning.

"Nothing for them individually," I say. "But perhaps a rebellion could help us all."

"I don't know. It just doesn't seem like more violence is the answer to anything."

I know what she means. "The star dwellers should never have attacked the Moon Realm," I agree. "That was the wrong way to go about things. But maybe my mom and dad can set things right. If we can just unite the two Realms like my father said, then maybe…" I trail off, unsure of where I'm going with it.

"Maybe it will make a difference," Tawni finishes.

I shrug. "Maybe." I don't even convince myself. Everything seems so out of control—like a lost cause.

"Why were you asking Trevor about the guns?" Tawni asks.

My dark mood disappears as my focus returns to my thoughts from earlier. I lay back onto the bed, thinking furiously. Something jabs me in my lower back. "Oww!" I yelp, turning to the side to grab at the thing. My hand closes on the steel and I remove the gun from beneath my tunic.

Tawni lies down next to me and we both stare at the weapon, as I turn it over and over in my hands. It's different than the gun I fired earlier. Older, marred by time, with scratches on the handle and barrel. And etched just above the trigger: *Rose*.

Tawni notices it at the same time as me and says, "It was your mom's gun."

I rub my fingers over the engraving, tracing the lines of each letter. "From the Uprising," I say thoughtfully. It's like she's passing the torch to me. She's done her part—now I have to do mine. I wonder how many times she's fired this gun, how many times she's killed with it.

"You would think all the guns would be old like this one," Tawni says. She's smart—Tawni. Not only a good person, but a real thinker.

"Exactly," I say. "Something's going on, and I think Trevor's involved. That's why he got so defensive when I asked him about it."

Sitting up, Tawni reaches down and retrieves our packs from underneath the bed. "Can we eat somewhere else? This place is depressing."

We take our packs with us, as we won't be coming back to the medical ward to sleep again. On the quiet balls of our feet, we weave our way back through the beds, careful to avoid any reaching hands, and exit back into the shadowy cavern. I know it's the middle of the day, but it always seems like night is falling in the Star Realm. The amount of electricity they're rationed is unforgivable.

"Where should we go?" I ask. The thought of eating in the streets with the beggars isn't ideal. But I also have no desire to go back to the military buildings—not yet.

"Are you starving? Or can we explore a bit, maybe find a better spot?"

I'm used to being hungry—I've been hungry my whole life.

We move through the streets, passing dozens of homeless people, who seem to be the majority. Although we should be paying attention to where we're going, we don't, making a left turn, then a right, then another left, zigzagging through the subchapter. Every street looks the same. Narrow. Dirty. Beggars. Stray animals. The smell is awful, but I'm getting used to it. I guess it's what it's like to be a garbage man—at some point you just adapt.

The next street is a light commercial district, although most of the shops are boarded up and empty. The sides of the buildings are covered with spray paint. Some of it's pretty good actually, showing that even delinquents have talent. One in particular catches my eye, a massive, colorful mural of a red dragon. The message is dark, with the dragon breathing bright orange flames on a group of people, setting their clothes on fire

178

before they can flee. Their expressions are filled with horror. I shiver. But most of it is just random scribbles, or obscene messages about someone's mother, or where to go for a good time.

A couple of grizzly men light up cigarettes as we pass by, staring at us with dark eyes cast in shadow by their hats. The tips of their smokes appear bright against the dim backdrop. When I look back at them they remove their hats and I cringe as their fully tattooed faces are revealed, gleaming with metal piercings in their eyebrows, noses, lips, and chins. They laugh at me, deep and throaty, and I usher Tawni forward at double the speed.

We make another left and enter the narrowest alleyway of all. To our surprise, it's deserted. After the other streets, which were jammed with beggars sitting shoulder to shoulder, this one seems peaceful, serene even. I was hoping for some kind of a big plaza, with high-backed stone benches and the soothing sign of a bubbling, decorative fountain, but I don't think that exists in this world, so I stop.

"Want to eat here?" Tawni asks, reading my mind.

"It's as good a spot as any, I reckon," I reply, sliding my back down the wall. I look up and see the building rise three stories before connecting with the low cavern ceiling. All the buildings are built all the way to the top of the cavern, out of necessity, I expect. With a growing population and limited space, the star dwellers are forced to use every last square inch. I thought we had it bad in the Moon Realm, but at least we had space to spread out. The subchapter 14 cavern feels like a land of plenty compared to this foreign country. My heart beats rapidly as I realize how spoiled I've been.

179

Tawni slides in next to me, sitting close, our shoulders touching like the street beggars. We each open a pack and retrieve some wafers. I know they won't satisfy my hunger, but at least they might stop the gnawing pain in my gut.

"You know, the star dweller army probably provides better food to the soldiers," Tawni says.

"I expect so."

"Maybe we can have dinner there."

"Sounds good."

We munch for a few minutes in silence, each lost in our own thoughts. Just as I'm finishing my third wafer, a sound breaks the silence. A cry, soft and pitiful, carries down the alley. It sounds weak and childish, like a baby or a small kid. Peering into the gloom, I see a boy, no more than five, his face red and tear-stained. I watch, slow to action due to my surprise, as the kid staggers forward and then collapses face first, barely cushioning his fall with his hands.

I spring to my feet and race to him, expecting the worst, like maybe he's contracted a fast-killing disease, or been shot by some thug on the streets. Any number of atrocities seem like a viable option in this place. I hear the soles of Tawni's shoes clapping the stone behind me as she follows.

When we get within a few steps of the boy, he miraculously springs to his feet, whoops, and then darts away, his small legs churning like the propellers on the boats in subchapter 19 of the Moon Realm.

"Hey! Wait a minute!" I shout, but the boy just keeps on running. I start to chase him, but stop when Tawni yells something behind me. Whirling around, I see her running back toward our packs. Past her a group of kids are whooping and hollering and—

—stealing our stuff.

"Get away from that!" I yell, following in Tawni's wake. I realize where the kids came from when they leap on the wall, climbing it like spiders. Except it's not the wall they're climbing; rather, the rope ladders strung along the stonework.

Fourteen

Tristan

My palms are sweaty as I stare at the screen. I don't know why, but I'm nervous. I can tell Roc is nervous too, because he's biting his nails. My anger at my father is gone, and I'm just worried about what he's going to say, what he's going to threaten. Like he might tell me to come home or he'll bomb the crap out of the other Realms. The only thing is: I am home. Or at least more home than I was up there, in the Sun Realm.

I feel sweat trickle from my armpits and beneath my knees and I try to calm my nerves by gripping the table. This is one time I need to be strong. In this instance, being angry is better than being timid. I can't stop thinking about the press announcement. I don't care that he lied about me, but why did he have to bring my mom into this? Why now? Righteous anger rises in my chest once more because I know the answer: to get to me. Because he knows that dragging my mother's name through the mud once more will piss me off. And for some reason, he thinks that will help him in some way.

I'm staring at the table, but I feel the screen change from black to white. When I turn to look, Roc's already gazing at it, waiting. His now-bitten fingernails have moved to his lap and it almost looks like he has to pee.

And then the nightmare is made real, as my father's face appears on the screen. Away from the crowds and the press, he looks much older, age lines surrounding his eyes and mouth. Gray flecks pepper his short, light-blond hair. He's getting old, having turned forty-two earlier in the year. Less than two decades away from the average life expectancy for males in the Moon Realm. But he's not in the Moon Realm. Sun dweller males get to live for another six to ten years, averaging sixty-five years old on their deathbeds.

His eyes are cold, black, as if the blue pigment I inherited from him has been darkened by a life of sins. His lips curl into a smile, but it's not real.

"Ah, Tristan, my son. It's been a while. How are you?" My heart pounds rapidly and my breaths become ragged, but I clench my face so I don't show my discomfort.

"As you well know, I'm in my bed, recovering from the ordeal of trying to find my mother," I say, not trying to hide my sarcasm.

He laughs, deep and throaty and repugnant, and hot blood churns through my veins. I'm a coward because of it. If we weren't separated by miles of rock and cables and video screens, I'm not sure it would be anger I'd feel.

"I see your little adventure has added to your charming wit. And I also see that you brought your servant boy, *just* like I asked you to." His voice is even, as if we're just having a friendly father/son conversation, but beneath the natural timbre of his voice I can feel an icy cold. Even when he knows he can't touch me, he's trying to show his control over me—that his words are commands, to be obeyed by any who hear them, especially his own son.

"He's not a servant anymore," I growl. "And he has a name: Roc."

"Tsk, tsk, Tristan. Have I taught you nothing? Getting emotionally attached to the help? I warned you about that."

"I learned nothing from you. Except what not to do," I say, forcing the grit out of my voice. Anger is okay, but I need to control it. Need to show him he can't get to me—no matter what.

"Anyway, enough chitchat. I can already see you don't want to do this the easy way. I requested this conference because I want to right some past wrongs. Make amends, so to speak. No, no, don't worry, this is not a deathbed thing—I'm far from my grave." There's a smile on his face, like he thinks he's funny. I just stare at him. "I requested that Roc attend because he is involved. More than involved, really. He *is* the topic. Well, technically you both are."

My mind spins as I wonder what Roc could possibly have to do with anything. I don't mean that in a bad way; it's just that my father has never had anything to do with Roc's life, other than to order him around like a slave. Out of the corner of my eye I can see Roc's hands clenched under the table, his knuckles white. I can tell he wants to look at me, but is afraid to remove his gaze from my father, as if by doing so, he'll open himself up to an attack.

"Keep Roc out of this," I say, surprised at how venomous I sound.

"I'm afraid I can't do that. I feel bad about lying, and I just want to make it right." His words are remorseful, but his tone is not. He's not even trying to make his lie believable. "I did something a long time ago, something I've kept hidden."

"Out with it!" I demand, slamming my fist on the table.

Even my father, the master politician, is unable to hide his shock at my outburst. His face flinches slightly, like he has a tic, but then returns to his normal, unreadable, placid expression. "Patience, my son."

"Don't call me that."

"But it's true. Surely not even you can deny that. Flesh and blood and DNA."

"You are my father only biologically," I say. "In love, I never had a father."

"Spin it any way you want, *son*, it is of no concern to me. But back to why we're here. The truth. Do you remember the day Roc was born?" He shakes his head and chuckles. "Of course not, how silly of me. You were only a day old, as pink and helpless as a piglet. Well, it was a good day. A day in which I buried a secret that could have destroyed me—all of us. The Nailin tradition."

My head is throbbing, perhaps from the anger pumping through my skin, my bones, my blood. Without thinking, I raise a hand to my forehead and start to massage it furiously. There's a sinking feeling in my stomach. It's fear. Despite the strength of my anger, I can't drive away the fear of what he's about to tell us. I know it will be bad—with my father it always is.

"I couldn't let something so insignificant destroy something so grand, now could I? No, of course not. So I did what I had to do. As soon as the child was delivered, I ordered the doctors from the room. I wanted it to be personal, because the situation was personal. At least to me it was. So I used my own bare hands, curled them around her throat—I could feel her pulse thrumming under my fingertips—squeezed hard, hard, harder, harder, until the pulse weakened, died. She died."

"What?" For a moment I'm confused. Clearly my father murdered someone, but who? Who were we talking about? It all comes rushing back. *Do you remember the day Roc was born?* I gasp, as the horror of his tale splits me in half, spilling my heart and my guts and everything out of my body. At least that's how it feels. *Roc's mom didn't die giving birth to him. She was murdered by my father.* I'm shaking and the tears are coming and they're like a train and I can't stop them. But I must. I must, for Roc's sake. I need to be there for him now, like never before. And I can't be a whimpering mess in a ball on the floor if I want to be there for him. I let the anger take over, surging through me until I *am* the anger. My face is contorted with rage, but I don't care. "She didn't *die*; you murdered her."

"Call it what you want, but the end result is the same."

To my right, Roc's body is slack, all fear and nervousness and emotion gone from it. His head is slumped into his chest, his eyes are closed, his arms are loose at his sides. He almost looks dead. Inside, I think he is.

I face my father again and I realize that if he was here in person, and not just an image on a screen, that I'd kill him. For the first time in my life, the idea of killing appeals to me.

186

He's grinning, which should make me even angrier, but for some reason it doesn't, and I pause, trying to figure something out. *Something's not right*, I tell myself. *Of course not, you idiot, nothing's right*, I reply to myself. *No, not that. It's something else. He's not done yet.* Even as I think the words, I know they're true. My father's grin widens as he sees the recognition in my eyes. My head churns through all his grotesque words, trying to latch onto the right ones:

Roc...is involved...he is the topic...you both are.

Do you remember the day Roc was born?

You were only a day old, as pink and helpless as a piglet.

...it was a good day...I buried a secret that could have destroyed me— all of us. The Nailin tradition.

Nooooo! My mind has put it all together, but I scream again and again in my head, refusing to believe it. *No! No! No!*

But he won't let it go—has to keep talking, like he always does. "I only gave the bitch what she asked for. I would think that would make you happy, considering who you keep company with. She wanted me—who was I to deny her? It's not my fault she got pregnant, although I was quite tickled when she gave birth the day after your mother."

His words are like darts, each one penetrating deeper into my heart. I don't know how to speak at a normal volume anymore. Can only scream. "You liar! You raped her! You killed her! I hate you!"

Roc abruptly stands, his motions jerky as he steps past the chair, shoving it under the table. His eyes are moist as he staggers from the room, slamming the door behind him.

"I. Hate. You." I spit the words out, one at a time, like I'm trying to eject a foul taste in my mouth. The image of my father smiling blinks over and over in my mind as I stride through the door and away from him.

* * *

I lie in bed staring at the rough ceiling without really seeing it. I want to be out looking for Roc, but they won't let me. Ben said I would just get lost too, and then they'd have to find us both. Ben's lying on the bed next to me, his injured leg elevated on a couple of pillows. He doesn't try to talk to me, for which I am glad. He said I could take as long as I need before we talk about what happened with my father. But from the way Roc charged out of the room and the way I was shaking with anger and sadness when I emerged, I think he knows it's something bad.

Roc is my half-brother. Of that I am certain. Although my father is not one to be truthful very often, in this case the truth served his purpose so he went with it. From the smile on his face at our reaction, I know in this case he relished the truth. And who knows how many other half-brothers I have out there. Knowing my father, there could be dozens. Dozens of motherless children. Dozens of dead mothers.

I close my eyes. All these years…

I've considered Roc to be my brother all these years, but in a loyalty sense. In a friendship sense. But it seems our bond is built of more than just shared experience. We share a father. I feel bad for Roc right away, because now he's stuck with my father, which I wouldn't wish on my worst enemy, and certainly not on my best friend. We share the Devil as our father.

The question that I can't seem to answer, though, is why did he reveal this to us? Why to me? Why to Roc? My worst fears were that he would threaten me through those I care about, but that didn't happen. There is seemingly no purpose to what he did. It's as if he did it just to…spite me, to break my spirit. Perhaps he thinks it will drive a wedge between Roc and me, thus creating chaos in my life. Maybe he believes in his sick and twisted mind that I'll give up on the cause, go into hiding somewhere, or even return to him. He's so arrogant he might just think that.

But I won't. He's only succeeded in lighting a fire in my belly, one that won't be extinguished until he's destroyed and his power usurped.

I open my eyes and roll my head to the right, where I can see Ben, who looks like he's sleeping. On the floor is a piece of paper. Roc's drawing. The side with the portrait of Tawni is face down, leaving the drawing of the woman who is half his mom and half my mom revealed. Not just my mom—his stepmom.

It's weird, how none of it makes sense at first, but then *all* of it seems to make sense. That he always felt like my brother, always felt like my mom's son. Us playing, laughing, growing up together. The only part that doesn't feel right is that a guy who turned out as honest, caring, and awesome as Roc should have a father like mine. I guess that gives me hope that I'll turn out all right in the end.

A nasty thought pops into my head and I squeeze my eyes shut again, trying to make it go away. But it won't, not until I think about it, so I let it in slowly, playing it around in my mind. Could my mom have known Roc was her stepson? Is that why she always treated him the way she did? My initial reaction is *No way, José*; my mom, the kind, loving person I grew up with, would never do that, would never keep such a secret from us.

But then again, I never thought she would leave me alone with my father, no matter how bad things got for her.

I pound my forehead with the heel of my hand. I hate these thoughts. My anger should be turned on my father, not on my mother. This is exactly what he wants—for me to doubt things, to doubt my mother, to doubt myself. I'm playing right into his hands. If my mother left, then she had a damn good reason, one that was for the good of everyone involved, including me. She wouldn't do something like that, and she wouldn't keep a secret from us, like the one my father revealed today.

"She didn't know," I say out loud, opening my eyes and trying out the words to see how they sound.

"Who didn't?" Ben asks, his own eyes blinking open.

I glance at him. I'm ready to talk about it—at least as ready as I'll ever be.

"My mother," I say. I tell him everything, the whole dark and twisted story. I even tell him how I felt, about Roc's reaction, about my father's smug smile. By the end my vision is blurry and my cheeks wet, and for a moment I'm embarrassed, using the back of my hand to wipe away the tears, turning my face away from Ben. Adele's father. My judge. My jury.

"I don't think she knew either. Your mother," Ben says.

"How can you say that? You don't even know her." The words come out angrier than I planned and I feel like I'm defending my mom, even though what he said was what I wanted to hear.

"Call it a hunch," Ben says, ignoring my tone. "I'm sorry you had to find out this way."

He's such a genuine guy that I can't hold onto my anger. "It's okay. I suppose it's better to know the truth, even when it's hard."

"Those are mature words."

My embarrassment waning, I turn back to face him. His green eyes are shining with the moisture in them. While I was protecting some silly requirement for manly pride, he was crying, too, maybe not as much as me, but still. It makes me feel better. He's the leader of the Resistance, strong, a fighter, a hero to his daughter. And becoming a hero to me. A true man. So if I'm crying and he's crying, then maybe I'm just a little bit like him. For the first time since the meeting with my father, I have hope again. That there's good in the world. That evil can be vanquished. And that I can help to do it.

"Let's go find Roc," he says.

Fifteen

Adele

Without time to consider my options, I close the distance to the rope ladder in three long strides and leap onto it just before someone starts pulling it up. My knuckles scrape against the stone block wall as the rope starts to swing, but I force my fingers to hold on. I hear Tawni shout below me but I don't look down as I feel the earth moving away from my feet.

Instead, I peer up and see a set of eyes attached to a small body looking down at me. A boy, older than the crying kid, but no more than Elsey's age. He's hanging onto the rope ladder casually, using just his knees, as if he does it all the time. And in his hands: a slingshot, which he's already pulling back.

I duck sharply, afraid to let go of the rope, but making sure my eyes are protected.

Twang! The slingshot sings and I feel a sharp pain in my shoulder as the stone deflects hard off my collar bone. "Arrr," I growl, desperately fighting off the urge to massage the wound with one of my hands. It hurts like hell, a stinging pain that shoots through my nerves like a fire cracker.

I grind my teeth so hard that my jaw starts to hurt. But it takes my mind off my shoulder and I start to climb, keeping my head down and starting with one hand up, then one foot; the other hand—the other foot. All the while the rope is careening side to side and being pulled upward by an unseen force. I repeat my climbing cycle twice more and then risk another glance up.

Another kid, a girl this time, is staring back at me, as if she was waiting for me to look up. Her hands hold a tube to her lips like a straw. Not a straw—a pea shooter, like we used to play with when we were kids. I hear a sharp exhalation of breath and feel a pin-like prick on my cheek.

This time I can't help but to raise a hand to my injury, and I feel the warmth of fresh blood streaming down my face. *That filthy, little…* I think, once more lowering my head to climb, moving faster, less worried about falling, more focused on getting my hands on the brats who are attacking me. A few more stings pepper my body in various places—my ear, my neck, the crown of my head—but I ignore the pain, determined to—

Thud!

Something heavy crashes into my skull and sparkling fairy stars dance before my eyes. My head suddenly feels heavy and my hands too tired to grip the rope. In the back of my mind I know I'm pretty high up and that a fall could kill me, but the thought of going to sleep just sounds so good.

Luckily, when my fingers relax on the rope, I fall a little forward and my hands slips through the ladder, pushing the rung sharply under my arms, burning my skin. The sensation of falling loops wildly through my stomach, sending warning signals to my brain. It snaps me out of my stupor and I manage to grasp the rope once more.

I look up just as the foot comes down on my head, trying for the knockout blow. Turning my head sharply to the side, I avoid the worst of it as the dirty, shoeless foot glances off my shoulder. Able to think once more, I grab the foot and pull down hard.

"Ahhh!" a high voice yells as a small form tumbles into my arm. It's the girl with the pea shooter. The kicker. I desperately cling to the ladder with my other arm, while trying to hold onto the girl, who is kicking and thrashing wildly, trying to unhinge herself from me, completely unconcerned with the potential three-story drop below us.

"Stop squirming," I snap. She doesn't listen—just wriggles even harder.

I hear a shout from above and look up to see the boy with the slingshot, once more taking aim. He's now dangling outside the top-floor window, where I'm headed, as the ladder continues to ascend.

"Don't shoot or I'll drop her!" I shout, muscling the girl away from the rope so she's hanging precariously over empty space. Finally she stops fighting me as she realizes the danger she's in.

The boy's eyes widen and I see doubt register in his eyes as he lowers the slingshot slightly. If he shoots me and I fall, she's going with me. Although clearly he's not afraid of violence, perhaps he draws the line at bearing responsibility for the death of a friend.

"What youse want?" he says.

The ladder rises another couple of feet. I can almost touch him.

"Just to talk," I say. *And wring your little neck.*

He pulls back and helps to pull the ladder over the windowsill. With a final grunt, I pull myself and the girl into the window, crashing awkwardly to a crinkly floor below. I feel my tiny hostage scramble away from me, scraping against the papery floor with her fingernails.

For a moment I can't see through the gloom, but then a bright light is flashed in my eyes and I raise a hand to shield them.

"Don't move," the boy says, wielding a slingshot next to the light. His confidence is back.

"Yeah, don't move," the girl repeats, holding the light.

"I'm not moving," I say, considering my options. I don't particularly believe in hitting children, but for these two I might make an exception. They put the *rats* in *brats*.

"Youse said youse wanna talk. What about?" the boy asks.

"About you and your friends giving me my stuff back, for starters."

"Forget it," the boy says. "Finders keepers."

"I'm pretty sure that's not a real rule," I say.

195

"Yeah, it is," the boy says. "And anyway, it ain't ours to give back. Not anymore."

What is *that* supposed to mean? "Well, then, whose exactly is it?"

"Mep's. The Gimp. Only don't call 'im the Gimp—he don't like that."

I feel blood trickle off my scraped knuckles, and my shoulders, neck, and head are throbbing in at least six places. *Damn kids.*

"Where can I find this Mep?"

"You cain't. He finds youse."

Screw talking—it's not getting me anywhere. I fake right, move left, and feel the air from the rock as it rips past my head, missing me by mere centimeters. I crash into the boy, rip the weapon from his hands, and swing around him to grab him around the neck from behind.

The girl plays the flashlight on our faces and I can tell she's scared. I feel bad for a second, but then I remember how she bashed me in the head with her heel. "Let him go!" she cries.

"Only if you take me to Mep."

She nods furiously. "Follow me. He's just down the hall."

"He's here?" I say incredulously. After all the talk about how *He finds youse*, I thought for sure we'd have to go to some secret hideout in the city.

The girl doesn't answer; instead, she moves away from me through the room, her feet crinkling on the floor, which I now see is covered in old newspapers. In some spots the newspapers are rolled up, and next to them are large squares of paper, knit together to form sheets. I realize: *the kids are sleeping here.*

I feel sick as I begin to put it all together. These kids are orphans, living without adult supervision, stealing to stay alive, sleeping on newspaper and reporting to some gimp named Mep.

I hesitate for a second. Tawni's still down there by herself and she's not exactly a fighter. And the Star Realm's not exactly a safe place, as we're quickly discovering. With the kid still in a headlock, I peek out the window. Tawni's looking up at me, her face masked with concern. "You all right?" I shout.

She nods. "Should I get help?" she yells back.

"No!" The last thing I want is Tawni traipsing through the narrow subchapter streets by herself. "Stay there. I'll be back in a minute."

We tramp across the sleeping quarters and out of the room, passing through a short hallway with moldy, pockmarked walls and a crumbling floor. At one point the boy tries to stamp on my foot, but I just tighten my hold on his throat and his body goes slack, forcing me to drag him with me.

The girl pauses at a closed door on her right, takes a deep breath, and then knocks. There's a muffled sound and the door opens slowly.

She whispers something I can't hear to someone I can't see.

"Enough with the mysterious bull crap," I say, pushing past the little girl and into the room. The room is well-lit, with lanterns in each corner and at least a dozen candles. It reminds me of a séance, like the ones Madame Sonia used to hold that my mom wouldn't let me go to. Three kids, wearing tattered white tunics that are so dirty they appear gray, bar my path with serious arms folded across puffed-out chests. "Move it if you don't want to get hurt."

The kids look at each other, like they're unsure who to be more scared of—me, or this Mep character.

"Let her enter," a remarkably high and whiny voice says from behind them. They shrug and part in the middle, allowing me to pass through them. I dump my "hostage" on the floor and move forward. The kid immediately races out the door. *Little wimp*, I think, *not so confident without your slingshot*. I'm still clenching his rock-slinger in my hand.

Mep's sitting on a big cushion in the center of the room, surrounded by a half-dozen other kids, who almost look like his worshippers, such is the meekness of their postures. He would have been sitting cross-legged; that is, if he had any legs. Instead, he is just sort of resting on his torso, the stumps of his legs no more than half a foot long. I keep a straight face, but inside I'm horrified. This poor orphaned boy is stuck in the crummy Star Realm with no legs. It almost makes my time in the Pen look like a vacation.

As I look at him closer, I see that despite his tiny stature—due to his missing limbs—the boy is older than the rest of the kids—perhaps fifteen. He gazes at me with curious brown eyes that dance with questions.

"Why have you come to see Mep?" he asks.

"Why you are speaking in third person?" I retort.

A hint of a smile crosses his face. "I'm sorry, I'm used to speaking to children," he says. "Why have you come to see *me*?"

"Your thugs stole our packs," I say, "and when I chased them they shot rocks at me." I don't mention the heel-in-the-head incident. I'll save it for later if I need it.

"You shouldn't have chased them," he says, like it's the most obvious thing in the world.

"They stole my stuff."

"Finders, keepers."

"Yeah, rock-slinger boy already tried that on me, but unless you can tell me the Tri-Realms law that states that, I want my packs back." I can't believe I'm actually relying on Tri-Realms law in my defense, which is the biggest bunch of BS there is, but I can't think of anything better to say, except maybe *Give them back now or I'll sock you in the nose.*

"Mep's Law," he says.

I'm getting bored of this conversation, which is beginning to transition from somewhat silly to laughably loony. "Listen, you little punk," I say, stepping forward. Immediately, about twelve feet are planted in a circle around Mep. Some of the kids have pea shooters, some slingshots, and all wear fearsome glares. Well, maybe more comical than fearsome, but still, under the flickering glow of the candles, it's somewhat intimidating, especially because I'm hopelessly outnumbered.

So what do I do?

No surprise there—I fight.

Three kids are down before they even know what hit them, my foot arcing through the orange light. I take a little strength off the kick, as I want to intimidate the buggers, not kill them. The other kids drop their weapons and run for the door. I let them go. Like I said, my tactics are for intimidation purposes only.

I fake a punch at Mep's face and he flinches, throwing his hands across his face in defense, as if that could really stop my fist. I know I'm just being cruel now, but I don't care. I've had enough.

"Give me the packs," I growl.

"I think we might have gotten off on the wrong foot," Mep squeals.

"Give me the *freaking* packs. NOW."

"Okay, okay, they're right here," Mep says, reaching behind his back and retrieving our two packs. He hands them to me and retracts his hand quickly, as if he's afraid I'll claw him or something. I check each bag to make sure nothing's missing. Stale wafers. A handful of leftover Nailins. Some clothes—our only spare clothes. No canteens, but that's because we chucked them away when they were contaminated. All there.

"Thanks," I grumble sarcastically, making for the door.

"Wait a minute, please." I stop, but don't turn around. "Why don't you stay a minute and have something to eat or drink."

"I'll pass," I say.

"I want to make you an offer," he says, his voice going up in excitement.

"You can't possibly have anything I want," I say, although I am curious as to what the little guy has to say.

"Just five minutes," he says. "Take a seat." He motions to another cushion, and grudgingly, I place it in front of him and sit down. "Thank you, I appreciate it," he says.

I just stare at him. This day is getting weirder and weirder.

"Some protectors they are," he says, motioning to the door. I sense movement to my left and I jerk my head to the side, seeing the three kids I kicked to the ground sneaking for the door. When my gaze catches theirs, they break for it. I laugh as I watch them go.

"They did all right," I say, massaging my sore shoulder.

"They're good kids," he says, at which I cringe, again remembering the kick in the head. Noticing my reaction, he says, "They *are*. You don't know what kind of lives they've had—where they come from."

"That's just an excuse," I say.

"I like you," Mep says. I raise my eyebrows in surprise. It's not what I expected him to say to the girl who penetrated his defenses, accused him of stealing, and beat up his gang of minions. "I do," he says, flashing me a smile. He's boyishly cute, with dimples in each cheek when he grins, piercing, turquoise eyes, and messed up brown hair.

"Why?"

"Because you're tough—like me. You don't survive in this world without being tough."

"I'm not from this world," I say. "I'm a moon dweller."

"I guessed that much," he says with a wink. "But I wasn't talking about you. I was talking about me." I stare at him for a second, letting his words sink in.

Oh. The Star Realm. I wonder what tragedies have occurred in this boy's life that he would end up legless, an orphan, master to a bunch of kids who steal for survival. I want to ask him, but know I cannot.

"You don't want to hear my story," he says, as if sensing the question on my lips. "It's not a happy one." Unlike the other children, who sound rough, with harsh language from harsh upbringings, Mep is well spoken, seems mature even.

"You speak well," I say, hoping he doesn't take it the wrong way.

He seems to like that, his eyes opening wide. "My mother always…" He trails off, his eyes going misty.

"Your mother always what?" I prod.

He looks away and then right back at me. "She always read to me when I was little. Taught me how to read, to write. Made me smart. She's still taking care of me, even now."

I'm not sure I understand. I assumed he was an orphan, but maybe I was wrong. "What do you mean?"

Waving a hand, he says, "Oh, not like you think. She's not around anymore. But the kids around here feed me, cloth me, practically worship me—all because I can read them stories." He motions to the corner and my eyes drift to the spot. There's a stack of old books that I hadn't noticed earlier, with worn covers and broken spines.

It all suddenly makes sense. Mep gives the children in this place a chance to escape from the horrors of the real world, to places where there are happy endings, where heroes really do exist, where parents are alive and take care of their kids. My vision blurs and I blink furiously before I return my gaze to Mep.

I change the subject. "How'd you know I was a moon dweller?" I ask, choosing a safer question.

He laughs. "It was obvious the moment you chased after my gang of misfits," he says. When I raise an eyebrow, he explains. "The people here are broken, their bodies, their spirits. They don't even think we're worth the energy. One of my kids grabs a loaf of bread off a passing cart and they barely react. You, on the other hand, it was like I'd stolen your baby."

Now it's my turn to laugh. Remembering the items in my pack, I realize I probably did look a little crazy chasing after a bunch of kids for our meager possessions, particularly when the star dweller army evidently has significant resources at their disposal.

Mep's face is still lit up, as if it makes him happy to have put a smile on my face. "I've got to get back," I remember, letting my thoughts flow freely. "My friend…"

"You haven't even heard my proposal."

Oh, yes, this great offer he has for me. "Make it quick."

"Be my bodyguard," he says, his eyes twinkling under the candlelight.

I sigh, pretend to consider. "And what'll I get in return?"

"Food, shelter, information."

"What kind of information?" The food and the shelter are covered by the army, but information is something I haven't been getting a lot of lately.

He grins, like he knows he's got me now. "I know most everything that happens in this town. Anything in particular you're after?"

"How's the army getting so many supplies?" I blurt out.

"Nothing's free," he says.

"I'm not going to work for you," I say.

"I didn't think so, but a couple of Nailins might do the trick." He's rubbing his hands together, like he can't wait to feel the smooth weight of the gold against his skin.

I reach in one of the packs and flip him two Nailins. I see the face of the president flashing in and out of view. Tristan's father. *But not like Tristan*, I remind myself.

Mep snaps them out of the air with unexpectedly competent hand/eye coordination. He bites down on the gold coins like he doesn't believe they're real. "I haven't seen one of these in a long time," he muses, his eyes greedy.

"The information," I say.

"Right. I'm not sure if this helps, but there's a supply truck that comes in every week, on Mondays. They back it up right against the loading dock so no one can see what it's carrying. If you find out where the truck comes from, you might be able to solve your mystery."

"Thanks," I say, moving for the door. "And Mep…"

"Yeah."

"Hang in there. Change might be coming faster than you think." Before leaving, I grab the bag containing the last of our wafers and toss it to Mep. These kids need it more than I do.

Mep grins as he catches it, like he knew I'd see things his way in the end. "Farewell, my fair maiden," he calls to me as I exit.

I'm no fair maiden. And this is not one of the hero- and adventure-filled worlds from the pages of the books that Mep reads to the kids. No, it's nothing like that at all.

As I navigate my way to find the stairs, kids duck into doorways, hide in the shadows, watch me the whole way. My heart is sick. It shouldn't be this way. Kids running wild, forced into a life of crime. We have to do something for them. And it all starts now.

The only problem: when I exit the crumbling building, Tawni is gone.

Sixteen

Tristan

Ram finds Roc before we do so I'm glad to see he hasn't been pulverized. Maybe Ram's decided to take it easy on us because it's obvious something really bad has happened.

Or maybe not. "If you get lost again, sun boy, I'll destroy you," he says to Roc before handing him over to us.

Roc just stares at him, and I can tell he's thinking getting destroyed by Ram might be a good thing. It might take his mind off of what he's just found out.

"What the hell do you think you're looking at?" Ram says, and I think for a second Roc might lash out at him, but to my relief he breaks the stare, and moves past me with his head down.

As I move to follow him, I hear Ben ask, "Where'd you find him?"

Ram laughs condescendingly. "He was near the edge of the eastern border. If he'd managed to get out into the broader Moon Realm, he'd have been a sitting duck for some star dweller soldier with a chip on his shoulder."

I'm too far away to hear Ben's response, as I jog to catch up with Roc. "Roc," I say, "wait up!"

He ignores me and keeps walking. "Roc!" I try again.

"Leave me alone," he says, bringing me up short. I watch as he disappears around a bend in the tunnel. I want to chase him, to force him to talk about things—I desperately need to talk to him about all this—but I let him go. He's never asked me to leave him alone before, and it scares me. But I have to respect his wishes—have to give him time to come to terms with what my father told us.

Ben catches up with me and I'm glad to see Ram's not with him. "Why's that guy hate us so much?" I ask.

Ben shrugs. "He doesn't trust people easily, especially sun dwellers. But believe me, he's a guy you want on your side." I believe him. Ram's the last guy I'd want to face in combat.

Nodding, I say, "Roc won't talk to me."

"Give him time."

"How much time?"

"A few hours."

"He's already had a few hours."

"A few more."

"Okay." I don't want to wait a few hours, but I'm glad he didn't say a few days. I don't think I could go that long without

206

talking to my best friend, my half-brother. Especially with all this crap on my mind. "What do we do next?"

"Vice President Morgan has arranged a meeting with the other Vice Presidents who she believes will support us in a motion to join the star dweller rebellion. I need you there to help us convince them."

"What if I can't?"

"Then we're screwed," Ben says honestly, and I raise my eyebrows.

"Great."

We both continue in silence, the only sound coming from our boots as they scuff and scrape along the rough tunnel floor, broken up only by the tap of Ben's walking stick. He says his wounded leg is okay, but he's limping heavily and seems to be relying on the staff. We come to a crossroads, and where we'd normally veer right past our sleeping quarters or toward the common area, we slip left down a broad corridor.

"Shortcut," Ben says when I glance at him.

The gray rock walls continue to widen as the pathway heads uphill. Moisture trickles down the walls from the ceiling. As we move further along, the tunnel levels out, and the walls are fully slick from the rivers of water sheeting down them, pooling along the sides. Thirty feet later the puddles cross the breadth of the tunnel floor and meet in the middle. Our boots slap and slosh through them but still we don't turn back.

When the water level nears the tops of my boots, I fear I may be getting wet feet very soon. "Uh, Ben? Are you sure this is the right way?"

He laughs, in a way that my father never could. "You scared of something?"

I turn away sheepishly and keep plodding through the water. I can handle wet feet if I have to. Just when I think my feet are doomed, the tunnel curves sharply to the left, spilling out into an underground pond. The water at our feet is pouring down a natural step, emptying into the tiny lake. The water is crystal clear, and I can easily see to the bottom, which glitters like diamonds. Beyond the lake is a beautiful fall of water, coming down in a mist of tiny droplets, creating a cloud of moisture. Every now and then I see the sparkle of something shiny drop from above, as the glow from the lamps along the sides reflects off of *something*.

"Wow," I murmur. "Are those—"

"Yes," Ben says. "This is the Diamond Lake. The water falls from hundreds of feet above, just a small waterfall. By the time the droplets get down here they've split apart multiple times creating the spray you see in front of you. Every once in a while a diamond comes down with it. We have no idea how far the gemstones travel before reaching us, but it could be miles, or even hundreds of miles."

"What do you do with them?" Immediately my mind grabs hold of everything I know about the gemstone trade. This many diamonds would surely be suspicious if they started popping up on the commerce reports hitting my father's desk.

"We haul them out, hide most of them away, and use a small number to fund our operations. We've been dormant for so long that we don't need much to get by."

It makes sense and explains a lot. How they're able to keep the electricity on. How they can feed the Resistance members. Some of the technology, like teleboxes and videoconferencing. Not typical luxuries for the Moon Realm. All paid for by untaxed diamonds. "Awesome," I say. Anything that helps the

Resistance and withholds a few Nailins in tax money from my father is cool by me.

"Yeah, we were lucky to stumble upon it when we were constructing our command center."

Ben skirts around one of the edges and I follow him. The edges are dry and so are my feet. As we move around the mist, I feel a cooling sensation when the edge of the falls glosses over my face, my arms. It feels wonderful and I wonder if it's what rain feels like.

Behind the mist the tunnel continues on, leading us away from the Diamond Lake, and presumably toward the Vice Presidents. Well, not all of the Vice Presidents, just the nice ones—or at least I hope.

We reach a staircase, which cuts back on itself every dozen steps or so. It's man-made and in good condition, evidently having not been used as much as some of the other steps around the place, which are crumbling and in need of repair. By the time we reach the top, my thighs and calves are burning; I haven't done a good stair workout lately.

There's a heavy metal door blocking our path, and Ben has to use a key to open it. It's the first door I've seen that requires a key—it must be guarding something important.

Before Ben pulls the door open, he looks at me. His eyes are black in the dim lighting and seem to have a deepness to them, as if they are fathomless, filled with wisdom and experience. Despite the fact that he's staring at me, I don't feel uncomfortable. "Tristan, this is your time to shine. I believe in you, and I know Adele does too."

At that, I smirk. "She barely knows me."

"And yet she seems to trust you. She has always had good judgment. Speak from your heart, and everything else will work itself out."

"I'll do my best."

"I know you will."

With that, he pulls open the heavy door, which groans in protest. Inside, there's a flurry of activity, in utter contrast to the nervous silence when I met with the Resistance leaders. Men and women move around a massive stone table, chatting and drinking cups of coffee and tea. I recognize all the faces, but I can't necessarily put names to them from the one or two times I'd met each of them in a year. The Vice Presidents. *The nice ones*, I remind myself. Maia and Jonas are there, too. Oh, and Ram, which makes me think that Ben's so-called shortcut wasn't so short after all.

The only one missing: Roc. Although I didn't expect him to be here, my heart turns over when I realize it.

With a wave of his arm, Ben invites me in first. I hesitate only for a moment, and then step inside, look around, trying to take it all in. One by one, the Vice Presidents notice me and a hushed silence falls over the room. Although I'm used to being in the spotlight a lot, it's never been in this context. I'm no longer a diplomat from the ruling body. No longer a contract negotiator. I have zero power. I'm an unproven potential enemy combatant, and I know it, which makes my face warm with embarrassment under the scrutiny of their stares.

Then the whispers start, some behind hands, but others from visible lips, which I unsuccessfully try to read.

Ben steps past me and I follow him numbly to a seat near the head of the table. The rest of the attendees silently take their seats. I preferred the buzz of conversation from before to

210

this awkward quiet. Vice President Morgan gives me a comforting smile as she sits down at the head of the table, which helps calm my rare nerves.

Evidently she's in charge of this meeting, because she says, "Thank you all for attending on such short notice. Many of you have traveled far and wide to be here, and I appreciate it."

"Not all of us!" a man halfway down the line growls jovially, breaking the weird feeling in the room like glass. He wears a thick, gray beard, a bowler's hat, and a smile. He's one of the few Vice President's names I actually remember, because he was always funny and made me laugh when I'd visit. Byron Gray.

"Thank you, Mr. Gray. It's always been a pleasure having you just next door, in subchapter 2." Morgan keeps talking, exchanging niceties with the other VPs, but I don't hear her words, as I'm thinking furiously about something. We're in the command center for the Resistance and all these VPs are here with us. Which means they support the Resistance, or have in the past. Which means they really are the good guys and perhaps I don't need to be so intimidated speaking to them. They'll want to hear what I have to say.

I do some quick math. There are forty-two subchapters in the Moon Realm, and therefore, forty-two Vice Presidents. I quickly tick off the people around the table, not counting the non-VPs like Maia and Jonas. Thirteen. Not a lucky number, but a good number. Thirteen out of forty-two isn't bad for a start. If these are the ones who already support the Resistance, and will agree to unite with the star dwellers, the rebellion may have some legs under it. And that's not including any other subchapters who might be convinced. For just a minute, my heart soars, before being crushed by a slew of harsh words around the table.

"This *boy* has screwed over subchapter 39 more times than I care to remember, and you expect me to trust him?" a woman with a flash of red hair in a bun exclaims incredulously.

"The star dwellers are throwing grenades in the street, and you want me to join with them, *and* with the son of the Sun Realm President? Have you lost your mind?" shouts a short bald man whom I can barely remember from my travels.

A huge man with no neck, who looks more like a miner than a vice president, stands up and slams both fists down on the table, causing me to jerk my head back. "Blasphemy. I won't listen to a word that *Nailin* says." Right on the word *Nailin*, he slams both fists on the table again.

My eyes are wide and I realize I'm holding my breath. I let it out in a slow stream. Looking around the table I see mostly angry faces. The huge dude's face is all red and I'm glad he's all the way at the other end of the table, or I feel he might lunge across to hit me, or head butt me. Byron Gray is the only one who doesn't look angry, but he's not smiling anymore under his beard. As usual, Ram's in the corner, and he *is* smiling, but not because he likes me, but because he likes watching me get ripped to shreds, whether by words or by fists. In this case, I think I'd rather it be fists.

Because I was thinking at the time—about how we might actually have a chance—I didn't hear how the chaos all started, but I know I'm losing support fast, and even Morgan and Ben might abandon me soon.

Speak from your heart. In my heart, there is only darkness.

I'll try Ben, I'll try.

I stand up. Look around the room. "I just spoke with my father," I say, and I hear gasps around the table.

"I knew it," the red-haired lady mumbles.

"Not like that," I say, my voice hard. Her eyes widen in surprise at the harshness of my tone. I hate that I'm relying on anger to get me through another hard time, but it seems the only way I can handle things lately.

"He told me he raped and murdered my best friend's mother, that my best friend is actually my half-brother. His name is Roc, and he's not here because he's all alone, grieving. He won't speak to me. I hate myself for not knowing. I hate my father for who he is, and what he's done, not only to my friend and to me"—I glance at Ben and he nods, as if he knows exactly what I'm going to say—"but to the Moon Realm and the Star Realm. He's raped and murdered you, too. Not actively, but passively, through his taxes and his laws, all under the guise of a government that is really a dictatorship. It ends now. Whether you let me help unite the Tri-Realms or not, I will fight to the bitter end. I will kill my father! I will kill him!"

I stop when I realize spit's flying from my mouth and my hands are clenched at my sides so hard that they ache. Morgan's mouth is open slightly, as if in disgust. Ben's face is expressionless, and I know that I've failed him.

I shove my chair under the table and walk out.

* * *

My hands are shaking as I stride down the steps. Shaking with anger, shaking with frustration, shaking with pain at what my father did to Roc's mom. I can't wait any longer—I have to talk to Roc. Try to make things right, somehow.

213

I'm down the stairs in half the time it took to climb them. The glittering diamonds and misty falls are just a blur as I race past them, my legs churning into the water-filled tunnel. Each step is quicker than the one before it, and by the time I reach the dry part of the tunnel I'm sprinting, as if the entire sun dweller army is chasing me. But they're not chasing me; and if they were, I wouldn't be running. I would be standing, fighting, killing as many of them as I could before they killed me.

I'm stunned at my thoughts, numb with the pain. Who is this murderous shell of a person I've become?

Because I'm running, the Resistance center of operations is far smaller than I initially thought. I reach our sleeping quarters in just a couple of minutes. Sweat is dripping from my nose, my chin. My breaths are heavy and ragged. My fists are still clenched and shaking.

I open the door.

All fight goes out of me when I see Roc. He's on his bed, just sitting there staring at his hands. His dark hair is like midnight in the gloom. As he looks up at me, his cheeks are tearstained, but not with dried salt rivers like before, but wet with new flows.

I approach him, massaging my sore hands.

He closes his eyes, angles his head down once more. Defeated. He looks defeated.

Sitting next to him, I say, "Roc, please. Talk to me."

His eyes blaze open and he turns toward me. I was wrong. There's no defeat in his eyes. I only see...anger. Fierce anger and pride with a hint of sadness borne by his tears. "Your father is sick," he snarls between clenched teeth.

"I know," I say.

"No, you don't know! You pretend to, but you can't. Can't actually know how sick he is. You've been sheltered your entire life, protected, behind walls of marble and gourmet food and piles of Nailins! Nailins!" he scoffs. "Named after your family. Your sick, sick family."

"Roc, you don't mean that," I say, the sting of his words visible all over my face.

"I do mean it. Your father stole my childhood, stole my happiness, and now he's stolen my father from me? The man who raised me. And my mother? My poor, sweet mother who I thought I killed when I came into this world. I've harbored the guilt of her death my entire life and now I find out that my pain shouldn't have been directed inward, but at the very man who hates me because I'm the one who serves him. And you tell me I don't mean it?"

I feel like I've been slapped. Not because of what he's saying about my father, but because he's lumping me in with him, like I'm guilty by association. "I never had a choice, Roc. I never wanted to be a Nailin, never wanted a life of privilege. I left, remember? I left it all behind, and you helped me to do it. We're supposed to be friends—no matter what. Isn't that the way friendship is?"

And then Roc's breaking down, his angry shoulders slumping, his head dropping into his hands, the jerk of desperate sobs wracking his body. My arm is around him in a second and he lets me pull his head into my chest. We're two guys, two friends, but it doesn't feel weird or awkward. I've loved him like a brother, and now he really is one—and I'm there for him. Will always be there for him. I can't change the past, but I can be a part of his present, his future.

"My poor, sweet mother," Roc sobs.

215

"I know, Roc. I know," I say soothingly. I realize the anger is gone from me. I'm just Tristan again. Not the raging shell of a person I've been lately. Roc's sorrow has brought me back, which makes me feel ashamed. "Roc, I hate my father for what he's done—believe me, I want to kill him—but I can't hate the fact that you're my half-brother. You mean too much to me for that. I'm so sorry," I say.

Roc's head bobs back up, and through blurry eyes he says, "I know, Tristan. And I know you're not like him, not like them." I know he means my younger brother, who is becoming a clone of my father. "Your mom was the best mom I could have ever asked for," he sniffs. "And you were—are—the best friend I could ever want."

"Thanks, Roc," I say, and we hug, tenderly and firmly all at the same time, which should be embarrassing, but it's not and never could be.

When Roc pulls away there's a question in his eyes. "Do you really want to kill your—our—father?"

"Yes," I say without hesitation. "Roc, I think I've really screwed things up."

He wipes the tears from his cheeks and waits for me to continue.

I tell him about the meeting with the "supportive" VPs. "I can't control this anger inside me, man. It's like the rage takes over my brain and controls what I do, what I say. I feel like if I don't get control of it soon, it'll destroy me, and destroy everything the Resistance is planning. It's just…I have the urge to kill. To kill my father. To kill the sun dweller soldiers. To kill anyone who supports them. I'm afraid I'm becoming my father. Does that make sense?"

216

"No," Roc says, shaking his head. "You are nothing like your father. He's angry, but it's cold, calculating evil. Your anger is righteous, Tristan."

I believe him. Because he's my brother.

Seventeen

Adele

I whirl around twice, hoping that maybe I'm just not seeing Tawni in the shadows. The lighting's pretty crappy so it's possible. But she's not in the shadows, not in the alley, not anywhere. Would she have left when I told her not to? I took quite a bit longer than the minute I promised her, so she might've gone to get help. Or she's in trouble.

I pause for a second, trying to decide what to do.

The only place she would've gone is back to the army offices, so I head in that direction, retracing our turns through the cramped subchapter streets. I'm maybe halfway there when

I see a flash of shiny, white hair that is completely out of place in the dismal city. When I see Tawni striding toward me purposefully, her head down, I let out a deep breath. Trevor's just behind her.

I holler and her head snaps up, her expression changing rapidly from surprise to delight. As she jogs toward me, I hold up the packs like trophies, handing one to her as she nears.

Her smile twists into a frown when she meets me, her eyes darting all over my face. "Oh my gosh, Adele, what happened to you?"

"Those damn kids happened," I say. "But it's okay, it's nothing." To be honest, I'd forgotten about my minor injuries, but now that Tawni's reminded me, I feel their sting again like I'm being hit by the rocks (and the foot!) all over again. Trevor approaches, but I ignore him and relay the story to my friend, telling her everything except the part about the supply trucks— I can tell her that later in private.

"I was worried when you didn't come out, so I went to get help," Tawni says, continuing to inspect my injuries.

"Tsk, tsk," Trevor clucks. "I can't leave you two alone for five minutes without you getting into trouble."

I glare at him. "It's none of your business."

"It is when I'm going to look very bad in front of your mo—I mean, the General, because I'm failing in the one task she assigned to me."

"Like I said before, I just need to talk to her, and then don't worry, you'll be reassigned and we won't be your problem anymore."

He shakes his head. "You can be impossible sometimes, you know that?"

"C'mon, Tawni," I say, pulling her by the elbow the way she normally does to me. I hear Trevor's footsteps follow behind us, but I don't look back. Who does he think he is anyway? Yeah, we might've gotten into trouble, ended up on a street where we didn't belong, had our stuff stolen…but I took care of it. My dad sent me down here because he trusted me to take care of things. Not to be watched over by some babysitter who's "just following orders."

"Are you really okay?" Tawni whispers to me.

"Yes, now stop worrying. It's those poor kids we should be worried about. They have nothing, Tawni. They might be little brats, but it's not like they have any other choice. They're just trying to survive." Funny how your perspective can change so quickly. Get a little new information and everything you think can get turned on its head. The *brats* have become the *poor kids*.

"What are you going to do?"

"There's nothing we can do. If we stop to try and help every street rat that comes along, we'll never accomplish anything. The only way to make things better is to fix the bigger problem."

"The sun dwellers."

"Yeah."

I sense that Trevor's closer behind us. I whirl around. "Do you mind?" He's practically right on top of us.

"Just trying to join in the conversation." He looks kind of sheepish, a far cry from his normal arrogance. I'm glad.

"Private conversation," I say, grabbing Tawni's arm again and pulling her away from him, walking faster.

We make it back to the army offices without further incident. "The General should be just getting out of a meeting," Trevor says, as if he's trying to be helpful. For a second I wonder why he's telling us that, but then I remember that it's *my mom* he's talking about. The General. It's going to take me a while to get used to that.

I nod and enter the building, zeroing in on her door, which stands wide open. "We'll wait in here."

Tawni follows me into the room, and when Trevor tries to follow, I say, "You're dismissed."

He frowns and pauses for a moment, as if considering whether he'd rather deal with my wrath or my mom's when she finds out we've been hanging out in her office unsupervised, and then shrugs and closes the door behind him, leaving us alone.

I flop into a chair, sigh, and close my eyes. Immediately I start thinking about the supply trucks. If I could just get on one of them after they've been unloaded, ride it back to its origin...

"Adele," Tawni says, her voice motherly with concern.

I ignore her, trying to formulate a plan to deal with the supply trucks.

"Adele," she says again, more insistently this time.

"Tawni, really, I'm fine," I say, opening my eyes to look at her.

"No, it's not that," she says. Her thin, white eyebrows are furrowed, as if she's trying to solve a complex problem. Something's happened that I don't know about.

"What?" I say. She pauses for a moment, as if trying to work out the right words. "Tawni, what is it?"

She looks at me, holds my stare. "When I went back to find someone to help me I overheard something," she says slowly, looking away at the end. When she pauses, I wait patiently for her to continue. "I went straight to your mom's office and the door was ajar. I was about to knock—I swear I wasn't eavesdropping on your mother—but then I heard Trevor's voice and I perked up. He was telling her about how you were asking him questions about the weapons, how he didn't know what to tell us."

What? My mind is racing as I try to fit the pieces together. "What did she say?"

"She said to leave it to her—that she would handle it."

"What the hell is that supposed to mean?"

"I don't know, but it all sounded a bit…suspicious. That's why I'm telling you." If Tawni, one of the least skeptical people I know, thought something sounded off, then it was probably off.

"You think my mom is hiding something?"

"I don't know, maybe."

I frown. Perhaps she just hadn't gotten around to telling us yet. I mean, we've only been with her for a short amount of time, have practically just arrived in the Star Realm. Or perhaps there's something to it. Especially considering I've recently learned that my mom has kept secrets from me my entire life.

My thoughts are cut off when the door opens, and the subject of my thoughts walks in. "Adele, Tawni, I heard what happened," she says, slipping past us and sliding next to me on the padded bench.

"We're fine," I say, crushed gravel in my voice.

"It doesn't sound fine," she says, reading me like a book as usual. "Plus, your face is a mess," she says, reaching up to touch one of the welts.

Inadvertently, I shrink away from her touch, like it might burn me. It feels so weird, being scared of my mom for the first time in my life. "Adele," she says, concern etching her face, "what is it?"

I consider telling her what's on my mind, even glance at Tawni for support, but then just shrug my shoulders. "It's nothing," I lie. And then, "I don't want Trevor following us around anymore."

My mom sighs. "He told me you might say that. Adele, I'm not trying to smother you. It's just, this place isn't like the Moon Realm. It's not as safe. You found that out already."

"They were just kids. And I handled it without *Trevor*," I say, spitting his name out like a swear word. "Besides, the last time we were in the Moon Realm it wasn't exactly a safe zone, what with the bombs destroying every building in sight."

"Good point," she says, nodding her head. "But I'd still feel more comfortable if you keep Trevor close."

"Okay, we'll use an escort. But not Trevor." *Anyone but Trevor.* "I don't trust him."

"Well, I do. And trust me, he's the best person for the job." If only I *could* trust you right now, Mom. "I know this is all a lot to take in," she says. "Why don't you just relax for the rest of the day, and we can talk tomorrow if you're up for it."

I feel like I've been punched in the gut. I've crossed hundreds of miles of danger-filled caves and tunnels, only to find that my mom doesn't need rescuing and doesn't listen to me anymore. "Fine," I say evenly, standing up and walking to the door. Out of the corner of my eye I see Tawni shrug at my mom, as if to say *sorry*. Tawni, always the peacemaker.

To my annoyance, Trevor is waiting for us outside. My fury's not going to go away anytime soon.

"Have I been replaced?" he says snidely, which makes me even more annoyed.

"C'mon," I say, slinging a pack over my shoulder, "where are our bunks?"

He laughs, but I ignore it and let him lead us down a corridor, up a spiraling stone staircase, and into a large room that's buzzing with activity.

"They're done for the day," Trevor explains, motioning to the dozens of soldiers milling about the bunkroom, changing out of their training tunics, whipping each other with towels, and generally carrying on like members of a traveling circus. They're all guys, some young, some old.

"Umm…" I say, "…I call bull crap."

Trevor smirks. "Oh, I must've taken a wrong turn somewhere, these are the guys' bunks. Right this way."

It would have been a reasonably funny joke if it wasn't Trevor. We exit the room and make our way down a long hall that runs along the wall of the male bunks. At the very end is a door on the opposite side. "The women will get you all set up and get you to dinner. I'll see you there."

I ignore him and push into the room, hearing Tawni say, "See you later," behind us. Stopping, I take in the room. It's maybe half the size of the guys' room, but still contains at least fifty bunks, each about three feet apart, built from gray stone, with thin pads and pillows atop them. Fifty or sixty women are milling about in a much more civilized manner than the men, changing their tunics, chatting away. It reminds me of the Pen. Home sweet home.

One of the younger-looking girls notices us and approaches. I remember seeing her at morning training. A decent shooter but not so good at the close combat. Blond hair tied in a ponytail. Close-set, bright blue eyes. A small nose with lips for which smiling was a struggle. She's attempting to smile now. "Welcome, Rose," she says, addressing me by my last name. "I'm Lieutenant Marshall, and I'm in charge of the twenty-third barrack, which is this one. I don't think I've caught your friend's name yet."

"I'm Tawni," Tawni says enthusiastically, pushing her hand out so Marshall can shake it.

"This'll be your bunk," she says, leading us to an empty set of stacked beds with fresh towels and clothes folded neatly at the foot. Fourth one on the right side, I memorize. "Showers are through there," she says, pointing to an opening at the other side of the room, where women are passing through with towels wrapped around their bodies. "Dinner's in an hour," she finishes. "Don't be late or the food'll be gone."

"Thank you," I murmur, sitting on the unforgiving bed. Tawni plops down next to me.

"Maybe it's not what we think?" Tawni says, picking up our conversation from before my mom interrupted us.

"What do we think exactly?" I say.

"That your mom is up to something bad with Trevor."

I smirk. "So you're not so pro-Trevor anymore?"

Tawni laughs and it reaches her eyes. "I guess not. I mean, he's not so bad. But you're right, something seems off about him."

"Like something seems *off* about my mom?"

"I don't know." She's been saying that a lot lately. But it's what I've been thinking, too.

I reach behind me and remove the gun. Tawni's eyes are like saucers as I turn it over in my hands. I doubt if she's ever held one in her life. Not that I'm much better, having just held one for the first time today. I shove it underneath my pillow and out of sight.

Suddenly I feel dirty, not from my injuries, or from the sweat-inducing physical activity of the day, but just from being

225

in this place—the Star Realm. I know it sounds bad, but it's how I feel. "I want to take a shower," I say, "but not with all the others in there. It reminds me too much of the Pen." The idea of showering with a bunch of other girls has never appealed to me.

"I'll go first," she says, wrapping one of the towels around her and slipping off her clothes discreetly, so as to not embarrass me. She's a good friend.

While she's gone I lie on the hard bed, feel the lump of the gun under my head. The gun my mom gave me. My mom *the general*. God, it's bizarre. I don't want to think about my mom the way she is now—this strange person.

So instead I think about the Star Realm. It's so different than I expected it to be. Growing up, I always believed the other Realms were these magical places. I wanted to travel to them, to take in the sights, to meet the people. It's funny how when you haven't been to a place before, sometimes you picture it so much better than it really is.

That reminds me of a book my grandmother used to read to me. It was one of the ones my relatives saved during Year Zero, handing it down from generation to generation. A book about the Beach, a strange open place where people go to lay in the sun and waste the day away. My grandmother read about the ocean, too, sparkling and cool under the heat of the afternoon sun, washing sand and shells up on the shore. Tickling the toes of the people on the sand. In the story, the ocean is endless, going as far as the eye can see—and then farther still, beyond the horizon. I picture it as a beautiful place and I want to see it for myself. I hope it's as beautiful as I pictured—not like the Star Realm.

226

Tawni is back, hair wet and smiling. "The shower's empty now," she says.

"Thanks," I say, my vision of the mythical ocean vanishing like a cloud of rock dust.

"The water's cold, but not icy."

"Awesome. Not icy. What a review."

"Are you okay?" Tawni asks.

I know I've been in a mood lately, which is somewhat strange, considering I've got my family back. Well, sort of. "I'm sorry," I say, my pained expression softening. "I know I've been difficult. It's just that none of this is the way...I pictured it."

"I know what you mean," Tawni says, which makes me feel better.

* * *

Despite the iciness of the water—yes, Tawni's idea of *icy* most certainly differs from my own—I leave feeling refreshed. From now on, I'm going to grab control of my emotions and try to be positive, like Tawni. My resolve holds when we leave the bunks, when we walk down the hall, when we descend the stairs, and even as we approach the mess hall.

But then I see Trevor and it shatters like blown glass.

I'm angry again and I don't know why. I mean, I don't even know what's going on with Trevor, not for sure, but I feel like hitting him, punching him, kicking that arrogant smirk right off his face.

Of course, he's waiting for us in front of the mess hall. And his smirk is because he's still responsible for babysitting us—and he knows I hate it.

Deep breaths, I think. I try to hide my clench fists behind my hips.

"Hi, Trevor," Tawni says remarkably cheerily, despite the fact that even she doesn't trust him anymore.

"Hello, ladies."

Ignoring Trevor, I sniff the air. The warm aroma of hot food and tangy sauces wafts through the entrance. A choir of voices rumbles beyond. My stomach growls, a result of our meager wafer lunch being interrupted by Mep's four-foot-tall goon squad.

"Sounds like something is trying to claw its way out of there," Trevor says, pointing at my stomach.

"It's a moron-eating alien baby," I retort, "and you'll be first on the menu." The meanness is becoming so natural it's scary.

I don't wait for a reaction or a response, striding past him and into the dim glow of the mess hall. This time, the only similarity to the Pen is the long, cafeteria-style tables filled with eaters. Everything else is different. The sounds: the room is abuzz with excited conversations, almost as if there isn't a war happening miles above us. The soldiers almost seem…happy— if that's even possible in this place. The smells: rather than gummy and putrid like in the Pen, the aromas are sweet and hot and flavorful. The décor: dark walls and orange lanterns give the room a mysterious feel, unlike the bright, sterile whites of the juvenile detention center where I was a guest for six months.

There's no one else in line as we're the last to arrive, so I go right up and start filling my plate at the self-service food counter. Real sticky rice. Slabs of beef thick with brown gravy. Creamy mashed potatoes. I think I've died and gone to heaven.

I find a seat at the end of one of the long tables, leaving a few seats between me and the other soldiers. When I take my first bite of the delicious food I almost gag. The taste isn't the problem, or the texture, or smell, or anything to do with the actual food. On the contrary, the food is amazing, everything I expected it to be. But I realize it's just another example of how the Star Realm army is better resourced than they should be. Not just better. *Way* better. Like they should be eating stale bread, but instead they're eating prime rib. Something's not right, and so I can't seem to swallow the food, like my mind won't let me.

I take a swig from my cup of water and force the bite down my throat and into my belly, which feels like it reaches up with starving hands and grabs the chewed-up food, pulling it the rest of the way down.

Tawni and Trevor sit down. "How's the food?" Trevor says. He knows *exactly* how it is.

"Delicious," I say, taking another bite and repeating the water trick to get it down.

Tawni looks at me strangely, like she knows I'm only telling half the truth, but then shrugs and starts eating.

When Trevor focuses on his dinner, I hazard a glance at him. What are you hiding, you little creep? How have you managed to gain my mom's undying trust? I will find out. And when I do...

"Training begins at seven tomorrow," Trevor says into his food.

"When do we leave for the Moon Realm?"

Trevor looks at me with one eye closed, as if he's sizing me up, and then says, "I dunno. No one does. Everything's on hold while the moon and star dwellers send messages back and forth, trying to come to an agreement."

A bad feeling begins to squirm within the pit of my stomach and it's not from the food. How can I trust the star dweller generals to do the right thing, to listen to the moon dwellers, when they were the ones who decided to bomb us to hell and back again? I make a mental note to ask my mom about that, among other things.

Because of the delightful taste, and despite my dark thoughts, I manage to finish the whole plate of food in front of me. Which is good, because I need my strength.

"What next?" I say as we're leaving.

"Whatever you want," Trevor says. "Evenings are your time."

Tawni yawns. "I'm pretty tired. I might just hit the hay."

My body feels tired but my mind is sharp and there's no way I'll be able to sleep. "Can you walk her back, Trevor?" I ask. He raises his eyebrows—an unspoken question. "I won't leave the army grounds," I say, determined not to get angry at having to answer to him.

He bites his lip. The last time he left me I got into all kinds of trouble. Another decision point. To my surprise, he says, "Fine. Don't do anything stupid."

"Yes, sir," I say, mocking him. It's a dumb thing to do, but I can't help myself.

Thankfully, he ignores my impudence and says stiffly, "Goodnight."

"'Night."

Tawni winks at me knowingly before she goes. Her fatigue has granted me a minor reprieve from Trevor's watchful eye.

When they're gone, I take a deep breath. Today has felt like it's lasted a week or more. The shock of finding my mother and discovering she's a general in the star dweller army, the physical training activities, my half-crazed assault on Mep's hideout, my suspicions about Trevor and Mom's involvement in the army's seemingly unlimited resources: all add up to one thing—one hell of a long freaking day. But it's not over yet.

I go to find my mom to confront her.

Eighteen
Tristan

Roc's asleep, which I'm glad about, because it gives him a break from the emotional turmoil of the last few hours. I'm lying on my bed, staring at the picture Roc drew of my mom/his mom. Somehow it gives me hope because I know that their genes are in us, and not just my father's.

The door opens and a crack of light cuts through the dim glow of the lanterns. My heart sinks when I see who it is.

Ben.

Come to tell me I'm a screw-up. Come to tell me to leave.

"How's Roc?" he whispers.

It's not the first thing I expected him to say, but I guess it makes sense because Ben's such a good person. He cares about people. He's everything my father is not.

"We're okay," I say.

At that he raises an eyebrow, but doesn't pursue it further. Instead, he sits down on the foot of my bed. "I'll pack up my things and we'll leave as soon as Roc wakes up," I say, preempting him and trying to make the conversation easier.

Now both his eyebrows are raised. "You're leaving? But why?"

"You don't need to do this, Ben. I know I screwed up. I know I ruined all your plans. Maybe if I just go silently into the night you can show the VPs that you're listening to them."

"You think I'm here to kick you out?" Ben asks, the hint of a smile in his tone.

"Uh, aren't you?"

"Quite the opposite. The VPs have agreed to support us, support you." When my mouth drops open, he adds, "All of them."

For perhaps the first time in my life, I'm completely speechless. It's not that I don't have words fluttering around in my brain, but there are too many of them trying to get out my mouth at the same time, so it's like they get stuck on my lips as I continue to gawk at Adele's father.

Finally, I manage, "That's not possible. But I—"

"You spoke from the heart, Tristan. Just like I told you to. And they got it—every word of it. Nice touch stomping out of the room, I might add."

Bizarre. This whole thing is bizarre. "But I just went crazy angry like a bitter child," I protest.

"Look, I don't know how else to say this, but it worked. Whether you planned it that way or not—it worked. We've got thirteen of the moon dweller VPs on our side. But the hard part is still to come. They've arranged a video conference with the rest of the VPs, who won't be such an easy sell, that I can promise you. And there's a catch," Ben says, raising a finger in the air.

I'm still in shock, but my mind is slowly catching up to the situation. "What catch?"

"The cease-fire with the Star Realm will be expiring soon, so there's really no time to delay our discussions with their leaders further. So they'll be invited to the conference, too. They'll be listening in, and available to comment, if necessary." He pauses, looks me in the eyes. "We'll need you to be a part of it—to show everyone you're serious about this. Are you ready for that?"

"Uh. I guess so."

"Good. And Tristan?"

"Yeah?"

"A word of advice. Don't stomp from the room this time." Ben's smiling, and although I know he means it, I also know he's joking.

I grin back. "Thanks, Ben. Thank you very much."

* * *

I've been here before. I feel the air exit my lungs as I'm slammed against the hard stone wall. "Do you always have to do that?" I gasp.

234

Ram's face is as hard as the stone he's just flung me against. "I don't know how you do it, sun boy, but you haven't fooled me."

"I didn't know I was supposed to be trying to," I reply smartly, still trying to get a full breath in.

"You might have convinced a few VPs, but the rest won't fall for your lies. Just remember—"

"I know, you'll be watching me. I get it. Now freaking put me down."

Grudgingly, Ram lowers me to my feet and stomps away. I slump against the wall, my chest heaving and my heart racing. *God, I hate that guy.* No matter which side he's on.

Although Roc's invited to the conference—because I insisted—I've left him in the room because he's still not feeling up to it. Everything's fine between us, but it will take time before he's ready to get involved in things again. And that's okay. I can do this on my own—for him.

Ram was supposed to escort me to the videoconference, but I guess that's not going to happen now.

After a few minutes of haggard panting, I'm able to start moving again, thankfully without my escort. I don't take the shortcut past the Diamond Lake this time, because I want to see other humans before going into the room full of VPs.

As I cross through the common area, I relish the sound of people talking and eating dinner. The Resistance. Men and women and some kids, too, all acting like they're just having a normal meal together in a normal place. There's laughing and joking and smiles. If it wasn't for responsibility, I'd want to be there next to them. As it is, the last thing on my mind is food and companionship.

I'm not sure exactly how to get to the top floor from here, but I figure it won't be too difficult. At one end of the commons is the tunnel that leads to the steps that go up one level, to the room where I originally met with the Resistance leaders. Further along the curving atrium wall are three other tunnel entrances. Two look narrow and twist sharply out of view as I peer into them. The third is wider, taller, and looks like a main tunnel, so I enter it quickly, watching my shadows dance along the brownish-gray ground as I pass each wall-mounted lantern.

Shortly, I reach an opening to the right, the entrance to a spiral staircase. The tunnel continues on past the opening, but I need to go up, not onwards, so I duck under the archway. I count the steps as I climb, ignoring the door on each landing as I pass by.

One hundred and twenty-five steps later I reach the top. Although the door is metal and heavy and thick, I can hear the buzz of activity beyond. As usual, I'm late to the party.

Slowly, I pull the door back. The murmured conversations grow louder as I enter and close the door firmly behind me. From the VPs, I get a few glances, a few frowns, and even a few smiles. All I get from Ram is a disgusted upturned lip from the corner of the room. Vice President Morgan is at the head of the table again, with Ben next to her. I round the table toward him even before he beckons me with an open palm.

Along one of the long walls is a large screen, which wasn't there earlier in the day, but, at the moment, is displaying only white fuzz.

The instant my butt hits the seat, Morgan says, "Order!" and thumps her fist twice on the table. The murmurs die down quickly and those who are standing—except for Ram—take their seats. Although Morgan is speaking, most of the eyes are on me, and even when I look away from them to focus on Morgan, I can feel them on my face. Heat rises in my cheeks, but I try to ignore it so it'll go away.

"We only have a few minutes before we go live with the other moon dweller VPs," Morgan starts. "As you all know, the star dweller leaders will be watching, too, so keep that in mind. We are in a difficult position, because we don't have a majority opinion prior to involving the Star Realm, which I don't think any of us wanted, but they've left us with no choice. The cease-fire will expire at the same time tomorrow, so we need to reach an agreement quickly, and this is the only way." I'm thankful for the recap, since I left the last meeting before all of this was discussed. No one speaks as Morgan pauses to take a sip from a coppery jug of water.

"Now, I want to reconfirm our position to ensure everyone is still in agreement. After hearing from Tristan Nailin earlier…" she says, and I cringe when I hear my last name spoken out loud. My father has made me ashamed of it. I want to be Tristan. Just Tristan. "…we all agreed that he is telling us the truth and wants to help the Resistance overthrow his father, and that we could use his help to convince the other VPs. Given we have all had additional time to think about it, are we all still in agreement?"

The room is silent and I'm afraid to take my eyes off of Morgan to scan the faces around the table, but I know I have to. I have to show I'm not hiding anything—that I meant what I said earlier. I turn my head and gaze around the room, lingering on each VP's eyes, not flinching from their stares. I'm doing my part, in an odd sort of way.

With every person I look at, I expect them to shout "You're a fraud!!" but they don't. They just look back, some nodding, some seemingly indifferent. After a few minutes of silence, Morgan says, "We've got one minute. I need positive confirmation of your positions. Abbott, I'll start with you." The woman to her right says, "I'm with you."

As they move around the table, each VP affirms that they're on our side—on my side. I'm still shocked by the incredible turnaround from earlier, when their words were harsh and their expressions harsher.

When they get back to Morgan, she nods at me encouragingly. "Okay, here's how this will go. I'll begin and then hand over to Tristan to speak. Then the other VPs will have the chance to ask questions, make comments. Understood?" She's talking to everyone, but only looking at me. I jerk my chin down. I'm more than ready for this. I'll do anything to help stop my father.

"Right. We go live in three, two, one…" Clearly some technician is watching the proceedings because suddenly the screen goes all white and then flashes back to life, as the picture comes into focus. At first there are raggedy lines of static running across the panel but soon the clarity improves.

The screen is made up of a series of boxes, each with a live shot of one of the VPs. Evidently the meeting was called on such short notice that there was no time for any of them to gather together. As I scan each of the faces, I recognize most of the leaders, but if it wasn't for the names at the bottom of each box I wouldn't remember them. There's Bruce and Quinton, Perez and Morrison, Winters and Queen. Oh, and I notice Ogi, too, the Vice President of subchapter 14 of the Moon Realm. Adele's subchapter. Ben's subchapter. He's a sheep, one who will follow my father off the edge of a cliff. There's no way we'll be able to get his support.

Altogether there are thirty boxes, twenty-nine for the moon dweller VPs and one for the Star Realm. The Star Realm's box is the biggest, located at the bottom right-hand corner of the screen and the height and width of four of the other boxes. Across the bottom of the box it reads "Star dweller generals." Not the star dweller VPs, but the *generals*. The military is making the key decisions in the Star Realm. Things are even worse than I'd thought.

A number of people are seated across a table, staring at the camera, seven in total. Three women, four men. I take in their faces, trying to remember if I've ever met them during my visits to the Star Realm. Gazing at the first six I draw a blank—they're just faces with vague features—but the seventh…the seventh looks familiar for some reason. A woman, perhaps mid to late thirties, hazel eyes that look sad but intense, dark, dark hair, jet-black and beautiful, and features that appear soft at a first glance, but harden the more you look at them. There's something about her that—

My heart stops when I realize. The end of my thought was *reminds me of Adele*. Vice President Morgan is speaking but I don't hear her, my eyes locked on the seventh star dweller general. Unwillingly, my eyes close and I picture the woman next to Ben. They look nothing alike, but when I add my last memory of Adele—her green eyes shining with confidence, her soft but strong cheeks so pale and beautiful, her lips pink and parted slightly, all framed by the cascades of obsidian hair rippling around her shoulders—into the gap between them, they are somehow connected. She has both their features in her, like the missing link between two people who were always meant for each other. My eyes flash open.

And then Morgan is speaking directly to me, her eyebrows raised slightly. "Tristan? Would you care to say a few words?"

I don't know how many times she addressed me while I was daydreaming, but all eyes are on me, and more than a few of them are looking at me strangely. Although I'm flustered, my training kicks in and gets me started. "Yes. Thank you all for coming," I start, trying to buy some time while I find my words. I force my eyes away from the bottom right corner of the screen, away from the woman who might be Adele's mom, alive and well, not in some star dweller prison, a *general* in the *freaking* star dweller army, but my gaze keeps coming back to her. It can't be her—it can't. She's in prison. Not a general. Not possible.

I pause, my thoughts tumbling over each other like a team of acrobats, flipping and spinning and leaping, none of them coming out of my mouth, which is probably a good thing. But then one thought takes center stage and I hear myself gasp. *Ben.* Ben is here and this woman who resembles Adele so closely is here—well not *here*, but connected to us via the video screen.

My eyes dart to the big man sitting next to me, and beneath his well-trimmed goatee I see a slight smile. His eyes aren't on me, but on the screen, and I don't have to follow his gaze to know what part of the screen. His gemstone-like green eyes— that remind me so much of Adele—are wide and watering and full of emotion. It *is* her; the intensity of his eyes all but confirms it. He's looking at his wife for the first time in months, knows she's okay.

"Tristan?" Morgan says again, and I have no idea how long they've been waiting for me to speak. I clear my throat and desperately try to focus on the task at hand.

"I don't have time for this," I hear someone snap through the speakers. One of the boxes on the screen is lit up. Peroni. A white-haired VP from one of the Moon Realm subchapters; 20 or 21 or something, I don't really remember.

"No," I say. "Wait. This is important." Fire is coursing through my veins again—not anger this time, but determination. To do the right thing. To convince these people of the way forward. "I know all of you through my role as heir to the presidency of the Tri-Realms. My father, President Nailin, sent me to all of your subchapters to negotiate contracts that were unfair to your people, contracts that you never should have signed."

"Like we ever had a choice," Peroni says.

"I know that. It was wrong, what I did. I always knew that and yet I did nothing, and for that I'm sorry. But it's time to make amends. It's time for me to make amends, by helping you rebuild the oppressive government that gives you nothing and takes everything."

"They provide us with leadership! The Sun Realm is responsible for everything good we have!" This time it's Ogi speaking, and I have to bite my tongue to stop myself from telling the weasel to *shut up!*

"No, that's wrong. I'm the only one here who has seen the inner workings of the government. All they care about—all my father cares about—is sucking the life out of you each and every day, so that they can continue to enjoy their lavish lifestyles. The time has come to take a stand. The time has come to stand together, united with the Star Realm, and take back the Tri-Realms!" I'm on my feet, my fist raised in the air, but I have no recollection of either action. My whole body feels hot, but this time I'm not running for the exit; this time I want to see the reaction.

I should have left.

"Rubbish!"

"We will never fight with the backstabbing star dwellers!"

"I'll die before I support the Resistance!"

A chorus of other angry rebuttals pounds through the speakers and soon I can't make out the individual comments. The boxes on the screen are all lit up and filled with a flurry of activity. Some VPs are on their feet, screaming and pointing fingers at the camera, obviously aimed at me. Some are pounding on their desks, their faces red. A handful of the VPs look as mortified as I do; they're either staring at the camera with wide eyes or looking down at their hands awkwardly. The generals in the star dweller box are whispering to each other, shaking their heads, frowning. Only Adele's mother is doing something different. She's ignoring the others, looking at the camera, almost as if she's looking right at me.

And I swear her lips are curled into a smile.

Nineteen

Adele

I find my mom in her office, and I'm starting to wonder if she ever leaves it. Her chair must be ultra-comfortable, or surely she'd have a sore butt by now.

I tap lightly on the door, which is open, and her head jerks up from some papers she's reading.

"Well, hi there, honey." Her greeting sounds so normal, like I'm just getting home from school and she's at the wash basin, preparing our meager supper of dried beans and week-old bread. Like she's not a general planning the next attack on the

Moon Realm. Her voice puts me right at ease, and I feel like maybe I can talk to her like a friend again.

"Can we talk?"

"Of course we can. But I thought you'd have crashed by now. It's been a long few weeks for you." Her smile reminds me of when I look in the mirror. *You're so much like your mother.* My father's words, not about my looks, but about my fighting style; and yet, still relevant here.

I go to sit down on the other side of the desk, but she says, "Not here," and stands, steps around the desk. Puts an arm around my shoulder, and I don't shrink from her touch this time. I didn't realize how badly my body has been craving my mother's touch until now.

I melt into her side, wrap my arm around her back, and we walk like mother and daughter through the halls. We don't speak and I don't really notice my surroundings as we pass by. I know they're gray and stone, but any subtle details escape me. I'm just living in the warmth of my mom's hold, the slight thump of her heart beating, the gentle motion of her hand rubbing my shoulder.

We reach a door, and she momentarily releases me as she unlocks it, pushes in, flicks a switch to turn on the thinnest of lights on the ceiling. Inside is her bedroom, private and plush compared to the packed Spartan bunk rooms. A thick, red comforter hides a largish bed with at least four pillows at the head.

"This is home...for now," she says with a wink.

I close the door behind us and she goes and sits against the bed's headboard, her feet sprawled out on the comforter, using two pillows to prop herself up. "Let's talk," she says, patting the space next to her.

I so want to just start firing questions at her, stay on my feet, maintain a position of power, but my heart won't let me. Instead, I obey, sliding next to her, my head resting on her outstretched arm, almost like the old days, when she used to comfort me after one of my nightmares about drowning.

"What do you want to talk about?" she asks innocently.

What *did* I want to ask her? My mind is blank—I'm lost in the beautiful glow of my mom's love. I can feel it surrounding me and it's so real—so different than the side of my mom that Tawni said she overheard, the side of my mom that makes her give me a gun and send me off to be part of the army. The side of my mom with secrets. Right, secrets—the army supplies, I remember. "How is the star dweller army so well-supplied?" I gaze into the fathoms of her eyes, seeking the truth.

"Trevor said you might ask me that."

"Why are you talking about me with Trevor?" I ask. I should be angry when I ask it, but I'm not. I'm more sad, because she's keeping secrets from me.

"It wasn't like that, sweetheart."

"Then what was it like?"

"He just told me you were asking him questions, questions he didn't know how to answer, and I told him I'd take care of it."

That's consistent with what Tawni told me. "So what's the story?"

"To be honest, I don't know. The other generals have blocked me out. I had power when I was a Resistance leader, but down here I'm just the new general, with very little influence. They respect me because I can lead the soldiers and because of my experience, but they won't let me into their inner circle. I don't know where the money's coming from, how they can afford all the weapons, the equipment. Trevor's trying to find out for me, do some undercover work. He's taking great risks for me, Adele."

It's not the answer I expected at all, so for a moment I'm not sure what to say. I thought my mom was at the center of some big conspiracy, involving bribery and theft and maybe even worse evils. But I can sense she's telling me the truth—and I believe her. Perhaps she's not the problem. Perhaps...

"What if Trevor is just pretending to help you? When really he knows the truth—is *part of* the truth—working with the other generals? Did you think about that possibility? That maybe he's a spy for them?" My questions are coming fast and I know there's heat in my words, so I look down when I finish, play with my hands, try to control my emotions.

"I thought that at first," she says, and I look up at her. Her lips are pursed. "So I did my own digging. I'm pretty sure Trevor's clean."

"What if he's not?"

"Then he's a damn good liar," she says, and I'm surprised. I've never heard her curse before.

"That fits with my impression of him," I half-joke.

She laughs. "Sometimes he doesn't make the best first impression."

I realize then that Trevor has my mom's complete and utter trust, and that she's not going to believe me without proof. I'll have to get that proof. I change the subject. "What's going on with the communications with the Moon Realm?" I ask.

Her face falls. "It's not going well," she admits. "Those papers I was reading when you came in were the transcripts from the meetings. That's where I was all day—with the other generals, speaking to the moon dweller Vice Presidents. The

246

majority of them are not being reasonable, are not willing to join the star dweller rebellion. But we have a few advocates, and I sense your father's influence behind their words."

"Dad?" I say. "So you heard him?"

"Not exactly. But I saw him—he was there. But trust me, he's behind the scenes helping to convince them to join the cause. Oh, and your friend is there, too."

My friend? I stare at her blankly.

"You know, Tristan."

My heart hammers in my chest. Tristan promised me he would help and he is. He's not like his father, the President—nothing like him at all. Excitement rushes through me, buzzing all over my skin and swooning in my chest. Memories of the last time I saw him race through my mind. The tenderness in his touch as he pulled me close to him. The way he looked at me, a tear escaping his eye. How his lips yearned for mine and mine for his, and how I had to use all of my strength to pull away from him, thus ensuring that our first kiss would not also be our last. How he surprised me by pressing his lips against mine anyway, filling me with more warmth than a warm blanket. "Tristan," I murmur.

"Yes," she says. "He spoke today, tried so hard to convince the moon dweller leaders to join the rebellion, was successful with a few of them. But it wasn't enough. The majority are still supporting the contracts with the President, maintaining the status quo."

"We have to go up there, meet with them in person, not hide down here like a bunch of rats."

"I agree, but the other generals refuse. Not until they have the support of the Moon Realm in writing. They've given the moon dwellers three days, or they'll attack."

247

"No! They can't do that! Dad, Elsey, Tristan, Roc—they're all up there! Did you tell the generals about the sun dweller soldiers me and Tawni saw?"

"Yes, I did, but they're skeptical. They think maybe you were seeing things, or dreamed it, or something, perhaps after you contracted the Bat Flu."

"But it was *before* we got the Flu!" I object.

"I know, honey, I told them that, too, but it didn't help. I'm trying, Adele. So very hard. But I'm outnumbered." *It's Trevor*, I think. He's a spy. The generals know exactly what my mom's trying to do before she does it, because she shares everything with Trevor.

"If the other generals won't go, then we have to go ourselves," I say firmly.

"Yes," she says softly, as if it's a decision she's been trying to delay as long as possible. "We will."

Finally, I feel like I've truly got my mom back. We're working together—on the same side. No more secrets. I flop my arm across her stomach and lean into her side, curl my legs underneath me.

Warmth and love and fear and exhaustion surround me and I drift away into the darkness of the never never.

* * *

I wake up naturally at five in the morning. I only know that because the dim lights are still on and I can see an old-fashioned clock hanging on the wall. The big hand is a minute past twelve. The little hand is dead on five. My mom is already gone, to do whatever it is she does as a general in the army.

I have a choice to make: to meet Brody or cancel. Something about the whole situation feels dangerous, not because he's a scary guy or anything—quite the opposite—but because I don't want to give him the wrong impression, especially not after it felt like he was flirting with me. But it's just training. No harm in trying to improve my shooting, right?

I take my time getting ready because I don't have to meet Brody for target practice until six, although it all seems kind of pointless now that I know we're going it alone. By five-thirty I'm in the mess hall, eating alone because I don't know anyone.

Just as I walk out the door leading to the training grounds, I see Brody emerge from a door further down the complex. He spots me right away and smiles at me, jogging over to intercept my path to the gun range. "I wasn't sure you'd show up," he says.

"I always do what I say I will."

"Mmm," Brody muses, looking at me curiously, "I bet you do." He pushes a hand through his hair to move his bangs away from his eyes. He's always doing that. "Ready to shoot?"

"Not really," I admit. "Guns aren't really my thing."

"But bows and slingshots and fists are?"

I shrug. "It's how I was raised. How'd you get so good with guns anyway? They were so rare in the Moon Realm that I wouldn't think there were any in the Star Realm." I ask the question nonchalantly, but I'm probing for information. Although I'm sure Brody wouldn't have more information than my mother, he might at least know when guns started popping up as if they were breeding.

His eyes are steely, as if the blue-green of his eyes have finally agreed to mix and form an iron gray. His dimple is there, but he's not smiling. Instead, his expression is wistful. "My

249

father taught me to shoot. We never had much money—or any money. But he had this old gun, handed down from generation to generation, a real dinosaur, you know? He'd take my brother and me out back to shoot tin cans using bullets he hand molded from whatever leftover metals he could scrounge up from the mines. By the time I was twelve I could hit those cans dead in the center every time." For a second there's a tear in his eyes but he quickly blinks it away, brushing his hair from his face once more. I know there's more to his story.

"Where's your family, Brody?"

His words are clipped, as if he practices saying them with as little emotion as possible. "Dad died in a mining accident. My brother got sick and never got better. My mom committed suicide. Any other questions?"

"No...I mean, I'm really sorry, I didn't mean to—"

"It's okay," Brody says, the smile suddenly popping back onto his face, lighting it up. "I'm not used to talking about all this. How 'bout we do some shooting?"

"Sounds good." I'm hoping he's just interested in being my friend—nothing more—because I'm starting to like Brody. He just seems so...real.

Brody moves in close, closer than I'd like but not close enough where it's uncomfortable, guiding a pistol into my hands, showing me how to hold it, how to aim it. "See, you have to hold it slightly lower than the target you're aiming at, because unlike a bow or a slingshot, a gun has some serious kickback. When you pull that trigger, it's going to squirm on you. That's why your first shot went way too high." I feel the warmth of his hands on my skin, as if they're burning through me. I have the sudden urge to push them away, but I want to learn so I don't. "Does all that make sense?" he asks, his eyes close to mine.

"Uh, yeah. I think so. Thanks," I add. We take the first shot together, a burst of flame, a jerk against my hands, and a shock through my arms. A wisp of smoke trails from the muzzle.

Finally Brody releases me and I feel the tension leave my body. For some reason, it's a relief.

"Do you see where the bullet hit?" Brody says.

"Wh—what?"

"The bullet? Did you see if we hit the target?" There's a twinkle in his eye and I know that he already knows.

"No. It went so fast I couldn't see it."

"It's not so much seeing it as *feeling* it. Trust me, you'll get the hang of it. Let's go check it out. Race me!" he whoops, and starts running.

Without thinking, I give chase, accelerating quickly to make up his head start. As we race, it reminds me of Camp Blood and Stone, when Tristan and I raced after we rescued my father. Except this time I'm not racing Tristan, a guy I barely know, I'm racing Brody, another guy I barely know. My life feels strange, like everyone I'm interacting with are just rocks in a swirling underground river, put in my path by chance alone.

With the head start, Brody beats me easily, but he would have beaten me anyway, his long legs gaining ground ahead of me with each stride. At the end we're both hunched over, our hands on our knees, breathing heavily from the exertion. Which I like, because it means Brody didn't go easy on me. He didn't underestimate me. Which means he respects me.

"Dead center," he says.

"What?" I say, wondering if that is what soldiers say in the army when they win something.

251

"The bullet you fired—it hit dead center."

I look up, still panting, and see that he's right. A hole the width of my thumb is drilled through the bull's-eye of the target, not even touching the edges of the painted-on red circle. I laugh. "It was *your* shot, not mine."

"True," he says, laughing.

Could Brody be like an older brother to me? "How old are you?" I blurt out, right away wishing I hadn't asked. It makes me sound like I'm interested in him—which I'm not.

Brody's laugh reaches his eyes and the single dimple is deeper than I've ever seen before. "Does it matter?" Matter for what? I think I know what he means, but I'm not going to say it.

"I was just curious," I say nonchalantly, looking away. "Forget it. Let's go shoot some more."

I start to walk back toward where we left the pistol, but Brody stops me with a hand on my wrist. I feel a crackle of electricity through my skin. "Twenty-two," he says.

"Oh." He's younger than he looks. I was guessing at least twenty-five.

I pull away from his hand and walk quickly back to the guns. The clop of his boots on the rock slab echoes behind me but I walk fast enough that he doesn't catch up. I need to get out of here; I feel like every second I'm with him he's getting bolder.

"I've got to go," I say as Brody pulls astride.

"But we've only just started the lesson," he says, looking at me with one eyebrow raised.

"I just forgot something I had to do." It's a bad lie, no detail, obvious.

But Brody doesn't question it. Just says, "Okay, no problem. How about one last shot with the pistol?"

252

I shrug. *Sure, why not?* Taking the pistol from him, I use both hands to line up the shot, like he taught me. Finding the target, I compensate for the gun's kick by lowering my aim ever so slightly. Keep my arms locked, my hands steady, my eye on the target. Pull the trigger. *Pop!* The gun is like a live animal in my hands, throwing them up and back, but I manage to hang onto it.

"Well done," Brody says. "That was much better. If my stellar eyesight is right, you nicked the top of the third ring up from the center. I've seen practiced shooters do worse."

"Thanks," I say. "I'm starting to get the hang of it, I guess."

"Yeah." Before I know what's happening, he leans into me, his breath on my lips, his eyes on fire. I know what he's going to do. I saw that same look of longing in Tristan's eyes before I left him, and I know my own eyes mirrored it back at him. But this time I know my eyes are only filled with horror. Brody's going to kiss me.

I pull away awkwardly. "Well, anyway…thanks for your help. I really appreciate it."

Brody sighs, pushes his feathery hair off his forehead. He looks stung, like I've just slapped him. "Uh, yeah, no problem." It's the first time he hasn't sounded completely sure of himself, and I feel bad about it, because it's my fault. He's been nothing but nice to me. He doesn't know that I'm thinking of him as a brother. "And I'm sorry."

Not what I expected him to say. What is he apologizing for? I'm the one who brushed him off. "No, Brody, it's okay. I'm the one who should be sorry. Look, I'll see you later, okay?"

"Sure." He sounds defeated and I have the sudden urge to put my arm around him, show him that I do care about his feelings, that I want to be his friend.

Instead, I just turn on my heel and walk away to find Tawni and my mom.

Twenty

Tristan

Sitting next to Ben the next day, I feel discouraged. The rest of the yesterday's meeting didn't go very well. We gained the support of five additional VPs, although the other Moon Realm leaders ridiculed them for it. So now we have eighteen out of forty-two, less than half. It's not what any of us had hoped for.

"Will eighteen subchapters be enough?" I ask.

"Jonas," Ben says, "you know how it works as well as I do. What are your thoughts?" I can tell Ben doesn't feel like talking about the rebellion right now. And I know why. His wife was there. Adele's mom. Like me, all he's thinking about is the fact that she's okay, that she's a general in the star dweller army, and he's wondering whether Adele found her, whether she is okay, too. All I want to do is get out of this strategy meeting and talk to Ben in private.

Jonas is speaking and I try to push aside my personal thoughts to focus on what he's saying. "…without a majority, the Moon Realm can't technically declare war on the Sun Realm, or form a military alliance with the star dwellers." He pauses, waiting to see if I have any questions. I nod at him and he continues. "However, each individual subchapter can act unilaterally if they wish. But then the other Moon Realm subchapters might align themselves with the Sun Realm, in which case we'd have—"

"A civil war," Ben finishes grimly. "Which is the last thing we want. Because then we'd be fighting our own people at the same time as the sun dwellers." Ben's voice is strong and determined. Evidently he's been able to temporarily store his personal thoughts, too.

"But I just don't see how we can get the support we need," I say. "You heard the others. I don't think any of the other VPs are anywhere close to supporting the rebellion."

"What do you think, Vice President?" Ben says across the table.

Morgan's been silent through the entire exchange, her hands clasped in front of her, looking calmer than a moon dweller subchapter after midnight. Unfolding her hands, she thumps the bottom of her palm on the table softly. "We have to get the star dweller leaders up here. Show the rest of the VPs that they're friends, not foes. Share information. Having them gawk at the proceedings like a bunch of ghosts at the bottom of a screen is not helping."

"The generals didn't seem like they would budge on the three-day deadline," Maia points out. "And they didn't seem interested in meeting with us until we've reached an agreement."

"What about your wife?" I say, immediately wondering if I should have brought it up. My eyes flick to Ben and I relax when I see the smile behind them. "I mean, can't she do anything to help get the generals up here?"

"So you knew the whole time who she was?"

"I just guessed it, but I was fairly certain," I say. "That's why I was so shell-shocked at the beginning."

Ben nods slowly. "She surprised us all. I had hoped she was alive and well, of course, but I never thought she would be part of the star dweller leadership already. But, knowing her, I suppose I should've guessed it."

"Tristan has a point," Morgan says. "Can she help us gain favor with the Star Realm?"

"I'm sure she is already doing everything she can. But, of course I will contact her. I've been itching to speak to her ever since I saw her on that screen." I can't help but smile when I see the look on Ben's face, the longing, the desire to be reunited with his wife, and to find out about Adele.

Before anyone can respond, the door flies open and Ram is here. I'd almost forgotten he wasn't in his usual spot in the corner. "Sir, there's something you need to see," he says to Ben, motioning to the screen, which is already descending from the ceiling.

We all turn to the video just as the screen changes from black to a live feed from the presidential steps in the Sun Realm, my father's usual press conference location. He's already addressing a crowd gathered before him. "...come to my attention that the Moon and Star Realms have been unable to reconcile their differences, despite the assistance that my son and I have offered. Clearly, the star dwellers have been the instigators, although it is my understanding that they have been able to garner some support within the Moon Realm. We all now face a very dangerous situation, one that could affect the lives of the citizens of the Tri-Realms for many years to come." He pauses and scans the crowd.

"It is my belief that the violence and acts of rebellion are being carried out by a small number of individuals, and that the vast majority of our people continue to support the government and their leaders. Therefore, after much discussion and the weighing of many potential peaceful solutions, I have had to make a difficult decision, but one that I know is the right one. The sun dweller army will step in to neutralize the rogues and arrest or destroy their leaders, so that our citizens can go back to the safe and peaceful lives they've grown accustomed to." The crowd is hanging on my father's every word, hushed and leaning in, as if he's some sort of a priest.

"We will protect the Moon Realm from those who seek to destroy it!" The crowd cheers as my father pumps a fist in the air. "Even now, we have stationed several platoons of sun dweller soldiers at key locations in the Moon Realm, and they await my orders to move in on the traitors."

A flurry of questions erupts from the reporters, but my father waves his arms to silence them. "I only have one more thing to say and then I must return to my duties." He pauses again, and this time looks right at the camera, his eyes darker than I've ever seen them. I cringe as I feel his eyes on my own. A horrible, sinking feeling enters my heart. I've seen that look on his face before, usually preceding a threat or punishment.

"For those of you who are traitors out there, whether you be star dwellers, moon dwellers, or *sun* dwellers...be prepared to face the consequences of your actions, which will be brought down like a hammer on you *and* those you care about. That's all for now." Even before the crowd explodes, he's off the steps and back inside the building. A shiver ripples through me. He was talking to me—I know it. *...consequences of your actions...brought down like a hammer...those you care about...*

Any anger I have for my father is lost in a cloud of fear at that moment. I don't care what my father does to me, but *those I care about?* If he touches Roc, or Adele, or Ben, or Elsey—I don't know if that's something I could bounce back from. My heart is hammering and I don't realize the telebox has been turned off until Ben says, "Tristan, why don't you and I try to contact my wife."

* * *

I feel like I'm on an emotional rollercoaster. The fiery pits of anger gave way to love and compassion for Roc, and then my father's speech sent me into a swirling vortex of fear for my friends and my maybe possibly hopefully *more-than-a-friend* (someday?). And now I'm giddy with excitement. Because I'm about to see Adele again. She's alive; as I always hoped, prayed, *knew*. It was confirmed via electronic message by Adele's mother.

Roc seems just as excited as I am. Finally, I've found something to bring him out of his funk and it takes all my self-control not to give him a hard time about it. Because his excitement is about a girl, too. We're acting like a couple of school boys. It took some convincing to get Ben to agree to

259

Roc being part of the meeting, but once he did he was able to persuade his wife to invite Tawni. And of course Elsey is here, too, and her level of excitement dwarfs both of ours combined, and that's saying something.

"Oh, Father, won't it be simply delightful to see Mother again," she says, beaming from ear to ear.

I expect Roc to mimic her, but apparently he's so stoked that he can't even bring himself to joke with his new best friend.

"I couldn't have put it better myself," Ben says, his arm around his daughter. Although Ben has been a lot of things since I met him—stoic, fatherly, wise, kind, level-headed—this is the first time he's seemed so *light*. It's like he's just floating around, not a care in the world, his head as light as a balloon, ready to lift him away to a better place, to where his family can be together. The contrast of his lightness against the heavy gray stone walls around us is strange.

"Do you think she'll remember me?" Roc says, chewing on his nails.

"Duh, of course she'll remember you, dork," I retort. We're all acting like a bunch of loons and I'm determined not to say anything crazy.

"Don't listen to poor, unromantic Tristan," Elsey says, putting a hand on Roc's shoulder as she counsels him. "Yes, she will remember you and all of your charm."

"Did you hear that, Tristy? I've got charm," Roc says, punching me lightly on the arm. At least he's joking again.

The screen goes white, and then black, and then white again, and for a moment I'm worried that technology will let us down and we won't be able to have the video call. But then the picture emerges and my heart flutters when I see her.

Adele looks the same but different. If anything, she's gotten more beautiful, her hair darker and fuller, her eyes greener and sharper, her face more heroic. She smiles lightly when she sees me—or so I think. I should say something, but my tongue is tied, so I just smile back at her. Now who's the loon?

"My dear," Ben says.

"Hello, Ben," Adele's mom says.

"Thank god you're alive. That you're all okay."

"And you," she says, smiling. "A fine mess we're all in."

I'm ignoring them and just staring at Adele. She's looking back at me and suddenly it's awkward and we both look away at the same time, laughing.

"Mother!" Elsey exclaims. "Oh, I've missed you so much."

"I've missed you, too, honey. How are you?"

"Oh, the orphanage was dreadful, but my dear Ranna was the best friend I've ever had. I'm okay now though. Adele saved me and Father is taking very good care of me."

Adele's mother looks at her with such love in her eyes—the way my mom always looked at me. "Yes, Adele has done much for our family."

Elsey's eyes light up. "Oh, and you have to meet Tristan and Roc—they helped save me and Father, too!"

"So I heard." There's a twinkle in her eye and Adele blushes. Sometimes she seems so strong, like an iron bar, unbreakable. And other times she's vulnerable, like now. Both sides of her excite me. "Well, any friends of Adele's are friends of mine. I'm Anna."

My tongue is still flopping around helplessly in my closed mouth, so Roc beats me to the punch. "I'm Roc," he says, winking. "You have two very cool daughters, Mrs. Rose."

Anna laughs, high and musical. "Don't I know it," she says. "And please, just call me Anna."

"It's so nice to meet you, Anna," I say, my voice quivery. I just spoke confidently in front of every last one of the moon dweller VPs and now I can barely string a sentence together in front of Adele's mom. I hope she doesn't notice.

"Thank you both for what you've done for my family, for my girls," she says. "We owe you a lot." The conversation seems to just be bubbling along casually, like an underground brook, and I haven't said anything of substance, anything that's in my heart.

"Adele, I—" My mind is like an old chest, full of odds and ends and balls of string, and I scrabble through it, trying to find the right words—the *perfect* words. She's waiting for me, her head cocked slightly to one side, her expression almost scared, like I might embarrass her in front of her parents. "I've missed you," I finish.

There's silence and I'm afraid I've upped the ante on awkwardness too far.

"And I've missed you, Tawni," Roc says quickly. I gape at him and then smile. Good old Roc. Elsey giggles. Ben chuckles. Soon everyone's laughing, except for Tawni—who's ultra-pale features have turned crimson—and Roc, who's suddenly found interest in a black mark on his left shoe.

The ice is broken—no thanks to me. Finally, Tawni says, "I've missed you all," very diplomatically, but I can tell her eyes linger on Roc's face slightly longer than the rest of us.

"We might be able to see you all in person soon though," Adele says, her first words since the conversation started.

My heart is thundering and I can't hide my excitement. "Really? When? How?"

Anna laughs again. "We'll get to all that. But first we need to get everyone up to speed." The next hour is an exchange of information. First Ben tells our story of escaping subchapter 26 and our flight to the Resistance headquarters. Then he talks about the political challenges we're facing, the animosity amongst the VPs, the pressure being added by President Nailin. When he talks about my father, I look away, chew on the side of my mouth. He doesn't mention what my father told Roc and me.

When he's done, I look back at the screen and Adele's eyes meet mine. My breath catches in my lungs and I feel pulled toward her, although there's no pain through the screen. I'd give anything just to hold her hand again, like that night. I can almost feel the pain as it morphed into beautiful shivers, caused by the simple act of her running her fingers up and down my hand. Almost.

"What happened to you after we left, Adele?" It's my voice, but I didn't plan on saying anything.

There's no awkwardness between us anymore. It's like we've known each other for years. She recounts her story as if she's talking directly to me, and I find myself unable to release her gaze. When she tells about the sun dweller soldiers passing so close to where she and Tawni were hiding, I feel my heart racing in my chest, hoping against hope that the next scene isn't one of violence. Thankfully, the sun dweller soldier passes from the story like a wraith in the night.

I find myself gripping the table as she tells of their bout with the Bat Flu and their unexpected awakening in the Star Realm infirmary. When she finds her mother I feel tears in my eyes, which I fight away. She finishes with, "We did it, Dad." She glances at Tawni and the two girls smile at each other with purpose, like their bond has been forever strengthened by what they've been through together.

"I knew you would, Adele," Ben says, pride in his eyes. His expression changes and he's all business. "So you're telling me what Nailin is saying is true—that you've seen sun dweller soldiers in the Moon Realm?"

Adele nods. "I swear it. But the generals don't believe us."

"Don't, or won't?"

I miss the subtlety of the question, but Anna nods in understanding. "I'm not sure and I may never know."

"So what's the plan? How do we find a solution before the three-day"—Ben pauses, looks at the ceiling—"make that two-and-a-half-day deadline?"

"We're coming to the Moon Realm," Anna says firmly. There's a twitch of excitement in my chest.

"Who?" I say.

"All three of us," she replies, and I can't keep the grin off my face.

"The generals?" Ben asks.

Anna shakes her head, her lips pursed. "Unfortunately not. The others won't support a trip to the Moon Realm. We'll be leaving secretly. Maybe having one star dweller general in person will be enough to convince the moon dweller VPs."

"It's a long shot."

"It's our only choice."

Ben nods grimly in agreement. "How will you get here?"

"The Resistance train line from subchapter eight here. But to get there we'll have to go through the tunnels. We can't risk using the public trains. They're being watched."

"Be careful."

"We will."

I can tell the call is wrapping up and there are so many things I want to say to Adele, but I can't bring myself to do it in front of everyone. I wish we could talk privately.

"Mom, Dad," Adele says. "Can Tristan and I have a minute?" It's like she read my mind.

"Of course," Anna says. "Ben?"

"No problem from my side," Ben says, giving me a wry smile.

Anna and Tawni stand up to leave and I swear Tawni flashes Roc a grin before moving out of the picture. I watch Ben and Elsey walk out the door. Roc lingers for a minute, waiting for them to exit, and then says, "Now, I don't want any funny business in here. I'll leave a shoe in the door."

I'm glaring at him, but I hear Adele laughing. "Don't worry, Roc," she says, "no funny business—I promise. And I'll do some probing with Tawni, see what she thinks of you."

Roc's brown skin flushes and he moves to the door. "Uh, thanks," he says before scrambling out.

"Thanks for getting rid of him," I say when Roc is gone.

"I knew that would do the trick."

I smile at her. "I really have missed you," I say, feeling more comfortable sharing my feelings with each passing second.

"I...wish you were here," Adele says. Her words sound sincere, but I can sense tentativeness behind them. "Look, Tristan, something happened I need to tell you about."

Here it comes, she's not interested in me, I think, but I reply, "Adele, whatever it is, we will get through it together."

"There's this guy..."

My heart sinks into my stomach. "Oh," I say.

"No, Tristan, it's not like—"

265

"No, it's okay. I understand. You barely know me, I chased after you like some crazy stalker, I shouldn't have expected—"

"Will you shut up!"

The power in her voice makes me stop talking and just stare at her. My heart hurts and my mind is blank. I wait quietly to hear what she has to say about this guy.

"I like *you*," she says, and her simple words send tingles through my skin. I ignore them, waiting for the *but*...

Instead she says, "You, Tristan. Only you."

Huh? "Maybe you should have started with that," I say and she laughs.

"I'm not very good with words," she says, "a side effect of not talking to humans for almost six months."

"So you were talking to animals then...or aliens?"

She laughs again, even though I know it's not one of my best jokes. It makes me like her even more. "Mostly myself, and even then I only spoke in my head."

I smile. "I'm not great with words either," I say. "Sometimes I just stick my foot in my mouth before I start speaking to save myself the trouble later."

I'm enjoying the conversation and I'm hoping we can just keep talking like this, and not go back to the thing about *this guy*, whoever he is. Or not. "So this guy..." Adele says, and I cringe, waiting for the hammer to drop. "Stop it! It's not bad news, I promise."

"Okay, just hit me with it quickly."

Adele   sighs. "There'sthissergeantnamedBrodyandhetriedtokissme," she says in a rush.

I heard everything she said but only four words really register: *tried to kiss me.* "What do you mean, 'tried'?" I ask. Fire

266

is pumping through my veins as I picture a little squirt of a guy puckered up and leaning into Adele, trying to sneak a kiss. And then my knuckles collide with his face, knocking him into the next Realm.

"He was teaching me to shoot a gun—you know, as part of my training—and then he just thought there was something between us, so he tried to kiss me." She rushes on, "But don't worry, I didn't let him. I pulled away. It was nothing."

"Then why are you telling me?"

"I just thought…we should be completely open with each other. That is, if we're serious about seeing each other."

I let out a deep breath that I realize I've been holding in my chest. I'm relieved. It really sounds like it was nothing, and she's just trying to be honest with me. "Thank you. I…I'm sorry if I overreacted. I've just had a lot of anger in me lately. Because of my father."

She smiles. "It's okay, sorry about how poorly I handled telling you. So we're okay?"

"Most definitely. Now if we could just bring peace to the Tri-Realms, perhaps we could go on a proper date."

"Oh, is that all we have to do," she jokes.

"Yep, that's it."

The door opens and Ben says, "Sorry, we're out of time."

"Adele, I have to go, but I'll see you soon, right?"

Her jaw is as firm as truth. "You can count on it."

Twenty-One
Adele

My heart is beating with all the strength of a miner's sledge. Talking with Tristan was incredible and reminded me all over again why I can't stop thinking about our kiss back in the Moon Realm.

Tawni and my mom are waiting outside of the conference room, chatting like best friends. My mom's telling stories of me as a kid and Tawni's laughing. "There were mashed beans all over the ceiling," my mom says, her words mixing with her laughter.

Tawni shrieks with laughter. "Somehow that doesn't surprise me," she chuckles.

"Ha ha. I can hear you, ya know."

"Oh, hi, honey," Mom says, pretending she just noticed me. "How'd everything go with…Tristan?" She raises her eyebrows twice.

"Fine," I grumble, wishing I'd never opened up to her about my feelings for him. For some reason I thought now that she's a general she'd be cooler about boys. But no, she's still just acting like a mom.

"Well, you two are very cute together."

"Mom! You haven't even seen us together."

"Call it Mom-dar. There are some things that a mom just knows."

"She's right, you know," Tawni says, not helping things.

"Whatever," I say, trying to brush them off the subject. "When do we leave?"

"Anxious to go see Tristan?" Tawni says, refusing to let it go. But this time I've got the perfect comeback.

"How did I miss the sparks flying between you and Roc?"

The crimson on Tawni's face is worth every word. "What? There's nothing…we're just friends." Her voice is about as believable as a politician's.

My mom's tone is back to business. "We'll leave immediately. There's no point in trying again with the generals—they just won't budge. Go get your things and don't tell anyone where you're going."

"What about *Trevor*?" I say, not trying to hide my sarcasm.

"He already knows and will be coming with us. He'll help you get ready and escort you to meet me."

My face feels like it's about to explode. How can she trust that creep? I'll be shocked if all the generals and half the army aren't waiting to arrest us. "Let's go, Tawni," I say coldly.

I grab her hand and leave my mom without saying bye. I'm just too angry.

We pass a few soldiers in the hallways but they don't speak to us, barely look at us. We're just a couple of random girls. We make it back to the bunkrooms, which are empty, with all the female soldiers off doing whatever it is that they do all day. Training, I guess.

For us, packing is like a thirty-second process. Tuck everything into our small packs, fill our brand new army-provided canteens, splash a little water on our faces, and we're ready to go. As we head for the door, I realize I'm missing one important thing: the gun. The gun my mom gave me, the gun I hope I never have to use. I'd rather just leave it hidden under my pillow, forget it ever existed, that my mom ever thought it wise to give it to me. But I can't. It's got her name on it. My name.

"One sec," I say.

I throw the pillow back and reach for the gun, but—

—it's not there.

I pull back, alarm crossing my face. "What's the matter?" Tawni asks.

"My gun—it's missing."

Tawni's brow furrows in that way that could only look cute on her. "Maybe you already chucked it in the bag and just forgot."

I know I didn't, but I check anyway. It's not there. Or in Tawni's pack. Someone took it. No, not *someone*...

"Trevor!" I exclaim. "He must've stolen it when he realized I was on to him. We've got to tell my mom right away!"

Squinting, Tawni says, "Hold on a minute. We don't have any evidence. I know he's been acting strangely, but it's quite a leap to say he's stealing weapons now."

She's the voice of reason, as usual, but I won't be deterred—not this time. "I know it's him, and I'm not going to sit by while he screws up everything for us."

I whirl around and storm toward the door, not caring if Tawni follows.

I gasp and my eyes widen when I see him standing before me, gun leveled at my head.

I freeze, my heart thudding in my chest.

Time seems to stop for a moment and I wonder if it will be my last.

"Adele, you shouldn't just jump to—" Tawni starts to say and then stops, letting out a tiny squeal.

"Hello, ladies," Brody says, standing in front of the open door. I didn't even hear it open when he came in.

"You?" I breathe. I'm in shock. Why is Brody of all people pointing a gun—no, not *a* gun, *my* gun, I realize—at my head?

He laughs, deep and not at all friendly. Not at all like the kind laugh I'd heard from him over the last two days. "For being the daughter of such a smart woman you're pretty dense," he says, sneering.

"I don't understand," I say.

"How could you?" Brody says. "I've had you wrapped around my little finger from the moment I laid eyes on you. I tend to have that effect on women."

271

The arrogance on his face is chilling. Even when faced with rejection, he thinks I was into him. "You're the spy," I say, as I finally realize what's happening.

"Obviously. You've been thinking Trevor the whole time, right? You really should have trusted your mother's judgment more. But alas, hindsight is twenty-twenty."

"Why are you doing this?"

"I'm not a complex person, Adele. The sun dwellers just pay more, that's all. They buy weapons, food, clothing, all of it."

"You work for the sun dwellers? But why would they want to fund a rebellion?" My mind churns through the facts, trying to fit them all together.

"A rebellion? Ha! Hardly. The only thing that's happened so far is the Star Realm fighting with the Moon Realm. A perfect opportunity for the Sun Realm to come in and reestablish peace, stabilize the Tri-Realms, play the heroes. And at the end of it all, the Sun Realm is stronger than ever and the others…well, they're more pliable than ever."

My mind is racing. All along I thought we at least had a chance if we could just agree on a common enemy. The sun dwellers. The President. But now I find out the entire thing has been orchestrated by the Sun Realm? I'm in complete shock—and angry at myself for not putting two and two together; I knew something wasn't right about how well-supplied the star dwellers were, if I only had more time I could have figured it out…

But I don't—and I didn't.

My feet are frozen to the ground. They may never move again. And even if they could, what could I do against Brody and my gun? If I tried anything he'd just shoot me between the eyes. Suddenly it all makes sense why he offered to train me to shoot. I thought he was being nice, trying to help me; but no, he just wanted to show me that he doesn't miss his target, so that when the time came for this confrontation, I'd be afraid, frozen, exactly like I am now. How could I be so stupid? So trusting?

Brody laughs again. "I see those cute little wheels spinning, Adele. Have I blown your mind? I had no choice. You were going to ruin everything with your rogue trip to meet with the Moon Realm leaders, so I thought I'd just stop by and share some information. You know, like any good friend would. And guess what? There's more, and this bit is for Tawni too."

"This has nothing to do with her," I say, my jaw clenched. Despite the gun in my face, I'm feeling fierier all of a sudden. He can do what he wants with me, but not Tawni. I won't watch another friend get hurt.

"Au contraire, my moon dweller friend. You see, Tawni's been beating herself up for a while because her parents turned your parents in to the Enforcers, right? I mean, that's what started all of this. The Enforcers kicked down your door, blah blah blah, grabbed your parents, blah blah, threw you in prison, blah-blibbety-blah." My fists clench and my leg muscles tighten. The pleasure he seems to be getting from all of this is really starting to piss me off.

"Get to the point," I growl.

"Now, now. Temper, temper. My point is: Do you really think Tawni's parents figured it out all on their own? I'm sure they're very smart people, but no one knew your parents' true identities except the Resistance. Well, it just so happened that I've been an honored member of the Resistance for more than a year now."

I freeze. He did it. He tipped off Tawni's parents. I'm two seconds from rushing him, from taking my chances with the gun, when I realize something.

"Why are you telling us all of this?" I blurt out.

He grins. "Now you're catching on. I just wanted you to know what I've accomplished. And in a minute it won't matter anyway, because you'll be dead. Both of you."

He's going to kill us. My mind is whirling. Everything he told me before now was a lie. Even—

"Was all that crap about everyone in your family dying a lie?"

"Ha ha ha!" he laughs. "I'd forgotten about that. No, they died, all right, but not the way I told you. You should have seen the look on your face when I told you the story. Pathetic, just like them. They were useless pawns with no ambition, so I killed them."

It's not until I hear him say it—no remorse in his voice—that I know what he truly is: a psychopath. We have no chance to talk our way out of it. The only option is to take our chances fighting. Even if I get shot, if I can just distract him enough for Tawni to escape, to tell my mom what happened, maybe...

"No more questions? I'm weary of this conversation anyway. Say goodbye to your friend, Adele." His finger tightens on the trigger as a smile flashes across his face.

One second before I die. *Make the most of every opportunity.* My dad's words. I leap to the side, hearing the crack of the gunshot, followed by a muffled thump and a groan. I feel nothing. No flash of pain. No searing heat spreading through my body. No tickle of trickling blood. Nothing.

More thumps and groans—the sounds of a struggle. The gun booms, much closer to my ear this time. I roll to my feet and spin around, trying to take in the scene before me with just a glance. Brody is on top of Trevor, who's lying in a pool of blood. The crimson rivulets are meandering toward me and instinctively I twist away from them, regaining my feet.

Tawni is next to me, screaming, her face contorted with fear and disgust. Brody has killed Trevor, and we'll be next if I don't do something. Our only chance is now, right now, no time to think, to plan, to strategize.

With a horrific yell I charge Brody, slam my shoulder into him, thrust him off of Trevor. At the same time, I search frantically for the gun in his hands, ready to wrench it from his grasp. To my surprise, his hands are empty, and I naturally scan the stone floor for the weapon.

"Adele," a voice says next to me. "It's over."

My head jerks to the left and I see Trevor pulling himself to his feet, my gun dangling loosely from his fingertips. His tunic is covered in red, slick and splotchy. Blood. But not his. Brody's. I turn back to Brody, who I'm straddling, nausea rolling in my stomach, churning and heaving. His dead eyes stare lifelessly at me and I notice the hole in his temple. Frantically, I roll off of him, throw my head to the side, vomit all over the floor. My hair is in my face, mingling with my regurgitated breakfast, but I don't care.

The guy who was so nice to me when I met him, who taught me to shoot, who nearly kissed me just this morning, is now dead. "You…you killed him," I manage to blubber, still staring at the floor.

"I had no choice," Trevor says.

"No—I didn't mean it that way." I pull back from the putrid scent of my upchuck, wipe my mouth with the top of my tunic, push my soiled hair away from my face. "Thank you. I meant to say thank you. You saved my life. Both of our lives."

Trevor's eyes are steely. "I'd do anything for your mother." Implying what? He only saved me because it's what my mother would have wanted?

"And for me?"

"Eh, I guess for you too, by default." There's humor in his words, barely betrayed by a wry smile he can't hide.

"Trevor, I'm, I'm—"

"She's sorry," Tawni interrupts, moving between us. "She's always had trouble with the S-word." Although I can tell my friend is freaked out, her face ashen, her lips thin, she manages to put a smile on my face with her words.

"I'm sorry—really sorry," I say.

"Don't worry about it," he says, thankfully not giving me a hard time. "I know you both must be in a bit of shock, but we don't have much time. We still need to leave for the Moon Realm soon, but given what's just happened we'll need to brief General Ro—I mean, your mom—right away."

"Can we get cleaned up first?" I say, motioning to Tawni. When I look at her, I realize she's perfectly clean and tidy and looks ready to go. It's me who's a mess. A nervous laugh escapes my throat. "I mean, can *I* get cleaned up first? Oh, and you'll probably want to change, too," I add, trying not to look at Brody's blood all over Trevor's clothes.

"Of course. I'll take you to your mother's personal quarters for all that."

"What about…the body?" I say, looking away so Brody's dead corpse is out of even my peripheral vision.

"Don't worry about that—I'll take care of it." Trevor's voice is so firm, so calm, I wonder how I never saw this side of him

276

before, how I never trusted him. But then again, after what happened with Brody, I may never trust anyone again.

* * *

It's one of the best showers I've ever had. Not only am I scrubbing away the dried blood, my own filthy bile, and sweat, but I'm exfoliating away Brody's lies and treachery. Although I'm shaken up, I'm alive, and I feel like it's a new beginning for me. A chance to stick with the people I know and trust. My family, Tawni, Tristan, and now Trevor. A lot of T's in the bunch, which is fine by me.

After toweling dry, I leave my dirty tunic in a pile in the corner of the bathroom, where my mom told me to. She said we'll probably never be coming back to this place anyway. My new tunic feels wonderful against my clean skin. When I move back into her bedroom, she and Tawni are waiting for me.

"Tawni told me everything while you were getting ready," she says.

"Mom, I'm sorry I didn't trust your judgment. You too, Tawni," I say, looking at the floor. I'm ashamed of myself.

"It's okay. I am completely shocked it was Brody, too," Mom says.

"Yeah, even though I didn't think it was Trevor, I was surprised it was Brody," Tawni agrees.

"You are?" I say, looking up.

Mom answers for both of them. "Yes, I never would have guessed him, which is probably why Trevor and I couldn't figure it out."

"About Trevor…" I say.

277

"That's okay, too. You'd only just met him, and it was perfectly normal for you to be skeptical of him, especially because I know he can be quite...grating sometimes."

"Someone must be talking about me, because my nose is itching something fierce," Trevor says, pushing through the half-open door. He's smirking in that way that I used to find so irritating, but now seems somewhat endearing. It's amazing how much difference a change in perspective can make to how you view someone.

"Trevor, I just want to say again that I'm so—"

"No more apologies," he says. "I know how much you hate that word, so I won't make you say it again."

"Thanks," I say, thoroughly humbled. He's being so nice to me. Why didn't I see this side of him before?

"I'm just glad you're all okay," Mom interjects. "Trevor, I already owe you so much, but now..." I'm surprised when I see tears shimmering in her eyes. My mother the general. Still the same compassionate woman I remember. She blinks them away. "Let's just say there will always be room for you at our table."

"I might just take you up on that," Trevor says. He maintains his smirk, as if everything is no big deal, but I can tell from the lightness in his eyes that he's touched. He claps his hands together. "Okay, the generals have agreed to meet. They seem very interested in 'the new developments' that I told them we want to share."

"Good. Let's go," Mom says, rising, no trace of the weakness that had clouded her eyes only moments earlier.

"Me too?" Tawni asks.

"Of course. You're all a part of this now and you all have valuable information."

For some reason I hesitate. "What if the generals are all working for the Sun Realm, too?"

My mom looks at me seriously. "I've considered that possibility. But don't let one person's lies affect your ability to trust anyone. While one or more of the generals may be against us, I don't believe they all are. We just have to trust that there are still good people in this world, Adele."

I don't know if I can do that, not after what Brody tried to do—what he *did* do—but I don't say anything, just nod. I ignored my mom's judgment once.

I won't do it again.

Twenty-Two
Tristan

I'm still feeling a rush of energy through my chest when Ben walks in. It's been over an hour since I saw Adele, but the effect is lingering. It's like there's a bubble inside me, leaving me airy and light. I expect I feel kind of like Ben felt when he saw his wife again.

The only thing that was weird was when she told me about this Brody guy. He seems like a real creep to me, trying to kiss Adele when they should be preparing for a war. Although I can't really blame him—I might've done the same thing if I was in his position.

I realize Ben is standing over me and I look up, surprised. I expected he was coming in to spend some quality time with Elsey, who's across the room reading a book with Roc, while I sit and daydream about Adele, bask in the few minutes of uninterrupted conversation I had with her.

"Something's happened," Ben says. He's wearing a frown, which concerns me because I haven't seen it much from him.

Adele's hurt—I just know it. Evidently my inner concerns make it to my face because he says quickly, "No one's hurt, thank god." I take a sharp breath out that I've been holding in.

"Then what?"

"A sergeant in the star dweller army was working for the sun dwellers. He tried to kill Adele and Tawni."

I suck in a short breath. "What? How? Why?"

"Unfortunately, I don't have all the details. I've only just received an encrypted message from Anna. Evidently my wife's second-in-command rescued the girls from their attacker. Shot the guy—killed him."

A thought flashes into my head. "Brody?" I ask.

Ben's head jerks slightly. "How did you know that?"

So Brody is Adele's mom's right-hand man. "Uh, Adele mentioned his name."

"What? In what context?"

I stare at Ben, wondering why he's so interested in the guy who saved Adele's life. I'm certainly not going to say he tried to kiss Adele. "I dunno. Just that she met him during training."

Ben shrugs, as if he was never really that interested anyway. So Brody saved Adele and Tawni, but—

"Who was the attacker?" I ask.

Ben stares at me strangely. "The guy you just said. Brody."

281

I put a hand on my head, run it through my hair. So Brody saved them from Brody? Are there two Brodys? "Wait...what? I thought you just confirmed it was Brody who saved them?" I'm getting more confused by the minute, as if Ben and I are running around in circles chasing each other, fake tails stuck to our butts.

"No, no. Brody was the attacker. Anna's second-in-command rescued them."

My mind is whirling. "But I thought Brody was her second-in-command."

"No, that's Trevor."

Trevor? Who the hell's Trevor? Some other guy I don't know about apparently. Some guy who didn't try to kiss Adele apparently. Soooo...

The guy who tried to kiss Adele tried to kill Adele? My jaw drops when I finally understand. Funny how changing two little letters in *kiss* transforms it into the deadly opposite: *kill.* Just thinking that word and *Adele* in the same sentence sends shivers down my spine. If he was working for my father, clearly he was trying to get close to her for information. I'm glad she didn't fall for that crap.

"Adele said Brody was friendly to her," I say.

"What do you mean *friendly*?"

"I don't know—a nice guy, I guess. Trying to get close to her. Perhaps trying to get information as it turns out."

"Well, he's dead now." Ben's eyes are as sharp as daggers. He's happy this Brody dude is dead. Not that I'm not.

"Remind me to thank Trevor when I meet him. So are they on their way here now?"

"No, that's the other thing I wanted to tell you. There will be a slight delay because of what happened. They want to tell the generals they had a mole in their midst, try to get them see what's happening, that the Sun Realm is playing games with us, hopefully convince them to travel to the Moon Realm with them."

"So what do we do?"

Ben shrugs. "We wait." Ugh. Already I'm tired of waiting. "There will be another peace summit, which my wife and at least one other general from the star dweller army will attend, so that's being planned, but other than that, there's nothing really for us to do right now."

"Okay," I say.

"Get some food. Get some rest. Hopefully by tomorrow they'll be closer to getting here."

"Okay," I repeat, because I'm all out of things to say.

* * *

I swear one of my least favorite things in the world is waiting. It's not my father's bad politics, or the sun dweller soldiers, or even the dust-filled moon dweller air that's killing me. No, it's none of those things. It's the waiting that's killing me. Slowly, second by second, minute by minute, hour by hour. Sucking the life out of me, making me grind my teeth and pick at my fingers, and bang my head against the wall.

I'd almost welcome Ram to stop by and beat me up again— at least it would kill some time, get my blood pumping again, break up the monotony of the gray stone walls and slap of cards against the table where Roc and Elsey are playing some game.

"I gotta get out of here," I mumble, to whoever might be listening. No one.

Or Roc. "Okay, master. Let's go for a stroll down that one tunnel—you know the one, right?—that leads to that other tunnel—the gray one with the brownish rocks. And then we can walk down that other gray tunnel that splits into two other gray tunnels. It'll be way more fun than sitting here playing cards with two of the coolest cats around."

I smirk. "One—don't call me 'master.' And two—Elsey's cool, but I'm struggling to figure out who the other cool person is, unless you're referring to me?"

"Ha ha, very funny. It's me, you dolt. Dolt—oh, I kind of like that. It definitely suits you more than 'master.'" He uses two fingers on each hand for the quotes around *master*.

Elsey giggles. "Are you sure you aren't brothers? You fight like Adele and I did when we were little."

I see Roc's spine stiffen, so I answer casually. "What do you mean 'were little'? You still *are* little."

"I most certainly am not!" Elsey scoffs.

"Are too! Would I be able to do this"—I leap off the bed, rush over to her, and grab her, picking her up and swinging her around—"if you weren't little?"

"Put me down! Is that any way to treat a lady?" she squeals, but she's giggling hysterically and I know she's enjoying it, so I don't stop for another ten seconds.

When I do set her down again, she brushes off her tunic with her hand and says, "Hmph. The scoundrel boys in the orphanage were more gentlemanly than you are."

I'm about to fire back a sarcastic retort, maybe tickle her, maybe pick her up again, when Roc says, "Elsey, we've got something to tell you."

The whole time I thought I was rescuing my best friend from a touchy subject, he'd been thinking about it, and I can tell he's ready to talk about things, starting with telling Elsey our big news. "Like a surprise?" she says, her face lighting up.

"Sort of like that," Roc says, staring at his hands. He gets up and moves to sit on the side of the bed and Elsey follows him. I remain standing nearby. Roc seems to want to do this on his own.

"What is it?" Elsey asks innocently, staring up at Roc with wide eyes.

"You know how you just asked whether we were sure we weren't brothers?"

"I just said that not two minutes ago," Elsey says, in that proper way that only she and people from the seventeenth century could say it.

"Well, as it turns out, Tristan and I, well, we actually...are...brothers. Well, sort of...I mean, we're half-brothers. We have the same father."

Elsey's eyes are bigger than the artificial suns in the Sun Realm. "Your father is the President, too?"

Roc nods. "We both just found out. Like a couple days ago. It's still a bit of a shock."

"Wow," is all she says.

"I don't really want anyone to know yet though," Roc says.

"Like a secret?"

"Exactly."

"I swear on my friendship with my truest friend in the whole wide world, Ranna, that I will never share what you have told me with another soul."

"Or you can just not tell anybody," Roc says, chuckling.

"That's what I just said!"

"Except it took you three times as long to say it," I add.

"Oh, boys," Elsey says, shaking her head, like we're the ten-year-olds.

"Who's hungry?" I ask, as I feel my stomach rumble. It's late, but the nice thing about this place is that there's always food to be eaten.

"Me, me, me!" Roc exclaims, waving his hand in the air like a child trying to get the attention of the schoolteacher. He's doing it to entertain Elsey and she giggles.

"I would be honored to dine with you two strapping young gentlemen. Thank you for asking," Elsey says grandly.

Roc and I just look at each other, laughter in our eyes.

We make our way to the commons, which are bustling as if it's the middle of the day. Members of the Resistance are streaming all over the place, carrying packs of supplies, weapons, and body armor. Everything looks a hundred years old but there seems to be plenty of it. It's as if the entire command center is readying to move out to war. The soldiers look like ants next to the heights of the honeycomb atrium above them.

Few of them are eating, however, so we easily spot Ben and his sister at a lone table, their heads together, their voices a whisper as if they're discussing something treacherous, like an assassination attempt on the President; maybe they are. They lift their heads and voices when they spot us, donning big smiles and motioning with their arms for us to join them.

We do. "What's all this about?" I ask as we sit down, sweeping my hand across the buzzing cave.

Jinny answers. "You didn't think we'd be going into subchapter 1 without some protection, did you?"

"They're all coming with us?" Roc asks incredulously.

"Sure," Ben says. "The Resistance is all about being prepared. In the event that something happens, we want to be ready for it."

"Will I be coming, too, Father?" El asks.

"Most definitely. You think after all we've been through that I'd let you out of my sight again?" he says, pulling his daughter into his side. For once, Elsey is just a kid, melting into Ben's side, closing her eyes, her face full of love for her dad. It's not something I'm used to seeing.

"Umm, food?" Roc says.

"Thanks, I didn't know you were serving tonight," I joke. "I'll take some mashed potatoes and bread rolls with gravy, if they've got it."

"Fat chance," Roc says. "Those days are long over."

I punch his arm and stand up. "For which I am glad," I say. "I'll get the grub."

After taking Roc's and Elsey's orders I go and retrieve the food from the counter, balancing all three plates on one arm like a waiter, while toting three mugs of water with the other hand. "Bon appétit," I say, dishing it out.

"You're good at that," Roc says, winking. "If this whole rebellious-son-of-the-President thing doesn't work out, you've definitely got a future as a servant in the Sun Realm."

"And you can become a comedian," I retort.

For a few minutes Roc and I manage to cease our normally nonstop banter as we strive to accomplish the same goal of stuffing our faces. As we eat, we listen to Ben and Jinny discuss the next few days.

"After we arrive in the subchapter, we'll head straight to the Big House to settle in and get the lay of the land," Ben says.

"The Big House is the code name for the place we'll be staying," Jinny explains for our benefit.

"Right. Hopefully Anna and Adele will arrive shortly afterward and we can have a big family reunion." At that, Elsey's eyes light up, but she can't speak as even she's forgone manners in order to fill her belly, and her mouth is full, her cheeks puffed out as she tries to chew.

"We're hoping we'll get a few minutes together before all the VPs are ready to begin the peace summit." *I'll drink to that*, I think, taking a big gulp of my water. It feels so surreal that I haven't hung out with Adele in days after having gone through such an emotional two days by her side.

"Then what?" I ask, licking the last bit of mashed potato off of my finger.

"Then we pray for the best," Ben says.

Twenty-Three
Adele

The star dweller generals listen patiently as my mom explains what happened. I expect looks of shock: wide eyes, open mouths, dropped jaws—something. Instead, they just stare with unreadable expressions and pursed lips.

The only one who reacts is General Baum, the one who's a member of the Resistance. She's older than my mother, perhaps by five years, but is in fantastic shape, with strong, sculpted arms and legs that boast years of athletic endeavors. Sort of like my legs. Strong and capable and far from ladylike.

Her aging brown hair is peppered with gray, but it's cut short, like a boy's, so it's not that noticeable.

Her eyebrows are raised and her knuckles white on the table. The exact opposite of the other generals who look almost indifferent. When my mom finishes, she rests her hands gently on the table, waiting for a response. The tension in the room is palpable and I have the urge to reach out and try to touch it, as if it's something solid in the air.

Finally, one of the older generals, a gray-haired man who looks almost fifty, leans back with his hands behind his head. "This doesn't change anything," he says.

General Baum slams a fist on the table and looks like she might jump across and throttle him. "Doesn't change anything? Are you cra—"

One of the other generals, a woman with long blond hair and perfectly smooth skin, silences her with a finger on her lips. *Shhh!* I can almost hear her say, although she makes no sound. Instead she mouths, *They're listening,* and then points to the ceiling. I look up, half-expecting a huge pair of ears to be hanging from above.

I glance at my mom and I can see her eyes are wide and serious. The blonde starts writing frantically on a piece of paper in front of her, as the old general continues speaking. "Honestly, I'm not sure what you expect us to do with this information. So there was a spy. You took care of him, so that's the end of it."

The woman finishes writing and passes the note to my mother. Tawni and I read over her shoulder. *The sun dwellers are listening to every word. They have our families. They'll kill them if we don't cooperate. I'm sorry we didn't tell you sooner, but if Brody had found out...*

My heart beats faster as the pieces fall into place. The unwillingness of the generals to listen to reason; the way they used the sun dweller weapons to attack the Moon Realm; this crazy three-day deadline: the Sun Realm—President Nailin—is controlling it all. And on the ground was the puppet master: Brody. Now that he's gone it will take the Sun Realm time to put another spy in place. We have a narrow window to act.

My mom's head stays down and she starts writing a note.

The other general keeps speaking as if nothing is happening. "But it doesn't change the fact that the Moon Realm is not willing to cooperate with us. In less than three days we'll have no choice but to declare war on the moon dwellers and use every resource at our disposal to crush them."

I read my mom's note before she passes it across. *We will do our best to protect your families. God bless.* She slides a separate note to Baum. *You stay here. Do what you can to help them.* She nods.

"Fine," my mom says. "I understand your position, even if I don't agree with it. For now, we'll wait and let the peace process run its course. If the Moon Realm won't join us, we attack." Her words are cold, harsh, believable. My mom's a good liar. I never would have thought it six months ago.

A final note from the woman general. *Godspeed and good luck.*

My mother nods. The old general says, "Good. This forum is dismissed."

Everyone rises and we leave.

* * *

When we exit the meeting, darkness has fallen on the Star Realm. My mom has a flashlight, which cuts a triangular arc

291

through the gloom, but because the lighting here is so poor even during the day, my eyes adjust quickly to the dark.

"We need to leave right away," Mom says.

"Shouldn't we tell Dad—"

"There isn't time. He knows about the spy, but the rest can wait. And some things are better told in person."

"I can't believe they took their families," Trevor murmurs. For the first time I see compassion in his expression. Perhaps it was always there and I just couldn't see it. But he's a different person to me now. Not a spy—a star dweller. And so he cares about the families of the star dweller generals. He's a good person, regardless of his faults.

"I can," my mom says. "Nailin is a heartless, soulless demon who will do anything for power." Her words are filled with fire. "The only reason they couldn't get to me is that I was brought in much later, as an outsider. Plus, they thought they already had my whole family imprisoned."

We walk in silence for a few minutes as we follow my mother through the narrow alleys of the subchapter. Occasionally I hear one of the homeless lying against the walls mumble something in their sleep, or snore. We pass through the alley where Mep and his followers tried to steal our stuff, and I look up at the window I clambered through what feels like years ago. Through the dark, I think I see the outline of legless Mep sitting on the sill, his arm raised, giving me a thumbs-up. I might be seeing things, but I return the gesture. Tawni gives me a questioning look but I just shake my head and picture Mep being carried back inside, where he'll read a story to the orphans huddled around him. The thought makes me happy and sad all at the same time. They're the ones we're fighting for. The unwanted orphans, the beggars in the streets, the wrongly convicted prisoners, the fathers working impossible hours in the mines, the mothers fighting like hell to turn a few potatoes and bags of beans into enough food to fill the bellies of their children: we're fighting for all of them. I feel adrenaline pump through my veins as I stride forward, following my mother, the warrior.

It's silent for a few more minutes until we pass by an open doorway in one of the buildings. Heavy music pumps through the opening and I can see bodies gyrating and writhing under crackling red and purple lights. One of them turns to watch us pass by, a genderless form with tattoos all over its face and a white-tipped Mohawk. Red lipstick stands out against its pale skin. Raising a single long-nailed finger, it motions for me to enter the building.

Holding my breath, I pass by the door quickly. Tawni's face is brimming with fear. I guess there's more than one dark side to the Star Realm.

Ten minutes later we reach the end of the subchapter buildings. A dark hole stands before us. "Do we have to go in there?" Tawni asks slowly.

"Unfortunately, yes," my mom replies. "The Star Realm tunnels are small and claustrophobic, but it's the only way to get where we're going."

"And where is that exactly?" I ask.

"The Resistance has maintained a train line hidden from the sun dwellers for many years. We need to access it."

"And we can't take a public train?" Tawni asks hopefully. She really doesn't want to go into that tunnel, not that I blame her.

"We can't risk it, especially after what the generals told us. There could be more spies that they don't even know about. If there was any other way, believe me, we'd take it."

"Let's get it over with," I say.

Mom nods and leads us into the tunnel, me then Tawni then Trevor, all of us stooping to avoid hitting our heads on the jagged rocks protruding from the ceiling. The walls close in on us immediately and I fight the urge to turn around and run out.

In ten minutes my back is aching from being hunched over and my arms and legs are scratched and bleeding from frequent accidental brushes against the rough walls. It's like everything in my life before this point—all the harsh living conditions, my time in the Pen, my harried escape through the Moon Realm—have been preparing me for this. I'm tough. I've been around the block. I can handle it.

An hour later I'm doubting myself.

"How much further?" I say, desperate for a chance to stretch out my back and legs.

"Not even close, honey," my mom says, somehow managing to sound like the kind and loving mother that she is, even under the harshest conditions.

"I don't know if I can do this," Tawni says behind me. She's a lot taller than me, which makes the hunching even worse. I realize this is a time when I'm going to need to be strong for her, another chance to pay her back for the strength she showed when Cole died, when I was at my lowest low.

"Yes you can, Tawni. You can do this. We all can. We all will. Let me know when you need a break, no matter how often, and we'll stop and try to stretch out."

I hear Trevor's voice carry from further back, agreeing with me. "We're all in this together." He sounds so supportive—nothing like the jerk I thought he was.

I hear her take a heavy breath out, and she says, "Okay. I'll do my best." We continue on, stopping almost every fifteen minutes to rest and so that Tawni—and all of us really—can lie down and stretch out our backs and legs. The splintered rocks on the tunnel floor dig into our skin, but none of us care—it's like a hardcore massage to us.

Perhaps two hours pass. The tunnel has been moving downwards the whole way, getting steeper and steeper with each step. The temperature has been rising, too, as if we really are descending into the bowels of hell. It certainly feels that way.

My body is dripping sweat from every pore, and the rock particles are clinging to my skin, making it appear gray and dusty. I start to feel faint as the heat feels like it gains another five degrees in an instant. "Mom?" I say.

"Almost there," she replies, reading my mind.

Two steps, three. Four, five. And then we stumble out of the tunnel, into a long cavern bursting with red light. I've never seen it before, but know exactly what it is, where we are.

"The lava flow," I murmur.

"One of many," Mom says.

There's a deep depression, brimming with flowing, churning viscous lava, crackling and popping with energy. The heat is stifling, pretty much unbearable.

I notice Tawni and Trevor stretching out and I follow their lead, touching my toes and twisting from side to side, trying to loosen out the crooks in my back. "Why are we here?" I ask.

Mom answers: "We knew the Sun Realm would never expect a hidden train line this close to the lava flow—nor would they want to come down here. It's very close to here."

She gives us a minute to finish stretching and pour delicious water over our lips and tongues, and then we must move on. Breathing is difficult in the oppressive heat as we pass the molten lava flow.

"How would you like to work down here?" Trevor asks.

"No thanks," Tawni says.

"People can't really work down here, can they?" I ask.

"They can, and they do," Trevor says. "My old man was a lava worker, hauling garbage from all across the Tri-Realms down to the flow, dumping it in, watching the flow devour it. He used to tell me stories about the stuff people from the Sun Realm would throw away. Stuff that we would kill for down here. Mountains of uneaten food, soft mattresses, furniture, all kinds of crap. He was under strict presidential orders that everything had to be destroyed, no exceptions. Those who were caught trying to forage through the garbage would have to pay the consequences."

"That's crazy," I say. "What were the consequences?" After my experiences with the Enforcers, I'm almost scared to ask.

"They didn't say. But this one time my dad gave in to temptation, came home with a beautiful new bed for my brother and me to share. When he gave it to us, he said, 'To hell with the rules.'" Trevor takes a deep breath. "He seemed so happy to give it to us, and honestly, I was so proud of my dad. He stood up for himself. The next day he didn't come home from work. We never saw him again."

My eyelids slowly close and I stumble when I step on a rock that rolls away under my feet. Trevor grabs my arm and steadies me. "Trevor, I'm sorry," I say, and this time he lets me say it, because I'm not really apologizing for anything, but showing him that I'm saddened by his story.

"It's okay. We got through it. We always do down here."

Supreme gratitude fills my chest as I realize how blessed I am that my entire family is still intact, regardless of all the bad stuff that's happened to us. *We are a blessed people.* I hear my father's words ring in my head, from a time long past.

We reach the end of the lava flow, where the reddish glow disappears beneath the rock, leaving us behind. The end of the cavern blocks our path. There's no tunnel here and I think my mom might have gotten confused, taken a wrong turn somewhere.

Before I can voice my question, she smiles and says, "Now we go up."

Tilting my head back, I gaze up along the pocked rock wall. Near the very top is a dark space, as if there's a hidden tunnel. You'd never even notice it unless you knew it was there.

"How do we get up?" Tawni asks, staring sharply at the thirty-foot wall.

I know the answer. "We climb," I say.

"Without ropes?" Tawni's eyes are worrying again. She's not the most coordinated and I can almost see the vision behind her eyes: her legs tangling as she falls away from the wall into the lava flow below.

I look at my mom, hoping she's got some brilliant—and safe—method of getting us to the top. "Without ropes," she confirms. "However, we'll tie ourselves together, so if one person falls, the others can try to keep them on the wall. Be vigilant with your hand- and footholds at all times and we'll get through this."

Tawni doesn't look convinced, but she seems better knowing she's not on her own. I put a hand on her shoulder comfortingly, and she manages an unnatural smile. "I guess the only way to conquer your fears is by facing them," she says, but I know she doesn't believe her own words.

"That's right," I lie.

We tie our packs tight around our shoulders until they bite into the skin under our arms. Then we tie our packs to each other's. It seems like a lame attempt at safety but I think we all feel better by doing it.

"This wall has plenty of good handholds," Mom says, "so don't settle for bad ones. Before moving up to the next one, make sure you're secure. We'll move up as a team. Ready?"

No one says anything, which she takes as a yes. She gets into position, reaching up for the first hold, a deep depression in the rock. And then she's up, born only by the strength and positioning of her own hands and feet on the wall.

I send Tawni up next, and despite her concerns, she seems to quickly get the hang of it, using her height to her advantage as she is able to access the best handholds simply by stretching herself out.

I'm third, and although I'm not afraid of heights, I feel a pang of fear thud in my chest. It's like I'm worried that after all I've been through, I might die because of a stupid wall—and it scares me. But I find my first handhold and manage to get up, pushing off with my legs. I don't see Trevor start climbing behind me, but know he's there because of the jostle of the ropes that connect us.

We move slowly upwards, like one organism, my mom as the head, Tawni the torso, and Trevor the legs. I guess that makes me the butt. One leg up, push off, reach with my arms,

298

grab a rock, raise the other leg, repeat. Again and again, until I know we're getting high. My heart continues to hammer in my chest and I fight the urge to look down. My palms are sweaty with exertion—and though I hate to admit it: fear.

I look up and see my mom clamber over the lip at the top, disappearing for a moment. Then her head appears, looking down at those of us still climbing. She offers a hand to Tawni, who takes it, allowing Mom to pull her up the final few feet. Finally, my heart rate slows. It wasn't so bad, after all. We're all going to make it.

You know how bad things tend to happen when you least expect them? Like right when a miner discovers a massive gemstone, and he's gawking at its beauty, that's when the roof collapses on his head. That's how it is now. I'm not paying attention and my foot isn't completely secure when I push off. I feel it slip off the edge and I wave my arms wildly, trying to find something to grab onto. Both hands find holds, but my sweaty fingers won't grip the slippery stone.

I fall.

I'm very high up and I fall.

I cry out and Trevor does, too. There's a twitch as the rope connecting me to Tawni tightens, and then I'm dangling in midair, swinging across the wall. I feel a jerk as my momentum wrenches Trevor off the wall, too, and now his full weight is pulling on my back.

Despite my better judgment, I look down. Below me is hell, frothing with fire and death. I gasp, let out a high-pitched shriek. Say something like, "Ohmygodohmygod!"

I hear my mom yell from above. "Reach for the wall—both of you!"

I look up and expect to see fear in her eyes, but instead there's a gritty determination as she hangs on to something I can't see. Tawni is also dangling precariously, barely clinging to the wall. My mom's holding all of us up.

I grit my teeth and reach out an uncertain foot to the wall, trying to stop us from swinging. As soon as my foot touches the wall, we start to spin, the rope twisting. It's disorienting and it takes all of my willpower not to look down again. "Trevor," I say, "reach for the wall on three."

"Okay!" he yells, his voice shaking.

"One!" I take a deep breath. "Two." My hearts slams against my ribcage. "Three!"

We both kick and scrabble and stretch for the wall at the same time. Our synchronized motion stabilizes the swinging, spinning rope for a moment, and I'm able to find a rock to grab on to. One of my feet finds a hold, too, and suddenly I'm back on the wall, secure, as if none of it ever happened. The only reminder is the sharp pain in my shoulders from having Trevor's weight pulling against the straps of my pack.

"Now climb!" my mother yells.

I don't look up, or down—just straight at the wall, focused.

"You can do it, Adele!" I hear Tawni yell from above. My trusted cheerleader has apparently made it. I push off once, twice, and then strong arms are pulling me over the top. My mother's arms. My rock.

I'm exhausted, but it's not time to rest yet. Immediately I turn and grab one of Trevor's arms as my mom grabs the other. We haul him up. The four of us lie in a row, panting, laughing stupidly, our tongues hanging out.

When I finally manage to push to my feet, I'm stunned by the sight before me. In the least likely of spots, there's a train, doors open and ready to whisk us away.

Finally, I'm going to see Tristan again.

And my family.

All together in one place for the first time.

Twenty-Four
Tristan

For once, I'm well rested. If I dreamt last night, I don't remember. The Resistance is situated so close to subchapter 1 that we're able to walk there. I feel like I'm at the head of a cavalry, me and Ben and Roc and Elsey, marching out in front of a few hundred stomping boots. Vice President Morgan left hours earlier to prepare for the peace summit in her subchapter. Jinny's here too, walking alongside Elsey, who is chatting with her like we're not heading to the most important meeting that the Tri-Realms has seen in a hundred years or more.

Naturally, my mind is on Adele. I wonder how she'll look. The last time I saw her, on the screen, she looked confident and beautiful, but that was before someone tried to kill her. Why would Brody do that? All we know is he was a spy for my father, but why target Adele? Is it because of who her parents are? Sort of a revenge for their efforts at resisting his rule? Or does he know what she means to me? Is he taking another shot at me? I remember his declaration from the presidential steps, when he was speaking to all traitors: *…brought down like a hammer on you and those you care about.* It felt like he was reaching through the telebox then, grabbing me by the collar and speaking those words directly to me. If he was targeting Adele because of me, he'll surely try again. When she arrives I'll stay by her side at all times just in case.

"Eww, gross," I hear Elsey say. It's about as relaxed a comment as I've ever her heard make, and I turn to see what has prompted it.

A bat lies twitching on the tunnel floor, injured, dying. For some reason I can't take my eyes off of it. A sense of dread enters my heart—like the dying bat is an omen, a sign of things to come. Not for us in general, but for me personally. One of the Resistance soldiers strides forward and stomps on the winged rat, and when he lifts his boot again, it is still. Dead. An omen, perhaps.

I look away and keep on walking. *You make your own fate.* My father's words, and yet they help to calm my troubled mind. Adele cannot die. I won't let her.

"What are you thinking?" Roc asks.

"Heavy stuff," I say.

"Thought so."

"Was it that obvious?"

"Only to a friend," he says, grinning.

I smile back, glad that he's here. "I'm worried my father will target Adele again, maybe as early as the peace summit." I told Roc what had happened before we slept last night.

"And Tawni, too?" he asks sharply, his brown eyes flitting back and forth like a caged animal. I keep forgetting he's got a crush on Tawni.

"I don't think so," I say. "I'm pretty sure she was just collateral damage. But if she's near Adele when he goes after her, Tawni could be in danger too."

"We can't let anything happen to either of them," Roc says firmly.

"We won't," I promise. "We won't leave their sides."

* * *

Less than an hour later we emerge from the tunnel and into subchapter 1. It's weird being out of the mysterious catacombs of the Resistance and back in a proper city. The last time I was in a moon dweller city it was subchapter 26, and the city was crumbling beneath the weight of the star dweller attack. I'm not sure what I expected, but it's not this. The city is untouched. Old and rundown, but not bombed, not full of smoking debris and rubble. Instead, it's just as I remember it from my last annual contract negotiation trip. The Water City, they call it, because it's literally built on an underground lake.

Heavy, stone blocks emerge from the water—which appears black in the early light of dawn provided by the overhead cavern lights—like majestic ships. The blocks are separated by thin canals, which run horizontally and vertically throughout the subchapter, intersecting like streets on a grid. Arcing stone bridges connect the stone blocks, on which the city is built. Compared to some of the towering buildings in other Moon Realm subchapters, the houses and buildings are built relatively low, rising two or three stories at the most. There is one exception, however, the massive dome in the city center, standing out like a beacon and dwarfing the other structures. They say you can see the subchapter 1 dome from anywhere in the city. It's code named the Big House—and is the site of the peace summit.

"At least they left us this," Ben says. My head jerks to look at him—I didn't realize he'd come up beside me. At the question in my eyes, he says, "It's the only subchapter the star dwellers didn't bomb. It's like they planned for us to meet here, almost wanted us to."

An eerie blast of cold air rushes through the enormous cavern and I shiver, both from the wind and from Ben's words. They don't give me comfort, not after everything that has happened.

We leave the edge of the city and tramp across the first bridge. On the other side a long thin boat is waiting. It might hold six or seven people—certainly not five hundred Resistance soldiers.

Ben shouts orders to a few of the soldiers behind us. Evidently they'll be taking the route on foot, through the city. We, on the other hand, are getting a lift. "Hop in," Ben says.

Roc gives Elsey a hand and helps her into the gondola. "Thank you, kind sir," she says, grinning.

"Be careful not to rock the boat, my dear lady," Roc mimics with his nose in the air, making Elsey giggle.

I follow my friends, sitting in front of them. The boat is so thin only one person can sit in each row. Ben and Jinny follow, and Ram stands in the center position, carrying an extraordinarily long stick, which he promptly uses to push off from the depths below. We shoot forward and I watch his technique as he shoves the staff hard into the water in front of us, lifting his body slightly to gain leverage before propelling us forward. He repeats this again and again, moving us swiftly toward our destination.

While the rest of the group are forced to twist and turn and cross dozens of bridges, we sail straight under them, reaching the city center in about ten minutes. Although I've seen what the locals simply call "the Dome" a half-dozen times before, I'm still not prepared for it as it looms up in front of us. The curved platelets that make up its exterior are a thin, shiny metal that manage to reflect even the dim light afforded to the subchapter, making the Dome appear bright and sparkling. From our vantage point in the canal, the result is dazzling, and I shield my eyes slightly with one hand.

We dock at a short platform and disembark, and strangely the gleam of the Dome dulls more and more the closer we get. The five or six sets of steps up to the entrance vanish beneath our feet in a blur. It's like just the sight of the Dome has given us a boost of energy, making our steps quick and light.

The inside of the Dome is just what you would expect from the outside. The massive stone roof curls upwards above us, reaches its apex, and then wraps back down, forming a semicircle that reminds me of half an orange, like my mom used to cut off the trees for Roc and me when we were little. Rows of steps wrap around the edges of the Dome, starting at the top and working their way down to the circular podium in the center. The space could easily seat fifty thousand people.

But today, there will be few. The forty-two moon dweller VPs; the leaders of the Resistance, like Ben and Jinny and Jonas and Maia and Ram; then there's me and Roc and Elsey and hopefully Adele and Tawni and Adele's mom—Anna, I remember—all surrounded by a few hundred Resistance soldiers providing protection for the whole event.

Already the VPs are milling around the center, shaking hands, talking and laughing as if this is just like any other gathering of Moon Realm leadership. You would never guess that the conclusion of the meeting could thrust the Realm into civil war, or worse.

As I'm still taking it all in, the Resistance soldiers arrive, pouring through the various entrances along the sides. They must have run to have made it here so fast.

"C'mon," Ben says, tugging me at the elbow. "We should get out of the way."

I resist, jerking my arm away. "But what about Adele? We need to be here when she arrives."

Ben looks at me with understanding eyes. "We *will* be here. Just below, in the private chambers. My men all know to send them down the moment they get here."

I look at Roc and he shrugs. "Okay," I say, moving to follow Ben.

We descend the steps as if we're going to join the VPs in the center platform, but then cut through an entrance to the seating area, tunneling beneath them. I know from my previous visits that there are dozens of rooms beneath the seats, where less public meetings are held amongst the politicians. It's dark, even though the lights are on, and I'm reminded of one of the more mundane reasons we're doing all this: My father refuses to provide adequate power to the lower Realms.

Not far down the hallway I can hear the murmur of soft voices. Soft orange light spills out into the tunnel. We make for the room—Ben enters first. "Vice President Morgan," he says.

"Hello, Ben," I hear her say.

We enter the space and I'm surprised to find a well-lit room with plush couches running along all four walls. There are only a handful of other people occupying them, including Morgan. I recognize them as a few of the other VPs who support the Resistance. They stare at us, hovering against the wall.

"Do you mind if my daughter joins us?" Ben asks politely.

"Of course," Morgan says. "I understand that you'll want to keep her close by your side during a time such as this."

"Thank you."

"Have a seat, everyone. We were just discussing the peace summit. Tristan, I'm glad to see you're here."

"I'm glad to be here," I hear my voice say automatically, but I'm not really thinking about my words. I'm thinking about how Ben is keeping Elsey close to him. He thinks something bad could happen. I've got to find Adele.

We sit down across from the other VPs and perpendicular to Morgan. "What's the situation?" Ben asks. "Do you have a sense of where the majority lies?"

Morgan shakes her head, but not because the answer is no. "We're still stuck at eighteen, Ben. Unless something changes drastically today, we're not going to get a majority for the cause."

Ben frowns, stares at the ceiling for a moment. I shift awkwardly in my chair. "Here's what we have to do. I'll speak to as many of the opposing VPs individually before the summit, see if I can sway them; I still have a few friends in high places," he says, winking at me. "Then we will start the conference with a speech from Tristan to do the right thing, to support an honorable cause, that sort of thing."

"But they haven't listened to me before," I blurt out. "Why now?" At that moment I feel a familiar buzzing along my scalp, and I gasp, but no one seems to notice.

"It's a one-two punch. They trust me a hell of a lot more than you, so if I set them up for your speech, it might change their reaction. If we're lucky we might grab the majority right from under their noses." *Yeah, we'd have to get pretty lucky*, I think, massaging my head as it continues to tingle.

"I don't know…" Morgan murmurs.

Before she can continue her thought, the door bursts open and Ram barges in. "I'm very sorry to interrupt," he says, "but they're here."

I freeze. *They? As in, her?* I'm on my feet in an instant, my chest buzzing with excitement, my mind racing, feeling more adrenaline than if I was in a swordfight. *She's here!*

I barely hear Ben say, "Just please set up the meetings, Morgan," before he sprints from the room, with me right behind him.

"They're in the first room to the right!" Ram growls after us.

Twenty-Five
Adele

The train ride was long and I didn't get nearly as much sleep as I would have liked, but still I feel wired. I've never been to the Water City before, and I'm taken by its beauty. And the Dome, which we've just entered, is the most beautiful of all.

I'm shocked by the buzz of activity inside. Men and woman are moving frantically about, dressed in dark-colored jumpsuits, some brown, some black, some gray. They're not uniforms, because, well, they're not *uniform*, but they look somewhat coordinated, like they're all on the same side.

The moment we enter I feel a shiver down my spine, although I'm not cold.

"The Resistance is here," my mom explains.

"What do we do?" I ask.

"Look for your father."

Dad! I think, as my head swivels through the crowd, trying to locate the grizzly man I left in subchapter 26.

"Excuse me," a woman says, approaching from the side, "do you need hel—" She stops suddenly, her eyes ablaze with recognition. "Ms. Rose?"

"Yes?" my mother and I reply simultaneously.

The woman looks back and forth between us. Initially her eyebrows lower in confusion, but then they slowly lift as understanding flows into her mind. "Anna and Adele," she says.

"And Tawni," my friend says.

"And Trevor," Trevor jokes. "I'll be down on the platform area making sure everything is ready." He walks off.

I laugh. "We're all here," I say. "Can you take us to my dad—I mean, to Ben Rose?"

"Of course, of course. Right this way."

Shivers of excitement are rippling through my body as we follow the woman down some stairs, into a darkened hallway, through an archway and into a room. "Just a moment, wait here," she says.

There are three beds and two benches. Tawni and my mother sit next to each other on one of the benches, facing the still-open door. I remain on my feet, unable to sit for fear that the energy coursing through me will be stifled.

A minute passes slowly. Then another.

311

Then he's there, the man from my childhood. Not the unkempt, unshaven, bloodied fighter from before, but the clean-cut, handsome man who raised me. I rush to him, but I'm too late. My mom is already in his arms, clutching him to her like releasing him would mean death for all of us. Over her shoulder his eyes are closed, his chin buried in her neck. I feel tears well up in my eyes.

As if by magic, Elsey appears at their side, hugging them both around the waist. My mom's arm curls around her and she says, "Oh, El. Sweet El."

The tears are bubbling up faster than I can blink them away. My mom's other arm reaches back blindly, beckons me into the fold. Two steps and I'm there, surrounded by the warmth of the family I love, the family who's been ripped apart, convicted, abused, battered—but not beaten. Never beaten.

And then, abruptly, the tears stop. I'm complete again so there's no need to cry. My body recognizes right away what my mind takes a few more seconds to understand. *I'm home.* Not at our puny house in subchapter 14, but in the place where home really lives. In the love of my family.

I pull away to see smiling faces, a circle of strength, of goodness, arms around each other protectively. I'll never lose these people again.

Someone clears their throat behind me. I strain my head backwards and my eyes lock on him, just like they did the first time, with the power of rock crushers, and bulldozers, and lava flows. My skull begins to ache from being near him. I wince, enjoying the throbbing in my head. The weird, mysterious, awesome pain. Not that long ago I wanted nothing more than to be rid of it. Now I live for it. But it dissipates in an instant, replaced with buzzing in my scalp and spine. In this moment,

Tristan's dark blue eyes are the most beautiful thing I've ever seen in my entire life. Perhaps it's just crazy hormones, or the emotion of the reunion with my family, or some force greater than any of that, but I feel a physical pull and I rush to him, slam into his chest, wrap my arms around his torso—feeling muscle and bone and *strength*—in his body and in mine.

His face is surprised, and I know I'm not acting like the timid girl who was scared to hold his hand from before. Because I'm not. I've stared down death in the barrel of a gun in my face. There are only so many moments in one's life, and then it's over. And I'm determined to make the most of every moment from here on out.

I don't wait for his chin to dip; rather, I lift up on my tiptoes and tilt my head back, jamming my lips to his. I don't know what the heck I'm doing, but I'm not thinking, not anymore. I'm not worried about whether this will be our last kiss, or one of many. I'm just acting, listening to my heart.

I must be doing something right, because his hand moves behind my head, sifts through my hair, pulls me in even closer, if that's possible. His lips are soft and tender and urgent as he moves them over mine. My mind is exploding and my heart is about to, but I keep kissing him, relishing every moment of pain until it vanishes as abruptly as it started.

Luckily, he has enough presence of mind to pull away from me, because I don't know if I can. It's a good thing for two reasons: One—I'm completely out of breath and I may have suffocated myself before I released us from the kiss; and two— my whole family is watching us, which is embarrassing regardless of the gravity of the situation. Elsey's beaming, my mother's smiling sheepishly, and my father's wearing something between a grin and a grimace. The only ones not watching: Roc and Tawni, who are sitting side by side on one of the beds, talking quietly and smiling at each other.

I turn back to Tristan, and, realizing my arms are still around his back and his around mine, I twist to the side and grudgingly release him, sliding my hand down his arm until it intertwines in his fingers. "Tristan, I'd like you to meet my mom, Anna," I say.

Mom steps forward and shakes his hand. "I'm so happy to finally meet you," Tristan says, and I know I'm beaming ridiculously, more like Elsey than myself, but I can't seem to stop.

"And you, Tristan," Mom says. "Thank you for everything you've done for my family, and what you're doing for the Tri-Realms."

Her words stir the last remaining bits of emotion out of me and I put my arm around her, pull her in close.

Dad says, "I've got to go meet with the VPs. Enjoy yourselves until I get back."

When the door closes I turn around to find Roc and Tawni back on the edge of one of the beds, whispering and laughing. It makes me smile.

Mom and Elsey are side by side on one of the other beds and Elsey's telling her some funny story, using her hands as much as her voice.

At the foot of the third bed, Tristan's watching me. The breath rushes from my lungs. I'd forgotten how handsome he is—seeing him through a video screen just doesn't do him justice. His blond waves seem to fall perfectly atop his head, framing a face so stoic and strong that it's almost as if he *is* a prince.

I go to him, sit down next to him on the bed. He takes my hand and I feel my heart rate increase as warm blood flows to my extremities. Bats flutter ceaselessly in my stomach.

"I'm so happy," Tristan says. It seems like such a funny thing to say considering we're still in the middle of a potential war of epic proportions, but when he says it I know I feel the same way. In fact, I feel like I've never been happier.

"I am, too," I admit.

He raises an eyebrow in a way that only looks cute on him. "What happened with Brody?" he asks, and my breath catches when I think he's talking about his attempted kiss. "I mean, why do you think he wanted to hurt you?"

I realize he's talking about the other K-word and I let out my breath slowly, trying to hide the fact that I was holding it. "I don't know for sure, but I'm pretty sure it was because we were going to come here, try to convince the moon dwellers to join the cause. Your father didn't want that, and since he was working for him, he acted to stop us."

"Oh," is all Tristan says, but I know there are deep thoughts behind the one-syllable word.

"Why do you ask?"

His shoulders slump forward and his expression darkens. "I think he's trying to get to me—trying to get me to give up."

"He's a fool for trying," I say.

Tristan shrugs. "I guess, but if anything ever happened to you, I don't know…"

"Promise me you'll keep fighting no matter what," I say.

Tristan looks into my eyes. I recognize the look because it's the same one he gave me just before he kissed and we parted ways in subchapter 26. The same look I probably gave him right before I rushed into his arms only a few minutes ago. My lips part slightly.

He leans in and kisses me, sending electricity through my lips and shivers down my spine. This time he doesn't pull my head in, he simply holds both of my hands, runs his fingertips along my skin, like he did when we fell asleep together on a night that now seems so long ago. Now that I know how good kissing can be, I wonder why I never tried it earlier. *Because I didn't know Tristan*, I think.

A thought pops into my mind that almost makes me laugh. *I guess it's official: we're girlfriend/boyfriend.* My mouth breaks into a smile while he's still kissing me, and he slides back to look at me. "I'm sorry, did I do something wrong?" His face is pale and worried, like he really thinks *he's* the problem.

"No…it's just—you're doing everything right."

Twenty-Six

Tristan

I'm crazy-over-the-moon-ecstatic right now. I'm hoping all the emotion of the last hour will help me give the speech of my life in just a few minutes. I mean, everything is going perfectly. After we kissed for the second time, we scooted back and sprawled out on the bed, my back against the wall and her head on my chest. We could see Adele's mom, but she pretty much ignored us, focusing her attention on her other daughter, whom she hasn't seen in months. And Roc seemed more than happy to be left alone with Tawni.

I told Adele about how Roc is my half-brother, and about what my father did. She asked if I was okay. I told her I am now. It was nice, just chatting with her and getting to know her. It almost seemed normal, like we were on a date, and not at some peace summit. But now Ben is back, which means the date's over.

"It's time," he says when he walks in. "Anna, can you take them to the platform?"

She nods and motions to us to follow her out the door. "Where will you be?" she asks.

"I'll be right behind you. There's just one more VP I want to speak to. Elsey can come with me."

Elsey beams with pride. She'll always be daddy's little girl.

Adele and I hold hands and follow her mom out the door. I flash Roc a grin when I see him take Tawni's hand and pull her along behind us. He gives me a sheepish grin in return, but behind it I can see how happy he is too. It feels weird that we're all so happy. Somehow it seems impossible. It's like the crumbling crest of a stone wave during a cave-in, and I'm just riding it down, hoping not to fall off.

My hands are sweaty with fear and expectation, but Adele doesn't seem to mind. She's filthy from her trip through the Star Realm, and yet I've never seen her more beautiful. She told me about how she almost fell while climbing the wall near the lava flow. I'm hoping it will be her last run of bad luck.

She also told me all about the treachery of this Brody guy, as well as the stranglehold my father has on the other star dweller generals. It only makes me hate him more.

Anna shows us the way out from the tunnel and down the inner Dome stairs, to the platform in the center. The bustle of activity has calmed significantly. The Resistance members are spread around the seating area, creating a thin barrier of protection. The VPs are seated in one quadrant, but in front of their protectors, in the first few rows. I'm glad they're not spread out because it means I won't have to turn in a circle to make eye contact with them.

Everyone stops talking when we enter. There's a pocket of folding chairs on the platform, at the end furthest from where the VPs are seated. We follow Anna to them and sit down, Anna, Adele, and I in the front, with Roc and Tawni behind us.

There's a guy with brown, curly hair to our right, next to Adele's mom. He's literally her right-hand man, I chuckle to myself. Adele gives me a funny look, but I wave off her question and stand up, move toward the guy. "Trevor, right?" I say, extending my hand.

"That's what my mother named me when the doctor slapped my pale butt," he says. He grips my hand tightly. "Are you for real?" he asks.

The question stumps me, but I answer any way. "I'm not a specter, if that's what you mean."

He laughs and releases my hand. "I just mean, are you really going to help us?"

Now it's my turn to laugh. "Yeah, I guess so. Is it that hard to believe?"

"Kind of," Trevor says. "I might have given Adele a hard time because of you. I didn't really trust you or her when we first met. Did she tell you about that?"

"No, but she told me you saved her life. And for that I must thank you." My hand is out again, and Trevor takes it.

"You're welcome. I'm glad I did."

When I turn and sit down next to Adele, she's smiling, having watched the entire thing with interest. "He gave you a hard time?" I whisper.

"I hated him," she says with a shrug. "But now I don't."

I don't have time to respond because Vice President Morgan is standing in the center, preparing to address the audience. "I know you have all been forced to thrust aside your plethora of other responsibilities to make time for this peace summit, but I can assure you, it is well worth your time. We have a grave responsibility to the people of the Moon and Star Realms, which, as you all know, are sometimes referred to as the Lower Realms.

"I know many of you are angry at what the Star Realm has done to your subchapter, wreaking havoc on your infrastructure and even causing the death of many of your citizens, and for that they should be sorry. However, there is a reason for all of that. I know many of you don't want to listen, want to say 'There's no excuse for their behavior!' but there is!" Morgan's voice has risen, echoing throughout the entire Dome. She's a mesmerizing figure even though we can only see the back of her head. She's going to be a hard act to follow.

"But it's not me that should tell you. It's Tristan, the son of the President, the one person who should be against the rebellion. Please give him a warm welcome."

Morgan swivels and sits down next to Trevor, leaving the round platform looking large and empty. I should be nervous, but I'm not. Adele gives my hand a final squeeze before I stand, and I take strength from it. If for no one else in the entire world, I'll do this for her, right now.

The applause is heavy from the upper rows, where the Resistance soldiers are seated, but more scattered from the VPs. It neither encourages nor bothers me though.

Then I'm in the center of the platform, although I can't remember my feet carrying me there. I scan the audience, making eye contact with as many people as possible before I begin. I've planned it out in my head: All *do the right thing* and *unite the people* and *rebellion, ra ra ra!* but that's not what comes out when I begin speaking.

"My father raped and murdered my best friend's mother," I say. A few gasps and loads of murmurs fall over the crowd. Ignore them and continue. "I just found that out. He told me and my friend himself. That's the kind of man who's leading the Tri-Realms. He also gave the star dwellers the money to buy the bombs that destroyed your cities. Oh, and he's holding the star dweller generals' families under a knife so they'll do what he wants. That's the kind of man you're protecting by not supporting this rebellion. That's all I have to say."

Although my brain is telling me it's too soon to end my big speech-to-end-all-speeches, my heart moves me across the stand, where I sit down next to Adele, who immediately takes my hand. I look at my feet for a few seconds, and then twist to glance at Roc. I hope he'll forgive me for what I've done.

He's smiling.

Of all the expressions I imagined his face might have, a smile was not one of them. He reaches over and slaps my shoulder. "Well done," he says.

Adele kisses me on the cheek, leaving a spot of warmth that lingers well after her lips leave my skin.

Morgan seems so surprised at the brevity of my remarks that she's unsure of what to do. The audience is restless, whispering to each other and coughing and shuffling their feet. *Oops*, I think. Perhaps I should have stuck with the planned speech.

But Morgan has experience with unexpected situations and she's quickly back on her feet, raising and lowering her hands to quiet the crowd. "We have much to discuss, questions to ask and answer, and details to work out, but first, I'd like to take an initial vote to see where we stand."

I look around for Ben, but he and Elsey are still not back, which is strange because all the VPs are now in attendance.

I watch as each of the VPs writes something on a piece of paper and then passes it across the row, to where someone collects them before bringing them forward to Morgan in a basket. It seems old-fashioned, but effective. Morgan extracts the first ballot. "Yes, in support of the rebellion," she reads, and my heart lifts an inch in my chest. The ballot drops from her hand and flutters to her feet, discarded. "One in favor, zero against."

She reads the next one. "Yes. Two in favor, zero against." My heart is in my throat. I want to rush the stage and grab the basket and frantically read the rest of them. Morgan's slow and methodical pace is killing me. I think Adele's thinking the same thing, because she's squeezing my hand so hard it's getting sore.

"No," she reads, and my heart sinks a little. "Two for, one against." There are still thirty-nine ballots and I'm living and dying by each individual one she reads. I try to relax.

"No," she says. "Two for, two against."

The next six are all against the rebellion. I'm no longer holding Adele's hand, and my head is resting in my hands as I balance my elbows on my knees. "Two for, eight against," Morgan says. Despite Ben's efforts with the VPs and my pitiful speech, we're still way behind, not even close to garnering a majority. These men and women are still too scared of my father to stand up to him.

But then it happens. The tide turns, almost as if by magic. First Morgan says yes once, then twice, and then it's like that's the only word she can say. By the time she's done, it's thirty-two for and ten against. I hug Adele and she hugs back. Anna is looking at us both and shaking her head in disbelief, like she's seen everything in her lifetime but not something like this.

For the first time since this all started, I actually truly believe the Lower Realms can be united in a joint cause. With a little bit of pressure, we could possibly get the other ten VPs to change their mind, to support the rebellion. If we could just explain—

A screen emerges from the platform floor, rising up next to Vice President Morgan like a phantom in the night.

From the look on her face, I know she's not expecting it.

"What is the meaning of—" she starts to say, but then the screen flashes and she gasps, along with nearly everyone else in the audience, myself included.

"No!" I hear Adele croak, the word rough and jagged in her throat.

The whole world spins upside down as I stare at that screen. Ben and Elsey are each tied to a chair, their hands behind their backs, their mouths gagged with thick black cloth.

A man, dressed in sun dweller red, holds a gun to Ben's head.

I know he's going to kill them, and all I want to do is scream *I'm here, Father, I'm here! Please, take me, not them.* But when I try to speak all that comes out are ragged breaths.

Adele is already on her feet when the voice booms through the speaker.

Adele

I'm scared but it's nothing compared to the determination I feel coursing through my blood. I will not let them kill my family, not after I've worked so hard to bring them all back together. I'm on my feet, prepared to charge through the Dome, rip the place apart stone by stone until I find them, when a voice thunders through the arena.

"Your traitorous ways are punishable by death and death alone!" the President threatens. I'd know his voice anywhere.

I hear the slam of doors and then a cacophony of marching boots fills the Dome, cutting through the air like bullets. Above us, dozens of sun dweller soldiers, decked in polished red uniforms—they look like the same ones we saw in the tunnels on the way to the Star Realm—point gleaming rifles and pistols over the edge of the topmost seats.

The Resistance soldiers are on their feet, aiming their own weapons upwards, but everyone in the room knows they don't stand a chance. The sun dwellers have the upper ground, the better weapons, the element of surprise. We're sitting ducks.

"Don't move!" the voice booms. "We have you surrounded. There is no chance of escape. You have all been found guilty of high treason and should be executed in accordance with the laws of the Tri-Realm."

I close my eyes. *We're all going to die.*

"However..." Nailin says, and my eyes flutter open. "...I am offering you one chance to avoid death. Lay down your weapons, allow yourselves to be taken prisoner, and watch the execution of the real traitor, Ben Rose, and his daughter…and I *will* consider a lesser sentence."

What? No! "No!" I scream. "You can't do that!"

All eyes are on me but I don't care. Tristan tries to put a hand on my arm, but I rip it away from him, charge from the platform. The bullets start flying, but not at me. The Resistance soldiers are firing at the sun dwellers! They're not going to give up either. They're fighting!

I see my mom pull a pistol from beneath her tunic and start shooting at the sun dwellers. One drops, and then another. She reminds me now of the day the Enforcers took her away. A fighter—a force to be reckoned with. My mother.

The sun dwellers fire back and I see soldiers dropping amidst bursts of red. In my heart I'm sorry for them and scared for my mom, who's still on her feet, but there's only one thing on my mind: Save my dad, my sister.

*   *   *

Tristan

I sprint after her, but the wings of angels seem to carry her away from me. The crack of guns going off all around us reminds me of when the sun dweller army used to train in the fields by our house. Except this is not training. They want to kill every last one of us.

Adele is already up the steps. She turns quickly and yells to those on the platform to "Run!" but she doesn't have to tell them—they're already on their feet and heading for the nearest exit.

And then I see it. A sun dweller soldier—his gun aimed from above, right at Adele. I'm too far—I won't make it; and he won't miss. It's over.

A body flies from the side, violently smashing into her and flattening her against the steps. She cries out in pain just as the bullet takes a chunk of the seats behind her.

It's Trevor. He's saved her again. Has done what I could not do.

I run toward them, but she's already pushing up, bucking Trevor off of her as if he weighs nothing. She doesn't thank him, doesn't even look at him, keeps moving up the steps.

Just before she ducks into the tunnel beneath the seats, I see her pull a gun from under her tunic. *Where did she get a gun?* I wonder.

When I reach the steps I take a moment to scan my surroundings, ensuring none of the sun dwellers are making a move to follow Adele. Trevor gets back to his feet and hurriedly follows Adele into the tunnel, and I'm about to follow when I see Ram, standing out in the crowd, dark and bulging with strength. But all the strength in the Tri-Realms won't save him from hot metal bullets. He's pinned down behind a row of seats, with three sun dwellers peppering shots at him. He's trying to hold them off by taking blind shots with his pistol, but he's not even aiming in the right direction. He'll die if I don't do something.

I take five long strides and then roll, grabbing a gun left by a dead Resistance soldier, and feeling the whiz of bullets as one of the enemy combatants tries to take me down. But I know they can't hit me. I'm too fast, too determined. Coming out of the roll, every bit of my training kicks in. I lock on the first target in less than a second, shoot him somewhere he won't get up from. But I don't watch him fall; instead, I swing to the next enemy, who falls when I pull the trigger. The third one has realized I'm targeting the ones shooting at Ram and he ducks before I can get him.

I curse and rush to Ram, who's watching me with a funny expression on his big face.

"You saved me," he says.

"Yeah, yeah," I say. "Get back to the main body of men. Take this," I say, handing him the rifle. I don't hear if he responds because I'm off, sprinting to the steps, taking them two at a time, hoping I don't get shot. As I approach the top I see two forms moving swiftly toward me across one of the rows.

I swing to the side, tensing myself for a fight, but drop my hands when I see that it's Roc and Tawni, eyes wide but fierce and determined. I don't question their presence—I just say, "Hurry!" and sprint into the gloomy hallway. Adele and Trevor are already halfway down the curve of the tunnel, running hard, Adele holding the gun out in front of her like she actually knows what to do with it. Maybe she does. She seems to know how to do everything. Gritting my teeth, I give chase, hoping to catch her before she runs into half the sun dweller army.

I can feel Roc and Tawni just behind me, moving on silent feet.

I know something isn't right when we make it a quarter of the way around the Dome without resistance. The place should be teeming with sun dwellers, but instead, all the action seems to be out on the platform. It's almost as if my father wanted us to go this way, to make it this far. The thought sits in the pit of my stomach like a rotten egg. The crack and pop of guns provides a symphony for the slap of our feet on the stone. I catch up to her five steps later, grab her shoulder. "Adele, wait," I say.

She whirls around, levels the gun at my head. Her eyes are wild and her hands shaking. She lowers the gun. "Tristan, I'm sorry. I didn't realize."

"Welcome to the party," Trevor says from the side.

"Where are they?" Roc says, coming up behind us.

"They have to be in one of these rooms. C'mon," I say, grabbing Adele's arm and ushering her forward. We've already passed dozens of open doors, all clearly empty, so we slow as we approach the first closed door we've come across.

"Shh," I say, tiptoeing in. *One, two, three*, I mouth, slamming my shoulder into the door and entering side by side with Adele, the others looking over our shoulders. It's dark and we can't see or hear a thing. "Wrong room," I say.

We leave quickly and continue our search. Another quarter of the way around, we hear voices and as we come around the bend we see five star dweller soldiers come into view.

They raise their rifles.

* * *

Adele

The adrenaline is dictating my every move. When they point their guns at us I don't hesitate, shoving Tristan hard against the wall, my body flush with his, just as we hear the crack and resulting zing of energy as the bullets fly past. Across from us, Trevor, Roc, and Tawni have managed to do the same. We rebound off the wall in one motion, Tristan and I, charging down the tunnel as the soldiers release their expended shells, readying themselves to shoot again.

But they're too late. I'm too close and my arm is already up, my aim zeroing in on one of the soldier's chests. Of all people's, it's Brody's voice that pops into my head: *Hold it slightly lower than the target you're aiming at. Keep it steady, because when you pull the trigger, it's going to squirm.* I lower my arm slightly, tighten my grip, and fire. The guy jerks back as the bullet slams into the same shoulder he was using to lift his gun. He's thrown back into his partner, whose gun is knocked aside by his flailing arms.

Beside us, Trevor shoots two of the soldiers in quick succession, while Roc comes flying in with an elbow, crashing into the last one.

Neither of the ones I hit is dead and all I want to do is kill them. I stand over their sprawled-out forms, my knuckles white on the gun, my finger tense on the trigger. Their hands are over their heads, pleading, but that just makes me want to pull the trigger more. "No, Adele," Tristan says.

"It's what they deserve," I growl.

"I know, but not like this. You can't go back from this."

I know he's right, but maybe I don't want to go back. My teeth are grinding against each other, my breaths sharp and animal-like through them, whistling slightly. The only thing steady are my hands, holding death over these fools like an executioner holding a guillotine. "We need to keep moving, find your dad and sister," Tristan says.

My head snaps toward him and I forget about these guys. All that matters is my family. I lower the gun. Tristan kicks each of the guys in the head and they slump over, unconscious.

Roc is grappling for the last guy's gun, but Trevor puts an end to it with a boot of his own to the guy's noggin.

We move forward.

Soon we hear voices, muffled at first, but then louder as we approach an open doorway. Light spills from the room and we hear a woman say, "Should I kill them now?"

Which means they're still alive. Every cell in my body is suddenly alive with energy, urging me forward.

We hear the crackle of the reply over the walkie talkie. "Yes, kill them now," President Nailin says.

I charge into the room, not waiting for my friends, and this time I'm not taking prisoners. The first thing I see is my dad, struggling against his bindings, his eyes fierce and steely. All he wants is to save Elsey, who is beside him, her face as white as a sheet, all childish dreams about to be torn away from her. A woman in a red uniform has a radio to her lips, but when she sees me she lowers it.

I shoot her point blank in the chest and she topples to the floor.

Two big soldiers close from either side, grabbing at my arm that's holding the gun. But then Tristan is there, his fist slamming into the left guy's skull and sending him flying. As he grapples with the other guy, I break free and charge toward my dad. His executioner stares at me as I approach, but I'm not looking at him. All I see are my dad's eyes, my eyes reflected back at me, green and full of life and loving and kind and—

Boom!

The sound is deafening but I barely hear it. I'm choking on my own sobs, but still moving forward as my father slumps to the ground, the light in his eyes extinguished. I'm crying and growling and screaming and shooting—one round, two rounds, three, four, and then I lose count when the gun starts clicking as I use every last bullet.

The executioner is full of holes, spotting red, falling to the ground like my dad, but he manages to shoot again in desperation. *God no!* I'm praying and willing and trying to use my mind to protect her, but I can't do a damn thing.

The bullet tears into Elsey's side, and I hear her scream and see the slick red of blood on her skin before I black out from anguish and exhaustion.

Twenty-Seven
Tristan

The world is black, but when I open my eyes all I see is white, the underside of my sheets. Flickering orange light dances through the thin fabric. I have no words to say to her; I have no words to say to anyone.

I pull the covers tighter around me, like a cocoon. Inside I feel safe. Outside is only death and pain and a black, black world. A world created by my father.

Anger plumes within in me, hot and gritty. My fists tighten, my knuckles turning as white as the sheets. I close my eyes, trying to control the fire building within me.

After all, Adele needs me now more than ever. Breathe. Breathe, breathe, breathe.

As the fogginess of sleep clouds my mind, my last thought is:

Adele first, revenge second.

* * *

Adele

Waking and sleeping are the same to me, a swirl of confusing madness, one disorienting and dizzying blur of time where my face is always wet, my nightmares are constant, and spots of red flash before my vision, whether I'm awake or not.

My muscles ache and my head is throbbing, but those pains are minor compared to the ache in my chest. The awful, awful ache in my heart, where it's split in two, rattling around. I can almost hear it clanging around in there.

I'm broken.

And I may never be fixed again.

I slip into another fitful sleep. Or perhaps I've just woken up from a nightmare. It doesn't seem to matter anymore.

Twenty-Eight
Adele

Everyone dies sometime. You would think that would make it easier when you lose someone, but it doesn't. As I lie in bed I let the tears flow freely. I'm not ashamed of them. I'd cry a thousand more if I could, but eventually I'm all cried out and I just roll over and jam my face between my two pillows.

They say his death was instantaneous, that he didn't feel any pain. A single gunshot to the head. *There's nothing you could do*, they said to try to make me feel better. But that's not the point. The point is he's dead and I'll never see him again, never hug him again, never learn from him again.

They say it's a miracle that Elsey survived. The bullet hit her elbow, shattering it and deflecting before tearing into her ribcage, narrowly missing a handful of vital organs. They could save her, but not her arm. Now she has to learn to do everything with her left hand.

After surviving the Pen, being pursued by Rivet, watching cities being bombed, trekking through the Star Realm, I thought I had proved I didn't have a breaking point. I was wrong. Everyone has a breaking point. This is mine. The world is dead to me. All that I cared about. All that I loved. Ripped away from me. Wrenched from my shaking hands.

Tristan is here and I know I should talk to him. I haven't said a word since it all happened. Not to him; not to my mother. Elsey's still too unwell for visitors, not even family.

But still Tristan comes every day, sits on my bed, talks to me. Lies to me and tells me everything's going to be okay, even though we both know it's not.

He told me all about what happened afterwards. How the Resistance somehow managed to kill enough of the sun dweller troops to overwhelm them, eventually driving them away. How they fought like wild animals, with tenacity and heart. How they found us clinging together, amidst the dead, me and Elsey, my teeth chattering as I rocked her back and forth while Tristan used his tunic to put pressure on her gunshot wound. Roc and Tawni, of all people, stood guard over us while Trevor ran to get help. I don't remember any of that. Although I was apparently conscious for it, my subconscious protected me from the memory.

His father was never there, was just a voice through a speaker. A madman using his pawns to do his bidding.

He sits on my bed, in his normal spot, rests a gentle hand on my shoulder. "I'm here, Adele," he says.

A day earlier his touch would have sent tendrils of excitement all through me, but now, it's just a touch, cold and meaningless.

Finally, I break my silence, although the words come from a new Adele. The old Adele is gone, dead. "I'm toxic, Tristan. Everything and everyone that gets close to me dies. First Cole, now Dad. Stay away from me. STAY AWAY!" My body's trembling and my fists are ready for a fight, against whoever is in my way, Tristan or his father or whoever.

But he doesn't leave like I expect him to, like he *should* do. He stays right there, grabs my hands, pries my claw-like fingers apart. I've got nothing left. No fight. My body goes slack and I fall apart in his arms as he holds me, rubs his hands along my back. He doesn't try to soothe me with words or shush my tortured sobs, just lets me get it all out.

I need something to take the pain away. Just for a minute, a second. My lips find his and I kiss him hard, then harder, practically throwing myself at him. He lets me at first, but then pulls away while still hugging me. "Not this way," he says. "We need to give it some time."

I'm glad he's still thinking clearly.

* * *

The next day I finally go to visit Elsey, who is recovering. With each step I take my heart is breaking. It's like despite everything I've been through, I can't bear one more tragedy. Tristan holds my hand to make it easier. It's strange, how different it is holding his hand now from the first time. I mean, I still get the

336

tingles, the tiny bursts of electricity up my forearm, but now it feels so normal, so safe, like we've been holding hands for a million years plus a million more. I like the subtle change.

But the strength of the magnetic pull I feel toward him has not subsided whatsoever. When he is near I can always feel him on my skin, in my bones, particularly around my head and down my back. It's the weirdest thing.

We enter a dim room—only a clouded lantern provides a soft glow. We see the thin outline of my mother, sitting on a bed, looking down at a bump under the covers. Tristan releases my hand and I kneel next to her, gaze at the pale face of my sister, who's sleeping. She almost looks dead and for a moment I think she might be, but then I see the gentle rise and fall of her chest as she breathes.

"How is she?" I breathe.

My mom has one hand on my sister, and now she places the other on my shoulder. "She's a little trooper, hanging in there. She can barely eat because she just throws it back up. The trauma of it all is affecting her entire body. But she's so positive about everything, it's hard to keep her down."

I manage a smile. That's my sister—a little firecracker. Even with the covers over her, I can tell she's lost weight. Weight she doesn't have to lose.

"How's she taking…"—my voice catches in my throat and I swallow—"Dad?"

Mom's eyes are misty but she doesn't cry. She's tough—like I used to be. "You'll have to ask her that, but I think she's handling it better than you or I."

I nod. "Do you think he's still somewhere?" I ask, surprising myself, because I didn't even realize the question was on my mind.

"Elsey does," she says. "I think that's one of the reasons she's handling it so well."

"Yeah, but do you?"

She tilts her head to the side and chews on the side of her mouth, like she's really giving my question some serious thought. "You know, I want to believe it and sometimes I do, because I can still remember him, can still feel him here"—she motions to her heart—"but other times I just feel this void and it's as if he's disappeared from within the caverns of the earth."

I nod. I appreciate her honesty. She's treating me like an adult.

Elsey stirs in her bed, yawns, and then her eyes blink open. "Hi, Adele!" Although her voice is weak, there's a certain energy in it, but the same energy doesn't make it to her face, which is ashen. She looks so pale she almost appears dead, if not for her half-open eyes and limp smile.

"Hey, El," I say, trying to keep my voice steady and the waiting tears from my eyes. "How are you feeling?"

"Like I just lost an arm," she says, smiling weakly.

I bite my lip, wishing I could laugh, if only to make her happy. Underneath the covers it's easy to forget that she's not whole anymore.

"It's okay, Adele," she says, acting the role of the big sister, as usual. "I survived. Because of you."

Despite my efforts, a tear rolls down my cheek, stinging my skin. "But you lost…and Dad is…." I can't get the words out, even now.

"I'm fine," she says, sticking her jaw out. "And Dad is…in a better place. Away from all the bad people." *Away from all the good people, too*, I want to say, but I don't. How can she be so strong when she's the one who lost an arm *and* a father? Why do I feel so weak? I try to think about my sister's words, try to take strength from them, like she does. *Dad is in a better place.* Is it true? Is he somewhere, his soul flying high, away from his broken body, away from the turmoil and strife of the Tri-Realms? Is he on Earth, aboveground, seeing the real moon and real sun and real stars for the first time, feeling the wind through his hair, the sunlight on his skin, the rain on his face? Maybe he is. Who am I to say Elsey is wrong? Warmth suddenly fills my chest and I know I'll get through this, just like all the bad times before. It's not about what I don't have, it's about what I do. My mom. My sister. Tristan. Tawni and Roc and even Trevor. Family and friends—that's all I'll ever need.

* * *

The funeral is a blur of tears and speeches and emotions and I don't remember any of it when it's over. As is the custom of the moon dwellers, they cremate him, which is good because I couldn't have handled seeing his face again, not like that. I prefer to remember him as the man who showed me how to kick and punch on our back patio.

Tristan's been following the news but I've stayed away from it. I'm just not that concerned with politics and rebellions and wars at the moment. I'm just trying to spend as much time with my family as possible. Half the moon dweller VPs are dead, but a vote will be held in a week's time to replace them. After everything that's happened, everyone's expecting that once the new leaders are elected, the VPs will unanimously vote to unite with the Star Realm and support the rebellion. Evidently the Sun Realm has already officially declared war on us, which I'm not too surprised about. Tristan tells me that people are saying the first battle could occur in as soon as a week's time.

My mother asked for and was granted a couple of days off, and she wants to use it to visit our old subchapter, 14. Elsey is still too unwell to travel with us, but Roc and Tawni agreed to keep her company while we're away. Tristan insisted on coming. He seems afraid to leave my side, maybe ever again, which is cute. Despite his good intentions, however, Mom said we needed to do this alone, and after much discussion and debate, he conceded, promising to tear the Moon Realm apart looking for us if we don't return within two days. I thought it a bad time to remind him that the Moon Realm is already torn apart, so I just agreed with him.

Although the train ride only takes half a day and we arrive in the afternoon, the lights are off in the big cavern I used to call home. The sun dwellers have cut off all electricity to the Lower Realms and for now we have to use flashlights and lanterns until the Moon Realm engineers come up with a solution to the problem.

As we walk through the city, the beams from our bouncing and bobbing flashlights reveal the destruction that took place a lifetime ago. Memories of the explosions as we climbed the fence to escape from prison flash through my mind like a slideshow. Buildings crumbling, cracks in the streets, the toppling of the fence. All distant memories now.

We pass a number of work crews, busily repairing the damage. They stare at us as we pass, and while outwardly they look haggard, tired, I see the fire of determination in their eyes. These are the men and women who will rebuild and then go to war for their very survival, and for the survival of their families.

The houses in our old suburb didn't fare much better than the city. Many of them have shattered windows and crumbling roofs. Some even have gaping holes in their sides which allow us to see inside. I'm surprised to find entire families inside, sitting down to have a meal together, to play games together, to simply be together.

"They can break our things, can break our bodies, but they can't break our spirits," my mother says.

I feel a shot of heat in my belly, as if a match has been lit within my gut.

We reach our house, which is in shambles, the entire front wall caved in. As we step over the threshold, I can't help but feel a twinge of pain as I remember the way my father used to look when he came through the door after work, tired but happy. We'd run to him, Elsey and I, and hug him.

When I lean against the wall, shocked by what I see, a memory is unlocked from some safe deposit box in my head, more vivid than if I was living it right now.

I'm ten years old and it's my birthday, but it's just like any other day. My dad wakes me up at six in the morning for training. It's still dark in the caverns, although even at midday, the thin, pale lighting from the overhead cavern lights is dim at best. We train on the tiny stone patio behind our shoebox house. My mom is already up and getting breakfast ready, but she doesn't say anything as I pass her. She does glance at me, however, and I can tell from the slight curl on one side of her lip that she knows it's my birthday and wants to surprise me. I pretend not to notice.

My dad is already outside, stretching his arms and legs. I follow his lead, because if I don't, I'll be sore tomorrow. As I stretch my arms above my head, I see the glittering flutter of wings as a bat slides noiselessly above us. The rough, gray cave ceiling is slowly coming into focus as the cavern lights begin to brighten right on schedule.

We start with hand-to-hand combat—my favorite—and, according to my dad, the most important part of training, because "you can always count on your own hands and feet," as he likes to say. I'm feeling energetic, which I try to use to my advantage, striking quickly with sharp stabs of my feet. But my dad is always up to the task, faster than me, blocking each attack with ease. Even when I start inventing my own moves, my dad just swats away my roundhouse kicks and judo chops like pesky gnats. He says my invented moves are creative and effective, although they never seem to work on him.

It gets frustrating sometimes, not being able to beat him, especially considering how hard I work. He says he pushes me harder than Elsey because I'm the older sister, and I can protect myself *and* her. That just seems like a free pass for El. He also says I'm getting stronger and faster with each training session, which sometimes is the only thing that keeps me motivated.

So I keep at it, chucking fists and feet at him faster and faster, until a thin sheen of salty sweat is coating my bare arms and legs, where my pale blue tunic won't cover. As I begin to tire, I become bolder, lunging forward and aiming a knotted fist at his sternum, at one of the places that he told me will hurt the most. To my absolute shock, my clenched fingers slide smoothly past my dad's blocking arms, connecting with his chest, and I feel the solid *thud* of bone on bone and muscle.

My dad grunts and lifts a hand to his chest, massaging it gingerly. I can't help but to lift my offending hand to my mouth as my lips form an O. "Dad, I'm so…I'm sorry. I didn't mean to—"

My dad laughs and I stop talking, my eyebrows rising along with my confusion. "Don't ever apologize for winning a fight, Adele," he says.

"Wha…what? You mean I…?"

"Won—yes." My dad is grinning. "You are learning so fast, Adele. In a couple of years I will have nothing left to teach you."

"So the student will become the master?" I joke. I am such a dork—but I don't care.

He laughs, deep and throaty. "I wouldn't go quite that far, but yes, you are doing well." Sometimes Dad can be so serious.

But I am grinning, too. I've never even come close to hurting him during training. The familiar rhythm of my hands and fists smacking against his hands and fists has become like a soundtrack for our mornings together. But I've added a *thud* to the mix, and for that, I am proud. I couldn't ask for a better present on my birthday.

"We'll finish early to celebrate your success," my dad says.

I frown. "No, Dad, I want to finish the whole session, please."

Dad laughs. "That's my girl," he says. "You're so much like your mother." I never understand what he means by that. My mom is a quiet, generous soul who would never hurt a fly. Me, I'm tenacious, feisty, and sarcastic. A redhead with black hair, my mom always says.

I'm not able to beat him again during training, but once was enough for me. When we come inside I'm exhausted but happy. Somehow our tiny stone house looks even smaller than before, but to me it's cozy, it's home.

A warm and tempting aroma fills my nostrils when we cross the threshold. My birthday surprise. Freshly warmed bread, not more than a few days old, from the bakery in the subchapter. Only half a loaf, but more than I've ever seen in our house before. A real birthday treat.

"Happy birthday, Adele," Mom says. "Go wake your sister."

I smile and sigh. Yes, we live underground. And don't have much money. And live in constant fear of the Enforcers, who ceaselessly roam the streets. But we have each other: my mom, my dad, my sister, Elsey, and me—a family. We're all we really need. Oh, and a warm half-loaf of bread for a birthday treat. For a moment, I am happy.

"Adele," my mom says, and the memory fades. Remembering my father, how things used to be, makes the flame that started in my belly flare up, heating my chest. It's a fire I haven't felt in a while. "Are you okay?"

I shake my head and the cobwebs disappear. "Yeah. I was just remembering."

"Your father?"

"And you," I say. "All of us. Before…"

"I know. This place is so full of memories. That's why I wanted to come here one more time."

My mom moves away from me, rummaging through the rubble, looking at old pictures and trinkets. I watch her for a minute.

When she turns around, there's a sparkle in her eyes. "There's something I want to give you."

I raise my eyebrows. "Give me? Mom, I just need you."

"Just follow me." She walks the three steps across the living area to the door to the bedroom that my sister and I shared with my parents. The door is hanging by a single hinge. My mom pushes it aside and enters. When I slip in behind her, I'm

344

surprised to find the bedroom mostly intact, although there is glass everywhere from the shattered window.

Using the hem of her tunic, Mom brushes the glass from atop the bed and motions for me to sit down. I do, wondering what in the Tri-Realms she could possibly want to give to me. I watch her while she scans the ground, as if looking for something she dropped, and then bends down. She uses her fingers to pry at a loose stone in the floor, which wobbles and then lifts. The gray rectangular rock is heavy and I see her straining at it, so I get up and help her lift it out and roll it to the side.

Beneath where the stone used to be is a wooden box. When I look at my mom, she offers me a slight smile and then reaches down to retrieve the chest. It's small and looks like it couldn't hold more than a few marbles at most. However, when she lifts the lid, I see a slight sparkle under the glow of the flashlight I'm holding. Using a single delicate finger, she lifts a necklace from the box. I gasp. Its band is thin and silver, polished and gleaming and well cared for, but that's not what makes me gasp, nor is that what sparkled when she first opened it.

Dangling from the end is a gem, big, perhaps the size of a gold Nailin, beautifully cut and a brilliant green hue that seems to catch every bit of light offered and then shine it all back tenfold in a dazzling array of green slivers. An emerald.

"Mom, I...I don't understand. Whose is this?"

"It's yours now," she says, handing it to me.

"But this must be worth hundreds—no, thousands—of Nailins. Where did you get this?"

Mom's smile is almost as brilliant as the emerald I'm holding. "It was your father's gift to me after you were born. I

345

don't know where he got it and I didn't ask. When he saw those emerald-green eyes of yours, he just knew you were going to be something special, so he gave me this necklace as a keepsake, something for me to pass down to you."

My eyes are watering. "But this is too much. I can't accept this," I say, knowing that I will.

Twenty-Nine
Tristan

While Adele is away with her mother I worry about her. Not because she's not capable of taking care of herself—I'd have to be an idiot if I didn't know that she was by now—but because there's some truth to what she said to me earlier. Awfulness does seem to follow her around. But I guess these days terrible things are happening to everyone.

I also feel somewhat lonely because she's not here. Trying to kill time, I rummage through my pack, organizing my stuff. As I toss out a few bags of dried meat and a dirty tunic, my hand brushes against something hard. *The diary.* Ben's diary. Well, not his diary, but the one he let me borrow. I never gave it back. And now he's gone. As I flip through the brittle time-yellowed pages, I remember him. His calm, solid demeanor; the ever-present twinkle in his trustworthy eyes; his rare combination of optimism and realism: he was a good guy. The best kind of guy. A friend, in the end.

He deserves some words from me. Something to honor him.

"Ben," I say, glancing uncertainly at the cave roof, as if he's above it somewhere, "I wish you were still here. You were...you were everything my father never was." *Were*. Such a simple word but with such an awful meaning. I choke on my words, my eyes brimming with tears. I fight them off, take a deep breath, determined to finish my personal eulogy. "In just a short time, you were my role model, mentor, trusted adviser..." The words are sticking in my throat; the pale tears overflowing and tracing lines to my chin. "You were my friend. I'll miss you so much."

I cry lonely and silent tears for him.

Ben should be alive and my father shouldn't. The world is broken, turned all upside down. Evil seems to conquer good again and again.

* * *

I spend a few hours with Elsey, who manages to cheer me up with her stories about her and Adele as kids. She's an amazing little girl. I should be the one cheering her up considering all she's lost, but it's the other way around.

When Elsey's shattered body gets tired after sitting up for only an hour, I go to find Roc. I'm walking down a random street in subchapter 1, hoping to run into him, when a shadow falls over me. Spinning around, I only have a split-second to react before a large, dark hand grabs me by the tunic and lifts me in the air, slings me against a rock wall.

It's Ram. Come to finish me off. After everything, I'm still not worthy of his trust.

"Thanks for that," I choke out smartly.

"My pleasure," he says, his lips curling into a broad grin. It's not his usual I'm-going-to-get-great-enjoyment-from-hurting-you grin. I look at him oddly.

"Am I missing something?" I gasp, trying to suck air through my crushed windpipe.

"I'm just messing with you, man," Ram laughs, lowering me to my feet and straightening out the collar of my tunic. With that, he walks away.

As I gulp in the air I chuckle to myself; I guess being friends with Ram isn't that different than being enemies with him. But I'll take it anyway.

Still smiling, I go to find Roc.

Roc's been spending so much time with Tawni that I don't see him much, but that's cool, because it's nice to see that they're getting on so well. Just before Adele's expected to arrive, however, I manage to corner him as he's returning from somewhere with Tawni. She gives his hand a slight squeeze and leaves him with me. She's a perceptive girl—always seems to know what's going on in the world around her. Right now, she knows I want to talk to my best friend.

"Hey, man," I say.

"Hey," he says. Roc's grinning from ear to ear.

"Things going that well, eh?"

"We have a lot more in common that you'd think," he says. "I really like her, Tristan."

"I'm happy for you. How are you really doing though? I mean, after everything…"

At first his face shows surprise, but then it falls and I see sadness in his eyes. "It's tough. I mean, we just met Ben and he was such an amazing guy, and now….now it's like he never existed. And Elsey—Tristan, I feel so bad for her. She didn't deserve any of this."

"I know. I feel the same way. Adele was a mess when she left with her mom. I just feel like there's nothing I can say or do that will help."

I'm surprised when Roc laughs. "I know how that feels," he says. I feel sheepish, because I remember how many times Roc tried to talk to me, to cheer me up, after my mom disappeared. But I just kept pushing him away, sort of like Adele's been doing. At least she finally let me hug her, finally talked to me, even though her words were filled with grief.

"I'm sorry," I say. It's too late for it, but I still feel like I should say it.

"It's okay. I understand. And maybe your mom's out there somewhere," he says. "I hope we find her someday. She was my mom too." Gravity takes his words and pulls them through my ear canals and all the way down to my toes. They are heavy words. The heaviest.

"Roc, I just want to say again that I'm so sorry about what my fath—"

"Our father," he corrects. "And it's okay. I'm not sad anymore, just angry. So angry that if I ever see him again, I think I'll kill him, Tristan. I really mean it."

I know *exactly* how he feels. If I ever see my father again, I think I'll kill him too.

* * *

As I wait for Adele's train to get in, there are so many things I know I want to say to her, to try to make things right, but I know none of them will help. A thought flashes through my mind, something I've almost forgotten about. Something I need to tell her, to tell someone, but it's so important I can't just go out and say it. While it won't necessarily help her with her grief, it might take her mind off of it, which could help—in a way.

The thought continues to tumble through my mind as the train pulls into the station.

When Adele steps onto the platform, she seems better, herself even. The fire in her that had seemingly been snuffed out when Ben died is back. I can see it in her eyes, in the way she carries herself, in the intensity of her hug when she greets me.

To be honest, I'm relieved. While they've been gone, I've been batting around one question in my head: How do you console someone when your words have lost all power?

That's how I've been feeling. Like anything I say to her just hangs in the air for a second, maybe two, and then drops in the abyss of lost and meaningless words. I guess she just needed time with her mom. The secret I've been keeping from her rolls around in my mouth, trying to take shape, but the time just doesn't feel right, so I swallow it back down. *There are Dwellers living on the Earth's surface*, I whisper in my mind, wondering why it's so easy to think it and so hard to say it.

351

We hold hands all the way back to the building in subchapter 1 where the Resistance leaders have been staying. No one wants to meet in the Dome anymore, not after what happened. There's been a lot of good news while Adele was gone and for the first time she seems genuinely interested as I tell her about it. The star dwellers realized their secure prison, the Max, was secretly being used, so they launched an attack on it. They found that sun dweller spies had been using it to hold the families of the star dweller generals. Now that they're free, the generals are able to lead the people the way they want to, without fear.

In fact, the remaining six star dweller generals just arrived today, along with three or four of their largest platoons. We expect more to arrive each day. They'll dispatch soldiers to all the borders with the Sun Realm, to protect us until we can prepare for battle.

"What are you going to do?" Adele asks suddenly, interrupting my monologue of news.

I gaze into her eyes, wondering what she expects me to say. "Fight," I say. "I can't sit on the sidelines while my father destroys the Lower Realms. I have to help stop him, kill him if I have to."

"Good," Adele says. "Me too."

Thirty
Adele

We're sitting around a very large courtyard. Me, Tristan, Roc, Tawni, my mom, all of the moon dweller VPs—both the incumbents and the newly elected—the star dweller generals. Discussing the strategy for the war. I don't feel like I or any of my friends should even be here. I mean, we're not leaders, except Tristan. He would fit right in. But for some reason they invited us.

Since my dad was killed, Mom has become the voice of the Resistance. "We've come up with a two-pronged approach to fighting this war," she says, her voice stronger than I've ever heard before. "The main body of our soldiers will be used in the subchapters we think are the most susceptible to attack. Although many of you were of the opinion we should attack first, the majority has decided that we will let the sun dwellers come to us. By doing this, we will stretch their resources and allow us to fight on our home turf. But don't become complacent, these advantages are minor considering the firepower President Nailin will rain down upon us. Any questions?"

Silence. I wait for her to tell us about the second part of the strategy.

"Adele, Tristan, Tawni, Roc," my mom says, and my heart skips a beat. *Why is she addressing us in front of everyone?* "We have something to ask of you, something that is hard for me as a general and as a mother." She pauses, takes a breath, continues, speaks directly to me.

"This is not a time to be complacent. This is not a time for fearful mothers to hide away their capable daughters. It's a time to be bold, to take risks. Your father trusted in your strength, in your abilities, and now it's time for me to do the same. God knows I don't want to. I've lost a husband already and my other daughter is in bad condition, but I cannot hold you back because I'm scared of losing you. You are a fantastically capable woman and I'm so proud of you, Adele."

Tears glimmer in her eyes and I know I'm reflecting them back at her. I don't know what she wants us to do, but I know I'll say yes, not because she's asking me, but because it's the right thing to do.

"Mom, just tell us. It's okay," I say.

She cringes as if in pain, like asking me this is physically hurting her. "We have a special mission for you. We want you to kill the President."

Her words are like a dark fog in the air, pressing down on our shoulders. It was the last thing I expected her to say. She rushes on, "Without him at the helm, we believe the sun dweller army will fall apart, will lose their resolve. He's the mastermind behind it all, and if he falls, we think we have a chance. Realistically, our armies don't stand a chance against the Sun Realm, but this might just give us the edge we need."

"Why us?" I ask.

My mom sighs. "You all have proven what you can do, and Tristan and Roc know the lay of the land in the Sun Realm, and, well, we knew none of you would go unless all of you go." She's right. I'll never leave my friends again—will never leave Tristan again.

Tristan grips my hand, squeezes twice. A signal. He's in. "I'll do it," I say, my eyes dry again, my face firm. I'll do it for my dad, for my sister, for my mom. For me.

"I'm in, too," Tristan says.

At the same time, Tawni and Roc say, "Me too."

My mom nods. "I thought you would say that. And Trevor and Ram will be going with you, too, as representatives of the Star and Moon Realms."

Trevor nods at me, a slight smile on his face. A week ago I would have cringed at the thought of spending more time with Trevor, but now grin back. He's a friend. Not because he saved me—twice—but because he stood by me when I needed him most. Just like Tristan, Roc, and Tawni.

A big, dark-skinned guy, who I assume is Ram, stands, looks directly at Tristan, and says, "I'll do whatever I can to help fulfill this mission. I'll even follow Tristan into the belly of the beast. But I'm warning you, if I ever so much as suspect you're working for your father, I'll kill you with my bare hands."

I glance sharply at Tristan, expecting his face to be red as he prepares to fight this Ram guy, but I'm shocked to see he's laughing. "I wouldn't expect anything less from you, Ram," he says.

I guess there's something I don't know about their relationship.

* * *

I go to see Elsey one last time before we leave.

"Do you really have to go?" she says right when I walk in.

I sigh. "Oh, El. If there was any way I could stay with you, you know that I would," I say, sitting next to her.

She's beneath the covers, like when I saw her the last time, just her tiny head sticking out. Her thick raven hair covers most of the white pillow she's resting on. Unexpectedly, she twists her left arm out from the sheets and pushes off, sitting up straight. I stifle a gasp when I see the stump of flesh sticking out from the short right sleeve of her hospital tunic.

"Does it scare you?" She giggles, waving the stump slightly in the air.

And just like that she's just Elsey again. My sister. Not my crippled sister. Despite myself, I laugh, although not as long or as loud as I'd like to for her sake. "You could never scare me," I say, putting my arm around her so she can lean on me. When I feel her minimal weight against my chest I feel complete.

We lay there together for over an hour, sharing memories of Dad, of Mom, of life, sometimes laughing, sometimes crying—

always loving. When she falls asleep I slip my arm from behind her head, covering her to her neck with the white spread.

"Goodbye, Elsey," I say, kissing my hand and touching it to her forehead.

* * *

The Resistance is full of surprises. We stand on a large overhang high atop the cavern walls in subchapter 1. The Dome looks like a giant bulge from up here, sticking out amongst the toy buildings around it. We're all sweating from the exertion of the climb. At least this time we got to use ropes.

We're shoulder to shoulder on the ledge, Tawni, then Roc, then Tristan, then me. My mom insisted on accompanying us this far. I take one last look at the Moon Realm, perhaps the last time I'll see it ever, and then turn around to where Mom is pulling away a big gray tarp from the mountainside, revealing a hidden ink-black tunnel into the rock. Like I said, the Resistance is full of surprises.

"We built this during the Uprising, but never had a chance to use it," she says.

"We're using it now," I say.

When she turns, her eyes are full of conviction. "You will succeed," she says.

"Of course we will," I say, trying to make it sound like the truth.

She hugs Tawni first, holding her for a long time without saying anything. Then she hugs Roc and says, "Elsey's sure going to miss you."

"And I her," Roc replies. He winks. "Don't worry, we'll see you again soon." It seems Elsey's optimism is rubbing off on him.

Next up is Tristan and she whispers something in his ear as she pulls him close. He just smiles and nods.

I'm last and we hug the longest. After all, she's my mom, and I'm going to miss her. Just as I'm pulling away, she tugs my ear close to her lips and whispers sharply, "That note your father gave you. Here's what it means: It's no accident that you and Tristan met."

My eyes widen and I open my mouth to speak, to ask her what she means, but it's too late, because she's pushed me into the thin tunnel and corralled the others behind me, blocking the path.

I grit my teeth, frustrated at my mom's cryptic message, but trying to focus on the task at hand: find the President; kill the President. I lead the way into the tunnel, flicking my flashlight on with one hand and gripping my mother's emerald necklace in the other.

Keep reading for a peek into the heart-stopping third installment in The Dwellers Saga, *The Sun Dwellers*, available now!

Acknowledgements

This time around I'm most thankful to all the readers who bought *The Moon Dwellers* and wrote the most wonderful reviews that helped inspire me to write the sequel. Your words of encouragement and your feedback mean so much to me, I can't even put it into words. I was literally tearing up as I read some of your reviews. I can't thank you enough for your support and for your willingness to take a chance on my books.

To my editor, Christine LePorte, thank you for helping me take my ideas and writing to the next level—the pearls of wisdom you provide do not go unnoticed.

A HUGE thanks to my marketing team at shareAread, particularly Nicole Passante and Karla Calzada, without whom there would be no buzz. You've taught me so much.

As always, thanks to my incredible team of beta readers who embraced *The Star Dwellers* from the very beginning and who have been so encouraging the whole way through. You are truly an inspiration. Without your feedback, *The Star Dwellers* wouldn't have been nearly as good! So thank you, Laurie Love, Alexandria Nicole, Christie Rich, Karla Calzada, Kayleigh-Marie Gore, Nicole Passante, Kerri Hughes, Terri Thomas, Lolita Verroen, Zuleeza Ahmad, and Kaitlin Metz. And of course, the biggest thanks to my ultimate beta reader, my always-honest wife, Adele.

To my friends in my Goodreads fan group, you are all amazing, I hope you know how highly I think of you, and I appreciate all your jokes, kindness, and comments. You brighten my life every day that you're in it.

I like to wait till near the end of the acknowledgments to recognize my awesome cover artists/designers at Winkipop Designs, because they are the first impression everyone gets, and so they should be the last two. Thank you for all your hard work within challenging deadlines and for finding a way to sum up an entire story in a single image. As one of my readers said, "After reading the book I realized what a work of art the cover is." I couldn't have said it better.

Discover other books by David Estes available through the author's official website:

http://davidestes100.blogspot.com or through select online retailers including Amazon.

<u>Young-Adult Books by David Estes</u>

The Dwellers Saga:
Book One—The Moon Dwellers
Book Two—The Star Dwellers
Book Three—The Sun Dwellers

The Evolution Trilogy:
Book One—Angel Evolution
Book Two—Demon Evolution
Book Three—Archangel Evolution

<u>Children's Books by David Estes</u>

The Nikki Powergloves Adventures:
Nikki Powergloves- A Hero is Born
Nikki Powergloves and the Power Council
Nikki Powergloves and the Power Trappers
Nikki Powergloves and the Great Adventure
Nikki Powergloves vs. the Power Outlaws (Coming in 2013!)

Connect with David Estes Online

Facebook:
http://www.facebook.com/pages/David-Estes/130852990343920

Author's blog:
http://davidestesbooks.blogspot.com

Smashwords:
http://www.smashwords.com/profile/view/davidestes100

Goodreads author page:
http://www.goodreads.com/davidestesbooks

Twitter:
https://twitter.com/#!/davidestesbooks

About the Author

After growing up in Pittsburgh, Pennsylvania, David Estes moved to Sydney, Australia, where he met his wife, Adele. Now they travel the world writing and reading and taking photographs.

A SNEAK PEEK
THE SUN DWELLERS
BOOK 3 OF THE DWELLERS SAGA
Available anywhere e-books are sold in December 2012!

Prologue
Subchapter 14 of the Moon Realm
Two years ago

Despite her nondescript gray tunic, the woman sticks out like a sparkling diamond in a coal mine, her shiny blond hair peeking out from beneath her dark hood. But it's not her hair, or her face—which is remarkably beautiful beneath the dark shadows—that identifies her as a foreigner in the Moon Realm. Instead, it's her gait, the way she carries herself: straight-backed and graceful and regal. Next to her the passing moon dwellers look hunched, their backs question marks and their faces turned to the dust.

She's knows it's the middle of the day—thus ensuring the girl will be at school—but the amount of light afforded by the overhead cavern lights is appallingly minimal, the near-equivalent of a Sun Realm dawn, or perhaps twilight.

Although she clearly doesn't belong amongst the rundown and crumbling gray stone shacks, she doesn't hesitate as she strides down the street, ignoring the stares she attracts. Unable to hold back her nerves any longer, she pauses—just a barely noticeable stutter step—as she nears her target: a tiny stone box, no larger than a medium-sized shed. She wonders how the two most powerful Resistance leaders could possibly be tucked in such an unremarkable corner of the Moon Realm. The front yard is barren rock, full of crisscrossing cracks and stone chips that roll and slide underfoot as she approaches the thin doorframe.

Before she knocks, her eyes are drawn to her feet, where she stands on the only unmarred stone square. Within the block is a single word—*friend*—elegantly cut with the skill of a professional stone worker. A hint of a smile crosses the woman's face before she looks up. Despite all her doubts and fears and indecisiveness while making the decision that's led her to this place, that one word chiseled at the entrance gives her hope that there's a better life out there for her eldest son—that maybe things can improve for him and for the Tri-Realms as a whole.

Her life is forfeit—stomped out by a loveless sham of a marriage, to the President no less—but her son's…well, her son's life could change everything.

After a single deep breath, she gathers her courage in a raised fist. When her knuckles collide with the door, the sound is final and hollow in her ears, but in reality is only a thud. Tilting an ear, she listens for footsteps, but is rewarded with only cluttered silence. The clutter: her mind, which trips and stumbles over a thousand questions. Is anyone home? Will the door be slammed in my face? Have I made a grievous mistake? Have I failed him? Have I failed my son? Have I failed myself?

Unexpectedly and without fanfare, the door swings open; a dark-haired woman wearing a plain brown, knee-length tunic fills the gap, her eyebrows raised in surprise. If not for the foreigner's information, which she received from a very reliable source, she wouldn't believe this woman to be a revolutionary. Except for her eyes, that is. There's a fire in her pupils that she's only seen once or twice in her life. It's the same fire she sees in her eldest son.

When the woman with the jet black hair doesn't speak, the intruder realizes her eyebrows are an unspoken question: *Yes? Why have you wandered onto my doorstep?*

Before answering the silent question, she pulls back her hood, releasing her golden locks and forcing away the identity-protecting shadows on her face. A spark of recognition flashes on the woman's face, but fades just as quickly. Finally she speaks. "First Lady Nailin—why are you here?"

"Mrs. Rose—I have a proposition for you. May I come in?"

One

Adele

Present day

The light gleams off the barrel of the gun with a brightness that blinds me if I look directly at it. My hands are sweaty as I clutch the weapon that once upon a time was so foreign, but now seems so familiar. The gun's every detail is burned into my memory, from the temperature of the cold steel against my palm, to its weight tugging on my wrist, to the strong yet delicate scent of burning gunpowder.

When I turn the corner and enter the room, it's all happening again. My dad is bound and lying prostrate on the rough stone floor, the executioner's gun to his head. A half dozen other sun dwellers bar my way forward. There's more than the last time, but it doesn't matter. A million of them couldn't stop me. Not this time.

I raise the gun and start shooting. Six booms later my foes are all dead, red and warm and blank-eyed. In the heat of the moment, I continue shooting, this time at the executioner, but the *click click click* announces that I'm out of bullets.

I toss the gun aside and charge forward, kicking his bland face with my heel. He slumps to the side, his own weapon discarded by his weakened fingers. I've done it this time. Saved him—saved my father. But I know something's not right as I realize my sister isn't by his side like she should be.

As I lean over the face of the man who I immediately know is not my father, the Devil's eyes flash open, the gateway to a black and soulless human shell.

"Didn't you know?" the President says. "Your father's already dead. And you're next."

My heart is in my throat as the demon lifts his hand, which is now holding a long glinting sword with a diamond-encrusted hilt, which I either didn't notice before or which has magically appeared.

As his white-knuckled hand darts forward, I scream. Although I don't close my eyes, blackness surrounds.

* * *

I'm still screaming and seeing darkness when a pair of strong arms cradles my head. "Shh," a voice says.

I quiet but I'm still breathing hard, panting like I've just run a long way, my chest heaving. An instant later there's a soft glow as a lantern is lit, casting dancing shadows on the rough, brown tunnel walls. Tristan's arm is still behind my head, and when he sees me looking at him, he retracts it quickly, his face flush with embarrassment. "You were dreaming," he says. "I heard you cry out."

I close my eyes, try to will the frantic pace of my heart to slow, as I remember where I am. In a tunnel on the way to the Sun Realm. On a mission for my mother, General Rose. As Tristan's father pointed out in my nightmare, my father's still dead—nothing can change that. No amount of fresh killing or revenge or trigger pulls will make one bit of difference. And yet the furnace of revenge burns hotly in the pit of my stomach. Kill his father. Kill the President. That is our mission.

I open my eyes and, despite my vengeful thoughts, say, "I'm tired of all the death."

Tristan's face worries its way to a tight smile. "Only one more person has to die, right?" The ever-present buzz whenever Tristan is near me hums along my scalp and down my spine. The urge to get as close to him as possible tugs at my arms, but I hide it well, not even flinching.

Even after the disturbing nightmare, I can't help but grin when I'm talking to him. "Yeah, just your dad—hope you don't mind."

He laughs. "He's no one's father."

"Not even Killen's?"

"Especially not Killen's," he says. "We were only ever puppets to him, used to do his dirty work, nothing more."

It saddens me for Tristan talk like that, but I know it's true. I'd rather have a dead father than a living one like his. I sigh, wishing I had the same boldness now as when I kissed him back in the Moon Realm.

"What was your dream about?" he asks.

I tell him, watching as his hands tighten into fists, curling and uncurling with each sentence. When I finish, I say, "I don't know if I'll be able to do it when the time comes."

"You're strong, Adele. I've seen it time and time again," he says, his dark blue eyes never leaving mine.

"Does it take strength to kill?" I ask, almost to myself. "Is that what makes your father strong?"

His hands relax and he folds them in his lap. "It takes strength to defeat evil," he says wisely. "In any case, I won't mind being the one to do it when the time comes."

Despite his more relaxed posture, there's a thirst for blood in his eyes that I've never seen before, which both scares and comforts me. Changing the subject, I say, "So what's with you and Ram?" I've been itching to ask Tristan about his strange relationship with the dark-skinned gargantuan who's part of our merry little death squad.

"What do you mean?" Tristan says, his eyes giving away his hidden laugh.

"Umm, I don't know…maybe the fact that he threatened to kill you at the council meeting, and you seemed to find it funny. Does that ring a bell?"

Tristan's laugh finally presents itself, lighting up his face. I bask in it for a moment as I wait for him to respond. "Let's just say our friendship has had its ups and downs. Right now we're on an up."

"C'mon, tell me," I push. "What were the downs?"

369

"He hated me," Tristan says bluntly. "He didn't trust me, tried to beat me up a few times, tried to block me from trying to help."

Wow. It's not what I expected him to say, but I guess it makes sense that he'd have opposition—even within the Resistance. Even still, a smile plays on my lips. "He *tried* to beat you up? The guy's a behemoth."

Tristan looks away, cringing slightly, but then turns back, his lips turned up once more. "Okay, okay, he *did* beat me up, but it's not like I tried to fight back—I didn't want to upset anyone by getting into fights while trying to convince people to trust me."

"Sure, tough guy," I say.

We're both quiet for a few minutes, but it's not awkward, which is one of the things I like about Tristan. Just being near him feels right. It's been that way since I met him. It's like all the nerves and nodes and synapses in our bodies thrive on our nearness. At least that's how it is for me, and how I hope it is for Tristan.

He must be thinking the same thing because he says, "Isn't it weird that we're here together?" He laughs and I'm silent, but I know exactly what he means. We saw each other across barren rock, through a barbed-wire, electrified fence, past hordes of his screaming, undergarment-throwing, adoring fans—me in freaking prison and him the prized attraction in a parade—and yet here we are, together; like *together* together. Weird is the perfect word for it.

"Have you ever thought that maybe it's more than just coincidence?" he says, his eyebrows question marks.

"Like fate?" I say, trying to hide my surprise at his question. I haven't told him what my mom said to me before we left the Moon Realm:

It's no accident that you and Tristan met.

"Maybe. I dunno. Something like that."

My thoughts come fast, careening around in my head like fish in a cave pond. In my world, the only fate is illness or death. We don't have much else. However, from the time I laid eyes on Tristan in the flesh, I *have* felt an indescribable pull toward him, like someone wants us to be together. But despite my mom's declaration that it wasn't an accident that we met, there's no logical explanation for any of it, which doesn't work for my pragmatic mind. I shake my head. "I don't think so. It's just plain random chance."

It's no accident that you and Tristan met.

Tristan frowns. "There's something I have to tell you."

I stop breathing. Here it comes. For a while now I've felt there was something he was holding back, something big—maybe life-changing.

"Did I ever tell you that I fainted once thinking about you?"

Huh? I'm guessing that's not what he's been keeping from me. What does that even mean? I sigh. "Umm…" Well. Hmm. No?

"I did. Roc and I were training, fighting with wooden swords. This was shortly after I saw you for the first time, mind you. The fight was over and your face popped into my head…" He ducks his head sheepishly and sort of cringes, like he's wondering why he decided to tell me this, but knows he can't go back now. "And, well, I passed out right then. In the time between fainting and Roc waking me up, I dreamt that my father murdered you right in front of me. It was creepy."

My head spins. Why is he telling me this? So I made him faint? I don't know what to say, but he's not done yet.

"Then I nearly passed out again when I saw you the second time, when you were trying to break out of the Pen."

I can't help but laugh now. "Are you sure it wasn't the fumes from the bombs blowing up all over the place?"

His face is dead serious. "No, it was you. I had a physical reaction to seeing you, almost like my body couldn't handle it."

This is definitely not the direction I thought the conversation was going. "I didn't take many baths while in the Pen so normally I would guess it was my body odor that caused it, but I had just showered that day, so that can't be it," I joke.

"Perhaps it was your remarkable beauty," Tristan says, sending warmth into my cheeks.

"Knock it off, charmer, I thought you were being serious."

"I *was* being serious," he says, which doesn't help stem my flush.

"Look, you probably just hadn't eaten in a while, or were dehydrated," I say, trying to steer the conversation away from what he thinks of my looks.

He tilts his head to the side, his eyes wandering to the tunnel ceiling. "That's possible..." he says, but I know he doesn't really think so.

When he looks back at me, there's resolution in his eyes. Although we're already sitting close to each other, he slides closer, right next to me. The normal strength of my pull toward him is super-charged, and the only desire I have is to hold him, to be held by him. He must feel the same way, because his arm curls around the back of my neck, drags my head to his chest.

His warm breath caresses the back of my neck, electricity shooting off his skin as he gently presses his arm against mine.

"This is the good part of life," he says, and I sigh, although I shouldn't. Not when my dad is dead, my sister maimed. Cole. No, I don't deserve this, I think. Not now. Not until the President is dead. Maybe never.

Going against every instinct, I unwind my body from Tristan's grasp, stand up, and walk away with the lantern in tow, wishing I didn't have to.

"I've got to get rid of this gun," I say over my shoulder, plucking the gun my mom gave me—*the gun I failed to save my father with*—out from beneath my tunic.

Made in the USA
Coppell, TX
30 January 2021

49211326R00207